FAIRY DUST

AND

Stripper

HEELS

LORRAINE WILLIAMS

FAIRY DUST AND STRIPPER HEELS

Lorraine Williams

Ebook: 978-1-7366268-1-8
Paperback: 978-1-7366268-0-1

Edited by: Alicia Russ
Cover art by: Mistvale Covers

I want to dedicate this book to my family. You have been with me through everything, and I couldn't ask for a better team.

I want to thank everyone who worked with me to make this book possible. The hard work, the beta readers, the coaching, and the support. I needed the advice, the support, and the laughter!

Table of Contents

Chapter One

Theodore always said that the strippers at Karnach had two jobs. "Dance and don't steal things." Some of Jada's colleagues managed both, while others managed neither.

Karnach was a dark smoky strip club that found its home on the corner of Rage, and some other street that screamed failure. Loud neon lights of the club's sign flickered on and off over suspiciously wet streets that had not seen any rain since the beginning of summer. The heavy bass from the music that spilled from the open door of the club filled the warm night air.

Theodore had told Jada once that he had chosen the name because of some mythical land involving fairies. "After

all, you ladies make my patron's dreams come true!"
Then he would always laugh at the end of his
explanation. Large whooping guffaws that expelled the
smoke that had settled into his lungs from years of cheap
cigars. None of the strippers got the joke, but then again
they did not have to. They were not there to laugh.

Theodore was the owner of Karnach. He was a round
balding man with sausage like fingers, who was not
above selling other services that the strippers were not
offering. Either way, dancing was how Jada made ends
meet once she left her day job. Being an inner city
runaway left her with few options. It was sink or swim,
and she learned quickly that sinking was not an option.
Therefore, off to work she went despite the danger that
seemed to settle around the club lately.

Lately, there had been a rash of missing girls. They would
show up for work, and never come back. Several of the
girls were quitting, but the others like Jada could not
afford to. Jada was not too worried, though. The bouncer
Gabriel was standing at the entrance. He kept the girls
safe on his nights there, and every girl was only too glad
to be kept safe by Gabriel. His black hair fell in short
deep waves that ended at the line of his jaw in a thin
chinstrap that Jada dreamed of tracing with her fingers.
He was 6'2, and had a smile that could light up the city
of Dallas, Texas.

Jada heard from the other girls that he came from Haiti to
work for Theo. Supposedly, Theo was Gabriel's uncle.
Jada did not necessarily buy the story but minded her
business. They all had stories, and most of the stories
weren't happy. Jada was self-aware enough to know that

Karnach was not the place for people who were working their way through college or trying to take care of their kids. Theo did not hire anyone who had a future. Not a foreseeable one anyway.

Jada nervously tugged at the stiff collar of her short light blue waitress uniform. Her warm brown hands moved to smooth out the rough material over her curvy figure. She self-consciously fluffed the curly blonde tips of her voluminous afro as she continued to make her way to the entrance of Karnach. Gabriel made Jada's heartbeat fast and her vocal ability a level of zero. She had a feeling he would not be working at Karnach for long. There was just something so … refined about him. Something just beneath the surface that made him different from any other man she had ever met. Just looking at Gabriel made her heart smile. Jada was doing her best not to get attached, but it wasn't really working for her.

Jada looked around mentally weighing her options. "Should I risk embarrassing myself in front of Gabriel, or should I sneak around back?"

In the end, Gabriel made the decision for her when his ginger-colored eyes lifted to hers. He gave her one of his heart-stopping smiles, and she knew she was not going anywhere. Jada continued her trek towards the door hoping he could not see how socially awkward he made her feel. Her lashes fell to her cheeks, and she took a deep steadying breath. "Hello."

"Jada, I hope your night is going well." Gabriel lifted the magenta velvet rope at the entrance and stepped aside to allow her through. He had not helped her onto a white horse, but Jada felt like a princess, nonetheless. She nodded with a smile and was about to continue on her way, but Gabriel grabbed her hand. The golden brown of his fingers twined with the deep brown of hers. Her teeth caught her lower lip as she tried not to say anything too stupid. Luckily, he saved her from herself. "Be careful tonight, Jada."

"I will, don't worry. I won't take any chances I'm not supposed to!" She looked up at him and smiled nervously unsure of what else to say.

Gabriel smiled, and Jada felt her face go warm. That had come out a little flirtier than she had planned. "I mean, uh, I feel safe as long as you're here." Jada's eyes lowered in frustration with herself. That was not what she had meant to say! She looked around waiting for a hole to open up and swallow her whole. Unfortunately, there would be no such grace extended to her.

Gabriel laughed and released her hand to cup her chin, gently guiding her dark brown eyes back to his. It might have been the light, but something seems to slither behind the gold of his eyes. It made them look almost reptilian. Jada frowned and tilted her head, but with the next blink of neon sign above them, it was gone. She kept watching his eyes for a moment to see if they would change again, but nothing happened. Jada shrugged it off as a trick of the light to focus her attention back on Gabriel. That man was every late night fantasy she ever had, and everything else at that moment could take a backseat. "Don't work too hard, Jada. There are those that would do a doll like you mischief if given the chance."

Jada nods quickly and gently pulls away. He did things for her that she thought she would never feel, and it threw off her equilibrium something awful! She knew he could feel how her pulse had sped up. Her breathing had become inconveniently deeper, and she rushed into the club without looking back. "I'm not running from him, I'm just late!" She mumbled the half lie to herself as she rushed through the club to get to the dressing room. She would be late if she did not hurry, and Theodore was not nice about his merchandise not being available on time.

It was a busy night in the dark black light filled club. Men were laughing over small piles of white dust that Jada studiously ignored as she passed by. Graffiti day glow mushrooms were painted in various corners around the room. Neon green script scrawled across black walls in a language that Jada did not recognize. She had asked about the words once. Theo had promptly snarled, "You can mind your damn business, go shake your ass." Jada had never asked again. In fact, after that she made a point of just trying to stay out of his way.

Jada frowned at the memory as she made her way into the dressing room. One would have thought he would have been nicer considering that he had a lack of girls to work with. Theodore had lost so many strippers that he had to make an open call for dancers. There were girls from all over the place trying to make their rent payments that night. Some of them were strange though. They were tall and beautiful. Not pretty with makeup, but naturally beautiful. They danced and moved about as if they had trained in some Russian boarding school. Jada could hear the angry murmur of the regulars who worked there as she entered the green utilitarian dressing room.

"Who do these trifling bitches think they are? Coming in here and stealing our tricks?" Kedra, otherwise known as "Lady Kay", was complaining off to the side as she twisted and turned in the mirror. Her long hot pink nails clicked together in irritation as she adjusted her bright pink G-string that rested in stark contrast to the dark gold of her shapely hips.

Kedra's background was filled with violence, and children that never wanted to see her again. She did not go into a lot of detail, but the line of cocaine Kedra snorted before fiddling with her clothes told the story for her. Lady Kay had been born into a world, where escapism had to become an art. Because of that, she made a lot of money as a stripper. She just had to be numb first. She promised Jada she was going to try hard to stay clean but trying to kick an addiction was no easy task. Especially, when all Kedra really wanted to do was forget. Kedra's slim honey-colored fingers shook out her long dark brown braids in irritation. "What was Theodore thinking?"

"Girl, you know Theodore only thinks with two things. His wallet and his other head." Leticia laughed, and a couple of the other regular girls laughed with her. Leticia was the mother of the group, the first stripper to work at Karnach, and Theodore's girlfriend. At least as much of a girlfriend as they could be in an environment that forced you to give the illusion of availability. She was as round as Theo was, but none of that stopped her from dropping it each night on the stage. She moved around that pole as if she was made of air. It was how she earned the name "Cocoa Puff". Jada had found Leticia's' laughs to be as warm as her hugs. Her pudgy but dainty fingers raked back her long flat-ironed hair from her green eyes. "Don't worry, Theo's got a plan. All of you will be taken care of by the end of the night! Right, Jada?"

"Right." Jada looked up as Leticia winked over at her with a wide smile. It was just something about the way Leticia phrased her answer that made a warning bell go off Jada's head. She shrugged it off and put it down to nerves. It was almost time for her set, and she did not know what she was going to perform that evening. The new girls had taken all the good songs. She fussed with her makeup and tried to roll the agitation out of her shoulders. There was something weird about the air tonight; Jada just could not put her finger on it. She finished her makeup and leaned over tugging at the straps of her impossibly high black heels wrapped around her ankle.

"Oh, Jada doesn't want to be taken care of by anyone other than Gabriel! Isn't that right?" Kedra laughed and moved to the stall right beside Jada's booth as she made some last-minute touches to her outfit. Teasing Jada about her not so secret crush on their handsome bouncer. "Not that I blame her." Kedra's fingers circled into an "ok" sign as her thick lashes dropped in a wink. "Gabriel looks like he could take care of a girl right!"

"Don't he though!" Leticia laughed and lifted her soft russet arms over her head in a languid stretch, before getting out of her seat. "It's all good, though, because he loves him some her." Jada looked up at Leticia as a slightly disturbed frown flits across her face. Leticia looked up at Jada's reflection in the mirror, and her eyes dropped in embarrassment. She laughs and makes her way to the door. "Better not dance too hard tonight, Sugar. Gabe might be a little on the possessive side."

Leticia walked out soon followed by Kedra who was good naturedly laughing at Jada's expense. Jada smiled and shook her head as they left her to get ready. Jada stands and moves through a series of stretches. In another life, she had taken ballet classes. The teasing did not bother her, as they were her family. Even more than the family she ran away from when her stepfather tried to put his hand in the cookie jar one too many times. He had drunkenly slipped into her room and unzipped his pants. Jada had screamed and hit him in the face with an iron. Her mother stormed in and commended to loudly not believe her. Jada packed everything she could fit into her bag and left that same night.

"And, here I am. Dancing for dollars at Karnach." Jada whispered as a deep sigh filled her lungs. Her hand skimmed over the short jade skirt, smoothing away her performance jitters. She turned towards the curtain that led to the stage, as she heard the song before her set. Suddenly, the feedback from the microphone made her wince. Jada knew what was coming.

"Jada get your ass out on stage!" Theo's bark snapped her back to reality. She had planned to step it up because of all the competition this evening. However, after what Leticia had said, she was starting to second-guess herself.

Jada peeked out from behind the velvet curtains, and the club was hopping! Lights were bouncing everywhere. Some of the girls had black light reactive tattoos that looked like the script on the walls running along their sides. Others had gigantic translucent wings and wore long gowns of every color imaginable. She was not sure what club they had come from, but it was much classier than this place. Those costumes must have cost a mint! She would have to do something special just to break even tonight. As she looked out over the club, she saw Gabriel standing at the DJ booth. She swallowed and dropped the curtain with a sigh. She would do her regular routine, and not try anything too crazy tonight.

Jada made her way to the booth and could hear Gabriel arguing with Theodore about the safety of the place. "Theo, you can't keep getting them hyped up! It's dangerous for the regular girls." Gabriel tried to reason with Theo, and it looked like it was going as well as could be expected. Jada caught Gabriel's eye and gave him a reassuring smile. He returns it, and Theo laughs derisively, having caught the exchange.

"Get on, with all of that. You don't care about any girls here, but this chick. They're all going to be rich tonight. You do your job, and I'll do mine." Theo rubbed his walnut-colored hand over his baldhead before turning to glare at Jada. "Where the hell did I tell you to be?"

"I... I was just going to give you my set list." Jada stammered and took a hesitant step back. She heard a low hiss, but she could not tell where it was coming from. She looks over to see if Gabriel heard it, but he gave no sign that he even noticed. Jada takes a deep breath and licks her full lips trying to steady her smooth Theo's ruffled feathers. "Set number four please."

"Set number four please!" Theo mocks her in a high pitched whine, and points to the stage. "You'll do whatever songs I give you. You got a special request! If

9

you want to have any type of future after this night, you'll get yourself on that stage post haste!" He snarls and turns to Gabriel who watches him steadily. "And you!"

The lights flicker and this time the black lights make Gabriel's look as if his eyes are glowing. Trick of the light or not, Gabriel did not look very amused, and Theo saw it. Theo coughed and turned away pretending to focus on the cassettes and knobs in front of him. "Just go back to bouncing like I pay you to do!"

"Understood, your highness" Gabriel's voice was sarcastic, but something about it sent chills up Jada's spine. He looks over at her and gives the barest lift of his lips in a grim semblance of a smile, and nods towards the stage. "Head on up Jada, I'll be watching you."

"Of course, you will" Theo grumbled, and glared at her as if asking what she was waiting for. Jada turned on her heels and hurried up to the stage. She did not want to get into any more trouble tonight.

Theo's words came back to Jada, as she moved up the steps. This place was the only spot she saw herself in the immediate future, and she could not lose this job.

A quick prayer was given as she moved to the stage. The colored lights were bouncing around in the darkness in a way that made the room seem ominous. Jada could not see the faces of the patrons. She could only assume one of the regulars made the request. Jada sees a man in the audience and tries to keep the dismay from her face. He was thin, pale, and did not look like he had a job that got him out in the sun much. His skin was almost milky. He was wearing a white button up shirt, and his dark blazer draped over his briefcase in the seat next to him. His red lips were wide and pressed into a hungry smile. The man looks up in time to see her watching him, and his grin spreads further.

She gave him a small polite smile and moves to the center of the stage. Jada looks around for Gabriel and sees him in a seat nearby. She could not stop the way her smile grew as she focused on Gabriel. She saw the man in the button up shirt frown and she fixed her face. She would have to tone the wattage down on her smile when Gabriel was around. She could lose customers that way. Jada could hear Theo in her head now. "Nobody wants a stripper who was taken!"

While walking to the stage, Jada took a deep breath and got into character. She put on a practiced smile as she sauntered up the stairs that led to the stage, her music was beginning. She glanced at Gabriel one more time before allowing herself to get lost in the performance. The heavy drums and electric guitar in the song told Jada that the special request was a semi slow rock song. They normally performed to rap music with quick beats that made you want to bounce in your seat. However, when someone asked for a special song, no request was denied, and no questions were asked. Although with the way Theo was acting, it was a no questions kind of night anyway. The beat dropped and her small hands went above her head to seductively grip the pole behind her, before slowly sliding them down the jade short dress she wore. A roll of her full hips brought her back to face the audience. The strange customer moved toward the stage, and her movements became less sure. Jada tamps down the sudden surge of panic and continues to dance. She leans over, and her hands slowly glide up her legs as she rolls back up. Each bar was another set of moves meant to sell the illusion of sex. Jada moves to the floor and lies on her back. Ignoring how sticky the floor was, and any thoughts of how it got that way. Her legs fan out then drop in a series of seemingly complicated twists that end with her back arched up from the floor.

Jada rolls over and crawls to where Gabriel was sitting; lost in the music she called him closer with a curl of manicured fingers. Due to the catcalls from the crowd, he could not say no. He moved to the stage, and the look on his face was best described as starved. Though he could not touch her, Jada had no such rules restraining her hands. Gently tracing her fingers over his jaw the way she had always dreamed of doing.

Gabriel's lips parted on a sharp intake of breath, as Jada continued to trail her fingers slowly over his skin. Skirted hips continued to rock with the beat of the music. The top of her light green costume fell away as the guitars in the music screeched. She was not nude, but the black bikini top did not leave much to the imagination.

As she gets ready to pull away, Gabriel catches her hand, and gently pulls her back against him. He takes a deep breath as he runs the tips of his nose along the column of her neck. It was as if he was trying to memorize her scent. The air came out as a sharp hiss against her ear. The sound made her heart skip a beat as his words grazed across her skin. "I told you to be careful Jada."

Remembering that other people were in the room he reluctantly releases her. Jada spins away to the other side of the stage where other people lined up to give her their money. She ignored the piles of bills on the stage. A crewmember would pick the cash up for her between sets. All she had to do was focus on putting on a provocative show.

On the other side, the thin ghoulish man slithered to the stage holding out what looked like a fold of mini portraits of Benjamin Franklin. With a pirouette and a roll of her body, Jada moves directly in front of him. He smiled, and it looked like his teeth were in a sharp jagged row across his gum line. She stops just short of gasping out in surprise but continues the show. Jada turns and gives a slightly panicked look to Gabriel, who inconspicuously moves towards her while trying not to disturb the rest of the patrons trying to stuff dollars down her panties.

The thin man looked between Gabriel and herself, then an ugly scowl stretched across his face. Jada turned and read the name badge around his neck that said "Bane Sidhe". Bane stroked the wad of hundreds down the bare skin of her leg and took the liberty of placing a reverent kiss at her feet. She did her best not to recoil at the touch of his skin against hers. Where Gabriel's touch was like fire, the thin man's was like ice.

The song ended, and Jada was about to walk towards the stairs to exit the stage. Long boney fingers grabbed her hand the way Gabriel had. She looked into his eyes, and she could not move. An abysmal emptiness held her tranquilized on stage. Bane took a step forward and could only watch as he brought her hand to his red lips. Jada tried to take deep breaths to keep her fear at bay as that desolate feeling continued to wash over her. Thankfully, Gabriel was able to pry the thin man's hand away from hers. The man turns to Gabriel to argue. Jada did not know what they were arguing about, but she did not waste any time leaving that stage.

Chapter Two

I'm going home! Theo can keep every red cent of his money." Jada snaps on her way to the dressing room, and notices Kedra in her usual booth. She jerks her bag from her locker and does not pass go or collect two hundred dollars as she starts stuffing things in. Kedra looks up at her with tired bloodshot eyes. Kedra was feeling that poison in her system, and it would be a while until she would ask about what Jada was doing.

It didn't matter Jada would call Kedra later to explain, but right now she had to get the hell out of there. "I don't care who he was or how much money he has!

Theo can fire me all day long! No, he can't fire me because I quit!"

"Jada are you okay?" Leticia comes in and sees her packing. Her eyes open wide, and she runs out. Presumably, to go get Theo, which was fine. Jada was ready to give him eight pieces of her mind.

Sure enough, they get back there, and Theo is watching her finish throwing her stuff into an overnight bag with a shake of his head. His plump fingers tiredly dragged down his face. "What are you doing, Jada? Did you see all that money you just made us this evening? I've got back to back lap dances lined up for you for the rest of the night!"

"I don't care. I'm leaving. That guy is the thing nightmares are made of, and I don't want him touching me!" Jada snaps back tossing the last of her makeup into her bag. She was fully prepared to never come back to Karnach. Her stepdad had the same look the night she left home, and she had never been back. "That guy is bad news, and I'm not going to put up with it!"

"You can't do this to me!" The look on Theo's face would have made Jada laugh if she was in a reasonable mood. He looked truly scared to be losing all of that money. You would think the club was not going to open tomorrow. Even Leticia looked a little pale.

Jada laughed, pulled her bag upon her shoulder, and nodded affirmatively. "The hell I can't!"

She took a step forward, and Theo stepped in her way blocking her exit. His voice doing that soft coaxing thing it did when he wanted you to do something you had a legal right to say no to. "What about the other girls? How do you think they are gonna feel covering your shifts?"

16

"Hell if I care. That man is evil, and if they were smart, they would leave before he gets his hooks in them. Now move!" Jada heads towards the door again, and Theo moves in front of her again. The tip of her tongue brushed against her cheek in irritation. She did not have an iron, but there was enough stuff in her bag to help her fight before she took flight.

"Look, be a reasonable doll. That guy was a little intense, but he wasn't dangerous. Gabriel took care of him no problem. He's not even here any longer." Jada looked at Theo suspiciously, and he waved her over to look out the dressing room door. Sure enough, the man was gone, and Gabriel was by the entrance leaning against the frame with his arms crossed.

All the patrons were having a good time, as if nothing had even happened. They were doing a conga line in a huge circle around the club. Even the mushrooms on the wall seemed to glow brighter with all of the drunken cheer. "See? You're overreacting. How about this, just go to the minute booths, and dance for a while. Maybe after you calm down, you'll feel like taking a few dances? If not, just finish out your shift, and we'll call it a night."

Jada looks over at Leticia and she smiles with a nod. "He's right Hun. Gabriel was a regular knight in shining armor trying to get to you!" She fanned herself with a roll of her eyes. "If only I was younger."

After a few minutes, Jada slowly nods and puts her bag down by the door and takes a deep breath. She did need the money and Gabriel was here. He would not let anything happen to her. The booths were like confessionals but wider. It had a metal curtain and a thick pane of glass that separated the two parts. She would do chair dances on the other side of the window, and the only way to keep the curtain up was to keep feeding money into the booth.

She felt something was missing and looked around for Kedra. Jada sees her bag on the floor, and her lips pull into a worried frown. "Where'd Kedra go?"

"Oh, she went home already. She had taken an early shift and left out the back. She had someone to meet you know." The soft tsk of Leticia's voice said that someone was Kedra's supplier.

"I'll grab her bag on my way out then. Call her and let her know I have it, please." She murmured to Leticia distractedly as she set her bag down next to Kedra's. It would be awhile before Kedra missed her bag. Though strange, it was not the first time Kedra had left something important at the club to chase her high. With multiple dancer's going missing it made Jada worry about her friend. Kedra had been both a confidant and family since she found Jada shivering in an alley over a year ago. Jada shook her head and walked out of the dressing room making her way down the corridor to the minute booths. She would stop by Kedra's place after her shift ended. This promised to be a long night.

Jada sat in a chair waiting for the curtain to come up. It was an ordinary guy on the other side, and she allowed herself to relax. Theo turned on some popular club songs and Jada started to dance. It was one of those songs that did not require any skill to move to. She just let the beat take over and left the rest to the imagination of the guy on the other side of the window. The metal curtain started sliding down, and she watched the man fumble with his wallet. She was glad to have the break, but she did not relax; he was about to put more money in the slot. The next song started, and the curtain came back up, only it was not the person from before. To her horror, it was her new nightmare with the red lips and jagged teeth.

"Gabriel!" Jada screams as she scuttles back knocking the chair over trying to get out of the booth but keeps her eyes on the monster in front of her. Adrenaline was making her heart pump painfully behind her breast. She scrambled into the dark hall, and all she could hear was loud music playing. Jada began moving to the exit carefully. She heard the door of the booth fling open and turned to see Bane crawling out of the booth. "Theo, where are you?"

One bone colored limb folded out from beneath the others in short jerky movements causing her heart to seize in fear. He gets into the hall revealing rows upon rows of teeth as he opens his mouth. An ear-splitting scream was released, and the windows in each booth exploded out into the hall in waves. Her hands lift to her ears as she runs back into the now empty club. Theo was gone, and so were all the other dancers.

"Leticia, we have to…" She makes it to the dressing room and pulls up short at the destruction before her. The empty room was in a confused disarray of thongs and bralettes. Costumes and chairs were strewn carelessly across the floor. Tubes and sets of expensive makeup were resting broken amongst stacks of cash and bits of glass. Whatever happened here had happened violently. Jada could hear Bane getting closer despite the heavy base of the music Theo had left playing. Another ear-splitting shriek galvanized Jada into action. Luckily, the bags were on the floor where she left them. Rooting around in the various pockets and praying that Kedra had left her car keys in her bag. "Please be here, please be here!"

Once her fingers engulfed Kedra's keys, she slid out of her heels and tiptoed out of the dressing room's side door that led to the parking lot. Jada tiptoed down the dark hallway stifling her scream as she heard furniture being tossed and broken behind her. The sounds of crashing furniture were moving closer. "Please don't let him know about the side door."

She continued to sneak out the back only to slip on something wet that was crumpled in the center of the hall. Her knee hit the ground painfully, and she looked back to see what she tripped over. Jada's hand instantly clamps over her mouth to muffle her screams. She tries to take in deep breaths to keep from hyperventilating, but nothing could stop the sobs racking her body. Kedra's body lay twisted almost inside out on the floor. The dreamy smile on her lips at odds with the bloody ruin her body had been left in. As if, she had been happy to end it all.

"Oh Kedra. I'm so sorry! I should have checked on you sooner. I knew something had been wrong. I should have listened to my instincts like you always told me to!" Jada sobs in a mix of fear and anger as she tries to cover her friend up as best as she could.

Another furious shriek filled the air, and Jada pushed herself to move. The thing had gotten tired of waiting for her. She could hear it throwing things around the dressing room. Jada looked back at Kedra one last time, hobbling to the door as fast as she could. Her hands pushed against the industrial grey pat on the door, and it took her a few tries to get it open. The monster must have heard her messing with the latch because it let out an ear-piercing screech that followed her out into the night.

Jada made it outside the club and made a limping break across the street to Kedra's car. Her knee was throbbing painfully, but she did not care. She could put ice on it later. Shaky fingers made it hard to get the key in the door, but finally she heard the click of the lock. She felt relief for just a moment before claw like fingers scraped across her scalp to grab a fist full of her curly hair. Her screams silenced as the monster pulled her head back then slamming it face first into the driver side window. Light exploded behind her eyes, and she dropped to the pavement. Jada could tell by the liquid warmth that poured down her face that her nose had been broken. However, that was the least of her worries. Bane leaned over to peer into her face releasing a high-pitched giggle that made her flesh want to curl away from her bones. He made a soft tut of disappointment, and he began to drag her back to the club.

"Look at you! I was supposed to get you undamaged! Unharmed. Perfect!" Jada really was not in the right frame of mind to apologize, so she let the monster continue his discordant rant. "I paid for you fair and square. Right as rain. Deals a deal. You belong to me!" Bane had not let go of her hair as he continued to drag her through the parking lot to the entrance of the club. "I have a music box made just for you! Just your size. Fit to be tied! You are going to be so pretty, pretty, pretty." He leaned over and showed his jagged teeth in what Jada could only assume was a smile. "Of course, some modifications will need to be made."

She tried to twist out of his grip, but it was like a fly swatting away a spider. Boney fingers only tightened their grip refusing to let her get away. She was in so much pain, but she refused to go quietly. She grabbed onto anything she could to keep from going back into the club. Bane gave a deep thoroughly annoyed sigh that she was still fighting. The loss of blood was making her lightheaded. Bane stopped with a snarl just as she was on the verge of giving up. She could not see what scared him, but anything that could scare him scared her too.

"When I get my hands on Theo I will make him sorry he ever hired me!" Jada was sure by the way he said modifications, he didn't mean a few piercings. She groans as she thought of all the things she would do to Theo if she ever saw him again. A prospect that seemed to get further and further away the longer she laid on the warm asphalt.

"She is mine! I bargained with that troll. I am taking her back through the Briars to my home." Bane roared angrily, but he made no more moves toward the club. The stiffening of her captor's fingers in her hair signified that he was scared. Bane took a step back and stumbled. In his haste, he had forgotten that he was holding Jada by the hair on the ground. For a minute, Jada thought he would turn tail, but the threat of someone stealing his new toy made him stop. He was jerking her up by the hair until she rested on bruised knees. "Go back to the fair lands and leave me to what's mine!"

Jada saw Something white was fluttering out the corner of her eye. She ignores the pain to roll over and get a better look at the monster in Bane's closet. Her eye widens as she sees Gabriel outfitted in platinum armor, like a knight from a fairy tale. Gabriel takes a step forward and kneels before her. His golden serpentine gaze flickers down to meet hers as she tries to crawl forward to get to him. Bane jerks her up by her hair to use her as a human shield. A white cloud of light haloed around Gabriel. If not for the dispassionate way he looked at them, Jada would have said he looked angelic. The cold light pricks at her skin the closer she gets. He lifts his hand to run his thumb over her busted lip, and his gaze snaps angrily to the monster that held her hostage.

"Release her! I had a prior claim, and I will not leave without Jada." Gabriel steps back and unsheathes his sword. Jada would have swooned if she had been in any position to do so. Bane, however, was less than impressed and roughly shoves Jada to the ground a few feet away, seeing that using her as a shield was not going to work. She watched Bane's claws stretch out into black knife-like points where his nails had once been.

"There is no need for this. Why don't we let her decide who she wants to go with? Make her choice. Pick and choose." Bane's voice was a soft coaxing taunt, that much to Jada's dismay Gabriel seemed to listen to.

They both turned to her, and Gabriel waved between them both. "Choose."

"Wait, what?" Jada blinked at how serious Gabriel was. She looked over to the monster, and something about the amused smile on his pale face scared her.

"Don't let Gabriel's looks fool, deceive, or trick you. He wants the same thing I do. At least I'm honest about it. I don't need to break your heart for eternity to get it." At his words, Jada looked over to Gabriel with a frown. Gabriel said nothing in his defense but gave her that smile that made her fall in love with him in the first place.

"I…" Jada was so confused. She did not know what was happening. She did not understand a world where someone she loved was more dangerous than the monster that wanted to make her a human jewelry box figure. Her head dropped in exhaustion, and her hand pulled blood-covered curls from her cheeks. She was in no shape to make any decisions, but they both seemed serious. "I just want to go home. Gabriel, please take me home."

"If you will not give me what's mine, I will make sure you won't have her either," Bane screamed angrily and came toward her talons first. At this point, Jada did not care; she just wanted it to be over.

Bane had slithered a few feet from her when Gabriel placed his sword between them both. A cold smile tugged at his lips with a slow shake of his head. "You lost. Now be gone. We'll settle up with Theo at the Court and Crown tomorrow."

Bane shrieked and dispersed in a pile of wriggling shadows, leaving a tired Jada crying on the ground. Gabriel comes over and wraps his cape about her shoulders before gathering her up in his arms. She curls into him and continues to cry into his armor. He rubbed her back, and she was almost weak with relief. "Thank you for saving me!"

"I will always come for you. You have nothing to fear."
He tilted her chin up to look so that she could see his
smile. Jada returned the smile with a soft one of her own,
but her eyes squinted as she peered into his face to get a
closer look at his eyes. Amused ginger eyes contracted to
points on each end, and she shivered in his arms. It was
like looking into the eyes of a cobra.

They made it back into the club, and fresh tears fell down
Jade's cheeks as she looked towards the dressing room.
The world may have thought Kedra was not worth
anything, but that had been her family for over a year.
"That thing killed Kedra," Jada sobbed.

"Oh… Did he?" Something in Gabriel's voice made her
look up at him. She frowned as something tickled in the
back of her mind. Something he had said about a prior
claim.

"So, you're not human." Jada was not sure if she should
be offended by the derisive scoff that left his lips, but she
ignored it and began looking at all the damage that had
been done to the club. In his defense, she was stating the
painfully obvious. "What was that thing?"

"He was a Banshee. They are normally very solitary. It's
surprising that he would make such a bargain with Theo."
Gabriel walked through the club and set her down on
stage and started to clean her up. Jada took a deep breath
at the warning bells that were beginning to go off in her
head again.

"I see, what about Theo?" Her face screwed up at the very
mention of Theo and Leticia. Jada continued to allow him
to clean her up, but the anxiety did not leave her.

Something about him was off. Gabriel had the same smile and touched her just as tenderly as always. It was just something beneath the surface that did not allow her to let go of the fear she had spent the better part of the night in.

"Theo and Leticia are trolls." Gabriel finally finished cleaning her up and inspected her nose. He shook his head and mumbled about Banshees and their lack of control. Then, he caught her confused look and smiled as he continued to explain. "They use the club to attract girls no one wants and sell them off in silent auctions through the Briars. Focus on my hand. How many fingers do you see?"

"One. You're all fairies…" Jada said slowly as she watched his armored fingers move back and forth in front of her eyes like a metronome. Her eyes started to droop as she watched his hand. Gabriel gave her another one of those beautiful smiles. She almost allowed herself to get lost in it, but something still was not right. Jada shook her head again, trying to clear it from the lethargy that was taking over her body. The longer she watched the movement of his hand the more exhausted she became. A weary sigh spilled past her lips as she looked around the destruction the Banshee had caused. "Aren't we going to call the police?"

"Why would we do that?" Gabriel lifted his snake-like gaze to her, and he tilted his head to the side just watching her. Meanwhile, his hand had dropped and reverently slid over her skin in a way that had Jada seeing stars for different reasons.

She shook her head trying not to be distracted by the wonderfulness of his touch, or the fatigue that plagued her system. Jada's eyes narrowed at his nonchalance about the night's events. "Someone has to find Kedra…"

"No one is looking for Kedra, eliminate her from your thoughts." Gabriel snapped, and his hand lifted to stroke along her cheek to comfort her from the sting of his words. "Anyway, who is going to believe that a group of fairies are human trafficking in a strip club?"

"But… We have to tell someone!" The alarm bells were going whole hog inside her head, and she started to feel uncomfortable beneath the gaze she once thought was benign. However, her limbs had started to grow heavy. "You are here to stop them after all!"

"How presumptuous." He laughed, and the sound made Jada's blood run cold. A roll of his shoulders released large gossamer wings that gracefully lifted him from the floor and brought him on to the stage. "I didn't come to stop anything going on in this club. I came to the surface to get you."

"If you are not here to stop the auctions, then you're…" Then, she remembered what the Banshee had said about Gabriel wanting the same thing as he did. Jada looked up into Gabriel's golden eyes, and he just watched the puzzle pieces fit together in her head with amusement. The metal-covered tips of his fingers continued to gently trail across her skin. Gabriel pulls her into his arms as she tiredly tries to make sense of the predicament, she now found herself in.

"Good, you understand. Are you ready to go now?" Gabriel asked, but it was not really a question. He gathered her in his arms and moved towards the back of the stage. A bright light shone behind the curtain, and Jada's eyes winced at the light's intensity.

"What are you doing? Let me go!" Even as the words slurred from Jada's lips, her head fell to Gabriel's chest. She fought to keep her eyes open even as Gabriel's vice-like grip held her steady in his arms. He gave a bemused shake of his head as he walked her bridal style towards the curtains.

"No, now hold still, and go to sleep. You don't want to get lost in the Briars. You won't like the monsters you find." Gabriel kissed the top of her head and hugged her close. His lips brushed against her ear as he whispered, "Don't worry. You'll get used to your new life after a while. Of course, some modifications will need to be made."

"Modifications?" Jada murmured, struggling to stay awake, but sleep was over taking any objections she had. She yawned once more, and this time when her eyes closed, they stayed that way. Her fitful dreams were filled with images of thorns, shadows, and Gabriel's smile.

Chapter Three

Jada's eyes slowly blinked open, and she stared at the ceiling for a few moments before looking around. She was wrapped in a sea of white linen, and down pillows the color of sea glass. She tried, but could not remember the last time she had felt so comfortable. Her eyes wandered over the washes of moss greens and ocean blues on the walls. The room was calming but empty. There was nothing in the room except for the colossal bed she rested in. Jada twisted around looking for the source of light that filled the room. It was a perfect cube devoid of windows, lamps, or doors. There was no comparison to the decrepit apartment on July Alley, but it was not somewhere she would have taken herself.

Gingerly, Jada pulled herself out from beneath the covers and sat back against the mahogany headboard. Her muscles screamed at her to be still. Minus a few aches and pains, she was physically fine. Looking around her prison, revealed that there were no doors or windows. It was a beautiful room, but a prison nonetheless. It was a perfectly sealed box with a bed inside. Her hand started to rub away the agitation that she started to feel, but she had to find her fingers through thick creamy bunches of lace that enclosed her fingers. She slammed her cloth-covered hands onto the bed in frustration. "What am I doing here?"

Then, it all came rushing back to her: The club, fairies, and Kedra lying lifelessly on the ground. Her beautiful smile was frozen in death. Tears welled in Jada's eyes, and her hands lifted to cover her face. Her shoulders shook as a sob wracked her frame. The next sound that left her lips was an outraged scream. The sound bouncing off the bare walls reminding her that she was no longer in Texas. Jada wiped away her tears in frustration, but forced herself to pull in deep, calming breaths. Her rage would have to be placed in a box marked for later. There was no time to be hysterical. She would mourn her friends once she got back home, and called the police. She needed to pull herself together and figure out how to get out of there.

"Oh, for goodness sakes!" Her hands furiously clawed at the comforter that wrapped around her. It was a fight to get out of the bed with its oceans of sheets, pillows, and the billowy nightgown she wore. It was a fussy Victorian number replete with ruffles and bows. Once she swam out of bed, she began pulling back the lace, and checking herself over. Her skin was devoid of any of the horrors that took place the night before. Save for the stitches, there was almost no proof that anything had happened to her at all. Her fingers lifted to rake frosted coils away from her dark brown eyes in irritation only to find her hair plated, and covered with a satin bonnet that matched the fluffy gown she wore.

She was not sure who had changed her, but Jada knew that she had not been in any shape to pull anything off. Let alone put herself into this complicated pinafore.

That left Gabriel, the man, no, the fairy that brought her here. Was it just last night that she had pictured a future with him? A deep, shaky breath pulled into her lungs as she berated herself aloud. "If I had just followed my first mind, and left that club, I would be home right now. Not in some windowless seafoam colored gulag!"

Fury soon replaced frustration as her thoughts shifted to Theo and Leticia. and. Leticia had been part of the little family she had made for herself at the club. Jada had confided in her, and told her everything. Even about the feelings she had harbored for Gabriel. Theo was another story, his actions did not surprise her in the least. "I should have known better than to listen to him. That jerk would sell his mother to hell for a pack of pop rocks and cola."

A door opened in the blank wall of the bedroom, and Gabriel walked through. The smile that had made her fall in love with him in the first place lighting up the room he now dominated. Chocolate eyes warily watched him, and she could feel the anger beneath her skin welling to the surface. Jada slowly backed away until the back of her knees hit the foot of the bed. He was no longer wearing the suit of armor, but he looked no less like a prince in his white breeches and knee-high black boots. The gold lining of his black frock coat almost glows against his golden tanned skin. He looked so good she almost forgot that the man was a monster that scared other monsters.

"Acclimating to your new surroundings I see." Gabriel's friendly words belied the amused malice in his voice. Snake-like irises rolled over her face and he frowned. Within two strides, he caught her within his embrace. Jada tried to wrestle out of his arm but his hold remained firm.

"I can't believe there was a time I dreamed of being exactly where I am now!" Jada's thoughts snapped as her hands lifted to press back against Gabriel's broad chest, trying to get out of his clutches. "Although in my defense, Gabriel had been human then. No, actually, he has never been human, and I'm going to have to make peace with that."

One of Gabriel's hands caught, and hauled her closer. Jada's breath caught in her throat at the speed and strength with which he moved. The angry midnight of her gaze met with the topaz of his.or a moment, she thought he was going to kiss her. Gabriel's lips tugged at the corner, and he loosened his hold. Jada was not sure if she was relieved or disappointed about it. Piano player like fingers lifted to cup her chin and examine her nose closer. "Damn Banshee. I should take the damage to your face out of his hide."

That was something Jada agreed with, but she had other things to worry about. Like how she was going to get back to her home from wherever this was. "I thought I asked you to take me home."

If Gabriel was annoyed, he did not say anything. He just continued to loosely hold her in his arms and watch her face curiously. His serpent-like gaze moved over her face once more. "I did, you are in my home, and you're welcome."

"Welcome!?" The word flowed past her lips in an incredulous whisper. Jada jerked out of his hold, and her fist balled at her sides. She was just this close to wreaking havoc all over his perfect face. She doubted she would hurt him much, but he would physically know how much she despised him for kidnapping her.

"Yes, you heard me welcome! That bug infested apartment building was a blight on the neighborhood's property value and your image." Shame and hurt started to burn beneath Jada's skin at Gabriel's word. His pale amber eyes glowed with anger, as he seemed to have a lot to say on the subject. "You should thank me for pulling you out of the life you were never going to escape from. Heaven forbid, I saved you from ending up like Kedra!" His dark sibilant voice lashed out, against the rage that she was feeling. As if stoking an inferno that was looking for a way out of its furnace.

The sound of her hand meeting his beautiful smug face was deafening within the emptiness of the room. Jada felt that he earned the slap she leveled at his face. Jada was far too busy shaking with rage, to pay any mind to the soft menacing hiss that she now knew belonged to him. What she had was not much, but she had earned every bit of that hovel.

"Say what you want about me, but you will not disrespect Kedra that way. She wasn't innocent, but she had been trying!" Jada had to pull in a deep breath, in an effort to control her temper. Something about being in this room, or maybe even near, him amplified her rage tenfold. "At least she never pretended to be anything that she wasn't. She sure as hell did not deserve to be twisted inside out, and discarded like trash. No one deserves to die that way!"

Jada could not remember her voice ever being so devoid of emotion, but she hated the way it sounded. Gabriel must have felt he deserved that slap too, because he had the good grace to look momentarily ashamed at what he said. Only in that moment though, because once his serpentine eyes blinked the only emotion left was amusement. Gabriel watched her for a moment. His eyes catalogued and weighed her in silence. He must have been pleased with something because soon his smile matched his eyes and stepped away and motioned behind her.

"You'll find something suitable to wear in the wardrobe, get dressed. I am taking you to the Court and Crown." Gabriel smiled and moved towards the door. Jada frowned and half turned to see what he was gesturing to in an empty room. There stood a tall mahogany wardrobe. The two wide doors were inlaid with light wood panels. While three draws beneath the doors slid open. Gabriel turned and walked toward the door. Jada could hear the amused warning in his voice rather than see the expression on his face. "And Jada, please don't do anything that will cause me to discipline you."

"Like what?" It did not sound as if he was playing. Not that it mattered to Jada. She was over both him and the place he had ferried her off to. If he did not like it, he could send her home. Her lips pressed thin at the threat, and her chin lifted to meet his gaze. He was not the first tyrant that she had escaped from.

Gabriel's sculpted lips spread into a smile that was both beautiful and cruel. "Please be downstairs in thirty minutes." With that, Gabriel closed the door, and left Jada wondering how she could have ever thought he was human.

"If he had wanted me to hurry, he could have at least grabbed my bag as he was kidnapping me." Jada snarked to herself as she watched the door contemplating sneaking out instead. Clearly, he did not trust her. As the thought of escape manifested the door sealed itself closed as Jada's mouth opened in surprised indignation. "The nerve of this b... oh!"

Angrily, Jade made her way to the wardrobe that had not been there when she had woken up. Her fingers glided over the decorative woodwork of the doors. The whole thing probably retailed what her apartment would cost for the span of two years. Her fingers pulled the gold latch, and there was a profusion of gowns. Green's, golds, burgundies, and a slew of other colors that almost blinded her. She was not sure exactly what to wear somewhere she had never been, but she had less than thirty minutes to figure it out.

With a deep frustrated sigh, Jada selected a pale gold gown with pearl buttons that lined the back. It looked like one of the dresses from one of her favorite slightly smutty regency novels. It had been filled with beautiful clothes and a dashing hero. Her thoughts wandered back to the evil fairy that was waiting on her, and her mood sobered. There were no heroes to be had here, so she would have to save herself Gabriel had not given her much time, and she was not necessarily sure how to operate the hooks on the gown she chose. A soft hiss filled the room, and Jada turned to look around the room with wide eyes. The sound seemed to emanate from somewhere, but there was nothing there to make it besides her. Warily she set the dress down and opted to do something with her hair.

Jada turned and a vanity that matched the wardrobe appeared in front of her. Jada barely contained the surprised scream, and hurriedly pulled her nerves together. She had to hurry and get ready. It was one thing to try Gabriel at the club, but another to try him on his home turf. She would have to play nice until she found her way home. Luckily, the vanity had a wide-tooth comb. In fact, the vanity surprisingly had many things that she would need to do her hair. Jada's lips pursed in concern but decided to focus on it later. She quickly but carefully detangled her coily hair and plated it into a spiral row that made a halo at her crown.

After completing her hair, Jada turned around surprised to see the dress resting open on the bed. All of the pearl latches spread out for her to get into. Her warm brown fingers gingerly lifted the dress and held it to her body, once she made it to the bed. The material was so satiny and soft, it was like a dream to hold. Jada guiltily spun around watching the bottom of the dress flare around her legs.

Another irritated disembodied hiss had the doors of the wardrobe open, and under garments were forcefully thrown at her before the door sharply shut once more. Jada scrambled to hold onto the dress and the new material that was foisted onto her. "Well, that explains the noise. What's wrong? Was I taking too long? Will his highness be upset?" Jada snapped, tossing the dresser a dirty look.

The wardrobe hissed back at her and disappeared as abruptly as it had appeared, leaving a pair of crystal slippers. Jada slid the lace and silk garments over her body with far more attitude than the action required. She was not sure where this sense of urgency was coming from. There were no clocks in the room after all. After she shimmed into the gown, she slid her feet into the dainty bits of crystal. Looking herself over, she did one more twirl, and hated the sudden child-like giddiness at the way the dress splayed over her feet. She stopped herself and looked around trying to figure out why her emotions were swinging so widely. "It has to be this room. There is now way I should feel anything but angry and scared."

A wave of urgency swept over her when the door reappeared. The back of her gown hung open, but there was nothing for it. She would have to show up half-dressed or risk whatever Gabriel called discipline. Jada was not sure what punishment entailed, but from the cobra-like look in Gabriel's eyes, she really did not want to find out.

Stepping out of the room put her in a long richly decorated hallway. Unlike the serene stillness of the room, the hallway was a cacophony of ticks, and chimes. The cream-colored walls were covered with clocks, and other time pieces. Jada moved down the hallway as quickly as her shoes allowed. Her hands lifted the skirts when they threatened to twist between her legs and trip her. The ticks of the clocks seemed to get louder and louder as she moved under vaulted glass ceilings towards the twin spirals that constituted the staircase before her. Carefully she made her way down the winding stairs into a wide light brown foyer and saw Gabriel watching an elaborate gold pocket watch with a frown. He looked regal standing in front of a wide stained-glass door. The large glass pane was an explosion of colorful doves, peacocks, and other birds of paradise.

Her hand lifted to rest on her heaving chest as she tried to catch her breath. Jada's face was flush with the effort she made in reaching him on time. Just as the clocks in the building hit noon, the sunlight that had been streaming through the windows suddenly darkened. The clocks filled the mansion with rings and gongs. Gabriel turned to her with a wide smile.

"Thank you for being on time. I had thought you were going to tempt fate and make me punish you. You had one minute to spare." He sounded as if he was disappointed. His lithe frame relaxed beneath his coat; Jada guessed he had been prepared to drag her out of the room. Gabriel looked back down at his watch, and pocketed it with a flourish. Jada pulled in a deep breath trying to still her rapidly beating heart, she mentally told herself was only racing because she had run there.

Gabriel moved into her immediate space and began inspecting her. The tips of his hands gently ghosting over the gown she wore. Jada's cheeks warmed beneath his touch, and she sharply stepped back. He was making it hard to think, and she needed her wits about her. "I'm not ready. I don't know how to close the hooks on my own."

Gabriel's brow lifted at the information that Jada had begrudgingly volunteered. His gaze widening and contracting over a bemused smile. "The dresser didn't help you?"

Jada quickly relayed the odd events that had transpired after he left her. Her hands animatedly moving about as she tattled on the wardrobe "The dresser threw my unmentionables at me and slammed the door in my face."

"Octavius must be feeling bitter." Gabriel laughed and moved behind her. His fingers deftly began to close the hooks that lined her back. He leaned in, and Jada shivered at the brush of his lips against her ear. He was too close once again. "Don't worry. He'll get used to you soon."

"The wardrobe has a name?" Her voice was shaky, but Gabriel would have to forgive her, she was only this close to men in very controlled spaces like the club. At the club Gabriel would be the one to save her when a customer got too close, but there was no one here to save her from Gabriel.

"Yes." Gabriel drew out the "s" in a soft hiss that seemed to be more pronounced the longer he touched her. By this time, his hands had moved to caress the bodice of her gown. The tip of his nose drawing a line over the column of her neck. "He used to work for me." Jada felt her skin heat beneath Gabriel's touch. She kept her eyes averted until he finished closing the hooks at her collar. The moment he was done, she stepped away and turned to look into his eyes. Jada's own narrowed in confusion and looked back in the direction she came from. "And he retired to being a wardrobe?"

"No, I retired him into being a wardrobe." His words were serious. A smile broke out over his lips although it never reached his eyes. Gabriel's hands lifted to straighten the pale gold cravat at his neck. His coat straightened with a roll of his shoulders. He turned toward the stained-glass door, and gallantly offered Jada his arm. "Shall we?"

"I see…" So, he could turn people into wardrobes. That information did nothing to bolster her chances of escape. Jada ignored his arm and stepped forward. This was not a date. She was a captive regardless of how nicely he dressed her. Gabriel ignored the slight and opened the door for her. She stepped out into the surprisingly cool air and stopped short. Pleasant puffy clouds hung overhead, but the sky was a strange mix of day and night. As if it could not figure out what time it wanted to be. Warm air brushed along her ear lobe as Gabriel leaned to whisper into her ear.

"No, Not yet, but you will." He straightens and pulls away with a purr. His hand moves to her lower back guiding her through the heavy doors before turning to close and lock them. "Come we'll be late, and I don't want to make up a story to explain our tardiness. I hate lying."

"Do you?" Her lashes almost met her hairline and her lips parted indignantly. "You just spent the better part of a year pretending to be a bouncer."

"Of course, I do." Gabriel's smiles and hooks his arm into hers, ignoring the rest of her statement. It was as if no matter how hard she tried to keep her distance he would find a way to touch or get closer to her. "You look perfect."

Her brow lifted, and she looked over herself with an appraising look. She had to admit that the gown was spectacular. It was surprising how well it fit her. "Thank you. Should I even ask how you knew my size?"

"Leticia, took care of making sure I had your measurements, likes, and dislikes." Gabriel's voice was so matter of fact as he led her into half of the sunlight.

"How thorough." Gabriel only smiled more at the tightness in her voice. She disengaged her arm, and stood apart from him. Ignoring the jovial laugh, he was having at her expense. The sound reminded her of the many times he would tease her before she went in to work. Jada forced herself to ignore the good memories she had of him. She wanted no reminders that she liked him, but it was hard to shut her feelings off after a year of holding them so close to her heart.

Jada followed him out into the part of the day that was much brighter than her mood. The clouds were high and fluffy. Birds were singing, and butterflies were dancing through the air. Her eyes scanned the high green rolling hills that stretched into the distance before they became greyish mountains. The part of the sky that was night covered low stone fences and a large expanse of a large grove of silver maples that twisted and reached towards the moon. "It's beautiful, wherever here is."

"It's cold here. I prefer warmer climates." Gabriel looked over the beautiful countryside dispassionately before focusing on something behind her. "The estate was a gift I received when I became a council member."

Jada tore her eyes from the pastoral scene before her to look back at him. Trying to reconcile the bouncer, she knew with the new information he gave her. "You're a politician?"

"Such as it is, yes." Gabriel smiled and nodded to something behind her. A soft neigh pulled Jada's attention away from Gabriel, and her eyes widened in amazement. There was a beautiful grey and gold carriage pulled by four white clockwork horses coming towards her. Gabriel stood beside her and they silently waited until the driverless horses pulled up to them. Jada's hand lifted to stroke the muzzle of the closest horse to her. The hollow beast gently nudged her hand in response. She despised herself for being charmed by something that lived in a world that she would grow to hate.

Gabriel collected her hands, and brought them up to his lips in a fond kiss. He pulled the carriage door open and guided her into an enclosed seating area. It was a mass of soft looking grey pillows and cushions. Once settled Jada watched him climb into the carriage before focusing on the view outside. After a moment she decided now was as good as time as any to get answers. "Where am I?"

"You are in the Fairlands, or as we say through the Briars." Gabriel settled back into the carriage and tapped on the roof. The horses gently pulled into a quick trot, and Jada could only guess at what made them operate. It felt like they were flying. She did not feel one bump in the road or any unleveled terrain as they began passing through the countryside. Gabriel closed his eyes and looked as if he was going to take a nap.

"That's where? Scotland? Haiti? I've only been asleep for a few hours. We can't be that far from Dallas." Jada frowned in confusion as she waited for his response. He said he hated lying, but it was not as if he volunteered the fact that he was a fairy. She had found out the hard way. When it came to Gabriel, she would have to accept that her judgment was not the best and operate from that perspective.

"Why do you doubt the things your senses are telling you?" Gabriel did not look at her. His eyes remained closed, but the soft smile on his lips told her that he was aware of everything that was going on around him. "You are in a carriage pulled by driverless horses. A wardrobe threw the undergarments I painstakingly chose for you. You watched me grow wings."

Jada angrily glanced at him from the side and took a deep calming breath to gather what was left of her patience. "I am trying to make sense of what is going on. Yes, you grew wings..."

"Which with anyone else would have gotten me laid, or at the very least a pledge of everlasting fealty. I truly miss the 1600's" Gabriel interrupted her crossly.

She turned towards him with a roll of her eyes. "There are things happening all around me that don't make any sense. Yes, I'm behind on the whole the Briars place as you call it, but that doesn't tell me what the Fairlands are."

"Fair enough. As I said, you are now in the world of Fairy. This means, though you are still on Earth, you are in a shady area between what religion calls purgatory and what you call reality. When your folklore tells you about wizards, witches, and warlocks using magic, they are pulling power from this world. Nothing is made from nothing." Gabriel's long fingers interlaced over his stomach, silently announcing that the subject was closed. Which was too bad for him.

"Fine, I'm not in Texas any longer. Why am I here?" One of Gabriel's eyes opened, to look at her over the barest of smiles. The mood in the carriage shifted, and the air of patient cruelty made her feel cold inside. Once again, he had let the gentleman like veneer slip into what she called the real Gabriel.

Both eyes opened as he silently watched her. It was as if he was trying to decide if he was going to kill or kiss her. After a few suspended minutes, his golden features softened from what Jada knew to be his true face. The cold, calculated assessment ended in a smile, causing Jada to release a breath she had not realized she had been holding. "Get some rest, Jada. We have to figure out the status of your ownership first."

"What's to figure out? I belong to me." Her voice dropped off as a pale golden glow lit his cobra-like eyes. His iris contracting and shrinking at their ends. Jada did not know what she said was wrong, but apparently, it made him furious. His movements became stiff as if his patience had run out, and he was one hundred percent done with her nonsense for the day.

"You will need that fire inside of you for what lies ahead." His words were short and clipped as he spoke to her. The smile that curved his lips was a humorless imitation of the one he normally gave her. She had crossed an invisible line, and landed on a land mine she had not known was there. Gabriel's voice was low and without the typical hiss that she had begun to attribute with lust or amusement. "However, don't say anything like that again. Aloud or to yourself. I'd hate to break my new toy before I've had a chance to play with it."

It was his turn to take a deep breath, and this time when his lids fell, Jada understood the subject was permanently closed. It took Jada a few moments to tamp down the rage that was boiling inside of her. He meant every word he said, and there was little if anything she could do about it. As he was no longer willing to carry on the conversation, Jada turned her attention to the scenery outside, angrily mulling over her options.

The countryside soon turned to what now looked like a busy village, Spanish tiles lining the roofs of various buildings. The sound of a merry church bell ringing in the distance told her it had just turned one. The sky was completely sunny once more, and the air had become warmer. The horses pulled to a stop in front of a large stately tan building with a blue seal above the door. In the center of the seal was a silver shield decorated with a blue crown, and scythe surrounded by what looked like silver ivy.

The clockwork horses happily puffed steam out into the air, and Gabriel stepped out of the carriage. He adjusted his coat and turned, holding out his hand to her. His serpentine gaze daring her to reject his outstretched hand in full view of the court steps. How many nights had she dreamed of taking his hand, and going anywhere that was not that dingy little club?

Refraining from embarrassing him on the court steps, thus deciding on the better part of valor, Jada took his hand. He had mentioned punishment, and she would avoid it for now. She was not at home, and she doubted the authorities here would be on her side. However, her nose, complete with its stitches lifted as she walked ahead of him. Going so far as to ignore his amusement as if the very prospect of acknowledgement was beneath her.

"What have we here?" A soft waspish hum brought Jada's attention off to the side. It belonged to one of two round portly men who mirrored each other in size, but were purposeful opposites in others.

The two gentlemen looked like jokers from a deck of cards played in hell. One wore a dark red suit and coat, the other wore a deep purple version. Where the one who wore purple had deep brown skin and blond hair. The one who wore red had a light olive skin tone with black hair. The one other thing they both shared was red irises that watched and weighed them both. Though Jada hated Gabriel, at the present moment she was not ashamed to step behind him. Anything to get away from the piercing gaze of the men who were openly assessing her. This seemed to do nothing but amuse the walking contradictions. They smiled, and Jada really wished they had not. They had long blunt rectangles of dried bone that rested in an offset pattern between their lips where their teeth should have been.

The creature in red spoke again, and this time the buzzing of his voice was louder, it was like the humming of angry yellow jackets. "Gabriel, so pleasant to see you. "

"Inquisitor Trinity, Inquisitor Trine, how are you? What brings you to the court and crown today?" There was an edge to Gabriel's voice, and Jada took another good look at the two men in front her. Her hand reflexively lifted to rest on Gabriel's back at the less than friendly greeting. Jada could feel by the subtle ways his muscles stiffened that he did not like them despite the words of greeting.

"Just here on council business. Nothing major, just a simple question of ownership." Trinity tossed the fringe of black hair that fell away from his eye, and shifted his gaze to Jada once more. His smile spread further as his red gaze slowly took her in. "What brings you here?"

"Just a clerical mix up over a new acquisition." Gabriel smiled with a shrug. Gabriel's muscles continued to coil as if preparing for a fight beneath Jada's hands. Whoever these two were, they were a problem. According to the way Gabriel's muscles bunched beneath his coat, he was prepared to fight.

Jada silently watched the exchange mentally trying to figure out what was happening, and how all the information could help her. "Was the enemy of Gabriel a friend or enemy to her?

"She looks delicious Gabriel. I hope whatever error was made is quickly cleared up for you. I would hate to see you lose such a tantalizing morsel." The words buzzed just against her ear by the one in purple called Trine. Most definitely not her friend. Jada turned sharply to swat at the angry buzzing sound in her ear.

Gabriel's hand shot out to grab her hand before the hit could land against Trine's face. He quickly twisted

her around in a swirl of gold skirts and into his arms as if they were dancing. When she next looked up, she was enclosed protectively in his arms. Gabriel pressed a quick kiss to her temple in both apology and smoothing of ruffled feathers.

"We'll be going; we don't want to be late. Give the rest of the council my best, won't you?" Gabriel disengaged her from his embrace and began leading her to the doors of the courthouse. His hand moved protectively to the middle of her back.

"I hope the acquisition goes in your favor Gabriel." The soft buzz of Trinity's voice was starting to grate on her nerves. The sound was meant to be disturbing, and as far as Jada was concerned, it was working. "When you get bored with her keep us in mind won't you?"

Jada's back stiffened against Gabriel's hand, and she turned sharply. It had been just a matter of time before she snapped, and as far as Jada was concerned now was the perfect time. She took a step forward and Gabriel stepped in front of her. She was barely able to contain the fury that was becoming a near constant companion in her life. The pale gold of Gabriel's amused gaze held a warning, that she reluctantly heeded. She gave Trinity and Trine a tight smile, then turned and headed through the doors that Gabriel had been leading her towards. It was hard to ignore the waspish sniggering coming from behind her back, but she succeeded.

"Thank you." A man in a dark blue suit who had the head of a lion handed her a ticket, and deeply bowed to Gabriel. Jada's posture remained rigid as she moved through the tall heavy oak doors into a small grey entryway. All of the wood trim in the building was a dark espresso color. It gave an air of importance and finality.

Waiting until she could trust herself to speak once more. "Who or what were they?"

"They are the council's inquisitors. They handle investigations in accordance with the bylaws of the council." Gabriel nodded to the flamingo with a smile. The whispering inside the large dark blue chamber became louder as Gabriel walked through. Though to Jada's ears most of the buzz seemed positive."

"Like the police?" Jada saw a group of women in lovely colorful gowns whose rapt attention stayed on Gabriel as they walked by. When he waved to them, their forms excitedly fell apart into three piles of autumn leaves. "Aren't you popular?"

"Executioners actually. Don't be jealous." Gabriel murmured from behind Jada. She heard rather than saw the smile in his voice.

"I'm not. I'm just trying to stay alive." Jada's reply was sharp as she curiously watched the mounds of leaves to see if they would reform once more.

"You're doing very well Jada. I'm proud of you." Gabriel sounded almost chipper as they made their way through the long equally blue hall of the Court and Crown. The corridor was filled with stark white marble, and plush dark blue carpets.

"And we both know how I live and die for your praise Massa Gabriel." Jada snapped, as her eyes looked towards the heavens for patience. Her movements continued to be taut as she moved down the marbled halls of the court building. The temperature inside was much cooler than outside. It served as a balm against her indignation. "Should I fetch your slippers when we get home?"

Gabriel continued guiding down the hall, but his voice had gone flat. He almost sounded cross as he spoke. "You have my word that you will never see that estate again."

"I won't? Wait, why not?" Jada turned in surprised confusion. She was tired of not knowing what was going on. Her gaze moved to his frustration. "Where am I going?"

Gabriel smiled but did not say anything. His eyes moved to focus on something further down the hall. Jada turned and her lips parted on a sharp scream. The monster who had tried to kidnap her from the club was standing there in a black coat and green breeches. She stepped back, and the only purchase she found was into Gabriel arms. The monster bowed and slithered towards them.

Chapter Four

H ello. Greetings. Salutations." Bane gave a disjointed giggle that made Jada's blood run cold. Though he was a thing of nightmares, he was smartly dressed in a black brocade frock coat lined with green satin. The long black rope of his hair was tied with a green thong. Here his skin had a soft shipper despite its milky appearance. Jada found herself sandwiched between Bane and Gabriel in a few quick strides. Her hands lifted to place themselves against the dark emerald green fabric and gently pushed forward to ease herself from between the two unyielding fairies.

Jada noted the way his pearlescent skin flushed at her touch and removed her hands immediately. Another high-pitched giggle filtered past his red lips. Long spine-like fingers wrapped around her hand and pulled her closer to him. "My dear, my queen, my prize! Cordial of Gabriel to bring you to me."

"The Crown will establish who she belongs to. Come along Jada." Gabriel stepped forward, and gently pulled her away. His hand moved to her lower back to steer her towards the doors and away from Bane.

Both men chivalrously put their hands flat against the heavy oaken doors and push forward to allow her to walk in before them. Jada would have found it noble if the situation were not leading to a lifetime of ownership and heaven knew what else. As the doors opened, Jada's eyes lowered as they adjusted to the blinding light that filled her vision. Her senses were overwhelmed in this wide navy-blue room. The room was a stately hall filled with various fairies. Some were a mix of human and animal, and some were just animals. A dashing hedgehog in a black military coat, and a dainty pelican adjusting her petticoats were standing on either side of a large brass scale. Both spiritedly and loudly defending themselves. There was pandemonium inside the courtroom, and Jada was not sure if she was amazed or frightened.

The Judge who listened to them looked as if he had been carved out of black stone. His milky white eyes were lifted towards the heavens beneath the pschent crown he wore. The golden hieroglyphs that scrolled along his ebony chest and arms seemed to shift and move across his skin like sand across the desert. Jada felt as if he could see right through her, blind or not. He sat upon a large ornate winged backed chair that seemed to swallow the diminutive man whole. The Judge's hand waved back and forth over a large papyrus scroll, as the hedgehog and the lady pelican bickered, each pass of his hands created braille-like rises in the parchment.

Jada lifted her long skirts from around her legs to move through the court audience. He led her to a row of seats roughly in the middle of the room, behind a partition that separated them from the scales. Jade settled down, between both men, and released a deep sigh. Whatever the Judge saw, she knew it was not going to be her freedom.

"Counselor, get your client under control, before I do it for him." The Judge's voice sounded like sand washing across the desert. It was neither hurried nor loud, but it did not sound as if the Judge was in the mood for any argument.

A tall cherubic looking man in a white pirate-like shirt flapped his gossamer wings and stood up quickly, throwing a worried glance at the dashing hedgehog. "Yes, of course your lordship. Mr. Oakley please calm down."

Oakley lifted his cane and began waving it around angrily. "I am calm, and within my rights! That old feather face pigeon stole my human and helped him escape!" Despite the severity of the situation, Jada was charmed by the Irish lilt of the hedgehog's voice. She found it hard to keep a slight smile from curling her lips. Her fingers curled over her mouth to keep from offending the furious hedgehog further.

"Yes, Mr. Oakley but..." The cherub started again only to be interrupted by a forceful wave of Mr. Oakley's cane.

"That man broke bread with me, and I demand 1000 years! That prattling horn swallow robbed me!" Oakley yelled at the Judge, and the Pelican gasped holding a handkerchief over her mouth in shock.

"I did no such thing. The human died in my bushes, and I disposed of him properly! I could not have him decaying in my snapdragon roses after all! I insist on all of my flowers being organic, and human fertilizer would be in violation with the Goblin markets." The Pelican sniffed angrily and turned to the Judge. "There is nothing left to serve Mr. Oakly, because there is nothing left of him."

"I demand satisfaction!" Oakley shouted again which caused another flurry of angry activity that Jada was having a hard time following.

"I rule in favor of Mrs. Fernhen. Bailiff, take them away." The Judge's voice swirled over the room, and the bailiff hurriedly removed the group from the scales. Those watching tittered, and whispered amongst each other, while the Judge continued to wave his hand over his book.

The Bailiff returned, smoothing out his gold and blue uniform before turning to the Judge. "Are you ready for the next case, your honor?"

"I suppose, but bailiff for your sake please don't bore me this time." The Judge's words made the bailiff grow pale, as he looked to Gabriel and Bane to save him. Jada's eyes widen at the steely tone of the Judge's voice, and the fear in the bailiff's eyes.

Bane leaned down, so that his lips were just above Jada's ear. "Whoever wins the cases here depends on how well you tell your story. Unlike your world where money decides much of who receives justice."

Jada rose as Gabriel rose, and smoothed out her dress with a frown. "Is it any fairer?"

Bane's amused smile stretched showing rows of sharp jagged teeth, and not for the first time Jada felt a shiver of fear race beneath her skin. One clawed finger extended to tap her lightly on the nose, before he moved ahead of her. "No."

The bailiff ruffled through his pages and began stuttering. "Y-your honor, the ne-ne-next case is about the ownership of a hu-human stripper."

"Oh excellent, this sounds promising already! Is everyone involved here?" The Judge waved his hand moving to a new page of the book as Gabriel and Bane moved to stand on opposite sides of the large scale. His eyes sightlessly watched them as they moved into place. Jada watched the chains of the scales shiver and creak beneath their weight.

"Yes, your honor." The bailiff took Jada's hand, and moved her to stand directly in front of the Judge.

"Don't dawdle, proceed!" The Judge's excitement seemed to send an electric current through the hall. It was the quietest Jada had heard the room since she first entered.

"Yes of course. Bane Sidhe versus Councilman Gabriel. Now that you have taken your places. You will each get a turn to speak after the lady in question has had her say." The bailiff gives Jada a kind smile that she returns. "Ms. Jada, is it? If you would please approach the Judge."

What would please Jada would be to go home. However, she did as she was asked and moved closer to the bench. The Judge leaned forward as if to see Jada better with his milky eyes. The Judge smiled displaying shark-like teeth and Jada took a quick step back, which seemed to tickle the Judge immensely. His dry chuckle filled the silent hall.

His claw-like hand waved over the book while his other hand waved in a motion for her to begin. "Tell me of the events that conspired to bring you here before me, my dear."

Jada looked back at the men on the scales and Bane's red lips were set in a slight frown, while Gabriel smiled as if nothing important like the rest of her life hung in the balance. Jada looked between them both and did the only thing that she knew how. She snitched on both of them.

Jada pointed at each one, as she explained why she was there. She had to get someone to understand her predicament. "Your honor, I was kidnapped by Gabriel from Bane, who tried to kidnap me from the club I performed at, called Karnach."

The Judge stroked his golden wrapped goatee and nodded. "The strip club?"

Jada frowned with a wary tilt of her head. There was always resistance to give justice to those who worked in socially unacceptable professions. Regardless of if, those in acceptable professions funded them. "Yes…sir, but I don't see…"

"Was there a runway?" The Judge suddenly jumped forward onto the podium that held his book as if to hear her better.

Jada took another nervous step back and continued again. "Uh yes, your honor, but…"

His hand rapidly waved forward impatiently. "And poles?"

"Your honor, yes, however…" Jada fought not to roll her eyes. This was getting her nowhere.

The Judge jumped back into his seat and nodded. "How did Bane find you?"

Jada swallowed and took a deep breath to steady her growing impatience. "The trolls tried to sell me off to him, and he followed me into the coin booths."

"He paid cash to watch you shake it?" Another shark like smile spread across the Judge's face, and Jada knew this case was not going to go at all the way she wanted.

That was the last straw for Jada, she recovered the two steps she had taken from the bench and glared up at the Judge. "Your honor!"

The Judge held up his hands in surrender. "Okay fine, but did you make it clap?"

Jada stood in stunned silence trying to process the Judge's last statement. "I am so sorry, what?"

The Judge sighed and moved onto the next question

"How did Gabriel find you?"

Jada watched the Judge warily and continued. "Gabriel was a bouncer at Karnach where I worked, but I fail to see…"

"So, he watched you dance for free?" Jada followed the Judge's line of sight to Gabriel who nodded with a wide smile that did not make Jada feel any better about her chances of receiving justice for herself or her friends. In fact, the ominous way Gabriel's scale lifted higher was a bad omen if Jada ever saw one.

Jada looked back at the Judge in confusion. "What in the irrelevance…That was his job, your honor."

"You pretended to be a bouncer, to capture a queen from the human domain?" A sharp sandy laugh was made as the Judge practically pulled out a verbal cigar to Gabriel for his cunning.

"Yes, your honor." Gabriel almost sounded bashful. He even bowed at the praise the Judge gave him. Jada on the other hand was sick at the way the court clapped and murmured their approval.

The Judge doubled over in laughter. His clawed hands resting over his stomach as gales of laughter filled the courtroom. The pages of the book he used fluttering rapidly to the next set of pages. He turned to Bane with a shark-like smile and waved his hands once more. "Bane, please proceed with your case."

The scale shivered tremulously with the aggressive step Bane took towards the bench. "Your honor, I am here, attending to press my claim of ownership." Bane waved his arm causing the scale to shiver once more. The scale tilted lower, and Jada doubted the trial would go the way he wanted to go. "I pretended to be an accountant and came to the club to collect my human."

"An accountant?" The Judge's voice was flat and the scale lifted higher on Gabriel's side. Bane grabbed one of the chains to steady himself from the sudden drop.

"Yes, I was told that the humans were very frightened of something called an audit." Jada's hand lifted to pinch the bridge of her nose at smug self-assurance in Bane's voice. It was not only awe-inspiring but also frustrating that an accountant was what he went with. By the silence that filled the room, Jada guessed the whole court agreed.

"Gabriel, call your first witness." The Judge looked to Gabriel as his side of the scale was practically soaring. Jada looked between Gabriel, and threw up her hands in frustration.

"Of course, your honor. If Theodore and Leticia Lungrot would step forward." Gabriel's deep voice was almost cheerful. Why would he not be? Bane had practically assured his win.

Jada's eyes lifted towards the heavens in an aggravated prayer for strength. The bailiff ushered the trolls in, and Jada saw red for one shining moment before she rushed forward to rend them to pieces. The bailiff barely caught her before her fist connected to Theo's nose. "You worthless trafficking slime ball! This is your fault!"

The trolls moved behind the bailiff, and Theo nervously adjusted his suit and tie. An unbothered Leticia examined her thick ring encrusted fingers, then smoothed out the white fur coat that wrapped around her thick curves. Like a piddling thing, like Jada's life was of no importance. They were no less round, but their skin had taken a dark green cast, and tusk protruded from their lower lip. Theo leaned out from the side to peer at her from behind the bailiff. "You got a hold on her?"

Jada turned sharply to release the bailiff's vice-like grip, as she attempted to murder Theo and Leticia in the middle of the courtroom. Her finger pointed at Leticia accusingly. "And you! I thought you were my friend! I told you everything!"

Leticia blew on dark red talons and shrugged. "I am your friend hun, and I do like you. But I have a certain lifestyle I enjoy and if it takes selling a few unwanted humans behind the Briars, so be it!"

"A certain lifestyle!" Jada still wrestled with the bailiff trying to get his hands to loosen up. "They killed Kedra!"

Leticia rolled her eyes and smiled with a shake of her head. "Kedra was killing Kedra. At least Bane was quicker than the poison she was snorting."

Jada was shocked still, and the bailiff breathed a sigh of relief as he let her go. As soon as his hands dropped, Jada launched herself at Leticia amidst the chortling of the Judge. Jada was determined to take out at least an eye. There would be justice, or there would be blood. Jada didn't care which. The bailiff narrowly catches her again and pulls her back to the front of the courtroom. Depositing her in front of a laughing Judge.

"Oh, I see what the fuss is about. She will make an excellent queen." The Judge wipes a tear away from his cloudy eyes. "Trolls give your testimony before I tell the bailiff to release her."

"It's like this, your honor. This bird was a waitress until Kedra brought her to the club." Theo's bulbous fingers raked back across his bald green head. "I took one look at her and knew we would have some interested buyers. Gabriel here expressed interest but didn't quite have enough to cover her fee. So being the upstanding troll I am, I let him work off the rest at the club."

Jada's eyes lifted angrily to Gabriel, who only smiled at her with an unapologetic shrug. He looked as if he was enjoying himself. The scale tipped so far in his favor, that it made it almost impossible for Jada to glare at him, as he deserved. Almost impossible.

"Bane came last night and saw her. The thing is Bane over here had all the money up front. I feel for Gabriel, but like my beautiful wife said. She likes nice things." Theo turns to Leticia and makes various kissing noises just before her face. His green fingers gently scratching beneath her chin. Leticia, in turn, giggles at the flirting in a way that made Jada want to retch. "So, I figured I'd give Gabriel Kedra, and call it square."

The Judge's head turned towards the troll, and his voice rumbled through the court like an oncoming storm. His voice was dangerously low, and Jada took a few steps away from the bench. "Had Gabriel worked off Jada's fee by that time?"

Theo must have heard it too. His eyes faltered and his long tongue furtively stroked over his upper lip. "Well technically, no it would have been up at the end of that night."

"So, yes." The Judge's voice was a slow growl. The bailiff grabbed Jada's arm and moved her out of the way of the Judge's line of sightlessness.

"I mean, sure if you want to look at it that way…" Theo moves in front of a wide eyed Leticia who was clutching his suit jacket in distress. "But your honor…"

The soft tapping of the Judge's claws on the wood of his bench filled the room, and Theo fell silent. "What happened troll, and do not try my patience any further."

"Well, like I said, I put Kedra in the back to wait for Gabriel. Unfortunately, Bane got there first, and thought I was double-crossing him" Theo tossed Bane an annoyed look over his shoulder.

Bane started to say something, but the sharp voice of the Judge cut him off. "But you weren't. You were double crossing Gabriel."

"Uh, I mean… anyway. Bane sort of lost control and… uh killed her." Theo looked off into the air, and the petty part of Jada enjoyed his discomfort.

Jada watched the Judge from her safe place next to the Bailiff, waiting for the judgment to come down. The scales had moved so high in Gabriel's favor that he had to sit down to keep from hitting his head on the ceiling. The Judge slowly turned towards Bane. "Mr. Sidhe. It looks as if you do not have a claim to this human."

"I want and will get what I paid for!" Bane's voice was just as low and flat. The narrowing of his eyes and the stiffness of his posture announced his anger far louder than anything he could have said.

"What, you want to be paid to belong to someone else." The Judge's replay was a low growl of warning. The court collectively held their breath in silent anticipation of his Judgement. Jada looked at Bane's scale to see that it was touching the floor. Kedra would not see justice, and those trolls were going to be let off scot-free.

Jada was fuming by this time. The Judge stood in his seat to render judgment. The trolls were adjusting their coats, preparing to leave. She was not property, Kedra was a person, and she was not going anywhere until someone paid for what they did to them. She escaped from the safety of her place behind the bailiff and stood angrily in front of the podium. "Make the trolls give the money back!"

The Judge stilled and abruptly swiveled his head to look in her direction. He leaped and landed on the podium on all fours. He leaned down from his waist so that he and Jada were at eye level.

"What did you say?" The Judge smiled as if Jada said something that amused him, and Jada took a deep breath before continuing.

"If they give Bane back his money, then he has no claim on me at all, right? It's their fault we're even here taking up your valuable time." Jada gave the Judge her best performance smile and lowered her lashes. She was not working for tips, but revenge would be just as good.

"You understand that your ownership will fall solely to Gabriel?" Row after row of the Judges jagged teeth shown in his malicious smile. His opaque eyes were trained on her from his place on the podium.

"Was there ever a chance of me going home?" Jada already knew the answer. She just needed that nail in the coffin of her dreams.

"None, whatsoever." The Judges brow lifted as he waited for her response. It was as if he was savoring a delicious meal.

"Then it doesn't matter who I go home with, doesn't it?" Jada smiled, cupping her hand to her lips and leaning forward almost as if she was going to impart a lascivious secret. I propose that the trolls be forced to give back all of the money, and Bane be ordered to pay Gabriel for killing Kedra. That will pay for the damage Bane did to my face, your honor."

The Judge's chin lifted, as if taking in her scent. Jada smiled just a little wider. It would serve both parties right if neither got to take her home. The Judge's laughter was both loud and cruel. His clawed hand lifted to stroke along her cheek. "You will make a formidable queen, my dear."

"Queen of what?" Jada was confused, but she had her eye on the prize of making the trolls pay. She could be the Queen of Texas as long as the trolls lost everything, starting with their money.

"Oh, you will soon find out my dear. How they will tremble when they see you." The Judge snatched his hand away from her cheek, and a gable appeared. "Trolls, you will give all of the money back to Bane, thus dissolving his claim."

"Give the money back!" Leticia screamed and fainted into Theo's arms. He almost dropped her in his effort to keep her up, and argue with the Judge at the same time.

"Wait, you can't listen to her! She's just some stray we picked up off the street!" Theo was almost rabid with the prospect of having to give back his money. Jada assumed he had already spent.

"Are you arguing with me?" The Judges voice was low once again, and Jada looked over her shoulder to see if the troll was going to argue. She hoped with every fiber of her being that the coward would defy the Judge.

Theo's green face pale at the implied threat and averts his eyes. "No, your honor. I agree, and shall obey." He struggles to pull Leticia from the courtroom, giving Jada a murderous look.

"Just the beginning." Jada mouthed with a smile as he left the courtroom. The look of fear on Theo's face was a cold comfort. It was a start, but not nearly enough. If she was stuck here, she would make sure that everyone involved would pay for their actions against her. .

"Bane Sidhe, you will pay for damages done to Gabriel's property." The Judge seemed to relish the announcement. No one could miss the emphasis on Gabriel's name.

"This is unsavory, unpleasant, unfair! Bane's talons unsheathed, and Gabriel jumped down from the scale to land in front of Jada. His hand moved to his sword preparing to protect her. Bane looked as if he was two seconds of losing complete control of himself. "What's mine is mine!"

"Sounds like you need to take it up with the Judge. Oh wait. You did. Unless you would like to challenge the verdict?" The Judge smiled and moved to stand between Gabriel and Bane. "Please say you want to challenge the verdict. I've been so bored."

Bane looks at Gabriel and his jaw unhinges as he screams in rage. His skin transformed from its normally pearlescent sheen to a sickly white that made him appear dead. Jada honestly did not know if she would have been able to stand under the onslaught of so much hatred. "You'll get yours Gabriel, mark my words. I will not rest until you have paid for what I have lost!" Bane roars and dissipates in a shadowy swarm of spiders and rats.

"Pity, he left." The Judge turns back towards the bench and begins walking away. "You are free to go."

"Thank you, your honor." Gabriel turns and pulls Jada's arm through his. He bows, and Jada promptly curtsies to the Judge.

The Judge nods with a smile and jumps back up to his podium. "Alright bailiff let's see what you have next!"

Gabriel continues to guide Jada through the building, and she tiredly allows herself to be directed back to the open air. The twin suns had started to dip towards the horizon, coloring the sky in deep oranges and purples. Jada rubbed her bare arms, and Gabriel removed his jacket and placed it over her shoulders.

The smell of warm coffee and honey wrapping around her as they wait for his carriage to pull up.

The trolls giving back the money was one thing, but it was not nearly enough to make Jada's pain go away. The clockwork mares arrive at the steps of the Court and Crown. Gabriel opens the door and helps her in before taking his place beside her. Jada watched his body relax into the cushions of the carriage seat. The carriage pulls away, and Gabriel leans back against the wall with a deep satisfied sigh.

Gabriel glances at her as the carriage rolls through the streets of the town. He crossed his ankle on his knee and lifted his arms back behind his head. His wide smile was as beautiful as it was magnanimous. "That's the second time you've chosen me."

"Did I have a choice?" Jada looked out of the window, there were so many conflicting emotions rolling around in her head. She pulled his coat closer around her as the cool evening air wafted through the carriage. "I can't even be sure that you are the lesser of the two evils."

Gabriel continued to watch her with a smile. "There is always a choice."

Jada continued to watch the world go by as the carriage moved forward to their next destination. "But did I make the right one?" Her voice a tired murmur as she replied.

Chapter Five

Gabriel had not lied when he said that Jada was not going back to the estate. Night had fallen and the streets were lined with lanterns filled with lightning bugs. The soft yellow light fills the streets with their warm glow. As they moved deeper into the twist and turns of the city. Each new city block looked like another period in history. Jada had dozed off in the Greco-Roman era filled with togas and olive leaves then awoke to streets filled with women wearing short dresses and long strands of pearls. The soft sound of jazz filled the air. A lovely fairy leaned against one of the streetlights merrily puffing into a long cigarette holder as the banana leaves of her skirt swayed softly around her legs. Clouds of smoke created various animals as a handsome suspender-wearing gentleman twined their chestnut fingers together. Jada smiled at the couple as they rode by, mentally crossing her fingers that they would be happy.

She turned to Gabriel who was wide-awake and looking over some paperwork as they passed into what looked like feudal Japan. A kitsune with a long sword moved down the street with a peaceful smile.

He nodded to a kappa who meditated on a nearby rock. "Where am I?"

"We are still over the Briars. However, we will be where we are going in a few minutes." Gabriel's voice was pleasant but distant as he continued to sort through the various papers spread around him.

The carriage continued past the medieval area with its jousting knights and was now moving into what looked like the early French Quarter. It was hard for Jada to focus on everything going on outside of the carriage. The sounds of music and laughter reminding her of home. Jada pulled Gabriel's coat tighter around her shoulders as they continued down the busy streets. The lanterns soon turned into fiery torches and snowflakes filled the air. Jada looked back at Gabriel, and he seemed unconcerned with the sudden drop of temperature. She focused her attention back outside, and the buildings that had once been cheery and inviting were now cold and intimidating.

"Ah, and here we are!" The carriage started to slow down in front of the only shop that's window was lit. Another puff of steam, and the horses pulled themselves to a complete stop. The storefront was a glassy red filled with toys and bright candles. Gabriel set down his paperwork and stretched in a way that made the shirt pull tight against every muscle he possessed. Jada's lashes fell to the side as she did her best to ignore both him and her reaction to him. When she looked back up Gabriel was holding his hand out to her, not bothering to hide the smug smile that tugged at his lips. "Shall we? Unless you need a minute?"

"Aren't you the perfect gentleman?" Jada's sarcasm was all the defense she had against her widely swinging emotions about Gabriel. His hand gently engulfed hers, as she climbed through the doors of the carriage in irritation at herself. The vision of the villain in front of her kept being interrupted by the memories of the bouncer who always helped her on stage. The same man who would ask about her day, and walk her home. When all along he was what she should have been afraid of.

"I could be more than a perfect gentleman if you let me, Jada." His smile widened as Jada's eyes raked over him, and she picked up her skirts to move past him without an answer. Gabriel tugged back on her hand in a way that pulled her against his chest in a tight embrace. His lips dropped next to her ear to ask a question that Jada had been asking herself the entire way there. "Would you prefer me to treat you differently?"

"Yes." Jada resolutely pulled out his arms and stepped towards the door away from the warmth of his arms. However, Jada had no answers to how she wanted him to treat her. She wanted to hate him for doing this to her, and didn't want to have flashes of affection she had developed before last night. Wisely she stayed silent and looked toward the area that seemed to grow darker as they stood there. The shadows seemed to shiver and crawl across the snow covered ground in horrifying shapes. "What are we doing here?"

It was Gabriel's turn not to answer, he took her hand again to lead her through the door. It was just as well, her attention had been taken by the shop where they arrived. They stepped into the brightly lit doorway, and Jada's lips parted in a mix of wonder and giddiness she hadn't felt since she was a child. The displays were overflowing with beautiful dolls and mechanical bears. Toy soldiers marched around a large castle and were greeted by a princess who rode on a black swan. The room was a modest size that as was warm and inviting as the exterior was cold and frightening. A monkey that frantically crashed his tiny cymbals together greeted them as they came in. A raccoon with a paper hat idly rolled across the floor over and under a blue and white spangled ball. Jada hands lifted to her lips in joy at the sound of all the whirring wheels and ticking gears.

Jada's eyes continued to roam across the room until her breath was stolen by a winged ballerino suspended from the ceiling. His deeply tanned arms were nailed over his head and crossed at his wrist above a short mass of inky curls. The pose was meant to be both horrifying and submissive, it succeeded on all counts. He appeared to be carved of smokey quartz, she could even see the mechanisms of his heart humming idly within his smooth chest. Though the dancer's muscled legs and lower torso were covered his chest was left bare. The love that went into sculpting every dip and muscle into the cloudy crystal was both beautiful and sad. The section to the left of his chest that held the mechanism of his heart emitted a soft glow that flickered steadily. He wore a black lace domino mask that displayed the electric blue of his glassy eyes.

"Good heavens," Jada whispers. He was a reverent testament to the skill of the artist. Her eyes widened as she walked over to the man as if being pulled by a magnetic force. Jada's hand cautiously lifted to stroke along the black wings of the statue. The tips of her fingers gently brushed along the spines of the feathers only to sharply be pulled back to her lips. Though the feathers appeared soft, they were carved from thin slivers of black glass. "How is this even real?"

"Should I be jealous?" Gabriel's voice was charming as ever, but there was an underlying tightness to his voice that distantly told Jada that he was only partially kidding.

She didn't bother answering him, as she was preoccupied with examining the carving. Her fingers gently followed the smooth lines of muscle etched into the statue's arms until her shaking hands moved to cup his cheek. There was such a sense of despair and loneliness about the sculpture.

"Jada?" Gabriel's voice sounded so far away as she looked at the statue. It was as if Gabriel was just a distant dream.

The spell was broken when something wet fell against her palm. Jada jumped back with a start. A blood red tear fell from the statue's beautiful eyes and onto her fingers. Jada's mouth opened and closed in horror, but she could find no words to explain the horror of what she was seeing. She started taking in deep sharp breaths, as her psyche tried and failed to make sense of the statue before her. There was only so much Jada's mind could hold, and she could feel it slipping away. "I…"

"Beautiful, isn't he?" Jada spins around at the husky voice behind her. A tall, beautifully round woman with a short afro watched her with an unreadable smile on her full plum painted lips. She wore a long western-style gown that puddled around her feet. The Woman's dark cinnamon brown skin seemed to glow with an unnatural light as cruel black eyes carefully looked her over. "I carved him myself."

Jada couldn't tell if she was being friendly or not, but what she did know was that the statue was alive. Her bloodied hand lifted to point up at what she had thought was just a sculpture. Jada looked back at the figure, and it seemed like all hope and light had gone out of its crystal gaze. As if nothing she had seen had been real. "He was crying. We have to release him. He's not a statue, he's alive!"

"My name is Dylaine. I am a Drosselmier." The woman who towered over her ignored her outburst and turned to Gabriel with a fond smile. She seemed to be surrounded by a swirl of violet light that seemed to follow all fairies. Long delicate hands held out for Gabriel to take in his. "Gabriel, my darling, it's a pleasure as always. Have you come to commission a doll from me?"

Jada looked back at the inanimate statue once more in distress. Glaring back at the woman who called herself Dylaine. "You're a toy maker?"

"I build champions." Dylaine's response was both quick and sharp. The violet light that surrounded her intensified

73

with anger. Jada didn't know what she was upset about, but Jada stepped back putting herself between the Drosselmier and the statue. There was nothing she could do to protect him, but she knew she had to try.

"Is he a champion? Because he doesn't exactly look like he's winning right now." Anger and her utter powerlessness in the situation was starting to make her mouth a little reckless. Jada continued to stand between the toymaker and the dancer. She was trying to ignore the dark frown on Gabriel's face as he glanced between her and the dancer. It promised both pain and punishment later, but she didn't care. She was not going to stand idly by while that man was tortured.

"Not yet. He is nothing more than a toy right now." Dylaine's lips curled, and she turned towards the back of her shop waving Jada forward. "If you'll follow me."

"I'm not going anywhere until you let him go." Jada snapped as her dark gaze watched Dylaine steadily.

Dylaine lifted her hand over her lips in a delicate yawn, and looked back to Gabriel. "How quaint. She's feisty."

"Jada follow Dylaine." Gabriel's deep voice filled the room causing the dolls and gears to rattle in place. Jada's lips parted, but Gabriel quickly cut her off. "Jada I won't ask again, and I doubt your new friend will like what I do to him if you cause me to punish you."

Jada looked over at Gabriel who smiled tightly, and nodded at her encouragingly towards Dylaine. She didn't want to follow the Drosselmeir, but Gabriel did not look like he was in any mood to be conciliatory. She also didn't want the ballerino to be hurt because of her. She

74

turned to the living statue then dropped her head and shoulders. "I'm sorry."

"One day that threat isn't going to work." Jada seethed as she passed Gabriel without looking back at him. Stiffly following the toy maker out of the back of the shop and into a dimly lit stone corridor.

Frames containing paintings and charcoal sketches of fairy anatomy lined the walls. The eyes of the paintings that hung on the grey stone followed them down the hall. Each person in the myriad of pictures stood in front of the same shop. Jada assumed they were all past Drosselmeir's. Jada rubbed her arms angrily as she tried will away the clammy chill that crept over her skin. The air in the hall had become wet and stale. The ground sloped down as they walked further away from the toy shop. The deeper they went underground, the more cave-like the passage became. They twisted and turned through the darkness, and Jada wasn't sure she would ever be able to find her way out if she lost sight of the woman before her. Dylaine continued to elegantly float down the hall unbothered by the change in atmosphere. They continued until Dylaine stopped at a thick wooden door with a black mushroom carved above it. With a delicate wave of her hand, the entrance opened into complete darkness.

The next wave of the fairy's hand indicated that Jada should go inside. "Please, come in."

"You want me to go in there?" Jada looked into the darkness trying to make sense of what she was being asked to do. The faint stirring of fear began to collect in her heart where righteous anger had lived right before.

Dylaine nodded and waved her hand once more. "Yes."

"Into that gaping darkness?" She leaned from behind Dylaine to peer into black nothingness. Jada would be damned if she willingly walked through that door. Gabriel and the toymaker could get wrecked.

"Affirmative." Dylaine's tone was both angry and running out of patience. Jada however didn't care. There was no way she was going into that room.

"By myself?" Jada said the words haltingly as if Dylaine was slow. She was trying a different pitch with her voice. Trying to convey that she had no intention of going into an empty hell pit.

"Oh, you won't be alone my dear." The toymaker's short laugh chilled Jada's soul. Dylaine smiled, and the dainty points of her canines flashed down at her.

"Yeah, I'm gonna hard pass…" Jada never finished her sentence. One of Dylaine's claws viciously curled into Jada's hair and tossed her into the darkness. Jada could hear her dress rip as she slid back over the stone until she forcefully came to an abrupt stop. The wind was knocked from her chest as she rammed back first into something hard and made of wood. She painfully pulled herself onto her knees as her hand held her chest as she tried to pull air back into her lungs. The sound of rattling chains and breaking glass fell around her. The commotion was followed by a low threatening hiss and small high-pitched giggles.

Jada shook her head as she tried to get her bearings in the darkness. Her hand jerked back as something skittered across her fingers. Hundreds of candles lit in a wave when Dylaine stepped through the doors, Once she could see again, Jada immediately wished the room had stayed dark. Her heart seized in terror as she stared at the room. This time the pictures on the wall were sketches of human anatomy. Jars filled with dead animals and doll heads soaking in some yellow viscous liquid. Bat wings were held flat against cork boards with jeweled pins. There were tables covered in sharp blades and jagged-looking tools. Large screws and knives to carve and stuff dolls rested on various tables. Axes stained within sprays of dark rust-colored drops hung from the ceiling. A cage swung over the table that Jada had been thrown into. It was filled with a gigantic black snake that shook its tail in sharp rattle as it bared its fangs down at her.

Dylaine locked the door, and with each step, she took into the room her skin color became paler, and her eyes receded back into their sockets. "Look at what Gabriel gave me to work with. You're so weak and emotional. I build champions. At best, you'll be an expensive sex toy."

Her jaw slowly unhinged and twisted outside so that her face looked more like the puppets she sold in her shop. She pulled on a set of white stained gloves with a sharp snap. "But he wanted the best, and I am definitely the best."

Jada weakly crawled backward in a futile attempt to get away, and her hand landed on something damp and spongy. She twisted to see what she had crushed, and a small black mushroom crumbled onto the floor. Her eyes were taken from Dylaine as she looked at the circle of black mushrooms surrounding the table. Unfortunately,, her lack of focus cost her. Dylaine grabbed her by the hair, roughly lifting her onto the table despite how hard Jada fought. A soft hum began to fill the room and intensified as the flames of the candles turned dark blue. Jada continued trying to struggle out of Dylaine's vice-like grip, only to have the toymaker lift and abruptly shoves her head back into the hard surface of the table. Jada's vision swam before her eyes, and she groaned softly as she weakly continued to struggle.

"Hold still. I'm beginning to lose patience." Jada kicked out into Dylaine's stomach, but the toy maker caught her leg and twisted the appendage at an unnatural angle. Muscles tearing apart as bones snapped through her flesh. The scream that tore through Jada's throat was so shrill she wasn't sure it even belonged to her. Jada would be lucky if she could ever walk on two legs again let alone dance. Dylaine tossed the twisted leg onto the table beside Jada like a pound of worthless meat. Jada gagged when she realized that the thick sticky liquid beneath her knees was her own blood. Angry tears began to fill Jada's eyes as her heart filled with despair. Instead of screams, heavy sobs wracked her body.

"You chose poorly, little doll. Just understand this could have gone a completely different way." Dylaine's laugh was shrill and unhinged. Her shoulders lifting in a pragmatic shrug. Dylaine moved to stand by Jada's head, her fingers gently stroking through Jada's sweat-soaked curls. Sharp manicured talons tilted Jada's chin, so Jada's tearful eyes met the black emptiness of hers. "I trust you will be a good girl. However, feel free to scream. I do love the sound of music as I work."

78

The lights intensified as the hum in the room became deafening. Jada's eyes narrowed against the brightness of the lights. She didn't care what happened at this point. Dylaine flicked open the cage that contained the snake as she moved to a cart set behind the table. Moving about the room collecting sharp blades and blunt hammers to lay on the cart with a flourish.

There was a soft skittering just below her ear, and Jada tiredly turned her head to the side. The mushrooms had not only grown in numbers but began growing arms that waved about. They pulled themselves from the ground and started dancing around. As they moved, they released red spores into the air from their ashy caps. Their incessant hum continued as they danced around the table. The tiny particles filling Jada's lungs as fear and pain made it hard to catch her breath. The dreadful hum turning into a frightful litany of words Jada couldn't even begin to understand.

"You're going to be in so much pain!" Dylaine locked Jada's wrist and ankles down into metal cuffs connected to the table with relish. The Drosselmeir moved to one of the blades covering the walls to Jada's right. Her sharp nails delicately tapping pouty plum-colored lips as she chose from a selection of saws and hatchets. Jada lifted her head to look at her now-useless appendage, and she laid her head back against the wood of the table in defeat. She tried to piece together a silent prayer, but the pain and failure made it hard for her to link words or repentant thoughts.

Something cold and smooth slid against her leg that was held together by raw strings of sinew. The snake that had been released from its cage slowly slid onto the table. Its head lifting to dispassionately stare into Jada's wide, terrified eyes. Jada tried not to give in to the impulse to laugh hysterically at the faint disgust in the snake's black and gold gaze. Instead, her breaths had come out in jerk hiccups that caused her shoulders to shudder painfully. The snake continued to watch Jada in disdain as Dylaine puttered about her workshop of horrors. The snake must have found her wanting because it bared its fangs at Jada and reared back, preparing to strike.

"No, you don't! You naughty girl!" Dylaine caught the snake by the throat as it lunged forward. Holding the snake aloft as it wriggled and snapped at her. The mushrooms had started to change colors as they continued their little macabre dance around the table. Their voices mixing with the angry hiss of the snake. Dylaine had finished preparing and brought all of the accoutrements of her craft to the table including the snake that coiled around her fingers in agitation.

"Let me go." Jada's voice was barely a croak above a whisper. The sustained screams had made her voice hoarse. Jada weakly tested the strength of the manacles that enclosed her wrist, heavily laying back onto the table when she found the binding to be secure.

"No." Dylaine looked at her leg with a slight suck of her teeth but an air of glee. "Since we've already started on your leg, why don't we do the other one?"

Dylaine deceptively strong fingers clenched Jada's other calve and jerked the fleshy segment entirely from the socket of her knee. Jada's back arched from the table in anguish. The only thing that kept her from getting whiplash at the were the restraints that held her down. Jada wasn't sure if the shock or the pain that kept her from going into hysteria. Blood poured out onto the table in dark rivulets that spread across the table to the small of her back.

A certain heavy numbness seemed to take over Jada's body as she went into shock. She thought that the toymaker couldn't hurt her any more than she already had. Dylaine came back with the short saw; Jada realized how wrong she had been. Jada's head rolled back, and she looked at the ceiling as Dylaine began to saw off each segment carpel of her fingers away from their sockets. Dylaine jerked apart every joint with jagged pliers. Dylaine would scissor away her skin, leaving Jada's nerves exposed to the air. Jada began to choke as more mushroom spores filled and replaced the air in her lungs. She didn't know why she was not dead yet, but she wanted to be.

By this time, the snake had moved to rest comfortably around Dylaine's arm as she worked. Dylaine's claws jerked the snake's neck from its coal to stretch it out over Jada's prone form. The snake angrily tried to snap at Dylaine. Once it figured out that it could not, the snake settled on the next best thing: a prone Jada. Jada's lips parted on a soundless scream as the snake sunk its fangs into her neck. Jada's body shivered as Dylaine roughly milked the snake's throat, injecting dose after dose of venom into her veins. Snapping the snake's neck in the process as Jada's body twisted and trembled against the table.

"Just kill me." Jada's tired whisper was so low that she wasn't sure if she made the request aloud or in her head. Dylaine laughed and moved away from the table only to return with a pleasant smile, buckets of sawdust, and several tiny needles.

After a time, Jada assumed she had finally given over into blessed darkness. The humming had stopped, but the sound of her heartbeat was loud in her ears. Thick doll-like lashes lifted once then twice as she tried to blink away the fog that filled her head. There were no mushrooms, no candles, and most importantly, no Dylaine. Jada looked at her arms and noticed that they were no longer cuffed to the table. She lifted her hand and curled them cautiously. There was a soft mechanical hum in her ears that she realized was coming from her chest like the dancer upstairs. Her hands moved to her chest and face and connected with cool polished brass armor. All nerve endings seemed to be intact. Still, she watched, horrified as each brass covered finger moved in odd angles independently of each other.

"Am I dead?" Her upper body swiveled around until her eyes landed on a dirty full-length mirror in the corner of the room. She quickly drug her body off the table to stand in front of its dingy surface. Black painted fingernails tore away her helmet as she got her first full look at herself. Her hand lifted to the smooth ceramic like perfection of her mahogany skin and into her hair. Her dark frosted coils had been combed and twisted out into glossy curls that spiraled around her face. Blessedly her features had remained her own. The fullness of her lips and nose rested beneath an unnatural wealth of lashes that gave her dark brown eyes an ethereal doe-like quality.

The polished helmet dropped from her hands as she stepped back from the mirror. The shiny bracers on her arms clicked together as Jada continued her horrified inspection. Her mournful scream was so loud it shook the dust and tiny stones from the walls. Her brass-covered hands moved over the rest of her armor encased her torso. Jada barely choked back a sob but could not keep the tears from falling down her perfect face as she examined legs that she thought were lost to her. Her thighs were bare until they reached the shiny brass that covered her knees and legs over tall black leather boots. She crouched down and wrapped her arms around her legs. Her whole body began to quiver as she cried into her knees.

She crouched with her nose buried between her knees as her mind played back the horror that she had been mostly awake for. As she thought of the tearing and ripping of her skin, her skin began to heat, and the tips of her fingers began to glow a dark fiery orange. Jada abruptly stood on the floor as rage filled her. Her fingers twitched, and the room exploded into a torrential inferno. A faint metallic scent filled her nose, and she looked back over her shoulder to see the saws that lined the walls melting away. She moved to the door and plated fingers curled into a fist, and she started swinging at the door until it splintered and buckled against the force of her fist.

"I'm certainly stronger than I was when I got here but am I strong enough?" Her lips curved into a satisfied smile as she stepped over the bits of door that now littered the floor. "Why don't we find out? Gabriel, Dylaine, where are y'all?"

"Come out, come out wherever you are." Jada moved down the hall's dark path, the fire from the room making it easier to pick her way through the cave. Jada went, still trying to sift through the rush of sensory information that came to her. Her chin lifted, and she caught the faint scent of honey and dark roasted coffee.

"Ollie Ollie Oxen free!" Another bout of fire leaped from her fingers as she made her way down the corridor. The fiery manifestation of her anger carelessly raged around the hall as she retraced her steps to the toy shop. If Jada had her way, she wouldn't leave anything left of that shop but charred toothpicks. Once she reached the landing, she was hit with everything her five senses could take in at once. The ticking of clocks, the tinkling of bells, twinkling light, and the trill of laughter. The faint sound of Gabriel's and Dylaine's voices met her as she climbed up to the shop level of the building. The scent of roses and warm bread mixed with the smell of honey and coffee as she reached the door.

The spinning of gears and the whistle of tiny horns made her lose focus and distracted her from her purpose. Dylaine and Gabriel were drinking tea at some fussy linen-covered table dripping with too much lace. Looking every bit like French aristocrats discussing something banal like the weather. As if she had not been left rotting on the same table she had been tortured on. The scent of their tea made her stomach lurch as she took her first step into the shop. She stood paralyzed until her rage fragmented thoughts coalesced and settled on the one who brought her into this mess.

"Gabriel." Jada's voice purred as she stepped into full view of the shop. Their conversation immediately paused as Jada slinked forward with a cheerful rock of her hips. Her mind quickly cataloging each of their moves and reactions. While Dylaine continued to sip her tea in boredom, Gabriel looked stunned. His tea and saucer resting forgotten in his hands. Jada's hand lifted, and the lace covering the table caught on fire.

"You little…! Oh!" Dylaine shouted in indignation as she further ruined the lace by quickly pouring tea over the flames.

"Jada, I understand that you're angry, but if you have a seat, we can discuss what's upsetting you." Gabriel's coaxing voice paused as he finally took a sip of his tea. Unbothered by the lace that smoldered on the table.

"But Gabriel, I thought you wanted to play? Isn't that what this was about? Getting your own private dancer?" Jada snarls, and her body seems to disintegrate into a thick grey mist that reassembles behind Gabriel's chair. She picked up a butter knife from the table and plunged the blade into his back. Before the knife can penetrate, Gabriel disintegrates into golden sand but reassembles in front of her. " "Is it good for you, daddy?"

"Is it everything you ever dreamed of?" She swung again, and Gabriel caught her wrist before the blunt knife pierced his heart. Chestnut colored eyes angrily flashed up into the gold of his as she tried to struggle out of his hold.

"Everything and more." Gabriel twists her arm around and brings her back against his chest. Bringing her hand up so that the knife rests against her neck. In turn, Jada sharply pulls her elbow back into his side. She mists away across the room to stand in front of the dancer once more. Gabriel turned to Dylaine with a wide satisfied grin. "Magnificent. Herr Drosselmier, you are truly an artist!"

The rage on Dylaine's face relaxes into an embarrassed smile at Gabriel's praise. She smooths out her skirts before bowing deeply from her waist. "Of course, she is. I promised that you would have an exemplary product. I can't take all the credit the shrooms helped. The spores, you know."

"She's beautiful." The reverent awe in Gabriel's voice grated on Jada's nerves. There was a time she would drug her tongue over broken glass just to hear him say her name in that soft worshipful whisper. Gabriel sets the butter knife down and makes his way toward her. The pale gold of his eyes watches her as if he cannot believe anything is as extraordinary as she is now.

"Stay away from her for a few moments, Gabriel. It's always like this when they wake up. I bet my workshop is in utter disarray." Dylaine's hand raises to stop Gabriel from going any further. The amused tone of her voice was not at all in keeping with the cold eyes that raked over Jada.

Jada smiled and lifted her metal-covered fingers to blow on her black nails. Feeling the first stirrings of satisfaction that she had felt that evening. "Oh, I burnt that hell pit to a crisp. Make dolls in that bitch now."

"I wouldn't be able to stay away if I wanted to. Look at her Dylaine, you have outdone yourself." Gabriel's hand waved in a motion that began at Jada's head down to her feet. The hunger in his eyes was not for the most likely dry cookies they had been eating on before she came in. Jada's mouth opened and closed a few times as they continued to speak as if she was not in the room. Dylaine simpered and batting her eyelashes bashfully at Gabriel's praise.

"Hello? Can we get back to the monster you two created coming back to smite you both? I'd give you two time to make peace with your souls, but since I'm sure neither you have one, just prepare to die." Jada knew she was being melodramatic, but they were not treating this moment with the gravity or fear it deserved. They were supposed to be cowering, but that doll making trout mouth and her cobra-eyed buddy were patting themselves on the back for a job well done. Her skin flushed in rage, and she focused on Gabriel once more. "What in the hell did you do to me?"

"Some modifications needed to be made." Gabriel's eyes continue their languid perusal of her form, and his broad shoulders lifted in a shrug as his forked tongue licking over his lips.

Jada's head tilted in annoyance, and she lifted a fiery glowing hand once more. "I am going to ask one more time what you did to me, and this time the answer better be a complete or, I will raze this freakshow to the ground!"

"I swear humans are so ungrateful. Gabriel, I don't know how you deal with it." Dylaine sighed in annoyance and moved back to the table to wearily continue drinking what was left of her tea. She took a sip of her tea and rolled her eyes towards the heavens. "You went into that room a scared, helpless little human stripper and came out a powerful goddess."

Jada turned to Gabriel furiously, and her hand itched to set everything he wore on fire. "You let her tear me apart! Do you know what I went through? She tore off my legs." She screamed and threw a fireball at him, which he dodged. His lips losing the smile that was usually a constant on his smug kissable lips.

"Drosselmier Dylaine equipped you to become a queen. She made you perfect." The smile had left his face, but he didn't seem nearly as concerned about the fireball as he was about something behind her. "It's time to go, Jada."

"I'm not going with you anywhere." "Jada screamed, taking a step back with a violent shake of her head. I am a monster! Just like you!"

"Eventually." Gabriel straightened his coat and picked up his cane. He walked over to Dylaine and took her hand in his. He turned her palms over and dropped a deep kiss to the inside of each wrist. Dylaine giggled and brought a napkin to her painted lips.

"Gabriel, you incorrigible flirt! You be careful out there. Please don't hesitate to come back for any of your needs." Dylaine's eyes dropped playfully, and the tip of her tongue danced between her lips in emphasis of the word any.

"I said I'm not going anywhere with you." Jada ignored the faint jealousy intead of focusing on gaining her freedom. She wasn't sure how she was alive after being torn apart, but Jada was going to make good what little chance of escape she had.

Gabriel straightened from his flirting with Dylaine and continued to keep his focus on something over her shoulder. His smile was cold as he held his hand out to her. "Be careful little one. You're powerful, but nothing a real fairy worth their salt couldn't handle with their eyes closed."

That wasn't something Jada wanted to hear, but it was good to know. So at this stage, she was stronger than a human but much weaker than a run of the mill winged human snatcher. That was fine: she would just have to make her moves carefully. "I said I'm not going."

"I'm going to ask nicely one last time." The deep labored sigh that lifted Gabriel's chest annoyed her on several levels. One, it made it seem like she was the problem, and two, she couldn't have cared less about how he felt about her leaving.

"I am..." The sound of her voice was cut off by the sudden grip that Gabriel had on her throat. Jada hadn't even seen him move. One moment he had been standing by Dylaine, and the next, his hand was wrapped around her neck.

Her fingers clawed at his hand as he lifted her from the floor. She kicked and struggled until something jerked her back out of Gabriel's grasp. The sculptured dancer that she had been drawn to earlier had protectively pulled her back into the feathered circle of his wings. The bright blue of his eyes was filled with an angry fire that was directed towards Gabriel. Despite his suspension from the ceiling, his gaze settled on Gabriel daring him to come forward.

"Nero, stay out of this. Gabriel is a valued customer. I will not have you insulting him." Dylaine leaned back in her chair with her teacup. She looked put out but not overly concerned at the actions of the handsome

doll she had created. "I'd hate for Silvestri to get you back damaged."

Nero's eyes flickered unsurely and moved to Jada as if asking what she wanted to do." Jada's hand lifted to cup his crystalline cheek. She wasn't strong enough yet to keep him from feeling the brunt of whatever punishment he would get for protecting her.

"I'm... I'm fine, Nero. I'll go with him." Jada lifted on her tiptoes,placed a quick kiss on the dancer's lips, and ignored the possessive hiss over her shoulder. Letting her hand fall away, she stepped out of the circle of his winged embrace with overwhelming sadness. She turned to Dylaine, spearing her with all the contempt that her eyes could muster. "I will come back for him."

Dylaine sneered and lifted her teacup in a mocking salute, unmoved by Jada's implied threat. "If you're alive later to try, I will let Silvestri know to expect a visit."

Jada gave Nero one last look before stalking past Gabriel into the wee hours of the night. She wasn't sure what would happen, but she knew she would figure out a way to stop this madness from happening to anyone else.

Chapter Six

The ride from the Drosselmeir's was a silent one. Jada sat staring out the window in quiet rage. The scenery changed from Victorian shops and townhouses to raucous nightclubs and tall glass buildings filled with neon lights. They seemed to be heading towards a rougher area of the town; it was familiar to her, from skyscrapers that disappeared into the clouds to the structured suits. It was the most at ease Jada felt since she had gotten there. She watched in fascination as a sea of blue jean-wearing fairies talked on their heavy cell phones. Their curly side ponytails animatedly bobbed back and forth as they yelled into their receivers. There weren't any light poles or telephone lines, so Jada didn't know what powered them. If Jada didn't know any better, she would say that she was back in Dallas. As they continued through the streets, a group of teenage fairies danced over a large sheet of cardboard as white terrycloth headbands held their moist Jeri curls out of their eyes. Taking turns practicing their popping and locking while a short but stout fairy beatboxed for them.

Jada tore her thoughts away from her homesickness. She had bigger problems right now, and her head was filled with questions and self-recriminations. Instead of going upstairs in a rage, Jada should have found a way out of the back. But where would she have gone? It is not as if she had a map of the world of Fairy in her head. Even if she escaped, how would she find her way back home? She didn't even know how she got there, to begin with. Jada was ignorant of the world she was in and it hindered her exodus from this very unpleasant place. She just did not have enough information about her location to make plans to aid in her escape.

"You're childish." Those were the first words that Gabriel had spoken to her since they got into the carriage over an hour ago. Jada studiously ignored the man on the other side of the carriage who seemed just as put out with her as she was with him, but that was his problem. She continued to ignore him while pretending to pick a bit of nonexistent fluff on her armor.

Gabriel lifted his hands in surrender. "I understand. Hurtful things were said, and threats were made that we both didn't mean."

"Who didn't mean it?" Jada scoffed at his words and looked around the carriage, ensuring she was the only one he was talking to. "I meant every word I said, and the ones I didn't say out loud."

"I'm just saying that we both had a hand in how this evening went." Gabriel sighed and held his arms wide open, giving her the space to come into his arms. "I will be the bigger person and apologize first. In turn, I hope that you will be adult enough to do the same."

"You're going to be the...." Jada's long lashes fluttered in confusion, and she leaned back at her waist to get a good look at him. "Did you just... Are you insane?"

"To be fair, Jada, you were on your way to cheating on me with another man. I have been nothing if not a perfect gentleman all day." Jada watched Gabriel try to control his own irritation. She guessed he did not want to be the bigger person any longer. "I think we can both agree that we both made some mistakes, but in the spirit of forgiveness, I'm willing to let bygones be bygones."

Jada turned to face him directly. Her brows lifted high over her wide eyes at the audacity of this man. "So, you feel that me reacting to the trauma of being beaten, kidnapped, sold, and dismembered in a basement is equal to you doing all of those things? Then add the whipped creamy topping of threatening another man who was helplessly strung up in that witch's shop?"

"You belong to me, and he clearly threatened that claim." Gabriel's lips twitched in dark amusement, and his long, graceful fingers lifted to cup her chin.

He gently tilted her head so that their eyes were level. "I was simply protecting what was mine."

Jada jerked her chin away and glared at him. "You, Bane, those trolls, and Dylaine can all go to hell." All the fury she bottled up over an hour began to bubble to the surface, threatening to spill all over the carriage. Her fingers curled into a fist as she fought to restrain herself from swinging at him. They were in an enclosed space, and she would lose. "I swear I will find a way to end every one of you."

"You're trying my patience, Jada." Gabriel frowned, his pale gold eyes almost glittering with his own suppressed anger.

"Go jump off the very next bridge we come to Gabriel. The. Very. Next. One." Jada seethed as she turned towards the window once more. Her face was hot despite the cool air that surrounded them. This time intent on ignoring him for the duration of the ride. She had no idea what fresh hell she was being taken to; knew if she kept talking to him, the situation would devolve quickly.

Gabriel threw up his hands and leaned back into the seats of his very expensive carriage. "Fine, but you will listen. Where you are going next is a harsh place. You have been given extraordinary abilities, and you will need to learn how to use them quickly. To that end, you will train to fight in the pits."

Jada stayed silent but lifted her eyes towards the ceiling in silent prayer for the strength to not murder the fairy next to her. To release tension, she moved her tongue along the inside of her cheek and rolled her shoulders. Jada took a deep breath in and held it for a few minutes before releasing the air heavily. Then mentally started to count to ten. Anything to keep from acknowledging the man beside her.

Gabriel moved closer to knead the muscles in her shoulders and the middle of her back. She did not want to admit to enjoying it, so she continued to stay silent. "You will hate me, but that's fine. You will need the hate to make it out of there alive."

The tension began to ease beneath his fingers, her jaw unclenched, and her shoulders helplessly relaxed. So wrapped up in the magic of his touch that she almost forgot that she hated the man intensely. She pulled away to turn around and back at him. Groping for the words to explain how crazy he sounded. "You're going to leave me in a-a…pit fighting…."

"Communal dungeon," Gabriel supplied helpfully.

"I don't need to fight to hate you. I already do! You expect me to fight my way out with no fighting experience?" Had Jada just enjoyed that man's touch? She could not remember because she was furious all over again. She could not find anything bad enough to call him. "In a communal dungeon, no less! Are you kidding me right now?"

"That was hurtful." Gabriel's expression was unreadable, but he ignored the rest of her tirade. The horses began to slow down, and Jada watched him closely. The slight tapping of his fingers on his thigh showed anxiety that Jada had never seen from him. This, in turn, made her worried because if something could worry him, it meant she should also be concerned. "It looks like we're here."

The carriage had pulled up to what looked like a nightclub. There were women with pointy ears half hanging out of windows in bright low-cut dresses that almost seemed to glow in the dark. Screaming out at every passerby in a happy but drunken stupor. Jada's nose scrunched as she inhaled the smell of tobacco, wine, and cloves that hung in the air. It was not unpleasant but overpowering. The carriage pulled to a complete stop, and Gabriel removed his fancy coat before climbing out. Ever the gentleman, he turned to help Jada descend from the steps of the carriage, but he didn't let her hand go as he usually did. Whether Gabriel was afraid she would get lost or run away was not apparent. His fingers entwined with hers as he led her through the night club's doors. His thumb was stroking back and over her palm as if he desperately needed her touch.

A neon sign over the door blinked the words "Hyena." They walked in, and if Jada had thought it had been noisy outside, it was thunderous inside. The smokey room was filled with lights and black lights that made the wings glow against their skin. Glasses clinked together as what looked like dominoes made with real bones hit the table amidst raucous laughter. She watched as fairies with long tatted locs speaking patois as they bluffed their way through a round of spades. That one on the left knew he only had two books and not three. All fairies were unconscionable liars it seemed. She made a short hum of disapproval and continued following Gabriel through the crowd.

Suddenly someone grabbed her hand, and Jada sharply turned to see who was trying to get the attention of a virtual stranger. He looked at Jada like an oversized Satyr. The man stood at least six inches over Gabriel with short horns just above his temples.

He wore an open brown vest over an impressive, bronzed chest and a loincloth that hung low over his hips, leaving his shaggy brown legs bare. His eyes never went higher than her chest, and Jada sighed inwardly. If there was ever a time that Jada was not in the mood to entertain some entitled prick's advances, now was that time.

"Hands off," Jada leveled a warning look at the fairy with a shake of her head. The tips of her fingers were itching to burn every hair from his skin.

"Who's going to stop me?" The large Satyr stood with a leer on his face that she was all too familiar with. The look was like the ones she got at the job when someone thought they could overpower her. He reached for once again, and his hand was knocked away as Gabriel stepped forward.

"I am." Gabriel pulled Jada behind him. She heard the warning in the low hiss of Gabriel's voice despite his civil tone. The room got quiet, and the Satyr's laughter seemed to echo in the now silent room. "She belongs to me. Don't touch her."

"Surprised to see your face around here, Gabriel. Thought you were too good for us down here in the pits." The Satyr sneered and looked around the room with a wave of his furry hand. "How is our lordship doing this fine evening?"

"Saturn." Gabriel's golden gaze swept over the large man dismissively. He pulled Jada further behind him to get her out of the way, but out of the way of what Jada had no clue. "Tell Faigen I'm here."

"Why don't you just be a good little lord and scurry out of here. Leave the woman. The way she was swinging her hips told me she wanted me or anyone really." The room laughed, and Jada did not know what they thought Saturn said was so damn funny. Not only had he called her a whore, but looking at Saturn told her he thought she was blind and tasteless as well.

"That was my one and only warning, Saturn" Gabriel smiled and continued looking for the man called Faigen. Jada watched the almost imperceptible tensing of Gabriel's shoulder and took a small step back. His hand tightened around hers reassuringly. Saturn might not have been able to hear the undercurrent of danger in Gabriel's deep voice, but she could. "Tell Faigen I'm here."

"You still think you're big and bad, huh?" Saturn moved directly in front of Gabriel and leaned down, trying to intimidate Gabriel with his size. Jada was not sure if Saturn really understood what he was asking for. Though Saturn was at least a head taller than Gabriel, his sheer size promised that he would be slower. Where Gabriel was lean boxer muscle, Saturn looked as if all his strength was earned through a lifetime of hard work. He would have to hope that he took Gabriel down with the first couple of blows. However, the way the Satyr poked his meeting finger into Gabriel's chest, he must have decided to take his chances. "You don't scare me."

"It doesn't matter how you feel; you'll be just as dead." Gabriel's voice was cold and flat. Jada knew he was running out of patience, and she nervously looked around. Hoping that someone would hurry up and get whoever Faigen was down there. Gabriel placed a quick kiss on the back of Jada's hand and disconnected her fingers from his. He gently moved her even further back from ground zero.

"What's all the ruckus?" A prominent voice filled the tense room, and every head swiveled to the direction of the stairs that lined the back of the room. "Who's asking for me?"

Jada's lips turned down as her own eyes scanned through the crowd. Though she could hear the low baritone of the man's voice, she could not see where it was coming from. Slowly, the crowd parted, and a short coppery-skinned man with bright red hair and a full beard stepped forward. An ebony cane twirling in his fingers before it hit the ground in sharp tap. He adjusted his red tuxedo and stood there glaring up at them. If the man were even four feet tall, Jada would eat the armor she wore.

"Gabriel is here. From the looks of the doll he brought, he paid a visit to Herr Drosselmier." The loathing in Saturn's voice told Jada that whatever this feud was between the two, it was a long one. That type of animosity took time to build.

"Has he now?" Faigen's voice sarcastically moved up an octave, and his hand rested over his heart as if in shock. The diminutive man pulled a monocle out of his pocket. He wiped it down with a black handkerchief before plopping it over his right. Green eyes peering at Jada curiously. "What business does council member Gabriel have with us, lowly pit dwellers?"

"I have a queen who needs to be trained." Jada was unsure if it was his wording or the request, but Jada was suddenly feeling less concerned for Gabriel as he turned to look down at the club owner. There was a flash of something in Gabriel's serpentine eyes. If Jada thought the monster had feelings, she would have thought he was sad. Did he miss being at this brothel? Gabriel's body relaxed some. He must have seen something in Faigen's reaction to her that pleased him.

"Do you?" Faigen's dark red eyes continued to restlessly bounce over her for a moment. "She's a pretty thing, isn't she? It would be a shame to scratch up that pretty face with scars." Faigen turned to Gabriel with a frown. "Though I don't see why we should let her train here."

"This is the best place for her to train." Gabriel's fangs flashed in a bright smile. They were down to bargaining. "And I think the money that she'll pull in would make her time here worth it for you."

"Bull, you just don't want your society friends to see what this little beauty can do before it's time. Which still doesn't explain why we should let your doll train in the pits." Faigen was starting to look bored, and Gabriel's shoulders tensed once more at the apparent insult.

Jada was torn, she had no desire to go to the pits, but she was also fascinated by anyone who could make Gabriel feel small. Gabriel pulled a sack of money from inside of his coat and offered it to Faigen. "I will pay you double the normal rate, Faigen."

"I don't want or need your society's money. Take your doll and go. "The small man turned and began taking short steps back in the direction he had come from.

Gabriel put the money away and glanced at Jada before turning his attention back to the man's retreating figure. "Faigen…" Gabriel was not begging, but Jada was pretty sure that the soft plea of his voice was as close as the evil fairy would get to it.

"I said leave before I let Saturn have you." Faigen continued to walk away. Not so much as turning around to issue the order that he levied.

"I'm not going anywhere; she will fight in the pits." Gabriel's voice was angry at the dismissal, and he took a step forward. He pulled off his coat and handed it back to Jada. Her hands closed around the soft material of his jacket, watching as Gabriel's first curl and his body coiled like a spring.

The Satyr laughed, and his gaze landed on Jada with a sneer. "Better leave Gabriel. I've been looking for a new toy, and yours seems like she would be fun." Jada wasn't sure what his idea of fun was, but she doubted she would think so.

"Faigen…" Gabriel was cut off when Saturn's sizable fist connected with his beautiful face. A line of blood trickling from the side of his lip. Jada winced as Gabriel went down on one knee. Under normal circumstances, the hit would have been satisfying, but right now, she was concerned.

Saturn's boot swung sharply into Gabriel's stomach before turning his attention back to Jada.   Leaving

Gabriel on the ground coughing and pulling in deep breaths from the surprise attack. "I hope you're as entertaining as you look. I bore easily, and I hate to be bored." Saturn grabs Jada's arm again, and her fingers immediately tingle with the fire that she is about to shove down his throat.

At that moment, several things happened at once. Gabriel disappeared, and the instep of the Satyr's foot was stomped in. Gabriel sent a quick punch into his stomach that caused Saturn to bend over with a huff as he tried to regain his lost air. Gabriel drove his fist up into Saturn's chin, causing Saturn to take an unsteady step back. Jada was pulled forward, but Saturn's face forcefully twisted to the side as Gabriel jabbed and twisted his fist into the larger man's nose. Saturn dropped Jada's arm as he brought his paw-like fingers up to his nose. Gabriel's white-hot aura blazed around him, and his face was a mask of fury. His snake-like eyes contracting and refocusing as he waited for Saturn's next move.

"I told you there would be no more warnings." The hiss of Gabriel's voice made a shiver of fear race up Jada's spine. She, along with everyone else in the room, moved back. Even if Saturn was too stupid to see what was about to happen, everyone else saw how furious Gabriel was.

"Didn't learn your lesson, huh? That's fine. I can hurt you some more." Saturn straightened up and cracked his neck. He spat out the blood that had collected in his mouth due to his nose being broken. The Satyr pulled his meaty fist up so that they could continue fighting. He leans around Gabriel to wink at Jada. "Be right back with you, sweets. Don't you go anywhere?"

Saturn barely finishes his sentence before Gabriel's fist strikes out at the soft part of Saturn's throat. The sudden loss of air had Saturn stumbling forward onto his knees. His enormous hands clawed at his neck as he tried to pull in more air. Gabriel's knee jerks up onto Saturn's chin. Jada's mouth and eyes went wide as Saturn went to the floor.

"Don't speak to her. Don't look at her. Don't touch her. She belongs to me. Don't ever forget again." Each curt sentence was punctuated with the heel of his boot driving into Saturn's stomach. Gabriel had begun stomping him out like a particularly bothersome cigarette. There was nothing left of the gentleman that Jada had been with for the better part of two days. What was left was someone who was barely human. A savage creature would willingly and gleefully tear the Satyr limb from limb.

"Gabriel?" Jada's voice was halting as she reluctantly tried to get Gabriel's attention. If someone didn't break up the fight soon, Saturn would die in the middle of the club. Jada looked around to see if anyone was going to pull Gabriel off Saturn, and no one else looked as if they wanted to get involved either.

"Let him be Gabriel. You proved your point." Faigen's angry voice snaked out amongst Saturn's moans of pain. Faigen tapped his walking stick on the ground impatiently before waving it to a set of stairs at the club's back. "She will get no special treatment here."

"I didn't ask for her to receive any." Gabriel's chest rose and fell as adrenaline bounced around his system. He watched Saturn writhe on the floor in hatred. Once he made sure that Saturn would not get up again, he focused on Faigen. "She won't need it."

Jada barely kept from rolling her eyes at Gabriel's words. It was all well and good for him not to want any special treatment since she would be fighting in the pits. Gabriel politely nodded to Jada as he took his coat back from her. He took her arm and examined the finger shaped bruises on her arm with an irritated hiss. Jada gently pulled her arm away as his eyes glowed with rage once more.

Faigen's lip tugged in amusement at the way Gabriel looked Jada over. "She will fight, or she will die."

"Hold on!" Jada quickly turns to look at Faigen. Her lips parted on another objection only to be cut off by Gabriel agreeing to Faigen's terms.

"She and I both agree." Gabriel's voice was solemn, but Jada would be damned if she just allowed this agreement to happen.

"Then it shall be done. Let's see what your queen can do." Faigen's hand lifted, and two men in sunglasses and black suits peeled out of a mural that had been spray-painted on the back wall. They were dark green with crew cuts and no facial features. However, it did not stop them from speaking into microphones that hung where their mouths would be.

"Wait!" Jada tried to speak again; guards approached her left and right side to guide her to the stairs that Faigen had gestured to earlier.

"Take her to the Lacuna." Faigen waved Gabriel forward after making his decree. The doors were opened by two men wearing bright yellow membersonly jackets. Presumably, they placed their hands on her upper arms and began guiding her towards the back of the club.

"Let me go!" Jada shouted angrily, and this time her whole body began to glow instead of just her hands. The guards paid no heed. They continued to do as they were bid and dragged her towards the waiting darkness.

"None of that, Missy. Gabriel can't protect you here, and though I would hate to explain why I murdered you, it wouldn't stop me from doing so." He turned to Gabriel and pointed with his cane towards what Jada assumed was his office. "You go wait for me upstairs.

I have to babysit your doll until we get her in the Lacuna."

Gabriel gave Jada a serene smile and turned to the stairs that would take him down the club office. Faigen followed her through the industrial swinging doors as the guards pulled her through into a landing where the lights ominously flickered. Jada wrestled with the men as they hauled her to a set of cement stairs. Jada broke away only to be caught by the guards once more. She didn't care about getting lost anymore. Being out in fairy alone was way better than being put into death matches for the amusement of others.

"You are a feisty one, aren't you?" Faigen's amused tone grated on Jada's nerves. His dry laugh filled the stairwell as she was frog marched into a large airy storage room with boxes containing booze and other supplies the club needed. They moved further back into the basement, and another door stood before them. This one looked ancient; the white marbled stonework was etched with glyphs that glowed soft blue beneath the incandescent lighting directly above them.

"Let me go!" Jada snapped and planted her feet in front of the archaic door. The guards tried to push her forward, but Jada wouldn't budge. Faigen sighed impatiently and wrapped his cane at the back of Jada's knees, causing her legs to buckle forward.

"She's strong, boss." The guard on her left painfully twisted her arm behind her back to forcefully usher her forward. Her lips spread into a full smile as the guard shook his out, trying to put out the fire that started on his suit cuff. Jada, in turn, scalded his hand, taking grim satisfaction at the irritated yelp he gave.

She continued to struggle as they dragged her through the marble corridor. The fluorescent overhead lights gave way to oil lamps that cast a bright glow through the passageway. Faigen laughed again with a deep shrug. "Maybe, but she'll feel pain readily enough."

Chapter Seven

Jada tried to set fire to the guard on her right. She only succeeded in causing him to growl at her angrily. Jada didn't have enough control of her newfound power to effectively use it as well. It only seemed to manifest when she was angry. She jerked her arm from his grasp and stomped on the foot of the other guard that held her. She turned to make a break for it as the guard hopped upon and down on one foot. Jada thought she was home free until Faigen's cane pulled out her ankle from under her as she passed him. She landed on her back and kicked at the guard who tried to grab her. Faigen pulled her up by her arm to peer into her face.

"Be nice. Gabriel will go through a lot of expense for you to fight here." Jada refrained from rolling her eyes as

Faigen tossed her back to his guards. Once he made sure that she was secured, they continued their ascent.

"Why are you even doing this? Don't you guys hate Gabriel?" Jada turned to Faigen and jerked her arm from the guard on her left with a glare. The procession halted once more, Faigen and Jada watched each other steadily.

Faigen nodded with a laugh and began walking once again. This time Jada followed without the guards holding her down. "We do, at that. But he is one of us, now and forever."

"One of you. So, Gabriel used to train here?" Jada rubbed her wrist where the guard had twisted and sent the man a glare that he only shrugged. The air started to get humid, and the temperature rose higher the further up they went.

"He wasn't always as you see him now. He used to be fairy trash like the rest of us. He used to fight here in the pits. Of course, the pits were run by my father then." Faigen continued walking, and soon the room let out into a vast marbled antechamber that split into several different directions. He took her through the one on the farthest right, and they continued talking.

"Why do they call it the pits?" Jada followed him, and her attention was rapt on the story Faigen was telling her about her captor. She knew nothing about the man who took her from the club and brought her here through the briars.

"It's a practical name for the area. A throwback from when my father ran the fights. We are four to five stories in the air. You'll see soon enough." Faigen murmured matter of factly as they continued walking. The tap of his cane was the only sound filling the passageway. "I believe humans call such a place a coliseum. A place where you survive by killing others. Gabriel was champion for a very long time."

"But he left." Jada's lungs filled with the stale air as they continued her journey through the dazzling corridors. Her arm was lifted to wipe away the sweat that collected on her brow. No air moved through the sweltering corridors that twisted and stretched into the air.

"Aye, he learned of the council games. It broke my father's heart when Gabriel gathered his pieces from our best fighters. Then left all of us behind. He took twenty-four of our best fighters and turned his back on us. We never saw him again until now anyway." There was an edge to Faigen's voice. He clearly did not appreciate Gabriel leaving and taking their fighting stock with him.

They arrived at a cell, and one of the guards pulled the heavy door open.He lifted the ebony stick with two quick taps of his cane, indicating that Jada should go through the doors. "Here we are, my dear. We'll come for you momentarily."

Jada sighed and walked through the doors, frowning as the heavy door was shut behind her. The room was filled with a soft blue light that seemed to shine brightly for a moment before fading to a more soothing glow. They reminded Jada of the candles in Dylaine's shop. The only steady light in the room was from the slot at the top of the door she walked through. The room was also filled with other people who looked like they were in a meditative trance. Everyone sat on the glowing stone with their eyes closed without moving. There were men of all shapes and sizes sitting at odd intervals against the wall. They were all dressed in battle leathers and armor. Each had the potential to kill her, a wave of angry despair hit her as she looked around.

"Jada," Gabriel's voice came through the slot in the door, and Jada turned and stiffly walked over. He was one of the last people she wanted to see at that moment.

"What do you want now, Gabriel?" Jada was in no mood to be conciliatory. She had lost her mind earlier feeling any sort of empathy for that beast.

"I want to apologize for the violence of my actions earlier. I didn't get a chance to explain, and I hate that you saw me like that." Gabriel sounded contrite, but that wasn't good enough for her. Faigen said he would be back in a minute which meant she would be fighting for her life soon.

"You're sorry you didn't explain? Explain what, Gabriel?" Jada's response was growing in levels of fury with each angry hiss of words that left her lips. "The violence is what you're sorry about? You stole me from my home, had me tortured at a doll shop, and now I'm being forced to fight for my life in a ring. But the fight with Saturn is what you're ashamed of?"

The amusement that seemed to be a part of Gabriel's ongoing personality was absent in his voice. Jada couldn't see him, but she was sure he was frowning. "Yes, but I see I needn't have worried about an explanation. I should have known Faigen would take care of the niceties."

"He also told me that you took off with a bunch of prized fighters." Jada shrugged but stopped as something in Gabriel's mood seemed to change. She stepped to the door and laid her hands flat against the splintering surface.

"Did he? He's grown vindictive in his old age." Gabriel's voice was clipped, and after a long, tense pause, he spoke again. She could tell by his clipped response that he was none too happy about her knowing he wasn't always noble. "Yes, I was born in a little village several miles from here. It was destroyed when the council found out that it was rich with fairy dust. I became an orphan scratching out a living on the streets. Faigen's father found me and threw me into the ring."

"Why am I here, Gabriel? If you know what it's like to be here, then why on earth would you put someone you say you care for through this?" Jada asked in exasperation.

"As I said upstairs, it's the best environment for you to train in. It's the only place that will get you ready for what's about to come." Gabriel's voice lost none of its stiffness, but he seemed ready enough to give her answers to any question she asked.

"And what exactly is about to come?" Jada could not imagine what could be worse than her last two days, but she didn't voice the sentiment aloud. Every time she didn't think it could get worse, the fairy found a way to make it so much worse.

"If you survive your time here, then I will tell you. Otherwise, it would be a waste of time. You constantly think about it and not focus on the fight in front of you.". Jada heard something metallic ring out into the silence between them, and soon a sword was passed through the shaft they spoke through along with her helmet. "I'll be back when your training is done."

Jada took the sword and immediately dropped it. She had never held a sword in her life, and now she was suddenly being charged with having to learn to defend herself with it. "Wait! You're leaving me here? For how long?"

"Correct. So don't die." He laughed when he heard the sword drop, and he ignored the question about how long she would be there. "Please accept my sword as a token of my undying affection and fight well."

"Why should I fight? Why not just die in the ring? I'm not opposed to your money or time being wasted." Jada touched the sword with her toe in disgust. When she thought about how many hours she had dreamed of a life somewhere far away from the club with Gabriel, she hated herself.

"You could do that, but I would just find someone else to be my queen." That was a dirty trick, and Gabriel knew it when he said it. He knew Jada would never let some other go through what she went through willingly. "Anyway, didn't you promise to kill me? How will you accomplish your goal if you're dead?"

Jada had nothing to say about that, and Gabriel took her silence as a conciliation. If she died, there would be some other person that would be tortured. The only way to get him to stop would be to kill him because he would resolutely stop at nothing to reach whatever goal he was trying to obtain. Jada's eyes lowered in silent prayer and damnation of the man before her. "I will kill you."

"I see that you understand. I will see you soon, Jada. I promise." There was something in Gabriel's voice that sounded like sorrow, but Jada was honestly too angry to process it. Gabriel moved away from the door, taking the scent of warm honey and coffee with him.

Jada stared at the sword on the ground in mute fury.. Armored fingers curled about the hilt of the blade, and she picked it up from the ground. After a moment, the anger dissipated, and her head hung in defeatShe would be on her own until Gabriel decided to come back for her, and she needed to get used to it.

The next time the door opened, a tall fairy with an executioner's mask draped in black leathers came through the door with a whip. A loud crack of his whip and he pointed at her and another fairy in the corner. "You and you."

"Fine, let's get this over with. "She tried not to memorize too many details about the man's face. She knew that to win, she would either have to kill or severely hurt him. She sighed and walked out of the door ahead of the man with whom she would be fighting.

"Don't worry. I'll make it quick so you don't suffer." The cocky voice made her turn slightly, and her eyes met his. The burly man was a troll. He held a large double-headed hammer against his shoulder. A shock of grey frizzy hair lined the top of his head, and his smile was interrupted by blunt tusks that rested at the corner of his lips. His green frog-like skin seemed to be perpetually wet and sticky looking. She wasn't sure if he was mocking her or if he was trying to be merciful. It didn't matter. One of them would not be returning to this cell, and it would probably be her with her lack of experience. Jada gave him a smile that could mean everything and nothing. She truly didn't have much to say in response. There would be no hard feelings. Things were as they were.

They walked up a set of marble stairs until they reached the arena floor. The executioner chuckled as Jada stared at the massive amphitheater. The pit was precisely what the coliseum like structure was. It was an inverted dome stained with blood and other bodily fluids that Jada didn't want to think about too hard. The entire room was a dingy white with evidence of battle in every square inch. The walls were lined with glassless arches that spectators hung out of and cheered. Jada could only marvel at the number of people who were here to watch the deathmatches.

"My lady!" The executioners' mocking voice accompanied a gallant wave of his hand as she stepped into the pit.

Jada tried to ignore the jeers and shouts of the gathered fairies. The crowds were both strange and humanoid. Where some had the heads of beasts, others looked like neighbors she had in her old apartments. She wondered how often she had passed by a fairy in human clothing. Dark eyes welled tears with thoughts of home, and she quickly brushed them away from her eyes. She didn't have time to break down right now. Maybe later, but not now.

"Look at her crying!" One of the fairies laughed and placed a bet against her. Her eyes found Faigen in the crowd, and he silently watched her. The tears gave way to rage, and she could feel her body heating up once more.

The woman announcing the match was tall, slender with yellow doll yarn for hair and wide black buttons for eyes. She smirked at Jada with her red zipper-like lips and raised her arms in their air. "Tonight, we have a very special fight! We have Blyssed from the house of Karnach. The crowd cheered, and Jada blinked at the name of the house that the other man was fighting for. Jada's eyes quickly scanned the crowd for those treacherous trolls but couldn't find them. They probably heard Gabriel was in the vicinity and ducked outback. The cowards.

"His opponent is Jada. Gabriel's...queen!" There were no cheers. Only catcalls at the announcement of yarn hair made. Pent-up hate for Gabriel was hoisted onto her, and it did nothing to assuage the anger that was building under her skin. The heat within her was a living, breathing, and tangible thing. She could almost touch it.

"This promises to be a short round, so don't blink, or you'll miss it." The button of the woman's eyes winked at the crowd, and Jada took a deep, steadying breath. She didn't have time to worry about the announcer being catty. She had a big girl problem to worry about. There was a lot of money being passed around, and most of it was not on her. The announcer dropped her arms, and a horn sounded at the beginning of the match. "Fighters fight!"

Jada's opponent swung his hammer, and she barely dodged the sudden onslaught. He had not been kidding about trying to end the match quickly. He swung, and Jada noted that her reflexes were heightened. There would have been no way she would have been able to dodge the troll's swing when she was just a human. This time when the troll swung, she jumped and landed on the business end of the hammer.

"You're only making this harder on yourself, dear." He swung his hammer again, and Jada backflipped out of the way. It was hard to think with the jeering of the crown. She had to come up with a plan, she couldn't keep dodging the troll forever. The troll must have gotten tired because he pulled the hammer back, and his fist clipped her in the chin.

Jada hit the ground with a skid that tore the skin at elbows split apart. She hissed in pain and pulled herself halfway up with a low moan. The hammer swung, and she barely rolled out of the way to sit in a crouch on the ground. Mentally weighing her options as she watched the troll warily. "I won't last more than twenty minutes if you can't find a way to end this fight."

Jada noted that it took Blyssed a few minutes to pull up the weight of the hammer. Her fingers tightened on the sword Gabriel gave her, and she swung it at the troll's dominant arm. The cut wasn't deep, but it was enough to cause the troll to wince out of annoyance. "Gabriel chose you?" The troll laughed as he swung the hammer again, but she hopped out of reach. At least, what she thought was out of reach. Suddenly the ground shifted beneath her, bringing her closer to the troll. This time he shoved the hammer into her stomach, and she painfully stumbled onto the ground. Her arm went around her bruised middle, and she barely blocked the next swing of the hammer with Gabriel's sword. She was moving on instinct because she was not lying when she told Gabriel she had no fighting skills.

The pain made it hard to think, and the shouts from the crowd were not making it any easier. "Looks like Gabriel should have picked a better queen."

The laughter of the crowd filled the arena. Jada gritted her teeth and stood once more. "What do you expect from someone who wasn't strong enough to stay champion in the first place?"

So many taunts from those gathered, Jada couldn't tell where each came from. "I'm glad I didn't put any money on her."

Another faceless voice soon joined the others. "I did! Get up, you harlot!"

"Oh, what's she going to do now?" The voices just kept going on and on. Jada was running out of energy, trying to dodge and block the blows coming at her in earnest.

She was starting to take more blows than she was blocking. The ground moved beneath her again, but this time the blow was coming for her head. Her reflexes saved her from having her jaw dislocated by the hammer, but it hit her shoulder instead. "Just die already, so we can get to a real fight!"

"Tough crowd, eh little lady?" The troll pressed his advantage and swung, but Jada dissolved into nothing

118

and gathered back together on the other side of the ring. The crowd continued their jeers, and Jada was low-level offended as she thought she had pulled off a fantastic feat. They didn't know Jada would win, and neither did she. But Gabriel must have seen something that told him that she would make it out alive. If not, why go through all of this trouble?

"If you die quietly, I won't mess up your face, yeah? You'll be able to be as beautiful as you are now." The troll's voice was coaxing and meant to be soothing, but unfortunately, he had the bad fortune to work for two people that she loathed completely.

"Thanks, but I'll pass." Jada disappeared again to the other side of the arena but forgot that he could move the floor to bring her closer. The troll brought her back but kicked her legs from beneath her. He proceeded to stomp down into her stomach with his powerful leg, but she twisted away at the last minute. However, he succeeded in punching her in the face.

Jada saw stars, but the second swing of the troll's fist met the blade of Gabriel's sword. The force of his punch against the sharpened steel severed four of his fingers. The troll's scream turned her stomach, but the blood splattering on her skin had her rushing to the other side of the arena to empty, retching until the only thing that came up was bile.

"Gabriel made the wrong call! The crowd continued their insulting calls, but Jada was too busy being sick to care.She can't even handle a few missing fingers, let alone be the Queen of the board!"

"You bitch! Look what you did! How am I supposed to swing my hammer now!" The troll's bellow filled the room in pain and the agony of his fate. He ran at her sans the hammer he could no longer lift. The long bulbous fingers of his other hand closed around her helmet, and she was thrown shoulder first into the stained marble floor. The sword Gabriel gave her dislodging from her fingers as she landed.

"Blyssed is going to wallop her good for that one." Jada wiped her mouth with the back of her hand, and she pulled her bruised form up from the floor. There were so many voices filling the arena.

Another voice in the crowd followed the first. "Hope it's not too fast. Gabriel needs to learn his lesson."

Jada was running out of steam, and she was in a lot of pain. Dodging and reappearing in other places was starting to take its toll on her stamina. She wasn't making any headway in this fight, and she needed to develop a strategy.

The ground shifted, and Jada's face was met with Blyssed's fist. Each word was punctuated with a swing of his fist. "You killed me! You were the only one supposed to die tonight, but you have killed me as surely as I'm going to kill you!"

"Yeah, give it to her!" They seemed to agree and cheer on the almost inevitable nature of her demise. Blyssed walked away long enough to pick up Gabriel's sword with his good hand. The cheers of the crowd became defining as the troll waved the sword in the air. "Kill Gabriel's whore with his sword!"

It wasn't all bad; there were some in the crowd lamenting her loss. "I've lost a whole week's wages betting on the quim!"

"Tell me! Should I start with her fingers?" The troll, emboldened by the cheers of the arena, started to play to the crowd. Walking around with his bloodied arm raised.

"What would I return to?" Jada tiredly whispered to herself. All she wanted to do was close her eyes and let it end. She thought of her tiny dingy apartment and wondered who would move into it. They would sell what little she had. They would hire another waitress to take her shift at the dinner she worked in. The club was gone, so were her friends. The truth was there was nothing for her back home. If she did make it back over the briars, she was barely human now, if at all. Even if everything was the same when she got back home, she would never be.

The troll leaned over to stare into her face with a smile. "You're actually gorgeous. Maybe I won't kill you right away? What about it? Should we give them another type of show?"

"What am I fighting for? Why not just let this nightmare end here?" Jada's thoughts ran incessantly despite her exhaustion. She groans and turns onto her side, trying to pick herself up off the ground.

Blyssed nudged her back over with the toe of his boot and kicked her legs apart. The lumbering troll dropped to his knees between her thighs. He brought Gabriel's sword up to her neck with his good hand. "Nothing personal, eh? What do you say? We'll both die satisfied tonight."

Jada weakly turns her head to look up at him. She could see her reflection in his glassy green eyes. She saw a scared little doll lying on the ground covered in blood. Weak and useless. "I can't even save myself.

How did I ever think I'd be strong enough to kill Gabriel?"

"Huh? What's that you're mumbling" The troll looked down at Jada uneasily. "What are you going on about?"

"Come on, Blyssed, get on with it!" The yarn haired announcer egged the troll on from the side of the ring. Stoking the bloodthirst that had spread through the crowd like a disease. "Where's the show you promised them?"

"You want a show?" The troll lifted his bloodied hand towards the crowd, which caused their hateful roars to become louder. The edge of Gabriel's sword pressed into her neck, drawing a thin line of blood. "I'll give you a show!"

"I can't die yet," Jada whispered as she looked up at Blyssed. Her lashes fluttering heavily as she struggled to keep her eyes open. The heckling of the crowd sounded distant over the blood that rushed between her ears. She caught her reflection in his eyes once more. That same scared little girl staring back at her as she laid on the floor. "I have to kill Gabriel."

"You'll never see Gabriel again. Relax and enjoy yourself." The sword bore down on her neck as the troll's knees spread her thighs further apart. His thumb doing its best to loosen the drawstrings of his pants without the rest of his fingers.

Jada's fingers twitched and curled into a tight fist at his words. Fury spread through her veins, and her hand lifted to close around the blade of Gabriel's sword. She could feel the steel cut into her fingers, but the pain was secondary to her anger. She violently pushed and twisted his wrist back into an impossible angle. Only stopping when she heard a wet popping sound as muscles tore and bone splintered beneath his skin. Blyssed's screams filled an arena that had gone completely quiet. They watched in silent horror as the troll fell back onto the area floor. His thumb tried to wrap around his wrist in vain as he tried to pick himself up using only his legs. Jada rolled up from the ground and walked over to the troll who had trouble getting his legs under him.

"I'll take this, thank you." Her lips curled into a tired smile as she pulled Gabriel's sword from useless fingers. "I don't know how to use this sword, but I'll learn."

She twisted the sword in her bloody fingers a few times. Jada swung and the ground shifted and drug her towards him. His head forcefully butting against hers, and the floor shifting and throwing her away once more. She rolled over the ground and landed on her left. Her hand slapped against the ground in frustration and pulled herself from the ground to run back to only to be pulled away again.

They continued to play keep away until Jada became fed up and ran at him. The troll shifted the ground once more, but Jada took a running jump and disintegrated in midair. The crowd roared as she reassembled in front of him. Jada scratches that stung her legs or the bruising to grip the sword in both hands. Jada watched Blyssed's red eyes

123

as they followed the blade that came toward his head. The arterial spray from his neck painted half of her face and arms in right red. She yelled and jerked her arms and continued to swing until his head rolled away from his shoulders. The coliseum was silent as Jada dropped the sword and fell to her knees. Her chest rising and falling with the effort of breathing normally.

"I want my money back!" The crowd stirred and soon the arena was filled with loud disappointment

"She's not fooling anyone! Drag Gabriel back here and tell him to get his ringer!" The sore losers tried to get a chant together to disqualify the match, but when Jada's eyes met theirs, the request died away as if it never happened. Even the ragdoll looked reluctant to look her in the eye.

Faigen stood with his hand and cane to bring the noise of the crowd down. Jada watched him in exhausted wariness. Disintegrating took a lot out of her, and she doubted she could handle another round if they put someone fresh in the ring. "She has won. Put her back in the lacuna and make sure they understand that they will pay with their life if anyone touches her outside of the ring. This is an arena, not a whore house!"

The crowd continued to jeer and scream about how unfair the match was. Jada put them out of her mind as she followed the guards down the arena stairs. She wouldn't be able to go back home, but she had found her purpose in that ring. A reason to keep on living despite all of the loss and pain her life had devolved into. There was nothing else for her to do but get strong and focus on killing her darling, Gabriel.

Chapter Eight

Jada had no idea how long she had been fighting in
the pits. She had stopped counting after the first year.
It was just an endless sea of faces she didn't
remember and didn't want to. Her humanity was stripped
away one soul at a time. The number of fairies looking to
use her to take vengeance on Gabriel was as endless as
her days. Each one looking for death, not knowing it
would be their own.

During that time, her powers grew. She leaned to wield
and control them with every match she won. One she saw
every time she went into the arena to fight.If Gabriel had
come around, she would have shown him. Jada never saw
him again after that first night. He was like a far-off
nightmare in her head. It was rumored that he would
secretly watch the games. It mattered not to her because

she could only focus on her goal of killing him. She wanted to make him hurt the way she was hurting and would die trying to do so.

"Jada, you're up." A guard called out to her, and she stepped away from her holding position in the cell. After the first night she fought, she found out that the Lacuna was a space for fighters to heal and let their mind go quiet after the screams of those they murdered filled their head. Apparently, the fairies had found psychology in their quest for entertainment. She pulled on her brass bracers and helmet as she walked to the door.

Jada took a deep breath of the humid air and picked up Gabriel's sword. The sword was very precious to her. It would be the sword she killed him with, and she wanted nothing to happen to it. She was stronger than when she started, but Jada wasn't sure she was strong enough to run Gabriel through. She wasn't even sure if she was strong enough to mount an escape from Faigen's pit. What Jada did know was that she would be by the time she left the world of fairy for good.

She stepped into the ring. This time, the cheers and chants for her were celebratory. She didn't do anything showy when she entered the ring. Though using her powers came easy to her, breathing now still took the energy she would need for the fight.

"Entering the pits is our current Champion Jada!" Button's eyes gave Jada a saccharine smile, and she was instantly put on edge. The woman never smiled at her. She hadn't forgiven Jada for not dying the first night she came. Jada had a suspicion that she had hoped to be the one to comfort Gabriel after her demise. Too bad for her. Jada had no plans on dying before completing her goals.

"This match is a special match!" The crowd oohed, and aah's loudly, and Jada barely kept herself from rolling her eyes. Special matches only meant they found someone that would be tougher for her to kill. "If Jada wins tonight, she will have her freedom!"

There were boos and cheers, and Jada didn't care about any of it. She wouldn't be free even if she did win. Her eyes lifted to Faigen, and his red eyes held her for a moment before looking off to his side. Jada's eyes followed his direction, and she saw the star of every one of her nightmares.

Gabriel sat amidst the riff-raff, and when their eyes locked, his head inclined. There was very little about him that had changed. His hair was a little longer, causing the dark curls to brush his impressive jawline in waves. The pure white suit he wore was a bold choice with the flung into the arena by the crowds. He also looked a lot richer. No doubt he had been betting on her to win. That was convenient because she had not planned on losing. His golden eyes remained steadily on hers until she ignored his presence all together with. Abruptly turning away from him to focus on the doors on the other side of the pit.

The doors to the arena opened, and there was a pale white fairy four times her size. The fairy was surely an Ogre and a starving one, from the looks of his red tinged eyes. The Ogre screamed out his rage, and the sound was virtually prehistoric. The Ogre's tusk dragged across the floor, making the arena shake as he moved. He lurched forward, and his spiked club dragged behind him. He wouldn't have to be fast to hurt her. The damage he could do with just one blow of his club could put her lights out permanently. Jada's mind raced despite how slowly she circled the ogre. She wouldn't be able to harm him with her powers; something that large would require physical force. At best, they would slow him down before he shook them off. If the mammoth of a fairy could feel it at all, it would just tickle.

"Let the match begin!" Jada looked over at button eyes, and the yarned hair cow smiled before twitching out of the ring to sit next to Faigen.

The fairy swung his tusk to look Jada in her eyes. His knuckles scraped the floor, and she glanced up at Faigen with a lift of her brow. Faigen shrugged with a slight smile. Jada guessed the plan was for her to never leave the ring if she was no longer fighting in it. His final revenge on Gabriel for leaving. The ogre swung the club at her head, and she rolled between his arms to buy herself some time to think. The next swing hit a pillar, causing some spectators to get nervous as the arena shook from the force. She rolled between his legs again and sliced into the back of his knee.

"That didn't even hurt you, big baby." Jada admonished the creature in irritation. His hide was made of thick scales that her sword didn't even chip at.

It would take forever for her to hack into the beast. She could try to temporarily paralyze the creature. Still the amount of energy it would take to do that to someone of his magnitude was daunting. It also would not leave her with enough power to do much else later.

She narrowly dodged another swing by turning into mist, and an idea suddenly came to her. If it worked, then she would be able to finish the fight quickly.

"Maybe…"

Jada jumped on top of the club and climbed up the ogre's massive arm. Carefully dodging as the other arm did its best to tear her away from his back. Her brass-colored legs wrapped tightly around his shoulders, and her hands covered his eyes. Jada focused her concentration on her palms, and her hands' fiery glow began to melt his eyes out of its sockets.

The room was silent but for the Ogre's tortured screams. He succeeded in ripping her off of his back and blindly tossing her across the ring. She rolled a few times but luckily landed on her feet. The blind Ogre began swinging his club around the room. Taking out pillars, boxes, and rows of seats. The fairies scattered like roaches trying to get out of the Ogre's way. They were fighting so hard to get out that none made any progress. The Ogre took out a section of seats, and screams filled the arena where there were once cheers. Jada would have been amused if she had not been at ground zero.

"He's coming this way!" Jada was unfazed by the cries of the crowd. How many nights had they been cheering for someone else to get hurt?

"He's out of control! Someone save us!" Jada rolled her shoulders in boredom as she waited to see how much of the audience would be left. She won the match; there was nothing left for her to do at this point. "He's going to kill us!" Jada leaned against an unaffected wall on the other side of the pit. She wondered how often the crowd had ignored the screams of mercy from those forced to fight for their entertainment. Now their blood would decorate the marble pit like countless fighters before them. Her lips curled as she watched the beast barely miss Faigen and Gabriel. The mammoth Ogre killing them would be poetic. Her arms crossed, and she relaxed as she decided to let the Lord do his work. Dispensing justice in the form of a blind rampaging Ogre.

The Ogre swung, and the announcer was decimated by the force of the club landing on top of her. The buttons of her eyes rolling and spinning at Faigen's feet like forgotten tops. Faigen's wide red eyes shifted to Jada's, and she shrugged. There was no reason to help them, and every reason to let them die. He turned to Gabriel, who was sitting off to his side just as relaxed as Jada was. "Tell her to kill the beast!"

"In her mind, she is." Gabriel's gaze met hers, and she made a kissing motion with her lips and made no move to help either of them. Gabriel's lips twitched into a smile, and he turned back to Faigen with his own shrug. "So, you are declaring Jada the winner then?"

Faigen ducked between Gabriel's legs, and they barely missed being smashed into a paste by the Ogre's random swings. "Yes, yes, hurry!"

Gabriel turned to her, his gaze decidedly friendlier than the one he gave Faigen. The arena master peeked at Jada between Gabriel's legs angrily. "Jada, kill the monster, please."

Jada laughed and waved her arm towards the Ogre and them. "Oh, believe me, I'm trying."

"Jada." Gabriel sighed with a roll of his golden eyes.

"Gabriel." Jada's voice was syrupy sweet. She saw no reason to help them at all. If the monster finished him for her, then that was fine and dandy with her. Plus, it would help her gauge how much stronger she would need to be to kill him. Work smarter, not harder.

"The Ogre will kill Faigen, but he won't kill me." Gabriel pretty much confirmed what she had been thinking, but there was no reason not to test his words.

Jada ignored the way his pale eyes glowed at the challenge and continued to watch the ogre tear the arena apart. She pulled off her helmet and tucked it under her arm patiently. "You can't control me."

"You don't know what I can do. Not really." Gabriel smiled with a shake of his head. She ignored the small part of her that was human and swooned at the memory of Gabriel's bouncer persona. Better to let that part of her die in the pit if it still lingered.

"Show me." "You better hurry. Faigen won't last much longer. Just as she was saying the words, the Ogre smashed another pillar down, and the ceiling began to crumble in various places. Jada continued to relax against the crumbling but not broken bit of wall.

Gabriel stood, and his halo of light that emitted from him surrounded the Ogre. Jada lifted her arms to keep from being blinded. She wasn't sure, but she could have sworn she saw a set of white wings behind him. Gabriel's reptilian gaze lengthened and contracted before a beam of light fried away from the arm the Ogre was using to swing his club. The Ogre began to pinwheel with one arm, and soon his opposing leg was taken in the same flash of white light. Leaving the monster to crawl pitifully across the floor in anguish on alternate limbs.

"Jada, this is the last time I'm going to ask." Gabriel turned to Jada and lifted both of his brows, and Jada frowned as she considered her options. Nope, not strong enough yet. Not by a long shot, but she was getting there. The time in the pit wasn't wasted, but she still wasn't where she needed to be yet.

"As you wish." Her voice was tight with disappointment. Jada's lips pressed into a thin conciliatory smile, and she sauntered toward the Ogre. She almost felt sorry for the mewling beast on the floor. Muttering a quick apology to the beast under her breath before severing its spinal cord where his neck and shoulders met. The beast went still, and thankfully its anguished cries stopped.

"Thank you." Gabriel walked to Jada and took her hand before bringing them to his lips in an affectionate kiss. His good humor restored, he turned to Faigen with a magnanimous grin. "Faigen, we will take our winnings and be on our way."

Faigen scrambled up, and even Jada was amused at how Faigen hopped up and down in anger. If he had been strong enough to murder them without his guard, he would have. "Collect what? Do you see what she did to my arena?"

Gabriel's gold eyes glittered dangerously over his smile. "Now, you were the one who chose her opponent."

"I thought she would die." Faigen glared up at her, and Jada stuck out her forked tongue at him with a wink. It was too bad; she couldn't kill him on her way out. Maybe she would come back for him later after killing Gabriel.

"I know. Our winnings if you please?" Gabriel gazed at Jada as he trailed his fingers from her cheek down the exposed column of her neck. Looking over the bruising with concern pressing his lips. The gesture was strangely affectionate. It would be something that she would expect a lover to do. "With that display of strength, no one will be willing to help you out if she decided to kill you right now. Deservedly I might add."

Faigen looked around at what was left of the cowering mass of fairies and threw his money belt filled with gold at Gabriel's feet. Faigen growled, pointing up at them and to the door. "Leave, and this time never come back."

"I won't need to. Jada, shall we?" He turned to Jada to see if she was ready to go. Jada gave Faigen one last look that he returned with a murderous glare before heading to the stairs that would lead them out of the pits. Gabriel picked up the money belt and began counting the gold as he turned away. Gabriel stopped, and his cold gold eyes looked back at Faigen. "I also trust that you will stop telling others that I used to be a fighter here?" Faigen averted his eyes, and Gabriel upped the wattage of his smile. Seeing that Faigen understood, he continued on his way.

"So, you're petty," Jada murmured as they made their way downstairs, away from the pits. The sword and helmet swung idly by her side as she walked.

"And vengeful," Gabriel said over his shoulder as they continued to walk. "Might I also add that you look beautiful this evening!"

"Thank you. Did you know that tonight was my last fight" Jada's voice was flat as they moved past the Lacuna and through the marbled hallways Jada had walked through three years prior.

"Of course." Gabriel barely spared the fairies that filled the stairwell a glance as they walked by. They had escaped down the stairs during the fight. Afraid of any retribution, their shameful behavior would garner them. They averted their eyes as the duo moved through them.

"I see." Jada left the topic alone for the moment. She was angry, but she also felt a keen sense of anxiety at the prospect of seeing something other than the arena and the holding cell.

They moved down each flight of stairs and into the dance club. Jada could hear the first stirrings of electronic music. She swayed a bit as she walked behind Gabriel. Jada had heard nothing but the sounds of heckling and screams since she became a fighter. Club Hyena was bumping when they opened the door. Dancers of all species moved to the rhythm of the synthesized music Blaring through the speakers. The heavy base of the music doing its best to deregulate the beat of Jada's heart. As they passed through the club, she saw Saturn watching them with a hateful sneer. Jada did her best not to make eye contact with him. They were almost out of there, and she didn't want any more trouble than she already had. Saturn's leer grew as they approached. Jada's chest lifted in a deep sigh and a roll of her brown eyes. Mentally making peace with getting into trouble on their way out.

As they passed by, Saturn took the liberty of grabbing a handful of her ass. The DJ's record scratched, and two things happened simultaneously. The offending appendage dissolved, and his other hand was sliced away by the sword she held only a moment before. Saturn yelled and rolled around on the floor in misery. Jada watched in surprise as Gabriel sheathed his sword to the empty scabbard at his side. She hadn't even felt him take it from her. Gabriel watched Saturn roll around for a moment and held his hand out to Jada. Pulling her in front of him in case anyone else got any ideas. The act was chivalrous and almost a little possessive. Jada shook her head and hoped no one else felt the need to jump them on the way out. His hand moved protectively to the small of Jada's back as they walked out of the door, moved to the small of her back as they walked out of the door for the last time.

They moved into the cool night air, and Jada pulled in as much as she possibly could. She barely remembered what fresh air without the stench of death smelled like. The clockwork horses pulled up and neighed happily when they saw her. Jada's smile was genuine as they came to a complete stop at the curb. Gabriel opened the carriage and allowed her to climb in first. Once they were securely seated, he tapped the roof, and the horses pulled away.

Gabriel watched the nightclub as it faded away from view. He watched with an overwhelming sense of sadness that made the atmosphere in the carriage heavy. It stayed that way as modern city streets turned to country roads and lamps turned to tall trees. Once they cleared the city without incident, he turned to

Jada with a tentative smile. "That went well, all in all.

'

"What fresh hell are you taking me to this time, Gabriel?" Jada was still watching the scenery go by as they passed through the countryside. She was tired and honestly didn't have a lot to say to him. They had nothing in common, and she hated him.

"Jada, don't be like that. It was necessary. Plus, we have grown wealthy!" Gabriel emptied the gold coins out of the bag and tossed the belt out of the window. She was glad he was happy about his blood money, but honestly, his winning did nothing for her.

"At the expense of my life." Jada's hands curled into fists. Now that the adrenaline was no longer bouncing around her system, she started to get angry.

"At the expense of other people's lives." Gabriel continued counting his money before pouring it all into a chest under his seat. He was so content like a well-fed python.

"My soul then." Jada tossed the words over her shoulder, refusing to look at him.

"Overrated." Gabriel's reply was flippant, and it was taking everything in Jada's power not to toss caution to the wind and try to murder him right then.

"Where are we going, Gabriel?" She asked again. Jada was running out of patience, and she guessed Gabriel sensed it.

Gabriel moved over so that his arms could wrap around her waist and pull her tightly against him. His chin moving to rest on her shoulder as he watched the scenery go by as well. "It's time to meet your true purpose. The reason you were brought here in the first place."

Jada didn't bother to respond. It was just another task on her journey to kill him. Whatever it was, she was sure it would be just as hellish as the arena. She focused on the beautiful countryside. The green crops and sapphire lakes were bathed in silvery moonlight. She felt like Cinderella on the way to the ball. Only her prince was actually Blue Beard. She stayed quiet. It didn't matter if he continued or not. She would have no real choice in the matter.

"Do you know what next year is?" Jada sighed, not in the mood to play any games with him this evening. His head tilted on her shoulder, and his lips pressed a kiss along the column of her neck.

"Gabriel, please get to the point." She resisted the urge to lean back into him and release the tension in her shoulders. This was going to be a very long ride to wherever they were going.

"It is the year of games. The council I am on decides how our world is run, but the games decide who is on the council." His arms tightened around her as if relieving a very unpleasant memory. It's a series of matches that determine who belongs to our ruling class. There are seven seats in all."

Jada squirmed, trying to keep herself from becoming too comfortable. She intended to hate him for the duration of her life. "One of which you already have."

"Correct, but the highest seat governs the council. That seat decides the fate of what happens across all of the fairies for an entire age." Gabriel's hand lifted and started to play with the curls of her dark hair. He twisted the coily strands wrapping them around his fingers absently. "Can you imagine it? One person who decides if one village should prosper or suffer. Who gets sent to work in the mines or sold off to the highest bidder."

"How long is an age?" If he thought Jada was about to sympathize with him, he was mistaken.

Gabriel pulled Jada into his lap and held her tightly. She knew she was not going to like what she was about to hear at all. "Roughly 100 human years, but 7 for us"

Jada removed herself from his lap and turned to look at him. His pale gold eyes rested on her steadily. "How long have I been here?"

Gabriel sighed as if his favorite toy had been taken from him. He leaned back with a shrug as if the matter had been so unimportant, he hadn't bothered to think about it. "In Fairy? Four years. In human years about

25. Time moves differently here."

Jada just sat there in shock, unable to move or believe what she heard. She hadn't thought that her world would have changed entirely without her. Jada had known that nothing of her life would be the same when she got back. She would be lucky if anyone left in her world would even remember she existed.

"Jada, I know it's shocking, but I need you to focus." Gabriel sat up straighter and took her hands in his. "To challenge for the highest council seat, you have to have an entire board of kings and queens. Meaning each player has taken over 100 pawns."

Jada numbly removed her hands from his. She didn't want to touch him. She hadn't remembered playing any games, but then it hit her. Her gaze met his, and her head tilted to the side. "How many pawns have I taken, Gabriel?"

Gabriel's thumbs brushed along the tips of his fingers where her hands had been as if trying to memorize the feeling. "Counting tonight? 150. I like to pad my pieces by 25 pawns or so. Bureaucracy is a pain no matter what world you're in."

"The fairies and humans I fought in the pits were… A-game. I have been killing and murdering others to fuel your dreams of grandeur for four years!" Her hands moved to her chest. She started sucking in a large amount of air and turned towards the window. Her stomach churned at the memory of every life she took.

"Correct, they were to be a part of someone else's board." Gabriel moved to gently rub her back in large circles. She didn't want to admit that it was helping but had no problem pulling away from his touch. "I know it's a shock. Take a deep breath."

"And now that they are gone?" Jada rested her head in her hands and knew the answer. She just wanted to hear him say it out loud. She did not have the stones of the Lacuna to manage her emotions or the adrenaline running rampant in her system. Each death was flooding back to her.

"They will have to go get more." Though Gabriel's tone was apologetic, he quickly moved on to a matter he felt was of some consequence. "That's not important, however. What is important is that my board is complete. I will be challenging Silvestri, the tyrant who rules now, for her seat this next year."

Jada did not bother commenting on anything that he said. None of it had anything to do with her. Not really. Her tyrant was trying to dispose of another tyrant. It was all sticks and stones to her at this point. She had enough to deal with now that she had time to think about all the things she had done over the past year or more.

Gabriel continued gently rubbing her back comfortingly. "Silvestri is an unimaginable snob who created the pits you fought in. The nobility trains their pawns in facilities that are not life or deathmatches found in holes in the walls in the middle of the city. Silvestri starved out my village for not producing enough fairy dust. I was sold to Faigen's father when I was a child to pay off my parents' debt."

During her time in fairy, she learned that fairy dust was basically the recreational drug of choice for the world over the briars. Stories like Rip Van Winkle were just famous humans that got hooked on the stuff until they were returned home years later. Ugly things happened to

141

those who became addicted, fairy or otherwise. Which still had nothing to do with Jada, who resolutely continued to stare out of the window. "My heart bleeds for you."

Gabriel's laugh was humorless as he lifted his boots to rest on the other seat on the other side of the carriage. His body languidly uncoiling as he made himself comfortable. "I wish you would see that I'm not the enemy Jada."

Jada wasn't sure if her eyes were rolling or if she was having an aneurysm. She half-turned in her seat to watch him as he stretched out. "You're my enemy."

"I don't want to be." Gabriel frowned, and the breadth of his impressive chest expanded as if she was trying his patience. As if he was explaining something to someone preciously slow. "I would have you learn to love me."

"Love you?" This time Jada turned all the way in her seat, looking at him as if he had grown another head. Her eyes locked with his. "Did you forget about the kidnapping, or was it the fighting in the pits you forgot? Herr Drosselmeir ring any bells?"

"You loved me once." Gabriel smiled, and one of his hands moved to curl around hers. At least Gabriel had the good grace not to deny any of the horrible things he did, but it still wasn't an admission of guilt.

"That was different! That was when you were…." Jada struggled to find a good word for who he used to be. The gallant bouncer from the club had just been an illusion. Like a dream that you wake up and forget about. No matter how hard you try to remember the details.

142

"Human." Gabriel finished the words for her, and she turned away once more so she would not see the pain in his eyes. She kept telling herself that she was not going to empathize with him. She wouldn't betray herself that way.

Jada's attention was taken by the passing landscape once more. The night she was abducted felt so long ago. She hadn't had time to even process and adjust to her new reality before more horror was forced onto her. Jada reminded herself that she hated Gabriel with every fiber of her being.

Gabriel was silent for a moment before his voice curled around her ear. In her distraction, she had not noticed that she had gotten that close once again. "Let's make a deal."

"You don't have anything I want." The rebuff in Jada's voice was loud and clear as far as she was concerned. He was too close, and he was making it hard for her to think on purpose.

"We both know that's not true." Gabriel scoffed, and Jada thought he was going to ignore the nonverbal cues. However, he surprised her by moving back and giver her space to breathe.

"Do we?" Jada's hand moved to rub along her arms. The night air had started to cool down, and the loss of his touch also meant a loss of heat.

Gabriel moved around, and Jada could hear the rustle of fabric. She wondered what he was doing until his white jacket wrapped around her shoulders. His hands rubbing up and down her arms to warm her. "I see that your time in the pits has made you mean."

"You get what I paid for." The coat smelled like him.

That familiar scent of roasted coffee beans and honey. Jada had to fight herself not to nuzzle her nose into the familiar scent. It reminded her of when she was safe and not a ball of rage and murder.

"Very true. Let's make a deal." Gabriel sounded contrite, but he went on. "The deal is when you win, you get one wish as the winning queen. It's a custom of the games to give the most important piece whatever they want."

"If I ask for your head?" Jada was not in the mood to play with him or listen to his lies. She was cold and wanted to go to sleep. She would be in the Lacuna now if he had not come to fetch her.

"If I die, I'll see to it you'll go to Bane, but it doesn't matter. There are rules to keep things like that from happening." Jada opened her mouth to respond, and Gabriel's elegant fingers lifted to forestall the coming argument. "Don't decide now. What you think you want now may not be what you want later."

Jada's eyes narrowed as she silently sized him up. He looked tired, but that didn't explain the sudden suspicious acquiescence. Gabriel's brow lifted, and her lips parted in indignation a moment later in realization. "You think I'll want you!"

"You already do. You're just angry right now. Not that I blame you. Jada, I want you to know that I didn't make any of these choices lightly. I hate every moment of what you had to go through. But trust that I'm not putting you through anything that I didn't have to go through. I just hope that you can come to see that I care for you. That I

144

love you." Gabriel turned from her after saying his piece. He laid back into the carriage and closed his eyes, leaving Jada to mull over everything he said.

Jada did not know how to respond to his words. The speech was pretty, but she couldn't trust it or him. She was too keyed up to go to sleep. She pulled the coat around her tighter and watched the road. She didn't know where they were going, but something told her that she would in fact, prefer to have been left in the pits.

Chapter Nine

Jada snuggled into her pillows and pulled her blanket closer around her. She must have dreamed everything. The pits, the Drosselmier, the entire ordeal with Gabriel. He would be there, ready to welcome her to work with that beautiful smile and his sparkling golden eyes. She felt so safe and warm. The carriage came to a lurching halt startling Jada awake. She hadn't slept that soundly since the day she had been dragged over the briars. Her fingers lifted to brush through her sleep mussed curls, and her eyes met Gabriel's. The mirth in his gold eyes filled with repressed laughter. Jada frowned until she noticed that the pillows she had been snuggled into Gabriel's arms. She threw herself back against the window of the carriage as if she had been scalded, and Gabriel laughed.

His broad shoulders rolled before lifting to rise over his head in a languid stretch. Allowing Jada the time to collect herself. "Good morning, Jada. I hope you slept as well as I did."

Jada's face was hot with embarrassment, but as she looked out the window to avoid his eyes, there were rolling tropical hills and palm trees as far as the eyes could see. The sounds of parrots and other exotic birds filled the early morning air. The sun was just starting to peek over the horizon. The moist salty air filled her lungs, and she could just make out the sound of the ocean. She couldn't, for the life of her, figure out where they were. It was as if they had been transported to a tropical island. "Where are we?"

"You're surely in the morning. We are at our new estate." Gabriel watched her looking out of the window and smiled. Jada didn't miss the "our," but she didn't comment on it.

"What happened to the old one?" Jada was astounded by the beauty of the location. The palm trees swayed in the oncoming rush of the wind. The butterflies danced over flowers in the small garden in the front of the white palace they had arrived at. There was a large fountain where the water fell from a pot held by a nude fairy with a coily crown of hair tied back with a scarf. She had never seen anything more beautiful.

"Let's just say we have both become more powerful during the last three years." Gabriel smiled at her, pulled her into a big hug, and gave her a quick kiss on her cheek. "Come on, let me show you your new home."

The door to the carriage was opened by a footman. He was a pelican with a white wig followed by a frog in a breach coat holding an umbrella. Each bowed as Gabriel held out his hand to help her exit the carriage. The morning was bright and cool. Jada adjusted his coat around her shoulders, it would warm up soon enough, but Jada didn't really want to let the coat go. If Jada had been in a good mood, she would have said that she was sentimental, but Jada was decidedly not in a good mood. She took his hand and allowed him to guide her out of the carriage like the gentlemen she had thought he was.

"Come on, you must be famished." Gabriel's voice was excited. He was almost glowing with boisterous energy. Jada was trying not to be infected by his enthusiasm. As Gabriel led Jada to the house, he was full of details about the grounds and their new home. "The workers belong to the house. At night the day servants become inanimate, and during the day, the night workers fall asleep. I see you looking at the flowers, don't worry. The flowers will bloom at all times of day and night. You will never be without flowers for your beautiful hair."

Jada was hungry, but she wouldn't give him the satisfaction of conversation. As soon as they got to the front steps, the statues were pillars on both sides of the animated doors. The stone effigies pulled the doors open, allowing them to enter the most beautiful room that Jada had ever seen. The sheer size of the foyer took her breath away. The room was filled with gold filigree and jeweled tones of purples, rubies, and sapphires. Large golden baskets holding flowers hung aloft from the ceiling in odd intervals. Gabriel pulled a white peony from the baskets they had and placed it in her loose coils behind her ear.

They continued through dark blue halls leading into a large dining half filled with the early morning sun and vaulted ceilings. Jada heard the call of birds of paradise and the soft coo of doves from somewhere outside of the room. A large lazy peacock outside of the bow windows caught Jada's attention. Once it caught sight of her, his tail spread in a magnificent plume of green and blue feathers. The eyes of his tail blinking at her curiously as he continued to walk by. A charming smile curved her lips despite herself.

Gabriel pulled out a chair for her and waited until she sat down at a table overflowing with food. "I see that you like your new home. Wait until you see your bedroom." He adjusted her seat as she made herself comfortable.

"Is it separate from yours?" Though she presented cool enough, Jada reached over to pluck a grape from one of the overfilled dishes. Taking a bite to hide the slight shake of her voice at the question. Though she forgot him momentarily. Her eyes almost crossed at the taste of real food and not the gruel-like sludge they gave to everyone in the pits.

"For now." Gabriel watched her eat with a smile, his eyes warmly resting on her full lips as she chewed. He took his own seat and spread a linen napkin across his lap.

"When will that change?" Jada started to fill her plate, half ignoring him at the prospect of getting as much on her plate as possible.

Gabriel's elbows rested on the table, and he leaned his cheek on his fist as he watched her. Jada couldn't overlook the fire in his eyes when he looked at her and made herself busy by focusing on her plate. "How chivalrous."

"I love you." Jada almost choked on the orange slice that she had been eating at Gabriel's declaration. She grabbed the glass of water that a teapot poured for her.

She took another sip and pulled herself together. Her dark eyes cut at him beneath her lashes as she continued eating. "Of course. How soon will the games start?"

"In a month. It will be just enough time to teach you how to play." Gabriel straightened from the table. A fairy butler with light blue skin and pointed ears arrived in an overly starched white suit to serve Jada coffee. Gabriel watched her steadily from his seat at the head of the overburdened table.

Jada tried to ignore Gabriel through half of her breakfast. He didn't say a word, just watched her with this indulgent expression that made Jada's face warm at her cheeks. "Just say it, Gabriel."

"You're beautiful in the sunlight. You're glorious by the light of the moon, but there is something ethereal about you in the light of day." Jada tried not to roll her eyes. She refused to fall for the adoration in his voice.

"Kind of you." Jada took another sip of water and took another bite of food to keep her from saying anything unnecessarily insulting.

Gabriel sighed and sat back in his chair with what could only be called a pout. "I hate that you don't understand that I am as much of a slave to you as you are to me."

Jada shrugged and picked up her knife and fork to continue working her way through her food. "Kill yourself."

Gabriel's serpentine gaze contracted in the first fissure of temper Jada had seen that morning. His head tilted to the side, and his lips thinned into a stiff smile. "That was ugly."

Jada smiled and took another sip of water. "But it proves a point. You don't have to do anything I say. Whereas I have no choice but to do your bidding. Do not pretend we are equals. There is no such thing as a good slave owner."

Gabriel grew silent and watched as she finished breakfast. It was a quick affair; she had lost her appetite halfway through. A shame really, she had dreamed of all the food she was going to inhale once she was away from the pits, and now she was no longer hungry. "I see that you are finished eating. I'll show you to your room." Gabriel rose, and Jada made a show of utensils down before following him out. The wattage of his smile had cooled several degrees.

Gabriel led her to a set of marble stairs that were at least three stories. His tone was polite but subdued from its earlier excitement. "The games consist of seven chess matches called bouts. We have special boards dedicated to such matches. We have one on the grounds so that we can practice. This is normally how the council ranks up their pawns before the games. It costs a considerable amount of money and time that most fairies can't hope to take part in."

She climbed the stairs, and her voice echoed throughout the corridor. "So, you couldn't afford a spot in the bouts, so you risked my life in the cheap seats?" Jada had nothing to distract her from the anger that had been bubbling beneath the surface, so didn't bother containing it any longer.

"No, I hid what you could do in Faigen's pits, so that they wouldn't have time to defend against it. Which not to brag, was an amazing idea! The way you look in a fight, the strength, the beauty, the savagery. Silvestri won't know what hit her! I couldn't take my eyes off you." Gabriel's voice picked up at his own brilliance. His smile was back, and the excitement filled his voice once more. He turned right and led them down a long hallway filled with glass and storm clouds on the walls. A slight frown flitted across his lips as he continued. "Along with the rest of the male population of the crowd."

"Bully for you." Jada ignored the swoon in his voice and the jealousy that followed. She was almost murdered several times on his errand. She was not in the mood to be congenial.

"You're petulant." Gabriel laughed and turned around to tap her on the nose. "You survived, and now you're back safe with me.

Jada's nose squinched, and she glared up at him. "I hate you."

Gabriel laughed aas they had stopped in front of a grand self-important mahogany door. Jada watched him open the door to a room that was filled with emeralds and gold. The bed was a decadent study in cushions and what looked like round black hooks that lined the bed frame. There was a large mirror over the bed and various high-backed chairs. Jada didn't want to be impressed, so she settled for just side-eyeing him.

Gabriel's smile was wide as he watched her look into the room. "Yes, my room is ostentatious but necessary. I have to observe the rule of hospitality soon."

"And that is?" Jada tried and failed to hide her annoyance at his attempt to drag the conversation out to gain her participation.

"Ahh, so you haven't lost your ability to hold a conversation! Thank you for asking. The fairy that challenges the head of the council must entertain the current council members while the matches are going on." Gabriel leaned back against the door frame, his eyes doing a slow sweep of her figure. "If you'd like a preview of the evening entertainment, I'd be happy to give you one."

"I'll pass, thank you." Jada stepped away from the opened doorway and pulled his coat around her tightly. Though it was warm outside, the air in the building was as cold as ice.

Gabriel shrugged with a smile before closing the door. "Should you ever change your mind, the invitation is a standing one."

"Decidedly not; which way is my room?" Jada's nose lifted in the air, and she took another step back from the door in case he got any ideas.

Gabriel stood from the door and recovered the two strides she took away from the door with one of his. Long fingers lifted to sift through her coils. It was as if he couldn't help himself. His eyes held hers, and Jada couldn't look away. "This all belongs to you, Jada. To us. Yours and mine. I will wait until you're ready."

Once Gabriel saw that she was not going to rejoin with any secret declarations of desire. He turned and guided her down to the other side of the stormy walkway. The colors became cooler the further down the hall they moved. There were drawing rooms and alcoves filled with music and different forms of amusement. Each room was filled with entertainment and staff cleaning each one. There was such a flurry of activity Jada doubted they even noticed their presence as they continued to move down the hallway.

The grey had become the color of cold mornings, and not the warm grey of clouds filled with lightning. Gabriel stopped at a silver door and threw it wide open with a flourish. The room was decorated with a rainbow of pastels and creams. The bed was far less decadent than Gabriel's, but no less built for the pleasure of the person sleeping in it. It looked as if it was made of clouds. There were shelves filled with every perfume and cosmetic item imaginable. Walls lined with books and beautiful plants. It was as if Gabriel had taken the perfect room out of a dream she had.

Jada looked to her left and saw something that was not in her dreams with a frown. "Really?"

Gabriel smiled at the look and moved into the room. He leaned back on Octavius, the dresser, who stood out in the space like a sore oppressive thumb. "I thought you could use a friend."

The wardrobe opens with a hiss and spits out a gown of pale blue at her. Apparently, he disapproved of the armor that she wore. "All of that money, and you couldn't afford a new wardrobe."

Gabriel laughed at the rejoining hiss of the wardrobe. His spirits had lifted once more. "He's not so bad. He's loyal and will protect you with his life." He softly pats the side of the wardrobe as Jada walks towards the door.

"If you say so." Octavius hissed, and Jada knew that he would sell her to hell for a new coat of varnish.

Gabriel stepped through the door but half turned. "Take some time to wash up and rest. I'll send for you when it's time for dinner. You may go anywhere on the grounds you wish as long as you stay on the grounds."

Jada glared at Octavius once more before turning her attention back to Gabriel. "And if I don't?"

Gabriel smiled and gave her a light shrug. "The punishment will hurt me far more than it will hurt you, but only emotionally. Physically it will hurt you more."

Jada stayed silent at the threat, deciding on the better part of valor. She had asked after all. Seeing that she understood, Gabriel nodded and began to close the door. Something made him stop, and Jada could only watch as he stepped back into the room. One of his arms moved around her waist as the other hand slid through the mass of long coils around her shoulders. Gabriel molded his lips to hers as if trying to memorize the way felt. He broke away just as Jada was getting over the surprise and started to pull away. "You have my word." Gabriel's words were breathless, and Jada couldn't think past the pounding of her heart. "That will be the last time I do that without your permission."

Gabriel turned and walked out of the room, leaving Jada in a mass of emotions she could do nothing with. The door closed behind him, and all she could do was sink to the floor, crying in anger, sadness, and frustration. She was trapped, and for now, her reality was whatever Gabriel was shaping it to be. She would get revenge, but she wasn't sure if she would enjoy it any longer.

Chapter Ten

J ada had taken Gabriel's advice and taken a long hot bath. Two fairies with large blue gossamer wings and white flower petals for skin drew the water. The tub was in the shape of a swan, and Jada's back rested against the slope of the quartz beast's neck. The dancer hadn't seen Gabriel since that morning, and she was grateful for it. Emotionally she couldn't stand him. Physically he made her want to throw everything away and wrap herself in the entirety of his being. Her mind kept trying to superimpose the monster she knew him to be over the human she had grown to love. Both had Gabriel's smile, his laugh, and the ability to make her feel like a queen. Then the memories of the past three years would cloud the picture, and she would be back at square one, unsure how to feel about the entire situation.

After a long soak, Jada reluctantly pulled herself from the luxurious bath. She had started to doze, and she would hate to drown in such a beautiful tub. The same fairies that drew her bath were the same fairies that brought her a towel. Jada walked back to her bedroom, and Octavius hissed at her once more. Her eyes lifted towards the ceiling with a shake of her head. "He left a whole house of valuable antiques, but that petulant wardrobe had to come along."

Her lips stretched into a thin smile as she adjusted the towel around her body with no thought to her modesty. Having spent the last three or so years with pawns in various states of dress, it had grown secondary to her safety. She stepped up to Octavius slowly. "And a good afternoon to you, Octavius. It's been a while!"

Jada ignored the hiss and tried not to murder the vengeful dresser. Then she smiled with a sudden resolution. "You know what! I'm going to kill you with kindness. I'm going to sit right here." She picked up the pale blue gown that Octavius had spit out at her earlier and placed it in her lap. "There is no reason for me to be at odds with a pile of matchsticks that chooses my panties. So, how's your day, Darlin?"

Octavius was quiet for a moment, and Jada thought they were making progress. At least until she was hit full square in the face with a pile of black lace undergarments. Which was immediately followed by a creamy white shawl. Jada sputtered indignantly from her place on the bed. Her hand glowing with a white-hot flame.

"I'm going to turn you into toothpicks, you overgrown vainglorious walk-in closet!" Jada pulled the towel tighter around her body heated as her skin prickled with rage. "I've had it. I'm not going to take another minute of this disrespect! I've killed people for less than what you just did. You pompous, selfrighteous nightstand!"

"I would appreciate it if you didn't burn Octavius into ash. As I said before, he's here for your protection." Gabriel's low husky voice brushed across her ear, causing Jada to turn sharply.

"For goodness sake!" She pulled up her towel and took an angry step back towards Octavius. Between Octavius' attitude and the dangerous fairy in front of her, she would prefer the company of the evil wardrobe. "Knock much?"

"I did, actually. I assumed you were taking a nap and didn't hear. I never dreamed you would be threatening Octavius with structural harm. Gabriel's eyes slowly appraised her towel clad state lingering on her hands before turning around with a laugh. "I was coming to let you know that I have arranged entertainment with dinner tonight."

"So, you're ordering me to come down?" Jada's voice was a bit terse. She had nothing political against going down to dinner, but Gabriel was there while she was undressed. He had turned around, but it made the moment no less uncomfortable.

"Not at all. I will not be ordering you to do anything.

Gabriel almost turned , his eyes widened as he remembered she was undressed. He resolutely faced the door and pulled his hair away from his eyes nervously. "I thought about what you said, and you're right. While I don't regret and will not apologize for giving you the tools to survive in this world by my side..." Gabriel's shoulder lowered, and a deep sigh filled and released from his lungs. His hand tucking his hair behind his ear. "I will not force you to play in the games. I will do nothing else that strips you of your choice."

Jada's eyes narrowed, looking for a trick. She began to pull on her undergarments beneath the towel. His voice sounded penitent enough, but Jada wasn't buying it. After all this time, he was just going to drop it. His plans for his triumphant win are just gone. Just because he was in love with her? "What about all of the money you spent?"

Gabriel's laugh filled the room, and he turned just enough so that his eyes met hers. "Jada, does it look like we're hurting for money?"

Jada had to admit that he was not. She stepped into the dress and quickly shimmied into the fabric. The sumptuous blue satin slid over her skin like a dream as she pulled it on. This dress had a lot of hooks, so she would have to depend on Octavius to close the back. "So, I'm just free to go then?"

She coughed, indicating that he should turn around once more. Gabriel smiled and turned back in the direction of the door. His smile widening as he caught his first look at her in the gown. "Yes."

Jada's lips twisted to the side in disbelief, and she stepped back to Octavius to let him magically connect the hooks at her back. She wasn't sure how he would make it happen, but right now, she was trying to decipher the meaning behind Gabriel's words. Her arms crossed, and when she felt the last hook on her gown close. She appraised Gabriel much the same way he was watching her. "What's the catch?"

"There is none." Gabriel stepped forward with his arms lifted as if he was going to pull her to him. Though at the last minute, he remembered that he promised not to touch her again without consent. His fingers flexed before his hands dropped to his sides. "You can stay here with me, and I'll spend the rest of our lives making up all of the pain I've caused you."

"Why not just send me back?" She refused to get taken in again. He sounded sincere, but she had thought he was human for over a year.

Gabriel's eyes averted, and Jada's eyes rolled. "Regretfully, I do not have that power. The only person that can grant that wish for you is the head of the high council." His voices had a soft undercurrent of anger.

"How did you manage to get me here then?" She supposedly had her freedom and could do nothing about it. How convenient.

"The trolls." Gabriel sighed, and his eyes finally met hers. Looking all over, he hated answering the question just as much as she was going to hate his answer.

"Son of bi...." Jada began to pace angrily. Her mind racing with what few options she had. She could either stay here and live with Gabriel in unholy matrimony. Or she could suck up her pride and go find Leticia and Theo. How they would love to rub her desperation in her face.

She also had killed their great troll champion, Blyssed. She would be lucky to get through their doors alive, let alone leave with a favor. She was troll enemy number one. "So, the only way for me to go home is to request to be sent home by the person whose seat you are challenging?"

"You, my darling, have a gift for succinct summations." Gabriel didn't look any happier about her asking Silvestri to go home than she was. "Not only would you be gone. The embarrassment of Silvestri doing what I was not strong enough to do would cause me to lose face in front of the other council members." Gabriel took a deep breath and gave Jada a tentative smile. "Then the hyenas would circle, and I would constantly be trying to fight them off because I would appear weak. You would get your revenge. If the whole council turned on me, I'd never make it out alive."

"What a load of bull." Jada pulled on the creamcolored shawl that Octavius had spit out at her and brushed past Gabriel into the hall. She made her way down the stairs with Gabriel hot on her heels. "You brought me here. You find a way to send me back!"

Gabriel gently grabbed her arm and took two steps down so that they could be at eye level. His smile was amused, and his serpentine gaze constricted as they moved over her face. "No, I brought you here with the help of trolls who have no intention of willingly helping us again. Not after the way you screwed them in court."

Jada pulled her arm away in frustration and continued to make her way down the stairs. She reached the landing and rounded on him as he came down the stairs. "Why is it that the trolls can go to my side of the briars whenever they please?"

Gabriel leans on the banister with a shrug. "To be honest, no one really knows. We think it has something to do with them not being very powerful magically. They are incredibly strong and can manage the odd glamour, but there hasn't been a troll alive who could compete in the games for ages."

Jada felt that familiar tingle of fiery rage crawling beneath her skin. Her fingers flexed. She wanted to incinerate him and the beautiful white shirt he wore. Her voice shook with the anger she was trying to suppress. "So, I can't go home. Not without winning the tournament and installing you as Silvestri's replacement."

Gabriel nodded and came down the rest of the stairs. His hand lifted as if he was going to cup her chin and pulled his hand away. His eyes looked deep into hers, and for one moment, Jada thought he would break his vow not to touch her. "I can't deny that taking Silvestri's position would give me the power to send you home."

"So, this is your way of pressuring me to fight in the tournament. Pretending that I actually have a choice." Jada's laugh was short and derisive. "Some freedom."

Gabriel looked angry as he stared down at her. "I don't want you to fight in the games at all. I don't want you to leave." Gabriel took a step forward, and Jada took a step back up. She had seen him angry plenty of times but never at her. His eyes were practically on fire. His body hummed with controlled power. "If I had my way, you would stay here in the palace I bought for you forever. Do you think I bought this place so I could live in it alone?"

Jada's eyes closed, and she took a deep breath, trying to assuage her anger. Gabriel seemed to be waiting for some type of answer, but when he saw that none would be forthcoming. He scoffed and shook his head.

"This way." Gabriel's turn was as sharp as his voice. He led her through rich jewel- toned rooms and out the back into the sultry evening air. Jada tucked one of her errant curls behind her ears and followed him in angry silence. The back of the palace overlooked a sheer cliff where the sea waves crashed against jagged rocks. He continued to stalk across the yard until they reached an ecru stone rail that followed a set of stairs to the right of the house. The stairs seemed to continue for another four levels. Gabriel led her to the second lower level, where one fairy waited to serve them dinner.

Jada stopped and looked down the slopes of stairs with a frown. "Where do these stairs lead?"

"You'll see in a minute. Come have a seat." Gabriel stiffly moved to one of the chairs and pulled it out for her to sit down. "I wasn't kidding when I said that I want you to stay by my side, Jada. I want you to choose me."

"That won't happen. Thank you" Jada sat down and pulled a napkin from the table to rest it in her lap. Gabriel made sure she was comfortable before moving to the other side of the table. Picking up a glass of what looked like wine before taking his seat. "I despise you."

"I know." He took a long drink from the glass and leaned back into his seat, silently watching her for a moment. "Which means your only real choice is to win the tournament. Would staying with me be so horrible, Jada?" Jada's lips parted to replay, and he held up his other hand with a shake of his head. "Don't answer right now. Wait until you see what I have to show you."

Dinner was silent, Gabriel didn't try to engage her in any more conversation, Jada was thankful. She didn't know what she would have said anyway. The fairies removed the plates and filled Gabriel's glass with more wine. Jada thanked them and watched as they placed a chessboard with a set of the most ornate chess pieces she had ever seen. They were almost lifelike. She picked up the queen and examined the lovely black onyx dress she wore. She was surrounded by waves and small fish. She looked a little worse for wear but beautiful, nonetheless.

Gabriel watched her sadly and took another drink from his glass. He smiled slightly when she picked up the piece and set his glass down. "Let's play a round. Do you know how?"

"No." She set the piece down and gently moved closer to the board. She found comfort in the plain alternating squares. Something familiar in an alien world.

"Good, take the night side of the board, and I'll take the dayside." Gabriel examined his pieces and smiled. "Before we start, take a look over the rail."

Jada leaned from her seat towards the railing and into the ravine below. The entirety of the expanse of land was filled with a large green and white chess pattern. It was early evening, but she had no problem seeing the two sets of people standing on either side of the vast field.

"Who are they?" Jada glanced back at the field before moving back to her original position in her chair. Her gaze warily watching him from across the table. Gabriel was hardly ever maudlin. Cocky and cruel, but never nervous.

"Are you ready to play?" Gabriel ignored the question, and his attention was focused on the board in front of them. She had never seen him so focused.

Jada looked at the onyx pieces on her side of the board. The exquisite carvings lay lifeless, waiting on her to take control of them. "Is it called the night side because the pieces are black?"

"No. You probably haven't had time to notice, but we have two suns here. One blue one red. Every day, at noon, they form a conjunction over the land." Gabriel lifted a pawn that looked like a large gargoyle. His long fingers set the piece down, and he looked back at her. There was a flap of wings, and Jada didn't bother to look up. She had other things to focus on as the seagulls began screeching over the water.

Gabriel's lips spread in the first smile she had seen him with since dinner, and he waved his hand, indicating that it was now her turn. "One side is covered in perpetual day while the other is filled with a shade that is akin to night. You'll see it for yourself if you choose to play the games. The boards are built and situated so that each side is cloaked in each variance of light."

Jada examined the miniature statues and picked up the queen that looked like a mermaid diving through a wall of waves. She set the figure down, and she heard a sudden rush of waves and gave Gabriel a look of concern. "Shouldn't the pieces be moved before they are submerged in water?"

"For the time being, they are fine. Look." Gabriel smiled behind the rim of his wine glass, and Jada refrained from lifting her eyes towards the heavens. She leaned back over the railing, and her lips parted in awe at the scene below her.

The Gargoyle that Gabriel had moved was surrounded by other Gargoyles. They filled the massive square that held their leader with anger roars. Their gaze was intent upon the other side of the board where Jada had moved the mermaid. The sound of waves had been the mermaid pulling the moisture from the air and creating a tidal wave that seemed to be contained within the square she held. The mermaid rode through the tsunami to land in the square Jada had moved her to on the board. The waves swirling and holding her aloft as she waited for her next move.

'The pieces are alive." Jada jerked her eyes from the field to see Gabriel seriously studying the board. "This is real."

"Very, and so are the consequences." Gabriel moved his Gargoyle forward once more and settled back in his chair. The smile left his lips amid the flapping of thousands of wings that filled the air. "Make your next move Jada."

Jada frowned at the seriousness in Gabriel's voice but turned back to the board. Her movements were hesitant as she moved the mermaid another space forwards. Another crash of waves filled the air, and the mermaid danced through the waves once more. The mermaid pulled a trident out of the water as if anticipating a battle. Oddly enough, thousands of other tridents filled the water, and what was one mermaid was now thousands. The tidal wave filled the crown-wearing mermen and maids of every color imaginable.

The gargoyles began to snarl and take to the air one more. Jada stood from her seat. She looked back as Gabriel picked up the gargoyle pawn once more. "Don't do it. Gabriel."

"Watch and learn, Jada." Gabriel's voice was cold and flat as he moved the pawn to take the mermaid that Jada had just placed in harm's way. Tears welled at the corners of her eyes, and all she could do was watch as the Gargoyles descended from the sky and into the oncoming swirl of ocean water.

Mermaids were soon plucked from the water and thrown to the ground outside of the wave of water. Left to gasp and claw at their throats as they tried to return to the water on legless tails. Gargoyles were dragged into the churning waters and deprived of air as they were pulled beneath the mermaid-controlled waves. Everywhere Jada looked was a scene filled with carnage. From mermaids being gutted within the waves as they swam. To Gargoyles trying to claw their way back into the air as water filled their lungs. Jada's eyes dropped sharply as a gargoyle's head was sliced away by a trident and rolled onto the square below.

Jada trembles with the effort not to break down and cry as she watches all the death before her. She had killed many in the pits, but this wasn't the same. It had been one on one fights with people trying to kill her. Not someone else dying as the result of her direct actions. "Make it stop!"

"I can't. Once the fight starts, it's not over until the square is taken or one of them dies." Gabriel's voice was right next to her ear. His hands gently running over her arms, trying to soothe her.

She turned in his arms, and her lips opened and closed as she found no words to express the despair she felt. Hundreds were dying, and it was her fault. "This is barbaric!"

"This is fairy Jada." Gabriel leaned over and placed a soft kiss at the top of her head. Burying his nose within the coils of her hair. "I wanted to spare you from this, but you insist on competing in the tournament."

Her hands lifted to cover her eyes as she broke down. Jada couldn't stop the tears from flowing down her cheeks and soaking into the material of Gabriel's shirt. There was nothing she could do. Her choices were to stay in a very luxurious cage or fight her way through a ruthless chess tournament. All she could do was sob into the arms of her captor. The very man she was trying to get away from. She cried until she was almost boneless within his embrace.

Gabriel held her until she had worn herself out and stopped shaking. His lips were still buried within the coils of her hair. "It's over now, Jada. You can look again."

Jada didn't want to, but she knew she had to bear witness to the result of her careless actions. She pulled away from Gabriel, fearfully moving back to the railing. The mermaid laid barely breathing on the square surrounded by the corpses of gargoyles and mermaids alike. The triumphant gargoyle's arms lifted in victory as it cried into the darkening sky.

"Is this what you brought me out here for?" Jada didn't look back at Gabriel. She had stopped being amazed at how many ways he could hurt her without trying.

"Yes, but you needed to understand what you were getting into, Jada. The games are a very deceptive name for the collateral loss of life and outright murder that takes place in them." Gabriel sighed and moved to stand next to her. Giving her space to collect herself as the sky started to fill with stars.

"I don't want you to have to go through this. I don't want to watch as piece after piece tries to kill you right in front of me." Gabriel's hands curled tightly into the stone railing, and he turned away from her to watch as the pieces left the field. They were done for the day, it seemed. "I make no secret of my ambitions, Jada. I have done a lot of things, and there is so much blood on my hands."

Gabriel's voice was tired as he watched the dead fade from view. Jada watched a tall, regal dark brown man wearing a helmet that looked like a canine, and a tall, pale man with a dark cloak and patch over his blue eye came to collect the fallen mermaid. The helmetwearing man gathered the mermaid in his arms, while the man with the patch glared up at them before fading from view as well.

"But... I think that I could live in peace with you by my side. I think I could be content waking up and falling asleep with you in my arms every night." Gabriel's voice was quiet, but Jada was not in the right frame of mind to appreciate the display of vulnerability.

"She failed... I failed her; will she be punished?" Jada finally tore her eyes from the empty field and rested them on Gabriel. "Is this what happened to Octavius?"

Gabriel shrugged and gestured towards the field. "If she survives to fight again, she'll die in the next practice round. With three-fourths of her army gone, she won't be able to take on the next onslaught. My board is particularly vicious." Gabriel dropped to his knees in front of her and wrapped his arms around her waist. His eyes closing as his forehead rested at her abdomen. Jada's breath caught at his touch, and she couldn't control the speed at which her heart accelerated behind her chest. "Jada, do you understand what I'm offering you?"

Jada ignored the tingles in her fingers that begged to soothingly run through his hair. He wanted what she couldn't give him. "What happens to them?"

"They have no queen to lead them. I have been using them to train my own board." Gabriel sighs and pulls her tighter into his arms. "I have enough pieces on the other side of the board to use as cannon fodder without sacrificing my own. This will offset any contenders who dare oppose my seat after I lose."

"You would let them die in a tournament you no longer care about winning?" her form went stiff, and she took a step back to see if he was serious. He fluctuated from cruel and kind so easily and quickly. Jada's hand went to her forehead as she tried to make sense of him.

"They mean nothing to me. The games will go on whether you participate or not. The challenge has already been issued. If you do not play, I have no reason to worry about amassing anything else. With you, I have everything I could ever want." Gabriel rose, and his golden eyes remained steady on hers. He was not lying, and Jada wasn't sure what to do with the declaration he was making.

"But they would fight and die for nothing!" Jada frantically tried to think of something to keep her world from spinning even further out of control. Either way, they died, and it would be her fault.

"The world of fairy is a harsh and unforgiving place. Vulnerability is only a virtue behind closed doors." He smiled sadly and stood. Moving over to her place, a kiss on her forehead. "Jada, I would give you everything I have, but I can't give you what you want. You'll have to do that for yourself. You must make your own choice."

"If I play, will I get to choose my own board?" She stiffened but did not move away as Gabriel pulled her into his arms. His shoulders sagged some, but he nodded sadly.

"As it is your life that is on the line, I will do whatever is in my power to do to aid you," Gabriel whispered fiercely into her hair as his arms wound around her tightly. "We will win this together, and I will show you that I am the better choice."

Jada didn't move from his embrace; she just stayed with him at that moment. She didn't have the strength to contradict him. As much as he wanted to comfort her from a choice he knew she would make, she wanted to take comfort in him. She would allow herself this moment because tomorrow, she would be on that board, and she would make sure no other lives were lost on that field because of her.

Chapter Eleven

What is the first rule, Jada?" Gabriel's foot stomped into Jada's stomach; whatever air was left over from the punch to her face was quickly pushed out. It had been a week since the night she had chosen to compete in the games, and the schedule had consisted of eating, sleeping, fighting, and chess. From the moment the two suns rose to the moment they set, every second of time was spent training. Gabriel would spar with her in the mornings to hone her fighting skills and then play chess with her in the evenings. Jada had never seen Gabriel so serious. "All of the rules of chess apply." She wheezed as she caught her breath. Jada rolled up from the ground just in time to avoid getting her ribs broken by the force of his feet. She turned and swung the borrowed sword at his shoulder, driving her fist into his beautiful face when she missed. The week had not been all wine, women, and song, of course. They had a massive fight about which board she would use to take on Silvestri. She wanted the opposing board, but he insisted that she use his. Some nonsense about his board would bring her back to him safely.

Gabriel's tongue stroked across his plush lower lips tasting the blood that seeped out of the corner. He nodded wordlessly and lunged at her once more. This time she had to dodge a beam of light that would have taken at least half of her face had it hit her. "Rule two?"

"The day side always goes first!" She snarled at him before allowing the fire in her hands to collect around her fingers. "If that's the way you want to play, Gabriel."

Another beam shot out, and before she could react, he brought the pummel of his sword into her stomach. She hadn't even seen him move. "No, my idea of play is nothing like this. If you would like to see what I find enjoyable, then I would be willing to take a break."

"No, I'd rather keep practicing." Jada ignored the warm flush his words brought to her face and kicked his legs from beneath him.

"Pity. What is rule three, Jada?" He moved again, and this time he appeared at her back. His foot kicking in her knee and bringing her to the ground.

A hiss of pain slid through her teeth as she went to one knee and rolled before his sword came down on her. It felt like she was fighting in the pits, but harder. If Gabriel wanted, he could kill her right now, and she wouldn't have been able to do anything about it. "When the players are not on the board, no harm shall come to them."

"When are they on?" A beam of light shot out from his hands and knocked her sword away. "Faster, Jada. When are they on?"

Jada shook out her hand and ran towards him. Sliding between his legs at the last minute to retrieve her sword. Narrowly blocked him from stomping down into her shoulder. She wouldn't be able to beat him head on, so she would have to take him down in small pieces. Slowly eroding his strength until she could win. "Their lives are to do with what the king wills."

"Why?" The sword was magically tossed away from her before she could retrieve it. Gabriel smiled in approval, but his foot aimed for her nose. Jada caught his foot and twisted it. Ignoring the way, the snap of bones that she heard as his foot went into the opposing direction it was supposed to. Gabriel cursed and dropped his own sword as he jerked his leg back from her grasp.

"Because they belong to him." Gabriel flashes away from Jada, and she is met with a barrage of punches from which she didn't come unscathed. One of her eyes was going to be purple by dinner time. "Excellent. What about rule four, Jada?" The last punch was the flat of his blade to her nose, and she saw stars. How did he get to be so fast?

She tried to put some space between them, and Gabriel wasn't having it. He caught her arm and twisted it behind her back. He pushed her shoulder down with a force that caused her knees to buckle. Her voice was taut with the strain of trying to keep from calling out. "Harming pieces off of the board is punishable by death."

"I will kill anyone who tries to harm you on or off the board, Jada." His fingers slid along her arms as he kept her in the locked position. His cool touch mingled with the fire beneath the surface of her skin.

Her teeth ground, and she forced the pain down. "What is rule five?"

"Do not cheat." Gabriel released her arms and allowed her to stand so that she could face him. Jada saw herself mirrored in the clear gold of his eyes. She tore her gaze away from his because they didn't reflect someone who was in the throes of vengeance. It looked as if she was having fun.

Gabriel laughed and pushed her away from him so that she fell on her hands. She stood and rolled her shoulders as Gabriel looked up into the sky. The twin suns were going to conjoin soon. The other pieces would already be out on the field.

"What is rule six?" Gabriel smiles and stretches. He looked thoroughly pleased with himself for someone who had mangled his sparring partner. The same woman he claimed to love.

"If you cheat, don't get caught." Jada couldn't help but smile in return. There were only five official rules, and the last two Gabriel made up.

"And what is the last one, my love?" Gabriel came up and put his arm around her shoulders. They walked amicably through the gardens towards the field. If they turned right at the bottom of the stairs, they had dinner as there was a giant hedge maze Jada secretly wanted to run through.

"Don't lose," Jada nodded. At the end of the day, that was all that counted. She knew that she wouldn't win with Gabriel's team. She needed the other board to make it through the tournament.

"I'm glad that you are a fast learner, Jada. It has been a joy to teach you." The compliment was genuine, so there was no reason for her to react to it hostilely. She glanced over at him before turning her attention to the field.

"Thank you." Her gaze moved to the field where what was left of the other board's players and alternates waited for them to arrive. Her eyes met the one-eyed glare of Odin, the king of the other side of the board. Two crows cawed at her vengefully as she was led onto the field. Ever since that day, her ignorance nearly got the mermaid killed; he had hated her. She didn't blame him; she hated herself.

"What happened to the mermaid?" The sorrow that crept into her voice had Gabriel turned to her. He lifted her chin up so that her eyes met his. His thumb gently stroking along her jawline absently.

"Yamja?" Gabriel smiled, and his eyes rolled with a fond shake of her head. "I felt that you would be cross if she got killed in the next match, so I retired her."

"You turned her into a wardrobe?" Jada's eyes narrowed at him suspiciously. That, and she didn't want him to see how much she had started to enjoy his touch. When he was like this, it almost made her forget the things he had done. Practically, she gave herself a mental shake and gently pulled away.

"Not a wardrobe." Gabriel didn't explain any further. He guided her to the square on his board then brought her hand to place a fond kiss on her palm. Gabriel clearly had a favorite, and it was the least tested one there. If the other pieces resented her, they made no mention of it. They just played their part as instructed.

"Where did the other board come from?" Each player had an entire football sized field of battle to fight on within their respective square. Jada had been amazed at how much larger the field was than she had initially thought.

"They belonged to the man whose council seat I took. A fairy by the name of Dima." Gabriel looked across the field with a lack of concern that Jada found chilling. The monster always peaked through to remind Jada he was there.

"Where is he now?"

"No one knows, and I was told it was best not to ask questions. I doubt he's alive though. I wasn't favored to win, and Silvestri is vindictive." Jada couldn't help but note the slight bitterness in his voice. She looked back out to the field with a soft sigh.

"When we are done training, what will happen to them?" What scared Jada was what kind of monster she was turning into that didn't mind so much.

"Some of them will be retired while others will become alternates. It's not unheard of for a piece to win the square and die anyway." Gabriel's fingers twined with hers. He was so tactile. It seemed he couldn't stop touching her. Unfortunately, it made it hard for her to think, so she disengaged.

Jada's tongue brushed the inside of her cheek in silent aggravation. If he kept wearing the other pieces down, then she wouldn't be able to use them as she needed to. "I take it we are on the night side once more?"

"I prefer to see what the other player is going to do first. If you watch the pieces as they move, you can see how aggressive the other player plans to be." Gabriel shrugged and lifted his brows to see if she had any other questions. The conjunction was about to begin, and the area had already started to go dark.

"One last question." Jada looked across the field, silently assessing each player. She had been inventorying their skills over the last week despite Gabriel's adamant desire to use his own board. "We don't have to kill the player, correct? We just need to subdue them to take the square?"

Gabriel frowned at her and pulled in a long-annoyed breath. "This is not the pits, Jada. There are things here that will do worse than kill you."

"But it's not necessary though. If you can persuade them not to kill you, then by all means, do so, Jada." Jada smiled up into Gabriel's frown, and his eyes rolled as he turned away from her to move to his square. "I'm sure they want to live too!" Jada shouted after him.

Gabriel half turned, and his head tilted to the side. Much like any other predator did when something easily killed came into their vicinity. He considered her actions weak.

"Still so presumptuous after all this time. I'll be running the game today. Let's begin."

Jada's eyes narrowed at Gabriel's retreating back and moved her attention to the field. All the players were as still as statues. The only thing that let you know that they were living were their eyes. Though the rest of their bodies were still, their eyes were filled with so many emotions, rage, anger, despair, and joy. Though the ones that held joy were the scariest. There was nothing to be excited about when you were ordered to kill unless you wanted to kill. Gabriel's board was filled with killers. They only perceived the death of others like joy, and she did her best not to engage them with any fighters. Which she knew Gabriel noticed.

Jada could hear the crows that followed Odin about. His eyes were always fixed on her. He clearly wanted revenge, and Jada didn't blame him. Yet, she had plans for him and the rest of the players on his board.

Odin lifts his arms, and his crows lift to circle over the board, their cries lost on the wind that started to pick up. The sound of distant thunder promising a storm. "King pawn to C3."

The knight in question was the man that had picked up Yamja the day she had gotten hurt. His tall, lithe body was covered in fine black fur that shone like polished onyx in the sun. The golden helmet he wore looked like the head of a jackal, but she couldn't tell what the carvings on the side of his muzzle were. They may have been hieroglyphs, but the rage in his eyes distracted her from trying to read them. He wore a short linen kilt, but the easy authority in his graceful walk told her he could kill her if she wished. Jada most certainly did not. She shuddered as the wind rose higher. Something terrible was about to happen.

She looked over at Gabriel, and he calmly watched the board. His lips set in a serene smile. The knight lifted his staff, and suddenly thousands of hyenas leaped onto the field. The hair around their ears was braided interwoven with beads of lapis lazuli and bone. The markings were those worn by warriors to account for the many lives they had taken. Some had so many they looked more like tigers than hyenas. The entire column moved to the center of the designated square. The half-starved beast stopped in the center of the square. Their terrible laughter filling the air as they waited for Gabriel's move.

"Queen to E5" Jada slowly turned at Gabriel's command. Her mouth was ajar as the hyena's braying laughter filled the air. The knight could easily take her from that position.

"How could you...." Jada's words die on her lips. He wouldn't make a mistake; he put her in danger on purpose. All the manners and gentle words had made her forget who he was momentarily. "Is that the call you want to make, Gabriel?"

"That is the request I'm making to you. I will not order you to go to the square, but if you are going to play this game, you will have to trust me." Gabriel's voice was grave, but he did not look at her again. He just waited until Jada walked the distance to the field in which she was.

"Trust you!" Jada's voice was a forceful laugh. The crows began to caw once more. Jada's eyes closed in frustration; she didn't want to hurt another of Odin's friends, but Gabriel was leaving her little choice.

"Call your army Jada."

"I don't have an army." Jada pulled in a large breath, trying to calm the seething hatred with which she spoke. The familiar burn of Jada's imposed magic rushed to her fingertips.

"It's possible. Some pieces do not have armies, but they have special abilities that keep them from needing it. I'm almost sure you have an army though." Gabriel remained unbothered. "I would hurry. Odin doesn't particularly like you."

"I see you have a gift for understatement." She glanced at Odin and the wide smile on his face. The large cloak he wore billowed in the wind as his crows continuously called for her head. The hyenas prowled around the knight, ready to rend her to pieces.

"Call your army Jada." Gabriel turned his attention from the army of hyenas to focus on her. His frown growing concerned as he waited for her to follow his direction. You need to do it quickly, Jada. You will certainly die if you do not."

"Where is it?" The worry in Gabriel's eyes raised her anxiety level. Goosebumps broke out over her arm as the air began to grow cold. The first rumbles of thunder could be heard. "One... two...thr...."

Thunder rolled again, and lightning arched across the sky."

"Stop fighting me, Jada, call your damn army!" Gabriel's voice snapped out at her in cold fury. It took everything in Jada not to turn around and march to his section of the field to take one of his eyes.

"I don't know how to call an army I don't have!" Jada began moving towards the square. But before she reached it, Gabriel's fingers curled around her arm and sharply pulled her back. His eyes ablaze with barely contained rage, and if Jada was not mistaken, fear.

"Knight to E5." The relish that Odin made the call to his piece was not lost on Jada. Revenge looked an awful lot like an impossibly tall man with a brown patch over his eye.

Gabriel released her arm and looked at the hyenas that were starting to move towards them. "I can't stop the game on their move, Jada. You have to call your army now!"

"I can promise you that I have no idea how to call an army I've never seen before" Her voice lowered to an almost soothing tone. "How do I do it?"

Gabriel's hand lifted to rake through his longish curls in frustration. "This is my fault. Normally it's an instinct. I forgot while watching you fight; you are not naturally a killer." Gabriel moved behind her, and his hands slid over her arms. He turned her so that she could face the oncoming army.

"Close your eyes, Jada." Gabriel's voice was like a balm against the disturbance his fear had caused. Warm air curled around her ear as she allowed herself to be lulled by his voice. "Take a deep breath and clear your mind. You will need to focus on the magic inside of you. It's just below the surface. You use it so reflexively, but you're going to have to concentrate on it now."

Jada's lips parted as she pulled in a deep breath and let it go. There was always this thing that she could feel. The source was just out of her reach. Once she found it, a warm flush spread beneath her skin. The hyenas were almost to her square, and they were starting to pick up speed. "Then what?"

"Now picture your army in your head. How big is it? What does it look like? What would make you feel safe right now?   What type of army would serve you?" Gabriel released her, and when she turned, he was gone.

The laugh of the hyenas was as evil as the intent in which they were sent, and they were fast closing the gap between them. "What army would serve me right now? With the blood on my hands, they wouldn't be angels. What would make me feel safe?" Gabriel's smile filled her mind's eye, and she quickly shook the thought away angrily.

"Jada, they are coming!" The hyenas were running at top speed, almost falling over each other to kill her. She would have to do something quickly. The anguish in Gabriel's voice would soon be assuaged with the blood that he would spill if she was killed.

Jada closed her eyes to block everything out, and suddenly the shadowy shapes of everyone she had been forced to kill filling her head. "Not angels. I'm surrounded by death." Her skin began to burn white hot under her skin. She could feel the magic trying to force its way out."

Her old enemies were almost a tangible entity in her mind's eye. "I need something that I can command, something large enough to stop what's coming." The ogre she fought rose out of the gathering of shades. The clanking of their shields and ring of their swords filled her ears and drowned out the scream of the crows and the sound of the hyenas. Every fighter she ever murdered began to spin around in her head.

"Jada!" Gabriel cried out in pain as if she was already lost. The hyenas were less than two hundred yards away, and the crows had begun to circle. Ready to feed on what would be leftover once the hyenas tore her apart.

Jada's eyes opened, and she could see the hyenas through a white haze. The first drops of rain hit her face, and her whole body went calm. Clawed skeletal fingers shot up from the ground, grabbing the Hyenas in mid-run. The angry yelps and enraged snarls were made at an enemy they couldn't reach. Jada lifted her hand, and the hyena army was pulled underground. Her hand pulled back so she could get a closer look at it. The nails elongated into black claws.

The rain had started to become torrential, and it was hard to see her opponent across the field. The crows continued their slow circle around her, but Jada paid them no mind. The knight's eyes glowed a bright ferocious red as he continued his march with what was left of his army. His staff urged the rest of his hyenas to move forward. Jada reached for Gabriel's sword and remembered that he had taken it back.

"With my bare hands then" Her lips curved into an amused smile as she watched the king's knight patiently walk towards her. The tip of her tongue slowly drew a line over her lower lip. She was filled with an energy she never had while fighting in the pits. Following the team of hyenas, he had ordered to kill her. It appeared as if he would stop at nothing to take the square, and Jada had every intention of taking him instead.

The next set of hyenas ran across the field that their predecessors had disappeared on. Skeletal arms reached towards the heavens and began to pull themselves out of the ground. Shields and swords were dragged out of the makeshift graves. Armored bone effigies that had once housed souls shrieked out with the promise of violence into the storm. The skeletons were a motley army of humans, fairies, and ogres. The skeleton of Blyssed looked back and screeched aggressively at her. Jada's brow lifted in acknowledgment, but her attention moved to the knight bearing down on her.

The skeletons subdued his hyenas, and Jada turned to the knight. "Do you yield?"

"Jada, kill him so we can end the turn!" Gabriel's angry voice ran out over the sounds of battle, but she ignored him. All her focus would remain on the knight.

"I won't kill him over a practice round." Her chin motioned behind the knight where his entire army including those pulled beneath the ground were being held down by the skeleton. "Your army would be dead if I wanted them to be, but they aren't. Please yield."

The knight snarled and stalked towards her. "So, you're angry. Okay, I get it." His staff raised with the intent to kill her. He swung his staff, and she blocked it with her arm. The pain shooting up to her shoulder with the force of his attack. He was strong, and if he wasn't fighting in rage, he would have been doing some serious damage.

"Practice or not, he will kill you." The fear had left Gabriel's voice, and he just sounded weary. Jada could practically hear his eyes rolling in his voice.

Jada was busy trying to block the swings from the knight's staff. He would take his pound of flesh, and she had to find a way to stop him. "Do you or do you not want to live?"

The knight continued to swing, but his head tilted in confusion. He caught Jada by her ankle and swept it out from beneath her. Jada fell back on her hands and flipped up onto her feet. The rain was falling in thick sheets around them as they fought. She wouldn't be able to hold her fire long in this rain, but it would be just long enough for her purposes.

"Jada, if he kills you, his life is forfeit anyway. Just kill him and be done with it." Irritation had settled into his voice. "Do you or do you not want to live?"

"You can choose to die here if you wish, but I would prefer you to live and fight by my side." The knight rushed her, and her clawed hand lifted to grab his staff. The knight tried to pull it out of her hand, but she wouldn't let go. "As an act of good faith, I am going to release your army."

One by one, the skeletons let the confused hyenas go. They looked to their leader, trying to figure out what he wanted to do. If Jada was lucky, it would smooth over the knight's ruffled feathers. The knight watched her through the rain for a few minutes then looked past her at Gabriel. He put his staff down and took a step back. His army lifted their heads and howled.

Jada turned in surprise at Gabriel's sudden presence. He looked furious, but it was a calm fury. Which made Jada worry for the knight in front of her. She slowly turned her body so that she was between him and the knight. Both the skeletons and hyenas shifted and moved around restlessly with so much contained power on the field.

"What if he had been trying to get you to drop your guard?" The cold clipped sound of his voice was like a slap to her face. His eyes were blazing and focused on the knight in front of them. He sounded ready to kill, and she was not strong enough yet to stop him.

"Then he would be dead." Jada stepped back so that her gaze could squarely meet Gabriel's. Her lips quirked slightly. Now that everyone was safe, she could afford to have a sense of humor. "You need to buy me a weapon with all that money I won you."

Gabriel's movements were stiff, and his eyes moved from the knight for the first time since he moved into the square. "Jada, you are not at all taking this as seriously as you need to. I didn't get you this far to lose you to overconfidence and some ridiculous sense of fair play."

"Well, according to you, it's my life to lose, isn't it?" Gabriel's furious eyes moved to hers, and for a suspended moment, she thought he would kill the knight anyway. His lips parted as if to say something scathing, but he turned on his heel and disappeared back to his square.

"The match will be called. Return to the oubliette." Gabriel's voice gave the command, and all the pieces slowly began fading from the fields. He didn't look at her again as he moved from the field, leaving her and the knight alone.

Jada winced and looked back at the knight. Mildly surprised that both of their armies were gone. The knight watched her steadily. "Oh, uh, you can go home for the day." Jada shrugged and looked around, trying to figure out what to say next.

"You mean back to the oubliette? My home is over the briars, same as yours. I can't go home any more than you can." His deep velvety voice bounced around within his helmet, but Jada was overjoyed to meet another human.

"Where were you dragged from? A male cabaret?" Her eyes did an informal sweep of the knight. He was athletic, but he looked more like one of those corporate America types. Like he sat behind the desk on a regular basis. Maybe he owned the club.

"When is a better question. When I was dragged, as you call it, into a fairy. Caesar was presiding over the coliseum. I was taken from Upper Egypt to be a gladiator. Although last I heard from the few humans, I have had contact with Egypt." His hands lifted to remove his helmet.

Once the long cascade of twisted locs fell past his shoulders, Jada could only mentally nod at the show he inadvertently put on. The knight was a very pretty man. His jawline and cheekbones were sculpted by the gods and framed by a Mephistophelian goatee. The kind dark almond shaped eyes were set within a wealth of lashes that shrewdly and silently took her measure. There was a restrained power about him. He looked savage, but it was a reluctant ferocity. Not the easy cruelty that Gabriel wore like a cloak. He didn't smile, but Jada was pretty sure when he did, it was luminous. He probably made a lot of enemies with that face.

"Yes, but that has been several thousand years ago now." Jada examined the grass of the squares to keep from staring at the man in front of her. She needed him to win the tournament so she could go home.

"I see. Why didn't you kill me?" He curiously watched her and had no problem looking at her directly. Jada's lips twitched ruefully. Her ego was going to get checked today, it seemed.

"I want to win the tournament and go home." Jada's shoulders lift in a helpless shrug. "I know that Gabriel's board won't be able to do it."

The knight canted his head, and his eyes narrowed upon her. "Why?"

"Why won't they win?"

"Why do you want to go home?" His shoulders relaxed as if removing some unforeseen stress, and his arms not holding the helmet rested by his side. "It won't be home when you get back. According to you, it's been thousands of years since I have been to our world, so it will not be the home that you remember. What are you going back to?"

Jada's lungs filled with air that she released on an annoyed sigh. He wasn't asking her anything she hadn't asked herself, so she would need to get out of her feelings. "I can't stay here."

The knight nodded, accepting the answer, and his arms lifted in a stretch that she was not above enjoying. He would make some girl very happy one day. He relaxed and regarded her from his impressive height. She was not short, but he stood a full head taller than her.

"My name is Irshad" He nodded, and Jada smiled. One piece down fifteen more to go. "As much as I hate to agree with Gabriel, he was not wrong. Someone else would have killed you."

"I'm Jada, and you're speaking of Odin?" Jada nodded, adding up the chances of success at such an insurmountable task.

Irshad's voice was flat but not unkind. To him, he was just stating an obvious fact. "I'm speaking of both boards. These games are not for the weak."

"No, they aren't." Jada agreed, running her fingers through her thick coils. "Will you go to the oubliette to rest?"

"Yes, it keeps me from thinking of all of the lives I've taken."

How Jada wished she could escape the wraiths of her kills in the oubliette, a larger version of the lacuna that she once stayed in. They stood as ghosts, ever ready

to Judge her. Waiting for her to make a mistake so that she would become one of them. "Mine seems to have followed me."

Irshad's locs slid over the impressive breadth of his shoulders as he nodded. "I noticed. You're powerful."

"How can you tell?" Jada didn't feel especially powerful.

"When you have been fighting for as long as I have, you can feel it." Irshad's eyes focused on something in the distance, and the first semblance of smile that Jada had seen from him tugged across his lips. She smiled slightly in return, not sure what brought on this sudden burst of amusement. "At the next match then."

Irshad stepped back from her and faded away from the board. Her gaze lifted, and there stood Odin. His cold cobalt blue eye watching her intently. She nodded to him, and he slowly did the same. There was no friendliness in the gesture, just an acknowledgment of presence. His crows silently judging her from their place on his shoulders. The little beast was not impressed with anything they had seen. Odin turned and faded away from the board, and Jada allowed her shoulder to lower.

"What was she returning to? Was it worth all of the pain she was about to endure?" Jada closed her eyes and tried to picture her home. The ratty apartment, the dirty streets, and the two jobs she would have to hold down to survive. Curiously the harder she tried to picture it, the less corporal the image became. It was as if she was trying to remember a movie she had watched and couldn't quite recall the details.

She turned back to Gabriel's palace with a renewed sense of purpose. She would make it back home or die trying. When Jada returned, she would find a way to burn their system to the ground. She would exact revenge for the atrocities that were done. She just hoped that she would not become the monster that she was fighting against.

Chapter Twelve

A re we human?" Gabriel had given her his sword back, and she had found a sparring partner in Irshad. He was an excellent partner. He was generous with his time and free with his advice.

"No, once the Drosselmier does their work, we are no longer human." His staff slapped at her fingers, and he shook his head. "Stop being distracted, Jada. Fight."

Jada's hand jerked back and from the slap. Her sword switched hands while her lips wrapped around her thumb to suck the pain away. "Will I become human when I get back home?"

"I have never heard of anyone losing their modification once they return home." He blocked her swing and shook his head. "That swing was extensive, Jada. I have also never heard of anyone making it back home."

"There was one mentioned at the court and crown." Jada succeeded in disarming him, but Irshad caught her hand and swung her around. She landed on the ground with a sharp hiss of pain.

Irshad pushed her forward to release her. His head leaned to the side, studying with a polite but disbelieving frown. "Someone survived the return home?"

Jada had the good grace to look away. She sucked her teeth and shrugged. "Not exactly."

The knight smirked and looked up at the sky. It was almost time for the match. "Then no one has gotten back alive or returned to being human."

Jada's lips moved in a silent mocking of his words. They continue to spar in earnest. Her hand caught his arm and brought him to his knees the way he did to her. Jada wasn't a trained fighter, but she was a fast learner. It had been three days since the last match. Gabriel had mentioned that she would get to choose her team, but she didn't know when that would be. He hadn't spoken to her much since that day. When he wasn't avoiding her, he was preparing for seemingly massive amounts of company coming.

Jada released Irshad, and he gracefully rolled away from her. Jada looked back at the house in concern before turning her attention back to Irshad. Her hand reached out to help him up. "What is the right of hospitality?"

"When a challenge is issued for the highest council seat, the games must be held at the challenger's home. The games are held in secret from the public, while the challenger entertains the rest. The rest, being the rest of the council and other minor fairy nobility." Irshad looked at her hand for a moment before taking it and pulling himself up. Once he was upright, his hands briskly brushed over his arms and legs. His smile was genuine as he nodded to her in thanks. "It's not like the general games where anyone can play. You can only take part in the rights of hospitality if you are a council member."

A warm flush washed over her skin. A displeased frown curling her lips at the idea of Gabriel's version of entertaining. Her imagination took over where words failed her. She wasn't jealous, of course, just concerned. "What exactly goes into entertaining?"

Irshad's dark eyes lowered to her, but his lips trembled in laughter. "It means exactly what you think it means. I wouldn't worry though. Gabriel doesn't strike me as the type to get too caught up in the festivities. Dima had always complained about how driven Gabriel was."

"Who's worried? I'm not concerned. He can entertain anyone he wishes as vigorously as he wants." Jada snapped and sheathed her sword. They were done for the day; the suns were about to meet in the sky.

"Pardon me if I'm prying, but you and Gabriel have an unusual relationship for a council member and his queen." Irshad turned and began making his way to the chessboard. Jada followed suit. They would need to take their places soon.

"What does a typical relationship look like?" Jada's question was measured but curious. She was brought to be the queen of his board. But that meant another queen was before her; where was she, and was she pining for him somewhere?

"There is none. The king's only objective is to win. He must and should remain remote so that he can dispassionately make decisions about the game. This is war after all." Irshad gave Jada a pointed look from the side of his eyes.

Luck was with Jada; they reached the field before she answered any question pertaining to her and Gabriel's relationship. Jada made her relieved goodbyes and made her way to her square. Gabriel's eyes narrowed upon her, and he glanced across the field where Irshad waited for the match to begin. Jada could feel the angry energy rolling within him. She turned to face the other board, mentally shrugging. There was nothing for her to apologize for.

"Jada."

"Gabriel." Jada knew from his stiff movements, and the tightness of Gabriel's voice that whatever happened next would be petty. The tension that had been building over the last week was heavy in the air. She had gotten used to Gabriel's attempts to flirt with her and get her to talk to him. Now he had flipped the switch, and there was nothing but silence.

"Pawn, move!" The pawn directly in front of Odin moved his army. The woman who stood there burst into millions of spiders that moved to a square that left Odin wide open. Odin's eye never moved from Jada's, and not for the first time she was glad that it would take a few turns to develop the board before she would have to move. She wouldn't be surprised if Odin tried something soon.

"Pawn to E5." Gabriel's voice filled the silence left by the spider's movements. The pawn directly in front of Jada moved.

The pawn was a simple wooden hut with a red roof. Jada watched in awe as the one lifted up on yellowed chicken feet and moved the square indicated by Gabriel. The thick raptor-like claws scurried to its square and settled down as if going to roost for the evening. Jada would have been charmed had the pawn not been standing in front of her. Jada's head tilted to the side and watched Gabriel. He wouldn't even look at her. The day side of the board was agitated. You couldn't tell by their movements, but their eyes were animated. Thunder rolled, and the first pattering of rain hit her shoulders. Her gaze moved to the sky to watch the clouds collect overhead.

Odin smiled, and the lightning arced across the sky. Jada watched the grisly gentleman's arms stretch out as the rain began to fall. Thunder crashed, and the clouds started to gather in earnest around them. If not for the threat of Gabriel, she was sure that Odin would have tried to kill her by now. Odin moved another pawn. This one frees his movements. Something was very wrong. Gabriel could have easily taken the pawn that Odin had carelessly moved across the board.

Another strike of lightning and Jada's gaze moved to Irshad. His eyes looked worried. Her lips pressed into a hard line, and she shook her head. Whatever was coming was not going to be good. Gabriel would have to be careful with his next move.

"Jada to D5." Gabriel's voice was clear despite the sudden burst of wind. It looked as if the tide brought a storm with it.

Jada blinked and looked over to Gabriel with a lift of her brow. That spot would allow Odin to take her easily. Her gaze flicked to Odin. The giant of a man looked as if someone had announced that Valhalla's doors had opened, but only for him. "Are you sure?"

Gabriel's lips quirked into half a smile, and his shoulders lifted into a shrug. His gaze, however, remained on Odin. "Why wouldn't I be?"

"I can be taken there. Is that what you want?" Jada's voice was flat but accepting. If this was the game, he wanted to play she would do so.

"If you have been practicing the way I assume you have, and not flirting with the dog then you should be fine. Please take your square, Jada." The smiles on both Gabriel's and Odin's faces widen. Whatever madness they shared seemed to bleed out over the board infecting all the pieces.

"As you wish." Jada's eyes left him to concentrate on her move. She could feel that the wind had grown colder across her skin. The storm had become a squall, that whipped and danced around them as the sky blackened.

The moment Jada moved to her position the crows that rested on Odin's shoulders took off into the air. Two crows become four, four crows become eight.

Each turn the crows took over Odin's head and amassed more crows. By the time Jada made it to her square the sky had blotted out what was left of the day side's sky. The sound of screams and feathers was almost deafening as it was tossed about by the torrential wind.

Jada looked back at Gabriel once more and turned to her second most pressing problem. A deep breath filled her lungs, and her hands lifted to summon her army. Skeletal hands emerge from the soil around her. The mass of bones rose out of the ground with shrieks that blended with the scream of the crows. It was hard to know where one began and the other ended as they moved into formation. Jada couldn't help but revel in the sudden rush of power that spread along her limbs. Her fingers slid through her hair to remove the wet strands from her face. She and the skeletons stood waiting for Odin's wrath. Her hand lifted towards Odin, and her fingers curled back beckoning him forward.

"King takes Queen." The crows screeched into the sky, their eyes glowing a bright blue that looked like stars against the galaxy of black wings that swarmed over Odin's head. His spear lifted to the sky, before pointing in her direction. Time seemed to suspend as the crows reared into a massive column in the air. Their wings obscured the second sun out of the sky before descending towards Jada's army.

"Shields up!" Jada called to her army, and the skeletons lifted their shields together to make a giant wall. Her fingers tingle with the familiar heat that always collected at her fingers. Jada's sword reached towards the night sky, and fire curled around the blade. The crows rushed towards the wall, and an eerie

silence filled the air right before the crows began to batter themselves against the wall.

Several crows broke through, and one whistled past Jada's ear. Thick lashes lowered once, then twice as a rivulet of blood welled from her cheek. Jada brought her arm down, and a wave of fiery energy disintegrated the first wave of crows that broke through the wall. The second wave began to fly up and over the panel in rage. The large birds caught boney arms and legs in their maw as they began to drag them away from the wall. The skeletons not responsible for the wall began to slice through beaks and feathers as more and more of them came at them. Once the crows broke through the wall, Jada was surrounded by flapping wings and ice blue eyes.

"Do you know what a flock of crows is called?" Odin's deep satiny voice rumbled around her. Jada's sword lifted in a defensive position as she searched for where the voice was coming from. Another burst of fiery energy sliced through a thick mass of birds, creating a hole that more crows came to fill.

"A murder," Jada answered grimly. Odin didn't seem to be in a hurry to make good on his silently implied threats just yet. "Come out."

"At least you're not completely stupid." Several crows moved into the shape of a seven-foot-tall Viking. His slate blue eye watching her from a mass of golden plaits pulled away from his face and beard. The tattoos that curled around his arms consisted of a giant life tree that continually produced crows. The other arm held two wolves. That seemed to ripple with surprising ferocity over his thickly muscled arms. "You have no place here. This tournament is for warriors. "

"Gabriel seems to think I do." Jada lowered her sword and slowly began to circle him. Like Irshad, the man before her was no joke. Unlike Irshad, Odin wanted to tear her limb from limb.

"Gabriel was the one who put you into my path." Odin grinned and ran his tongue over the blade of his spear to test the sharp edges. He disappeared into the throng of crows once more. "Maybe he has finally grown tired of you. What's wrong Dove? Lover's quarrel?"

Jada smiled but didn't answer him. What he said was true. Gabriel had put her there. The question was why. Something was happening here, and she wasn't going to be played that way. Nor was she going to be goaded into reacting to Odin's taunts.

"Find me, Jada." Odin's voice sounded almost hollow in the cloud of crows he faded back. "Prove that you are capable of leading his board. I have fought on the board of Gods. Do you know the humiliation of having those you love picked off one by one, and you are powerless to stop it? To be ranked lower than the Council members whore?"

Jada dodged to keep from getting hit with Odin's spear. She rolled up and turned to look around. All she could see was glassy black feathers. Jada's dark eyes tried to find the horizon line through the birds and found nothing. Full lips curved into a smile, and she stopped looking for him. "If Gabriel put his whore above you, then there's no reason for me to prove anything."

"I'll make your death a swift one!" Odin's enraged voice thundered from behind her. She turned, and his spear grazed her upper arm as he faded back into the darkness.

Jada barely had time to recover before she felt the hair on her arm lift. She heard the crack and sizzle of the air before Odin dropped out of the sky amidst a streak of lightning. Jada's sword lifted in time to deflect the lightning and keep from Being cleaved in two. The smell of singed feathers filling her nose as she looked up into the stormy blue of his eye.

He stared back into her eyes, and the blue receded empty white iris. Jada pushed him from her, and a smile that didn't reach his eye tugged at the corner of his mouth. "You're slow."

Jada's sword twisted in her fingers to adjust her grip. The giant was a vain and proud man. He wanted to taunt her before killing her. Like a cat playing with his meal. "You're no one."

Odin snarled and took a step back to adjust his stance. The spear arcing through the air between both of his hands. "Gungnir wants your blood."

"It shall not have it." Jada hissed and swung her sword towards his chess, which he blocked with his spear.

Far off, Jada could hear her army trying to fight their way to her, but the crows seemed to double in size and circle around them in earnest. Jada focused on Odin once more. She couldn't let herself be distracted by the number of skeletons that fell during the fight.

They would be overrun if Jada lost focus.

One crow turned its beak to nip at the back of her leg drawing blood. She turned and sliced the crow's head clean away, and the column of crows screamed. Her gaze flicked to Odin's arm, and blood ran down from the hollow of the tree.

"The crows are cute." Jada slowly backed away to give her space to maneuver. She had to think quickly if she wanted to keep Odin on her team.

Odin laughed and nodded his head in thanks. He threw Gungnir point first into the ground, and the board shook with its force. Odin's arms lifted as if welcoming any advance she would make, but his biceps rippled. The two wolves that were etched into his arm slowly peeled away in a mass of inky color to materialize across the field in front of her. The advancing beast were snarling and baring their teeth threateningly.

"Perfect" Jada's eyes rolled towards the moon that hung over the dark sun that hung over her board. Jada lifted her sword as they bore down on her.

The first one lunged, and Jada sliced the wolf in half.

The lupine yelped as it swirled back into Odin's arm.

The other one leapt and caught her forearm in his jaws. Jada screamed in pain as the wolf began to tear down the field through the crows and skeletons that fought around them. The muscles were torn apart with the force of the teeth that clamped down through her flesh. Jada's teeth gritted, and her fingers went numb before she and the wolf were surrounded by fire. This time Jada refused to let go; she staked the wolf into the ground through his paw as a burst of fire engulfed them both. The wolf howled in pain as it dissipated and swirled back to Odin.

"I see that you finally decided to play." Odin clapped before bloody arms rolled at his shoulders before he picked up his spear. His head leaned over as he cracked his neck. He moved towards her with the easy grace of a predator.

The flames cooled down and settled into smoke around her legs. Jada stood with her sword in her uninjured hand. The other arm hung by what was left of the sinews in her arm. The appendage was hanging at her side like so much meat.

Jada watched him walk towards her calmly. The numbness of her hands spreading through what was left of the shredded arm. "I don't want to kill you, Odin."

"Don't worry, Dove. You'll be dead before you have to make a choice." Odin brings down his spear, and Jada blocks it with her sword.

"Odin, listen, you don't want to die here. We can work together to save the rest of your board." Jada's foot lifted to the center of his stomach and shoved him back. She was ignoring the tingling of her limbs. Her instincts were screaming to take his life.

"I will save them. Once I kill you, Gabriel will see how useless you are, and will take members of my board into his." Odin swung his spear and scratched her leg as shifted out of his way.

"This is your last chance, Odin." Jada was slowly starting to lose the battle of keeping him alive. Her composure was starting to slip, and something in her wanted nothing more than to tear the Viking apart.

Odin didn't answer and began to swing at her in earnest. She continued to block him with one arm. "Look at you." Each word he spoke was punctuated by a swing of his spear. "Any queen worth her salt would have noticed that certain side of the boards gives different pieces special abilities."

Jada smiled and shrugged one shoulder, and her chin jutted towards Gabriel who silently watched them both. "I go where I'm told."

"Fair enough." Odin continued to swing at her, and Jada continued to block but not attack. Odin's movements were vicious but growing frustrated with the lack of battle that she was offering him. "Look at you! Is all you can do defend? Fight me, damn you! The Valkyries can't take me home without a glorious battle! Even your skeletons have more honor; at least they died with dignity. I only grow stronger!"

"Because you're on the night side of the board." Jada continued to defend but kept her eyes on his movement. Jada had heard the mournful slip about the Valkyries taking him home and understood what was at stake for him. She would not lose control of herself and fail at executing her plan.

Odin laughed as the thunder crashed overhead. Almost drunk with the power that the night side of the board was giving him. "Exactly. I am unstoppable, and you will die!"

"You are quite strong." It was an understatement, and Jada knew it. Both he and Irshad were powerful. They were roses dying on a vine on a board without leadership. Jada would fix that for them.

Odin snarled as she swung at her again, trying to make her fight him. "I am the strongest. I am the All Father!"

"You'll excuse me if I don't call you daddy." Jada smiled, and at this point, they were playing a game of keep away in the rain. The heavy sheets poured around them as they fought.

"It doesn't matter what you call me, and you'll be dead." He slowly paced her like a wolf stalking his prey. "Attack me, damn you!"

Jada shook her head, and a genuine smile broke out like the sun across her face. "I told you that I don't want to kill you."

"You couldn't kill me anyway." Odin threw down his spear, and lightning began to collect in his hand.

Jada's amused gaze flicked from the lightning in his hands to the milky white of his eye. "Your crows have become very quiet, Odin."

Odin paused mid step and notices the lack of battle sounds around them. Half of his crows were dead on the field, while the others balefully watched the skeletons that now surrounded them on the battlefield. He sharply turned to glare at her. "What did you do?'

Jada stuck her sword into the ground and slowly began to reattach her arm. "My soldiers are lifeless. They can't be killed. They just regenerate on the night side of the field."

"You planned this?" Odin watched her doubtfully. "No, but I knew you would try me eventually." Jada's voice was flat as she responded. This wasn't at all the way she had wanted their first meeting to go. "So, you drew me here to the night side?"

"I didn't have to do anything. You and Gabriel are apparently the same person." A fissure of anger slid along her spine, and she tamped it down. She was finally making headway, but she was finding it harder to keep her anger down.

"So, you planned to get your arm torn off is what you'll be telling me next?' Odin scoffed and ran his bloodied hand down his beard.

"No, that I had not counted on at all, but as you can see, my regenerative power also kicks in on this side." Jada's smile was feral, and she would win this game. She just had to maintain her patience a little longer.

"You think you can take me with one arm?" Odin glared at her, and his crows screeched, ready to begin fighting again.

"No, but my army has plenty of arms that I can use, and they will continue to grow back." She nodded to the blood running down his arms. "How many more

of them will go before you pass out? I just have to stall."

Odin looks up at the rustle of swords and shields. The entire force of skeletons surrounded them. The army having grown even bigger with the kills that they had made. "So, what you're saying is that you'll kill me?"

Jada's eyes rolled, and she took a deep breath before letting it out in frustration. "What I'm saying is what I have always been saying. I don't want to kill you. I want to fight alongside of you. This isn't the pits; we can't do this alone."

Odin scratched his head in deep thought, stroking his beard before letting out a deep laugh. "Then I yield on the promise that you will show me such a battle that will allow the Valkyries to take me home."

"We will both make it home. I swear it." Jada held out her hand and waited for him to take it. He would either agree or one of them would die on this field. He took her arm and nodded.

The match was over, and the square went to Odin.

Jada's square was captured, and the match ended.

"Game over!" The rage in Gabriel's voice surprised Jada enough to turn around. Odin and the rest of the board disappeared back to the oubliette, leaving Jada alone with the real monster.

"Has your mood been restored now that I have been suitably punished?" Jada's voice was seething as she turned to Gabriel. She lifted her damaged but healing arm where he could take a better look. It was times like this that she could forget how beautiful he was and remember the monster that rested within.

Gabriel was taking deep breathes to contain the rage that practically poured from him. 'He was supposed to die, and you were supposed to get his power! Damnit, Jada, how do you expect to get stronger if you don't kill?'

"What?" Jada took a horrified step back so that her eyes could meet his.

"Oh, what? You thought you were getting all these powers because you're nice? Maybe because you're beautiful?" He angrily scoffed as his power practically hummed around him. "Admittedly, if anyone could do it, you could, but did you not notice that your power grew as you killed?"

"I will not murder others to grow more powerful."

"Then you will die, and all of this effort will be for nothing." Gabriel began to pace deep in thought as he tried to calm down, but he was failing. "I love you with every fiber of my being, and the reason I even kept that board was to sacrifice them to make you stronger. Here you are, trying to keep them as pets! Like some sort of misfit toys that you can put on a shelf."

Jada felt so cold inside at the horror that she was unwillingly taking part in. Odin's words about the Valkyries not being able to find him replaying in her mind. "They know that you brought them here. As sacrifices for me?"

"Of course, they do! What else would they be here for? For Briar's sake!" The hiss in Gabriel's voice became more pronounced the angrier he got. His voice was deep and reptilian as his gold eyes rested on her, practically glowing. "What am I going to do with you, Jada.'

"You're going to trust me. You're going to give me the other board and trust me."

Jada felt a fear that she had not felt on the field. If she were going to save them, it would have to be now. A part of her wanted blood, and she would not take it from the other board. "Please."

"Trust you? While I've had to watch you play patty cake with that mongrel all week?" Gabriel's laugh was low and dark as he moved towards her. He looked deep into her eyes for a few moments. His hand moved to lift her chin so that his thumb rested beneath her jaw. His fingertips brushed along her pulse. "Your heart is beating so fast, Jada, but I don't think it's from fear."

Jada's heart stopped and fluttered as she waited for him to decide. She knew that if she fought with his board, she would never make it out of fairy. They were too far gone. They were the monsters that those on earth were warned of. They would not listen, only kill. "Gabriel…"

Gabriel smiled, and for the first time, she saw his fangs. The forked tip of his tongue stroked across his teeth as he watched her before letting her go abruptly. "Do as you please, Jada. You know that I could never refuse you anything."

Gabriel turned and strolled off the field with a smile, and Jada sank to the ground in the square that she had fought so hard in. She watched Gabriel saunter off, and she was no longer sure if she had won the battle or gave away the war.

Chapter Thirteen

Not that Jada got the chance to use it much, but there was a courtyard outside that she loved going to. She had claimed a small alcove just for herself when she needed to get away from Gabriel and the rest of the preparations for the upcoming tournament. She wore an airy white ball gown today. That pile of splinters in her room had chosen the outfit along with throwing a pair of white satin heels at her. Narrowly missing her head. "He has one more time to attack me before I turn him into kindling."

She sat down on the short wall of the new fountain Gabriel had installed with a slight grumble. A magnificent blue crystal that was so clear she could see through it. The centerpiece was a beautiful mermaid with afro textured hair pulled back by a band of carved seashells. However, those were the only seashells to be seen. Jada had to avert her eyes from the buoyancy of her anatomy. Water fell from the mermaids' crystalline hands as her arms lifted to the sky in a pose of joy and freedom. Whoever carved the mermaid loved the subject very much.

The board was taking a well-deserved break from the tireless training they had been doing. The air was warm, but the shade from the trees kept the area comfortable. She squinted up at the bright sky that peeked through the canopy of broad green leaves. Light dappled over Jada's skin as she dipped her fingers into the water, lightly trailing them over the surface. A deep breath filled her lungs and released with an even deeper sigh. The board was almost at a point where they had comradery. There were still those who mistrusted her, but she would win them over. She had to. It was a life-or-death situation, and that included their lives and deaths. Another sigh fell past her lips as she thought about the two they had lost in training. A priest and a dragon that had been so poorly taken care of that Gabriel's merry band of murderers tore them to shreds.

Her hands lifted to wrap about herself with the memory. The nightmares the battles had given her had lasted for weeks. Gabriel's board was as vicious as they were cruel. Jada hated to think what Gabriel saw that made her the perfect choice to be the Queen of his board. Her hand struck the surface of the water, sending droplets flying every which way. It did not matter what he saw; she would be damned if she became one of them. She looked up at the mermaid's serene face and shook her head.

"I wish I had your freedom." Jada rose from the edge of the fountain and turned to go back to the house. A sudden jet of cold water hit her in the back of her head.

Jada almost gave herself whiplash with the speed at which she turned around. Her gaze slid over the courtyard, and there was nothing to be found. She was the only one there, and there wasn't enough shadow in the small enclave for anyone to hide in. She frowned and turned back towards the statue, only to get hit in the chest with another jet of water soaking her white gown through.

Jada blinked owlishly at the mermaid fountain who had now changed position on her crystal pedestal. This time the mermaid sat in a pose of contemplation, looking out towards the field. The mermaid's hand cupped innocently beneath her chin.

"So, it's like that?" Jada snapped and wrung out her sopping dress. The white was positively see-through against her skin, and she sucked her teeth in aggravation. Though she felt contrite, it was her wrong move that had gotten Yamja there in the first place.

Remembering that little detail had Jada's features soften in guilt. "I know my apology is not worth anything because you're stuck here. However, had I known what was about to happen. I would never have played a game I couldn't win with your life."

"Talking to yourself, Jada?" Gabriel's voice made her turn around sharply, and there he stood in all his refined double-breasted suit glory. Dark grey was a color that had been made for him. The wide cuffs and the ruffle at his collar made him look like a very grim fairytale. Her gaze lingered on him longer than she would have liked. Her preoccupation with they he looked only made his smile widen as he gave her his own once over. "Though I appreciate how translucent your attire is, you'll need to change. We are having important visitors. Since you have finally managed to tear yourself away from the puppy, I require your presence by my side."

Then there was that. This random jealous streak Gabriel had developed over Irshad was nonsensical, but there it was. Irshad, Odin had the same desire she had, and that was to go home to whatever was left of their world. She felt no romantic feelings for anyone, period. At least that was what she told herself because there Gabriel stood looking like her favorite nightmare.

Jada took a deep breath to steady her patience. He had been polite if waspish as of late, and she did her best not to poke the bear. For the most part, he left her alone regarding the training outside of the odd comment about the time she spent with Irshad and Odin. "You turned her into a fountain. Gabriel… really?"

"Would you have preferred I let her die?" His head canted to the side as he studied her. He was always watching her as if he was waiting on something. Jada did not know what it was, but it set her on edge. "I thought you would like knowing she was safe."

"You mean constantly seeing my greatest failure on display from my window?" Jada returned to which Gabriel could only smile and shrug.

"If that's how you want to look at it." Gabriel's eyes moved towards the statue, and Jada stepped up on the wall between him and the mermaid. Jada refused to allow any ogling of the wave dancer while she was seashell less. Gabriel laughed and turned with a roll of his eyes. "I would worry about your modesty. That dress leaves very little to the imagination when wet."

Jada moved her arms around herself and shook her head. His laughter continued despite the glares she sent his way. "It's your fault for not making sure she was covered!"

"I had nothing to do with it, actually. Herr Drosselmier, you remember her, don't you? She sends her regards. She performed all the glorious work you see behind you. I must say the work she did with you two was inspired. It's a shame you two will be her last dolls."

A soft breeze wafted through the courtyard, giving her a chill, and she curled her arms about herself tighter. Seeing that Gabriel was going to be a good boy, at least for the time being. She stepped down from the fountain when she was satisfied that the mermaid was safe from his gaze. "Is she retiring? Did she develop a conscience and decide that murder and torture was a poor business to get into?"

Gabriel laughed, and his shoulders rolled as he removed his jacket from his impressive arms. He kept his eyes forward but held out his jacket behind him, which she gratefully took. "Hate the game, not the business model Jada. She was actually doing a very brisk business as a Drosselmier."

"So, what's making her stop?" Jada busied herself with slipping Gabriel's suit jacket over her arms. He was a maniacal sociopath, but his manners were exquisite.

"She's dead." Gabriel's words were so short and dispassionate that Jada could only stare at his back, trying to decide if she heard him correctly.

Jada's mouth opened and closed for a few minutes as she tried to find some way of making sense of his very blunt and unbothered statement. "I'm sorry, you said she was dead. As in someone ended her free trial of living?"

"Yes. Someone thought it was best that she was no longer allowed to make any more dolls." Gabriel's voice was flat, and his shoulders lifted in a shrug. "Go change Jada; our guest will be here soon."

Gabriel went inside, leaving Jada speechless and alone with the fountain. She half turned to look back at the mermaid. This time the mermaid was sitting facing Jada with her hands covering her eyes. The water of the fountain pouring from her eyes instead. Jada was sad for the fountain, but she couldn't say that she felt sorry for the doll maker. The things she had done to them both were horrifying. In fact, if Jada was honest, she had planned on having a long talk with the Drosselmeir after the tournament was over.

Jada left to give the fountain time to process and moved back through the winding corridors of Gabriel's home. The wall would change as she moved through each hall. Sometimes the walls were filled with images of the sky and other serene lifelike landscapes. Other times they would have images that would start off benevolent and end in unsettling images. The one she just passed held thousands of ceramic masks that would open their eyes as she passed by.

As she stepped into the room, she gave Octavius a wary look as she inched towards him. She had to pick out something new to wear, and she was honestly too tired to fight about it. The soft purr like sound of the wardrobe told her that Octavius was asleep. It seemed he spent the night watching her and then napped during the day. Her fingers gently closed over the gold fittings and the door opened without a problem. Jada took a deep breath as she eased a long dark emerald dress from the confines of Octavius's shelves. She held out the dress in front of her and mentally rolled her eyes at the deep cut of the neckline, but she had to hurry and get ready.

She made quick work of freshening up and pulling her hair into a French braid. She was halfway out of the door when she noticed that she didn't have any shoes. Her eyes closed in silent prayer for patience. Octavius wasn't purring any longer, so that meant that he was awake.

"Are you going to give me my shoes peacefully?" Jada called out into the silent room and edged closer to Octavius. "I just want some shoes. Can you gently hand me some shoes?"

Octavius must have felt benevolent because he peacefully set out a pair of clear green glass slippers. Jada took a few more steps expecting him to bombard her with stockings. When nothing happened, Jada lifted her hand to feel the wood panel of the door to see if he was warm to the touch.

"Thank you, Octavius. I appreciate you not hurling anything at me." She smiled and turned around only to have Octavius swing his door sharply tapping her behind. She turned to glare at him but remembered she had no time to waste. She needed to get downstairs. The house had gotten noisier, which meant that it was almost time. She lifted two of her fingers. She pointed at her eyes, and then at him, then back at her eyes before making a punching motion.

"Mistress, Gabriel sent me to escort you down." Jada frowned at the deep, somewhat familiar voice. In fact, the sound was almost mocking.

Jada glared at Octavius, who had gone back into a content purring slumber. She hopped gently as she put on her glass slippers. If Gabriel had sent emissaries, she guessed she was running very late. The door swung open, and Odin stood there in a white dress shirt. The sides of his long blonde hair were shorn and braided back away from his face. With his hair pulled back, Jada noticed how blue grey his eye were. She had just thought they were a pale blue, but his eyes were closer to storms rather than seas.

"He left Irshad in the oubliette?" Gabriel's coat, Jada stepped through the door with a roll of her eyes. Jada was both frustrated and amused by Gabriel's behavior. All she could do was shake her head. Odin offered his arm, Jada dipped in a mocking curtsey before taking it.

"So, he thinks you are the less likely to run off with me?"

Odin laughs, and his large shoulders lift in a shrug. "He knows my heart belongs to the sea."

They moved down the hallway, and there was a flurry of activity at the doors to Gabriel's room. Various fairies were carrying large boxes through the doors with something making a clinking sound. Jada's eyes narrowed as she tried to figure out what the sound was. Odin snickered and continued to lead her downstairs. There was so much activity happening between fairies hauling boxes and flying around that Jada was unsure where to look.

"So why are you here?" Jada's brow lifted as they moved past Gabriel's room, trying to avoid getting clipped by fairy wings.

"I am your protection. Gabriel needed something big and bad to scare the Boogey Woman away, and you can't get much bigger and badder than me." The Viking's other arm lifted to curl his bicep, and Jada tried not to laugh at how serious he was.

"So why did he send it to you specifically?" Jada ducked as a fairy flew over their head. Odin, who had refused to move, barely kept from being hit. "Be careful!"

"Because Silvestri has a minor crush on Irshad, she wanted him for her board. I suspect that Gabriel is going to use that to his advantage and stop that. It's beneath you to duck." Odin did not look at her, but his low gravelly voice was reproachful. He glanced down at her and shook his head with a scoff. "You are the worst evil queen ever."

"Life lessons from Odin, thank you." Jada feigned an imperious look that was ruined by her smile. She was just happy that he was not trying to murder her any longer. "I don't want to be an evil queen. I was evil enough in the pits."

Odin said nothing for a time as they continued to move down the busy stairs. "It won't be a matter of choice, Saeta. The games will show you who you really are. For you to have made it this far tells me that you are probably further gone than you think."

The smile that had been on Jada's face at the random Viking endearment soon faded away as he reminded her of the games and Gabriel's board. Those pieces were not human or fairy. They were just monsters that enjoyed killing others. Jada hated every moment of it. "If I end up like Gabriel's board. I want you and Irshad to promise to kill me. I don't want to become that twisted."

"Same, Saeta. Same." They reached the bottom of the stairs. The fairies must have caught the grim looks on their faces because they cleared a path for them to walk unhindered.

After two flights, they touched the ground floor. The fairies at the bottom of the stairs parted and allowed them through to the foyer. Jada could see Gabriel standing near the door greeting two people who had their back turned to her. As she moved closer, she saw the men she had met on the steps of the court and crown. Much the way they were dressed at court, they were dressed at Gabriel's door. The pale one with the black hair wore a magenta colored suit with a lime green cravat, and the darker one with the shocking blonde hair wore a lime green suit with a magenta cravat. Everything about them alternated. Including the grating buzz they spoke in.

"Gabriel, so lovely to see you again. We haven't seen you since that day at the court and crown." The one Jada remembered as Trine smiled in his magenta suit, and Jada hated him immediately. She had not forgotten them goading her on the stairs.

"Yes, we trust that the acquisition went well." Trinity tossed his blonde hair away from his eyes, and his smile stretched to show off rows of jagged teeth. "We missed you at the party, Gabriel."

"Welcome, and yes. As you can see, I have my hands full here." Gabriel's gaze moved past them to rest on Jada. They saw that Gabriel's attention moved away, and they turned to focus their red eyes on Jada and Odin as they approached. "Add yes, my acquisition went quite well."

Gabriel took her hand as Odin guided her to his side and took a step back. Jada turned and dipped her head cautiously in greeting both gentlemen. Her skin hated the feel of their energy. She wanted to step back, but not out of fear. Something inside of them was as sick as the monsters on Gabriel's board, and it made her want to attack.

"My my Gabriel. Is this lovely little beast why you have been missing all of the parties?" Trinity spoke to Gabriel, but his eyes remained on her.

Then we shall be back for Silvestri momentarily. We have to go and pick up someone!" Trinity's eyes moved over Jada once more with a smile that was less than cordial.

"Tah for now!" Trine Laughed and then both backflipped and faded from view.

Jada stood with Odin, and Gabriel watching the spot that they had disappeared from grimly. They had said they would be back, and Jada hoped that whatever errand they were running would take longer than they had expected. Way longer. Jada's lips parted to say as much, but the timid footsteps of one of the maids stopped her.

"Sir, High councilwoman Silvestri is ready to receive you in the main hall now." The blue fairy bit her lip and looked over her shoulder nervously. Jada could only imagine how the fidgety fairy felt about telling Gabriel someone was ready to receive him in his own home.

"Then let's not keep her waiting then. Jada, if you'll come this way?" Gabriel politely turned to Gabriel and held out his arm for her to take. A quick nod of greeting was given to Odin before he started to follow the fairy through.

The look on Jada's face said that she would rather not meet the horror that kept Gabriel up at night. However, she rolled her shoulders back, took his arm, and made their way towards the hall. There was nothing to be done about it, and it may not be as bad as she thought.

When they turned the corner, Jada saw how wrong she was. Her brows met her hairline as she saw the fairy that lounged in the center of the platform. Jada's saying that Silvestri was beautiful would not have done the vision of ethereal and physical perfection justice. She was like an obsidian statue come to life. The white gown that she wore shone like starlight against the richness of her skin. The dark cap of curls ended around her ears except for the feathery fringe that hung over her deep violet eyes. The large silver frame of the throne she sat in did nothing to hide the perfect figure that reclined back on one arm of the chair while her legs elegantly draped over the other. Jada's eyes had to drop at the woman's radiance as it started to make her feel uneasy.

"By my beard and spear!" Jada could only nod at the reverent exclamation from Odin. Power practically vibrated from the being who watched them approach in what used to be Gabriel's great hall.

Something moved, and Jada had to stop herself from quietly questioning her sexuality to focus on the floor. Her heart dropped as she saw Nero sitting at her feet, his cheek resting against Silvestri's leg. Her clawed fingers gently twisted his inky hair between her fingers. He wore a sleeveless white tunic over some black material that looked as if it had been painted onto his legs. His large black wings were closed and seemed to be relaxed. His electric blue eyes lifted to see who had walked in, but he made no move to acknowledge them as they moved closer to the throne.

Gabriel released Jada and gently moved her closer to Odin. He continued to move forward as he greeted his less than patient-looking visitor. "Silvestri, I see that you have made yourself at home and changed the venue of our meeting. Welcome to my home. You and Nero are most welcome."

"This chair is for the central and mist high council member. Which is me."

"And you look amazing in it."

"Thank you, but the chairs not made for my proportions." Silvestri's hands stilled their stroking motion through Nero's hair. "Why must you challenge me, Gabriel?"

"Because you ignore all of the new ideas that I bring to the council." Gabriel's smile was starting to wear a little thin. Jada could see in his movements that he was starting to lose patience.

"Honestly, Gabriel!" The snap of Silvestri's voice made Nero's eyes narrow on Gabriel, and he shifted as if preparing for an attack. Her hand lifted to stroke his shoulder, which made Nero settle back down at his place at her feet. "We don't need new ideas."

Jada watched Gabriel seemingly ignore Nero to focus solely on the capricious fairy in front of him. The small box of rage that sat before them seemed to be trying to decide whether she could get away with killing Gabriel. Jada's shoulders rolled in agitation. If Silvestri killed Gabriel, then there would be no need for her to fight in the games. If Silvestri killed Gabriel, she would be free. No, not free she did not know where exactly she would go if anything happened to Gabriel. Nero shifted again, and Jada's eyes rested on him. Would that happen to her? Would she end up nothing but a slave to Gabriel's whims?

"I do not agree." Thankfully, Gabriel's voice pulled her from her runaway thoughts and grounded Jada in the present.

"That's the problem. You disagree a lot, and about everything!" Silvestri unfolded herself from the throne, leaving Nero on the floor behind her. She moved to stand directly in front of Gabriel, her chin lifting to meet his pale gold eyes. "How have you been getting over the briars?"

"I wish I could claim to know what you are talking about, but I do not." Gabriel's smile went up in wattage, which only seemed to enrage the fairy more.

"You try my patience, Gabriel." Silvestri's hand shot out and captured his chin in her small talon-like fingers. She squeezed, and Jada could hear small bones cracking in his jaw. Jada took a step forward when Silvestri forced Gabriel into a kneeling position on the floor. Odin caught her arm and swiftly pulled her back to him. Silvestri's violet eyes shifted into a vengeful black as she addressed Gabriel once more. "And tell your pet not to make any more sudden moves. I'm feeling neither understanding nor charitable."

"I have done nothing." The clipped words were the only sign of the strain that Gabriel was under. His words were calm if impatient at an outburst that Gabriel seemed overused to.

Opaque black eyes moved over Gabriel's face searching for lies, but her posture relaxed, and she released the hold she had on Gabriel's face. Suddenly a childlike giggle spilled past her lips, and she skipped back to the throne. Hopping into the seat and draping her legs over the arm of the chair once more. Nero adjusted on the floor so that his long muscular leg stretch-out in front of him. He was displaying an inability to stay out of Silvestri's presence for long.

"Possibly, but you're crafty, Gabriel. You're also well-liked. One would even say well-loved." Silvestri continued to relax in her seat, resuming stroking Nero's shoulders like a cat.

Gabriel stood, and his hand moved to the handprint that Silvestri left on his face. "Not as well-loved as you, your grace."

"No, you're not." A content smile settled on Silvestri's lips as she practically melted into the throne she rested on. With the loss of rage, Silvestri's eyes turned back into their violet hue. Her gaze moved to Jada, and a slow sweep was made only to be dismissed before addressing Gabriel once more. "What's wrong, Gabriel? You used to love when I touched you."

"And so, it remains. I have been preoccupied with the touch of another." Jada's eyes lifted into a slight roll at Gabriel's words. "Ah, Trinity and Trine are back."

"So, it seems." Silvestri's smile grew wider at the sound of feet scurrying through Gabriel's halls. Silvestri's leg began to idly swing back and forth against the arm of her seat. Her gaze moves back to Jada, but her words were meant for Gabriel. "Here comes the one whose touch you are so preoccupied with."

Gabriel calmly turned towards the door at the sound of the distressing scuffle that announced the twin's arrival. Jada did not have to lie to herself about who she had thought Gabriel was talking about. Therefore, she was proud that she did not give herself whiplash trying to see whom Silvestri was speaking of. Trinity and Trine moved into the room in a flurry of colors dragging a woman wearing an ornate dark pink sari that glowed against her deep skin. The beautiful garment was askew as she struggled against them. All Jada could see other than her sari were the pierced tips of her tapered ears and rivers of long black hair. Her features were lovely, but her beauty was contorted in the tussle to get away from her sadistic ushers.

"Devanshi?" Gabriel's voice was both confused and concerned about the woman that the twins hauled in.

Jada could only look between Gabriel and the struggling trio, trying to figure out what was happening at that moment. She looked back at Silvestri to see the evil fairy was watching her in turn. Trine and Trinity threw the fairy unceremoniously to the floor. The woman Gabriel called Devanshi stayed huddled there until she could collect herself enough to move to her knees. Her body shivered as her sobs filled the room with their pitiful sound. When Jada finally got a good look at her, she assumed magnificence must have been something the women of the world of fairy received from drinking the water. Her eyes were a pale green set within thick lashes. They were in stark contrast to the dark gold of her skin. She had a classic regal beauty about her that would have made her famous on the silver screen.

"Where am I? Gabriel!" Devanshi cried out his name as she rose from her knees to rush toward him. Trine placed his hand on her shoulder to halt her progress with a sneer."

"That's far enough, Devanshi. "We are ready to start the interrogation when you are High Council Silvestri. I can't have you go wandering around in unfamiliar spaces. His attention moved to Silvestri in merciless pleasure.

"Excellent! It appears you've never been here before. Shame on you, Gabriel. I would have thought you would have brought the love of your life to your new home." Silvestri sat up straight in Gabriel's throne, and one shapely leg crossed over the other. The points of her fingers lacing together to rest in her lap. "No matter, you can give her a tour later. Now Gabriel, is there anything you wish to tell us before we start torturing your lover?"

Silvestri looked at Jada to see what her reaction would be to her words. Unfortunately, Jada was busy trying to figure out how to help Nero. He had switched positions on the floor again. He had to be uncomfortable. His black encased knees were pulled up to his chest. The electric blue of his eyes was dull and lifeless despite the activity in the room. It was like nothing mattered to him. Silvestri frowned at Jada's seeming interest in Nero, and Gabriel did not look thrilled at her actions either. Her brown gazed lifted to the pale gold of his, and she went back to minding the business that kept her alive.

Gabriel's brow lifted as Jada turned back towards him, and he turned to Silvestri with a shake of his head. "Silvestri, stop this! There is nothing she can tell you because nothing is going on. She is an esteemed council member like we are and should be treated as such."

Silvestri smiled and waved her hand. "As you wish. Trinity, if you'll begin the interrogation?"

"Of course, my liege" With a wave of Trinity's hand Devanshi's s skin begins to bubble and fry away from her slim ankles.

Devanshi screams and drops back down to her floor. Her chest was rising and falling as she tries to pull in deep fearful breaths. Jada's eyes closed as she looks away from the flesh melting away from her bones. Odin places his hand on her shoulder. But she isn't sure if it was an act of comfort or to keep her from going to help the fairy now writhing on the floor.

Gabriel's brow lifted as Jada turned back towards him, and he turned to Silvestri with a shake of his head. "Silvestri, stop this! There is nothing she can tell you because nothing is going on. She is an esteemed council member like we are and should be treated as such."

"Have you gone through the briars on any business of Gabriel's?" Trine's voice was as pleasant as the sounds of wasps could be but friendly under the circumstances.

"No! Gabriel, stop them!" Devanshi's begged from her spot on the floor. Her hand was reaching out to Gabriel pleading for him to come and rescue her.

"Silvestri, this is ridiculous. We have done nothing wrong. Let her go." Gabriel was no longer smiling, but Jada could see the first stirrings of anger light up his golden gaze. If something didn't change, soon things were going to get very bad very quickly.

"You don't call conspiring against me wrong?" Silvestri's brow lifted as her fingers laced to rest behind her head as she leaned back into the throne. Her feet were moving to prop up on Nero's shoulder.

"You've grown paranoid in your old age Silvestri." Jada's lips parted at the insult Gabriel tossed out. She had never seen him be rude to any woman, and the sound made her angry. She half-turned to give Silvestri a long look beneath her lashes. The angry fairy was courting trouble, and Gabriel looked like he was preparing to give it to her.

Both of Silvestri's brows lifted at Gabriel's words, and her hand moved to wave once more. This time the skin at Devanshi's wrist bubbled and pulled away from her bones. The acrid smell of searing flesh filling the room. Devanshi screamed and writhed on the floor, watching Gabriel with wide pitiful green eyes. Gabriel took a step forward towards Trinity, and Trine held up his hand. His index finger was separating from the rest as it waved with a click of his tongue.

"Ah-ah! You know the punishment for interfering with an investigation by the grand inquisitors is death. We would hate for you to be the first we've had to kill in ages." Trine smiled in a way that said they would, in fact, not mind it at all.

"Devanshi hasn't done anything." Gabriel grits his teeth as he watches Devanshisquirm in pain on the ground.

"We shall see, won't we?" Trinity shrugged and turned Devanshi over on the floor with his boot. "Deal Council member Virinka. Have you aided or conspired to take the throne from High Councilwoman Silvestri?"

"No! Why are you doing this! I've been loyal to the council since its inception!" Devanshi's tortured sobs continue to fill the room.

"Did you not take a prized board piece from Silvestri at the auction to aid in making Gabriel's board stronger?" Trinity ground his boot into her shoulder, and another wave of wails made Jada's flesh crawl at the sound.

Jada frowned at the mention of auctions, and her gaze moved to Gabriel to see if they were exactly like the slave auctions they sounded. From the look on Gabriel's face, they were most certainly. Jada took a deep angry breath in, and Odin placed a steadying hand on her other shoulder. He didn't appear to be any happier than she was now, but as the least powerful entities in the room, no one was going to ask their opinion about anything.

Out of the corner of her eye, she saw Nero adjust his position on the floor to watch the proceedings. Silvestri had removed her feet, and a small smile rested on her lips. Nero's eyes no longer looked bored but intent. Her dark brown eyes met the electric blue of his, and her heart ached for the desolation she saw there. She nodded, and he did the same.

"My Gabriel, it seems your women have the same taste in men." Silvestri's voice was nasty but amused.

"Jada, unfortunately, has boundless amounts of empathy." Gabriel gave Silvestri a distracted roll of his eyes before giving his full attention to Trinity and Trine.

"No! I brought Princeton for my board, I swear!" Devanshi screamed beneath the foot that Trine had placed on her back as she tried to squirm away.

"Oh really? then you also planned to challenge me for my seat?" Jada's lips parted as she had just about had enough of Silvestri's inquisition. Her gaze moved to Silvestri, and the fairy lifted one finger to her smiling lips, indicating that Jada should keep quiet. The silent request did not seem like a suggestion." Is that what you two are planning?"

"I wouldn't dare! Gabriel had suggested that I needed to build up my own board, and Princeton seemed like a good choice!" Devanshi crawled forward but not towards Silvestri. Her large green eyes pleading for Gabriel to do something.

"You wouldn't dare! Funny! Do you hear that, Gabriel? Councilwoman Devanshi wouldn't dream of opposing me. Yet here you stand, preparing to do just that. Ready to usurp my position." Silvestri's moved her hand so that it was propped beneath her chin. Looking all the world like a mother who was disappointed with her children.

"Are you denying my right to do so?" Gabriel's brows lifted as if he was hurt but made no move to deny the accusation of challenge that Silvestri levied at him.

Silvestri's lips pressed thin as her gaze met Gabriel's steadily. "You know I very well can't."

"Then let Devanshi up. She has no part of any nonexistent conspiracy. You're grasping at straws." The first stirrings of impatience started to creep into

Gabriel's voice, and Jada took a step back closer to Odin. She refused to get caught in the crossfire of them fighting.

"No, even if she is not conspiring against me, she was caught coming through the hedge." Silvestri smiled now that her trap had been sprung.

Gabriel's eyes closed in angry frustration before he looked down at Devanshi in annoyance. "In the name of heaven, Devanshi, why?"

"I...was curious! You talked about the human world so much. I wanted to see what was so special about it." Devanshi tossed an angry gaze towards Jada.

Jada barely kept her eyes from rolling. If Devanshi wanted her place on Gabriel's board and the bed, she should have asked. Now she was in the middle of two angry fairies connected by Gabriel. Jada watched Gabriel as he stiffly pulled in a deep breath.

"She went through the briars alone. It was stupid but not punishable by death." Gabriel's words were slow but measured. The conversation had become a lot more complicated, and Jada could only watch as he navigated through it. It was the tensest she had ever seen him.

"You two are going to look me in the eye and tell me she was not running errands for you?" Silvestri scoffed and looked to Nero in disbelief. Nero could only shrug and focus on Devanshi, who was still huddled on the floor.

"That's exactly what I'm saying. It's what I've been saying. Let her up now." The snap of Gabriel's voice filled the room, and Jada wasn't sure what was about to happen, but she knew that Gabriel was officially out of patience.

Silvestri smiled and waved her hand. Trinity released

Devanshi with a nudge of his boot towards

Gabriel. Gabriel strode over and kneeled next to Devanshi as he gratefully pulled his coat from Jada's arms to wrap about Devanshi's shoulders. Devanshi gave him a watery smile as he wrapped her in the grey woolen material. Carefully he picked up Devanshi's foot and placed a light kiss over the scarred area

above her ankle. He scooped her up from the floor and gently held her in bridal fashion out of reach of Trinity and Trine. Devanshi looked over to Jada with a smug smile, and this time Jada didn't stop herself from rolling her eyes.

Silvestri rose from the throne and walked down the steps towards the clustered group. The wide shark-like smile stretching across Trine and Trinity's faces was of no comfort to Jada at all.

"Then I shall take my leave. Devanshi you'll accept my deepest apologies, won't you?" The apology Silvestri was a syrupy sweet one, which meant there was no apology at all.

However, it seemed that now that Devanshi had gotten what she wanted, all was fine in the world of fairy once more. "Yes, of course, high councilor. It was a simple mistake after all."

"How gracious!" Silvestri slinked towards the door. "Although..." She half turns and smiles at Gabriel. "There is still the matter of you going through the briars."

Several things happened at once. With a flap of Nero's wings, he took to the air to swan dive towards Gabriel with his scythe drawn. Jada pulled Odin's spear from his hands and threw the sharpened point towards the on-coming seraph as hard as she could. The pointed end knocked Nero off course and pinned his wing into the opposing wall of the great hall. The whole room went still as they watched Jada approach Nero. Nero jerked forward, allowing the spear to slice through the feather-covered tendons. His body was slowly walking forward to the other end of the spear before disconnecting himself. His wing flapped gingerly, and Jada could see through the other side of the gaping wound.

"Nero, I'm sorry. Are you okay?" Jada's hands moved to gently cup his chin in her hand. The tips of her fingers gently stroking along his chin worriedly. "I just reacted... I... I didn't mean to hurt you!"

Nero didn't speak, but his chin turned in a cat-like nuzzle of Jada's palm before his undamaged wing brushed her back behind him forcefully. He moved towards Gabriel and Devanshi with the scythe in his hand, intending to carry out the mission his mistress had set.

"Silvestri, call off Nero." Gabriel's voice was flat and calm as he looked over to see how Jada was doing. Devanshi eyes were wide as they focused on the oncoming Nero. "I don't want to kill him, but I will. I can't have him distracting Jada or harming Devanshi."

"Oh, he's not after Devanshi. Just you. After you and, Jakeisha was it? Are gone, we'll be through. Devanshi, you can walk out when you're ready." Silvestri smiled over at the terrified fairy in Gabriel's arms.

Nero continued to move towards Gabriel with his scythe in hand. Jada frantically looked around for a weapon. She told herself it was Nero that she was worried about and not Gabriel. But having seen was Gabriel could do while he was not trying, she knew Nero wouldn't stand a chance if he cornered Gabriel with both hands tied around Devanshi.

Jada once again settled on Odin's spear. It was too large for her to maneuver with, but it was all she had at present. She jerked the spear from the wall cleanly.

She was mildly amazed at how much stronger she had gotten, but she didn't have to pat herself on the back.

She ran, and her body seemed to phase out of sight, and she was suddenly between Nero and Gabriel. She looked around in amazement but quickly gathered herself together to face Nero. "Nero, please stop before you get hurt!"

"Isn't that sweet? Your human pet is concerned about Nero's welfare! Isn't that just a whole bowl of sugar cubes!" Silvestri was leaning against the doorway next to Trine and Trinity. Their red eyes were almost feverish as they watched the spectacle in front of them.

"Silvestri. This is my last warning." Gabriel's attention focused on Nero, and that halo of light always accompanied by violence began to emit around him.

"I can always make another if he fails. " Silvestri yawned before her lips fell back into a sarcastic smile.

"Oh, wait! I can't! Someone killed Herr Drosselmeir. How inconvenient."

Jada held up the spear, ready to fend Nero off if necessary. She could feel Gabriel's light wrapping around her. She knew she had to think of something quickly. "Nero, stop this! You can't let her control you!"

"Aww, she doesn't know, does she? funny how you kept that from her." Silvestri's actually looked interested for the first time since they started this farce.

"Devanshi, hold on to me." And just like that, Gabriel's patience had run out. "Gladly!" Devanshi wrapped her arms tightly around Gabriel's shoulders.

Jada frantically racked her brain for something that could save Nero and could only think of her time in the pits. "I issue a challenge!" The room freezes, and Jada's words ring out through the hall.

Silvestri smiles broadly, and she leans from her waist from her place against the door. "Oh? Do you wish to challenge Nero? Such an unusual request. I mean, there are easier ways of getting your hands on him. However, if you want it rough, then I'm sure Nero would be more than willing to oblige you."

"No. I'm challenging whoever this Princeton guy is. That's the piece that started this, right? If I win, we will keep Princeton. If he wins, I go to Devanshi's board." Jada's kept her eyes on Nero, who watched her from a few feet away. His head canted to the side with a sad smile on his full lips.

Both femme fairies seemed to bright up at the idea of Jada being moved from Gabriel's board. Silvestri nodded with a clap of her tiny hands. Nero's gaze falls from Jada, and his graceful stride takes him to

Silvestri's side. "Very well then! since you insist, and Gabriel agrees?"

Trine and Trinity snicker as Gabriel turns with Devanshi in his arms. He watched Jada from the side of his eyes but shrugged. "I could never deny Jada anything. If Princeton is here, then we can clear this matter up today."

"Excellent! It's just darling how you worry about my dear Nero." Jada couldn't miss the emphasis that Silvestri placed on the word my. However, she didn't have time to worry about it. She truly had no idea what she was getting herself into.

"Trine, please find one of Gabriel's servants. It might take a few minutes. He doesn't have very many, to see to our refreshment. Trinity, please fetch the handsome Princeton." After Silvestri issued her orders, her arms wrap around Nero's, and she sways out of the room in good spirits.

Devanshi looks over at Jada from her place in Gabriel's arms and hugs him close. "How kind of you to save us, Jada! It looks like I owe you one!"

Jada's eyes disgustedly avert from Gabriel's, and she pulls in a deep, steadying breath. She wasn't sure what she was feeling right then, but it wasn't good. Her voice going flat as she replies. "Don't mention it."

Gabriel leaves the room with Devanshi in tow, and Odin walks up to take his spear from Jada. He leans down, and his beard brushes her ear as he speaks. "You are going to get yourself killed being soft."

Jada watches Odin walk out behind Gabriel and her eyes left towards the vaulted ceiling. A shake of her head was made as she follows them out to face her hasty challenge. "Yeah, I will."

Chapter Fourteen

They moved outside to the balcony where Jada was first introduced to the games. It had only been a few months ago, but it felt like a lifetime since then. The day was a pleasant one despite the unexpressed rage inside of her. The fairies gathered on the dais overlooking the board like the very model of fairy propriety and decorum. They looked like old friends having brunch. Not depraved murderous savages that stole people from their lives and forced them to fight to the death for their power and general amusement.

Jada lifted her skirt and made her way down the marbled stairs. Odin silently followed her down to the board, where three concentric circles were laid out. Two humans stood there waiting for her to come down. One was a fair brown, tall, and thin with a large curly black afro.

Musicals notes were inked along the muscles of his arms and chest. She could see the beginning of a treble clef peeking out beneath the collar of the white button up he wore rolled up to his elbows. The other was a medium brown beauty who had her small purple ringlets pulled into a tall Mohawk. The way they stood next to each other spoke of a deeper relationship than just friendship. The woman looked worried, but the male seemed to be serene.

They turned towards Jada as she walked over with Odin, and the male took a step forward and offered his hand. "Howdy, I'm Princeton. I will be your opponent today. Nice to harm you! This luscious lovely over here is Valkari."

"Prince!" Valkari's soft alto was scandalized but amused. The relationship was definitely not one of just being friends. It was refreshing to see genuine love in such a desolate place.

Jada's lips quirked, and she looked back at Odin, who nodded at Princeton and then Valkari. Jada shook her head in exasperation at the tall man and returned the handshake. "I'm Jada; this tall drink of surly water is Odin. I am both pleased and sad to be meeting you both under these circumstances."

Princeton raised Jada's hands to his lips in a chaste kiss before letting it drop gently to her side. "Well, if I'm going to get murdered, I'm glad it's by someone as beautiful as you."

Valkari rolled her eyes in exasperation, but Jada could see the deep fear that she had for Princeton. She took a deep breath and gave Jada a long once over. "Not to be rude, but aren't you a little over dressed for a duel?"

Jada laughs with a shake of her head. "This was not planned, I assure you."

"Enough of this! Fight already!" Silvestri's voices rang out over the board, and all four of them collectively frowned up at the dais where she sat.

Trine arrives on the field with a backflip that forces Jada and Princeton to step back from each other about three feet. The grotesque sneer on his face made Jada want to get violent. "The rules are as follows. There will be three rounds. The one who wins takes all. The object is to knock the other out of the last fairy ring by any means necessary."

Trine backflips off the field in a wiggle of feet, leaving Jada and Princeton in the circle. Odin guides Valkari from the field, where they wait for the match's outcome.

Jada, who still held Gabriel's sword, brought it up between them. "How about we make a deal not to use our powers? This way, we both make it out alive?"

"No offense, but I don't know you like that." Princeton frowned and pulled out a violin that was holstered on his back along with its bow.

"Fair, but you can trust that we both want to live, right?" Jada made a show of sending the army that was starting to rise from the ground away.

"I don't know…." Princeton looked to Valkari, where she fearfully waited for his return.

"If I use my powers, you have my promise I will abdicate the match." Princeton's eyes widened at the promise she made. Making a promise was no small thing in the world of fairy. It was a binding contract not to be taken lightly by the maker.

Princeton frowned, still unsure, but slowly nodded. The prospect of getting back to Valkari in one piece decided for him. "Looks like you have a deal, madam. No powers." He put away the violin and chose a flute from its holster. His hands pulled at the ends, turning the flute into a hollow staff twirling it between his fingers before lunging at her.

Jada dodged and kicked towards his midsection, causing him to jump back a few steps. Jada brought her fist down only to be blocked with the center of the long flute. Princeton, in turn, spun and kicked Jada in the stomach knocking the wind out of her.

"Tell your human to fight like she means it!" Silvestri snapped over at Gabriel, who only shrugged, not turning his attention away from the fight.

"Jada prefers a less murderous approach to win." Gabriel smiled and took a sip of wine, enjoying Silvestri's disappointment.

"How dull." Silvestri turned to Devanshi to angrily hiss at her. "Devanshi, make Princeton do something!"

"O...of course, councilwoman. Princeton quit playing around and try to kill her! I command you to be more interesting!" Devanshi blinked and looked at Gabriel beneath her lashes. She didn't want to lose Princeton, but removing Jada was also an important goal.

Princeton's teeth grit angrily at the orders, and he swings his staff low and behind her leg. Drawing the staff up towards her knee before pulling her forward so that her leg was now wrapped around his waist. "Shall we dance?"

Before Jada could be indignant, Princeton grinned before spinning her around and gently setting her down outside of the fairy ring. Jada's lips parted in awe as she tried to add up in her head how she found herself outside of the ring. Her eyes were narrowing at him slightly. "Did you use your powers?"

"Not at all, and that's one Queen B." Princeton sauntered back towards the center of the ring where he raised his staff waiting for her.

"How do you know I'm the queen?" Jada moved back to the center and raised her sword once more. Princeton was clearly more than just a pretty face.

"They don't go through this type of trouble for pawns, my lady. Engarde!" Princeton rushed forward, spinning the flute between his hands more.

Jada's eyes narrowed, and she took two large steps back toward the edge of the circle. As Princeton swung his staff, Jada caught the flute, turned staff in the middle, and dropped back with a roll. Her foot moved to the center of his stomach, using his momentum to toss him from the ring.

She smiled over at him as he picked himself up from the ground to dust himself off. He frowned at the fresh grass stains on his shirt before looking back at her with a lift of his brow.

"You didn't think it would be that easy, did you?" Jada laughed and settled into a fighting stance waiting for his next move. Whoever won this match won the lot.

"I expected nothing less from Gabriel's queen." Princeton's dark eyes sized her up as he moved back into the ring.

Jada glanced over at Valkari, who looked both relieved and sad. "Is she your girlfriend?" Jada indicated Valkari with a toss of her chin, causing her tiny braids to bounce over her shoulder.

"My wife, or as much of a wife as she can be under the circumstance." Princeton's smile was also a little sad, but he spun his staff determinedly, readying himself for the next round.

"I'm sorry." Jada's heartfelt heavy for the fae. He had so much to lose by not winning this match.

"Nothing to be sorry about. You didn't do this." He looked back and up across his shoulder. "They did."

"You ready?" Jada pulled his attention back to the fight, and he nodded.

"Yes. Last one, best one!" Princeton did two things at once. He holstered his flute and pulled out his violin. He plucked one string, and Jada found herself unable to move. The next sound that he pulled from the violin was the stirrings of a dirge. The sorrow filled melody wrapping around Jada pulling her towards Princeton one forced step at a time.

Jada looked over at Princeton, who was breaking their deal in disappointment. "I'm sorry to do this to you, but you're stronger than I thought you were. And I will do whatever it takes to stay with Valkari. I can't be separated from her. I love her. I hope you understand."

"Jada, watch out! You're almost outside of the fairy ring!" Jada could hear Odin shouting, but it sounded so far away from inside the music that played around her. She could see notes dancing around her body and scale lines tugging at her feet and arms. She tugged and fought trying to free herself from the literal pull of the music.

"Trust me when I say that I hate myself right now." Princeton's lament of his sacrificed honor could be heard in his voice. However, Jada didn't have time to focus on his remorse because she was getting closer to the edge of the ring. "You know when Devanshi gets you, she's going to give you to Silvestri, don't you?"

"It doesn't matter. One is no different than the other." Jada shrugged and pulled her foot free from one of the musical scales. "You understand that you're breaking our agreement, don't you?" Jada was busy trying to stay in the ring; she didn't have time to be distracted by who was going to be given to.

Princeton frowned, knowing full well that he was breaking the agreement. His eyes closed, but he continued to play. The bow between his fingers gently gliding across the strings towards its climatic end.

"You want to get away from Gabriel that badly? Then

I will oblige."

Princeton's fingers moved swiftly across the top of the violin. The tempo of the song picked up and forced Jada to come up with another plan. She was about a foot away from the edge of the ring, and she looked up at Gabriel, who silently watched. His smile still in place, and Jada took a deep breath. Her hand caught one of the music notes, and she used it to slice away the music strings from her wrist and ankles. Then threw the note like a throwing star at his violin. The movement caused the instrument to dislodge from his hands. Princeton shouted in angry surprise, but by the time he had picked his instrument back up. Jada was standing over him with a sad smile of her own.

She grabbed his hands and slowly began to waltz with him. Without his hands on the instrument, he could no longer control its melody and became caught in it. She twirled with him until they reached the edge of the ring. She spun him off towards Valkari, leaving her to catch her lover before moving to the violin, where the bow still strummed across the strings. She let the song end and picked up the instrument, slowly walking it back to the disgraced musician. He was on his knees in front of crying Valkari, who had her nose and fingers buried in his thick curls.

"That's it!" Silvestri scratched from the balcony. She stood knocking over all the refreshments from the table in one angry swoop of her arm as Trine transported the party on the field on the dais where the fairies congregated.

Gabriel's eyes moved over Jada, and he lifted his glass to her before. He turned towards Silvestri, doing his best but failing not to look smug. "Well, now that this is over, I hope you are satisfied with the outcome."

"Silvestri rounds on him as her small body begins to quake and glow in rage. "You tricked me! You knew that strumpet was going to win! You two planned this from the beginning,"

"No, you jumped to conclusions and acted irrationally. I just trusted Jada to be Jada. The match is done. Devanshi has been punished, and we will see you at the tournament." Gabriel stood and motioned for one of the nearby maids to clear the mess that Silvestri had made.

"You dare speak to me in such a fashion." Silvestri grew still, and her glowing body started to dissolve the nearby chairs causing Trinity and Trine to indignantly take a step back once their shoes became singed. "I will take your queen's head. That is the only thing that will conclude the matter of this insult.

Gabriel's face darkened, and this time his smile was neither amused nor pleasant. The halo of his aura was a dark vengeful red that coiled around him in a pulsing ring. The pale gold of his serpent like eyes darkened to a fiery orange. "Silvestri. You are trying my patience. Take Nero, the twins, and go. I will not ask again."

Silvestri walks up to Gabriel, and the light that surrounded her is collected in her hands. "Who do you think you're talking to?"

"I'm talking to a spoiled princess who has long outlived her usefulness. An overindulged brat who no longer has the rule of the council behind them. Did you forget that the twins don't answer to you but the bylaws?" The menace in Gabriel's voice was not lost on Jada. She looked to Silvestri, whose face had lost its pallor.

Silvestri turned to look at Trine and Trinity, and their grotesque leers spread in a way that connected their ears, but this time their red gaze was focused on her.

"Please." Trine's waspish voice began.

"Don't mind us." Trinity finished Trine's statement with the stinging rasp of his voice.

"You will pay for this, Gabriel." Silvestri's voice was both angry and low as she turned away from the twins. She snapped, and Nero turned to follow her away from the dais and through the doors.

The twins, in turn, bow, and backflip out of sight, leaving the groups in stunned silence. Gabriel took a deep breath working on getting his anger under control. Devanshi stood and threw her arms around Gabriel's shoulders peppering kisses across his neck and cheeks. He gently pulled away and continued to work on pulling himself back into some semblance of graciousness.

"You beautiful man! You saved me! How can I ever thank you!" Jada wasn't sure how Devanshi could both gush and be suggestive simultaneously, but she was performing admirably.

"Actually, Jada saved you." The fire of his gaze turned on Devanshi, causing her to take a few fearful paces back from him. He lost the fight by tamping his anger down, and the full force of his rage was turned towards Devanshi, "What were you thinking? How could you leave such a trail?"

Devanshi glared over at Jada as if this situation was her fault. "Don't be cross, Gabriel! I didn't have a choice!

251

Grimali took me there and left me because I told him you and I were in love! I didn't know he would take it so hard! I had to get Theo and Leticia to bring me back!"

"And they dumped you in a public place?" The soft annoying hiss of Gabriel's voice was a sure shine he was about to lose his cool. Jada gently pulled Valkari and Princeton back away from ground zero.

Seeing that Gabriel was not about to return or confirm the declaration of love made the curvy fairy pout further. "In Silvestri's garden...."

Gabriel cursed beneath his breath before he was able to calm down. He took a deep breath and through the fire in his eyes was, there he smiled once more. Jada did not feel any more comforted by his restored humor. "So, the trolls wish to be vindictive. That is fine. I will take care of them personally; no need to worry."

"And Grimali? It's all of his fault for not accepting our relationship." Devanshi was quick with spite. Jada assumed that vengeance-like promises were taken very seriously in the world of fairy.

Gabriel paused and looked at Devanshi for a moment, and his smile spread across his face slowly. "I know just what to do about Grimali. Don't you worry."

"I won't, Gabriel; you take care of me so well!" Devanshi was back to gushing, and Jada could not stop herself from looking at the healing scars on the fairy's wrist and ankles.

Gabriel glanced at Jada before following her gaze to the burn marks on Devanshi's wrist. "How are your wrist and ankles."

"All healed up unless you would like to examine the personally?" Devanshi was quick with two things, and that was replies and come ons. Jada nodded her head with her own smile as she was pretty impressed at how quickly Devanshi turned that into an offer.

"Another time, perhaps. I will be spending the evening taking care of Jada and the new piece she procured for me." He turned his hungry gaze to Jada, and she wished he had kept his focus on Devanshi. "Masterfully done, by the way, Jada. You never cease to both amaze and humble me."

"But Gabriel! I brought him for you!" Devanshi's tone was both mournful and grating.

"And nearly lost him and Jada to Silvestri." Hearing Gabriel confirms Princeton's words made her take another look at the tall willowy man once more. Princeton didn't not look proud to be right. Her attention turned back to Gabriel as he moved towards Devanshi.

Devanshi stepped back towards the door, seeing that her welcome was quickly running out. "I...I'm sorry, Gabriel. It won't happen again."

"Think nothing of it. Now head home and see to your lovely skin. I will contact you in a few days if Jada is doing well." Gabriel had lost the fire in his eyes, and his voice was once again pleasant.

Devanshi smoothed out her sari and suddenly looked as if she would rather be in any place but there at the moment. "Of course, Gabriel. Valkari, let's go!"

Valkari turned to Princeton, and her fingers lifted to brush the curls away from his forehead. She placed a sad kiss against his cheek and stepped away. Princeton grabbed her arms and fiercely pulled her back to him, unwilling to let her go. Jada sighed and prepared to get herself into more trouble.

"No." Jada turned her attention to Devanshi and moved between her and the couple.

Devanshi pulled her hand to her chest and exaggeratedly looked around as if she was missing something. After appearing not to have found it, she looked back at Jada with a blink of her green eyes. "Who are you to tell me no? You little human nobody!"

"I'm a nobody; you owe one too for stopping Nero from killing you. Valkari stays here with Princeton." Jada turned to look at Gabriel as he watched the tug of war over Valkari silently.

"How dare you!" If Devanshi was doing an impression of Silvestri, then she was doing an excellent job.

Jada did her best to remove any attitude from her voice as she continued. She knew that the couple would die without each other, and she wasn't willing to let the only happy humans in the fairy lose each other. "If we get Valkari, we can replace the two pieces we lost earlier this month."

Gabriel watched Jada's eyes for a moment as if searching for something and looked behind her to Devanshi. "Did you make a pact, Devanshi?"

"But Gabriel, you can't hold me to something I said in relief!" Devanshi stammered, knowing that she had made a mistake in her effort to be catty.

"Did you or did you not say that you owed Jada one?" Gabriel's voice was calm, and he had every reason to be. The mistake was Devanshi, and she would have to honor it or risk being punished by the court and crown.

Denshi pouted, and her shoulders sagged sadly. "Yes."

"Then it appears Jada is within her rights. She has made a request, and that request is Valkari's become part of my board." Gabriel turns to Valkari and takes her hand, walking her over to Princeton. Even he had not missed the love that the two shared. "At my queen's leisure, we are glad to welcome you to your new home."

The look Devanshi gave Jada could have frozen oceans at high tide. Jada ignored the death glare. Jada was in much too good of a mood to worry about the promise of revenge. Valkari stood in front of Princeton, who looked as if the world had upended itself. Like he hadn't seen kindness outside of their bubble for so long, he had forgotten what it looked like. Valkari, on the other hand, threw her arms around Princeton's shoulders, only to have Princeton lift her and spin her around in relieved joy.

Devanshi shrugged and turned to Gabriel sharply. "Gabriel, if you'll escort me out." "Of course. Jada, I will find you later." Gabriel took Devanshi's arm. He led her away from the stone dais, and with a last glare thrown Jada's way, Devanshi was gone.

Jada turned to Princeton and Valkari, who were busy being all over each other. They were a tangle of limbs and kisses, and for the first time, Jada felt sad that she had never had or seen that type of love up close. She looked over at Odin, who looked oddly pained as the affectionate display of relief in front of them. Jada coughed gently; in fact, she coughed a couple of times to get the couple's attention.

Valkari had to use her hands to physically stop any more of Princeton's efforts to continue to celebrate. A soft embarrassed laugh was filling the momentary silence. "Wait, so just like that? We are staying together. No string attached?" Valkari dark eyes were so infectiously animated that all Jada could do was smile despite Princeton's suspicious laugh.

"Well, the strings are that you will be a part of

Gabriel's board. That in itself is enough of a string." Jada smiled but shrugged. There was no getting past the reason they were all here.

"Gabriel's board." Princeton's cheerful voice was a little flat. He was clearly the less trusting of the two despite his jovial manner. Jada hated that this world could turn two such genuinely happy people hard. "You mean he has a team of serial killers."

"Princeton!"

"What? You saw what they did to Dima's board."

Princeton winced and lifted his hand to scratch the back of his curly head nervously as he looked at Odin. "No offense."

"None taken." Odin turned from Princeton took a look at Jada as if watching her with new eyes. "Well, you took care of the issue of the missing piece quickly enough." Jada felt like something heavier beneath his words, but she was too keyed up to examine it. She was as relieved the ordeal was over as everyone else was.

Jada held up her hands to forestall any argument that Odin was about to give her. She just wanted to feel her victory just a little longer. "I know it seems callous, but I'm willing to do what it takes to keep our board free of Gabriel's influence. I personally have no intention of fighting alongside any of them."

"If you say so. However, it's going to take more than just some switched pieces to win at the tournament. "Odin shrugged and put his spear back behind his back now that the danger was over. He stretched and looked out onto the empty board. "Plus, now you've made two of them angry."

"He's right about that. They are vindictive, and they won't forget today. You've bought us some trouble." Princeton smiled slightly, and Jada internally beamed at the use of the word "us". They would be a team if Jada had to drag each of them kicking and screaming to the field.

"Are you two afraid?" Jada asked the question seriously. It was fine to be afraid. Human even. She looked at each of them, they looked back dissolving into a pile of laughter.

Princeton pulled Valkari into his arms and placed a soft kiss in the middle of her curls. His eyes were closing in contentment before focusing on Jada once more. "I don't care where I'm fighting as long as I'm fighting beside my wife. I don't have anything, but I swear you have my loyalty."

Valkari nodded profusely from Princeton's embrace with tears in her eyes. "I agree, I don't know how to thank you for finding a way to keep us together, but if it's till death do we part, it will be on the board at your side.

Jada smiled at them both, and she suddenly felt hopeful about their chance at winning next month's tournament. Suddenly her wish to get home was spreading out to get all of them out of there. She laughed and held up her hands to staunch any more thanks. "Don't thank me. With pieces as strong as Nero, we have a lot of training to do, and unfortunately, all of this happiness is going to turn to hate fast."

"Aye!" Odin casually dropped a friendly arm around Jada's shoulders, and Jada could feel the excitement rolling off him. "We have a glorious death to earn!"

Chapter Fifteen

Horns sounded announcing the arrival of Gabriel's board. Rexserious was filled to its borders with the joy and cheers of thousands. The streets of the capital were overrun with fairies waiting to see if their hero Gabriel would slay the Silvestri's dragon. Jada's eyes were wide as she watched the crowd gathered to watch the parade. In front of their carriage were dancers on foot adorned in a rainbow of plumes and feathers. Jada barely refrained from leaning out of the window as she watched from her seat next to Gabriel. They moved through the city streets at a passive pace as their board walked behind them. Their krewe moved along the thoroughfares playing with the crowd and putting on a show for the parade goers. Fairies, every color, size, and appearance, applauded as they passed by.

Princeton was the only other member of Gabriel's board that was not walking. He was riding in a brass music box pulled by another set of white clockwork horses. His long thin fingers vigorously danced along with the ivory keys of the calliope he played. Music was not the only thing that was piped through the brass columns. There was a never-ending stream of sweets that fairy children clamored in the streets. There was so much laughter and happiness around them. Jada's dark brown eyes softened at the streets of adoring fairies. They held so much hope that Gabriel would save them from the tyranny of

Silvestri's iron-like grip on their lives. Her quest for the mining of fairy dust had laid waste to many of their homes. The regard and trust they had for Gabriel was almost a tangible entity of itself.

"It's beautiful here." Jada's awed whisper broke the silence of the carriage.

"Would it be inappropriate for me to say that the view out there is nothing compared to the view I have in here?" Gabriel placed a kiss on the back of each of her hands. A lingering touch of his lips was set against the back of each of her hands.

Her eyes dropped and cheeks heated, and she quickly turned her attention back outside. If Jada had to pick a season, it felt like an early spring day in the capital city of fairy. The day was bright, and the wing that made the various flags snap and wave at attention was cool. It was at odds with the perpetual summer that seemed to permeate Gabriel's home. Octavius hurled a full golden rococo gown that kept her from being cold as the horses pulled their carriage through the streets. This offset the

260

extortionate amount of time it took to have her make-up and hair done to Gabriel's exacting specifications. Though the process was tiring, she could not complain about the results. Half of her hair was braided back towards her ears while the rest was allowed to spread and curl around her head like a dark crown. Cosmetic magic had been performed that carved her lips into a black cupid's bow beneath the small black heart under her right eye.

All the women on Gabriel's board wore golden corseted gowns that cinched impossibly at the waist and white wigs. The men wore black brocade frock coats that were trimmed in gold as the gowns were trimmed in black. They waved and blew kisses to the crowd as they walked the parade route to the capital's castle. Where the other six council members were already waiting on Gabriel, Jada could barely see past the paper streamers and confetti butterflies that swarmed the air in a joyful array of bright colors. Jada lifted her hand to try to catch one of the paper butterflies that flew too close to the carriage. She almost hit herself in the face with the black lace that gathered over her hands from the bell sleeves. She glared over her shoulder at Gabriel for the inconvenience.

Gabriel caught the look and laughed in a way that almost made Jada forget that he was a mass murdering fairy. The carefree sound of his laughter filled the carriage. He leaned over and The look in his gilded eyes hypnotized jada. Gabriel's viper-like gaze widened and contracted before settling on her lips. Jada's lip's part and the tip of her tongue nervously moistens lips that suddenly ran dry. She forcefully pulled herself out of the momentary trance. A sharp turn of her body had her facing the fairies that lined the street once more. Her hand lifted over her heart in a vain attempt to stop the swift beat of her heart.

"What's wrong Jada, aren't you entertained?" Gabriel's words were warm against her ear. Though Jada had turned away, Gabriel had moved over to wave out of the window of the carriage. His dark curls brushing against her cheek as the scent of coffee and honey wrapped around her. The roar of the crowd was almost deafening with the adulation being thrown at their carriage. The closeness with his queen only making the impression of them being a team stronger to the outside world.

"I want to walk with the rest of the board." Jada unsuccessfully tried to keep her voice from sounding petulant. The camaraderie she had earned was hard to maintain when she was riding in a plush clockwork carriage without them.

"I know, and it's unfortunate because the image of you walking with the board would have been magnificent" Gabriel nodded in agreement.

Jada pulled in an exasperated breath and turned to look over her gold satin-covered shoulder at him. "Then why am I in here?"

Gabriel took her hand and gently pulled her around so that she faced him once more. Jada was finding it harder and harder to hate him, and in turn, hated herself for it. His large hands curled around her as he brought them to his lips.

"We both know that once this tournament starts, we will be spending very little time with each other. You may even die. I want you at my side for as long as I can. I know you pretend that you are not feeling what I'm feeling, but I decided to do us both a favor. Feel free to thank me any way you see fit." Gabriel's eye drops in a playful wink before he turns back to a crowd that was only too glad to have his attention. The sky was starting to darken as the twin suns began to conjoin above them, casting shadows on those gathered to watch them pass by.

Jada ignored his comment to keep from having to answer it. Her hand lifted to wave at the fairies that lined the parade route. Her hands raised, and she allowed a small fire to blaze just enough to heat the air around her. The hot air caused the paper butterflies to rise into the sky, creating a fluttering heart. The crowd cheered, and Jada held the shape in the aloft for a few moments before allowing the colorful bits of paper to light on fire. The paper crackled and sizzled before rising towards the clouds in a puff of colorful smoke that lingered for all to see. The excited roar of the crowd was almost deafening. She sat back against the soft cushions of the carriage and ignored the way Gabriel watched her with a knowing smile.

"Thank you for that. I expected nothing less from my queen." Gabriel turned back to the crowd and Jada bit her lower lip as her feelings were in disarray because of the man beside her.

Jada decided on the better part of valor and turned her attention back to entertaining the crowd. "Do you plan on keeping me on this pedestal forever?"

"What pedestal? I love and accept you for everything you are. Even when you deny who and what you are."

Gabriel's hands lifted, and a tiny ball of white light collected in his hands. He tossed it up towards darkened heavens, and a stream of fireworks burst through the afternoon air.

Jada watched the beautiful explosion above her and couldn't staunch the childlike awe at the myriad burst colors. Her hand lifted to brush away an errant curl from her shoulders, trying to ignore the rush of her feelings. "And what am I?"

Gabriel didn't look back at her this time. He was in full swing of entertaining the parade watchers. He didn't have to. His words were simple enough, and she heard them loud and clear. "Mine."

They continued in silence for a time. The procession was slow but filled with excitement. The enthusiasm of the crowd was infectious. Soon she was doing small tricks with her magic and telling herself that it was just practicing for the tournament. Jada found herself making fiery shapes in the form of dancing bears. The rest of the board began to follow suit. Soon the streets of the parade were filled with shapes and random displays of magical powers. Hyenas gave rides to the youngsters in the crowd, allowing them to be part of the parade. Crows caught bits of shiny paper and brought them to women along the parade route. Valkari even produced little rag dolls that she handed out as they walked by.

Jada watched her board fondly, taking in the rare smiles. She was glad they were happy for now. Though the parade was exciting, she couldn't forget why they were there. This parade was one step closer to her going home. There could be no failure; it was either home or death.

The board had spent almost every waking hour practicing and training to win. Jada continued to wave to those gathered around them; determined to soak up as much happiness as possible.

Gabriel turned from the crowd to watch her again. His proud smile prompted her own. She could admit to herself that despite the circumstances of her presence there, she was having fun. A small brown pixie with large magnolia petal wings flew by Gabriel to present Jada with a bouquet of white roses. She gratefully took the flowers and leaned forward to give the pixie a quick peck on the cheek. The pixie blushed and flew away as fast as it had come with a rapid flutter of gossamer wings. Jada made a show of considering all the flowers and selecting one to place in the lapel of Gabriel's coat. There was another round of cheers, and Gabriel's happy laughter filled the carriage once more.

"You're a natural at this. Not even nervous." Gabriel nodded in thanks and looked out towards the crowd, but his words were directed to her.

Jada's shoulders lifted in an amused shrug as she continued to wave at everyone outside of the carriage. "I'm used to performing for crowds."

"I haven't forgotten. Will you return to stripping when you return home?" Gabriel looked as if he was in the mood to take a break. He relaxed into the cushions of the carriage and concentrated solely on her.

"I haven't honestly thought about it. I'm focused on getting there first. I'll cross that bridge when I come to it." Jada mirrored his action as it appeared that they were coming towards the end of the parade route. It was almost time for them to put on an entirely different type of show.

"You could stay here with me and use your wish for something else?" The tone Gabriel had taken was meant to be persuasive, but Jada looked out at the crowd around them sadly.

"Let's say I did. I wouldn't know what to do with my freedom here either." Jada knew that no matter what world she chose, she would be an alien amongst the inhabitants there. She was no longer human enough for humans, and she was not a fairy.

"You could stay and marry me." Gabriel turned to her. His molten gaze watched the array of emotions play across her face causing Jada to avert her eyes in frustrated confusion.

"I'm sure Devanshi would be overjoyed at my continued presence." Jada's lips twisted ruefully at the memory of the only other council member she had met outside Silvestri and Gabriel.

"You're funny." Gabriel began to laugh so hard that tears filled his eyes. Jada side-eyed him as he fought to catch his breath amidst gales of laughter as he was doubled over at her expense.

"How so?" Jada's soft voice sounded tart even to her, but she wasn't focused on that right now. She was busy being insulted by his laughter at her expense.

Gabriel wiped his mirthful eyes and focused once more. "You say you don't want me."

"I don't." Jada snapped and pulled her arms in so that they were folded over each other waiting for him to get to his point.

"But you don't want anyone else to have me." Gabriel's beautiful smile was far too wide for Jada's pleasure.

"Is that what I said? Devanshi is welcomed to you." Jada lifted her nose and turned to the crowd to wave once more to avoid any more conversation.

However, Gabriel was disinclined to acquiesce to her silent reproval. "So you didn't mean to sound jealous just now?"

Jada twirled back around in her seat in righteous indignation. Her hand lifted to rest on her exposed bosom at his audacity. "I am absolutely not jealous! what in the world do I have to be jealous of?"

"Good, you shouldn't be. I belong to you. "Gabriel watched her with a bemused expression that made Jada roll her eyes towards the top of the carriage.

"I don't belong to you." Jada's voice was flat, but she wasn't as sure of that as she once was.

Gabriel's eyes contracted as he continued to focus on her. He shook his head and tsked in disappointment. "Jada, I never took you for a liar."

"Am I lying?" Jada watched herself in his eyes, and she didn't particularly like what she saw in the pale gold mirrors.

"Aren't you?" Gabriel didn't wait for her answer, and they had reached their destination. Jada was glad that she

267

didn't have to respond, but she was less than thrilled to start the formalities of the tournament.

Rexserious was the jewel of the fairy world. It was where all the policies that the fairy followed were made. Every decision was held to a vote, but each vote was based on the highest council member's policies. The castle they stopped at was like a highly polished mirror that reflected their world back to them. If you were happy with what you saw, then the system was working for you. If you were not, it was best to find a way to get a council person in your pocket.

When Gabriel stepped out of the carriage, it was as if a rockstar had entered a building. The applause of the fairies sounded like thunder. If Jada had thought that the area was crammed with people before, the sheer amount of people around them was overwhelming. There were so many fairies pushing and pulling to get a closer look at Gabriel Jada wasn't sure if she should even get out of the carriage. Gabriel held up his hand, and the crowd fairies went still in a ripple of movement that amazed Jada. Gabriel turned towards the door of the carriage and held out his hand for her. Jada stepped through the door and took his hand. She lowered her lashes to keep from reacting to the collective sigh of the female population at his chivalrous behavior.

The press of so many people up close caused a flare of anxiety to crawl up Jada's spine. Gabriel sensed her distress and placed a reassuring hand to the small of her back as he guided her up the wide round flight of stairs. Jada picked up her skirts to keep from tripping as they moved forward towards the row of mirrored seats before them. Each one possessed a member of the council that represented a different kingdom of fairy.

"Magnificent, isn't it? Just think if you stayed, you could rule the world of a fairy by my side." Gabriel's words were quiet, but the meaning was loud and clear as he guided her towards the council.

Jada smiled but spoke under her breath so that only he could hear her. "I think Devanshi and you make a lovely couple."

"You don't mean that." he laughed and shook his head. The crowd had stopped clapping, but the general rumble of excited conversation was all around them.

"Of course, I do; she's stunning." Jada's voice didn't waver as she gave Gabriel her assessment of Devanshi with a calm shrug of her shoulders. "I've danced with a lot of women, Gabriel. I know when someone is gorgeous, and I feel no way slighted or threatened that you think so too."

"You're right. Devanshi is truly divine. However, you are the one I love." Gabriel's whisper had sharpened with annoyance, but his smile stayed in place despite his irritation with her. "I wish you could see and accept how sublime we would be together. If you weren't so afraid of how you felt, we'd be unstoppable."

"Look..." Jada was starting to become angry as he verbally eviscerated her as they moved up the stairs.

He turned to her and pulled her hand to his lips to smooth out the sting of his words. They had reached the top step, and Gabriel's voice evened out despite his annoyance. "Fine, I will leave it for now, but this isn't over."

Jada fell silent as they continued the short walk to the seven thrones on the platform. One chair was empty, but that seat belongs to Gabriel. Jada felt the presence of two figures on either side of her, and she half turned to see Irshad and Odin at her back on either side. She wasn't sure what they were preparing for, but she was glad they were here. Jada gently disengaged her hand from Gabriel and curtsied to him before stepping back to stand between them. Gabriel's lips thinned fractionally as she moved to stand next to Irshad, but his audience kept him in check. He focused on the crowd and waved once more. The prolonged applause was so loud Jada thought the platform would crumble apart at its force.

To Silvestri's right sat another woman. The short, beautifully round woman had chosen a long white skirt and duster over a daringly low-cut navy blouse. The rich material draped attractively over her chest while exposing the cool umber of her clavicle. Her long, deeply curled brown hair was draped over her shoulder and tied loosely by a dark blue scarf. Her kind light brown eyes were surrounded by a wealth of thick lashes that watched them approach with curiosity. The white pin that held her sash together had the word "Council Member Ezuli." Scrawled across the front. She nodded to Gabriel with a polite, if stiff, smile. "Councilman Gabriel."

"You do like to make an entrance, my man." On the right of Ezuli was a tall man who wore an expensive double-breasted white suit with a tailored blue shirt beneath. The pin of his sash spelled out "Council Member Kionah."

Dark, intelligent eyes watched Gabriel with a sardonic smile. His long black hair was separated down the middle and braided with leather bands on each side. The wind tossed the beaded and feathered neckpiece he wore around his neck carelessly over his broad chest. His ancient eyes were as dark as his hair, and they were so serene they allowed Jada to allow her shoulders to relax upon meeting them. His russet fingers curled through the fur of a large grey timber wolf that sat at his side. The seat next to him was empty, and Jada assumed it belonged to Gabriel.

"Oh look, Devi, your savior, finally decided to show his face." On the left of Silvestri was a sturdy-looking man with broad shoulders and an olive complexion. His hair was short and slicked back from his high forehead and Roman nose. His eyes were a pale crystal blue that contrasted starkly against his dark hair. The expensive blue dress shirt he wore was tucked into the waistband of his perfectly pressed white suit pants. The white dinner jacket that accompanied his suit was carelessly draped across the back of his throne. His pin said, "Council Member Grimali" He was trying to get Devanshi's attention, but Jada assumed Devanshi was still mad about the troll incident.

The gorgeous Devanshi was resplendent in a white and navy saree that loosely wrapped about her figure. Though the ornate material was draped over her dark hair, it left her gold pierced nose and green eyes clear. She was dismissive of Grimali, and she was avidly speaking to the swarthy council member to her left. The man she spoke to was massive and easily the strongest looking member there. the pin on his sash read "Council Member Barron."

271

Warm russet fingers were interlaced and stiffly gathered into his dark blue covered lap. Everything he wore was precisely pressed, and not an inch of his blue suit was out of place. Not even the wind dared to muss his large crown of tight curls. He sat back straight against his throne, watching Gabriel and Jada approach with a silent disdain that was palpable.

Silvestri's cold violet eyes watched Gabriel approach over a placating smile. It wasn't hard to see how much the country loved Gabriel. He was their white knight despite being a nightmare to so many. The other six council members calmly watched Gabriel approach with varying levels of pleasure. Silvestri wore a formal white pantsuit and the navy-blue sash of the council. Her raven asymmetrical hair was tossed away from her cheeks in impatience. Silvestri's smile was pleasant despite the anger in her eyes. Her gaze moved over Jada dismissively before she moved her focus to Gabriel once more. Silvestri waved her hand towards the mirrored throne at the end. "How nice of you to finally join us, Gabriel. Will you take your seat as a member of the council?"

"Yes, but I am requesting your seat." The crowd had gone quiet at his statement, and there was no sound to be found amongst the throng of people surrounding the platform. "Will you concede your seat to me, councilwoman Silvestri?"

"I do not. Do you invoke the right of a challenge then?" Silvestri's voice was polite, but the rage in her eyes loud and clear.

. "Yes, and by invoking the right of challenge, I accept the responsibility of hospitality. I will share not only my bread but my home with you." Gabriel turned, and he focused on something behind Jada. Jada turned to see Valkari gracefully approaching the top step. Once she arrived, she swept by Jada with a silver plate of 7 small loaves of bread. She offered a loaf to each council member then took her place behind Gabriel.

"No!"

"Gabriel, don't do it! We can't lose you!"

"Oh, Gabriel!"

Despite the crowd's murmurs, all seven of the fairies broke their bread and began to eat half of the loaf given to them. Valkari held out the silver platter and waited for Gabriel to break the other half of his loaf into six pieces and place them back on the platter. She moved back to the council, and they traded their braid for pieces of Gabriel's on the platter. Valkari returned with the rest of the bread and presented the platter to Gabriel with a deep curtsy. He turned to the council and bowed.

"Let his bread be a symbol of our pact to see the tournament through. I thank you for your recognition of my challenge and the acceptance of my hospitality." Gabriel bowed to the council, and the council bowed from their seats in return.

"In eight suns, there will be a convening of the council. As the council member challenged, I invoke the right of death. Should you lose the challenge you and your board will be summarily executed." The shocked gasp that followed Silvestri's proclamation created an angry buzz amongst the citizens of fairy.

"That's not fair!"

"Fairy, help us!"

"She can't do that!"

"Who will save us if he loses?"

The conversations around them went on and on. Jada was starting to get a headache from the palpable fear that surrounded them. Gabriel seemed to glory in the loving attention of those around them. He was a drop of serenity in the lake of panic around them. He lifted his hands to the crowd of fairy, and they nervously settled down to hear what he had to say.

Even Jada was wrapped up in the theatrics that Gabriel played out before them. He walked to his empty throne and removed the flower that Jada had put in his lapel. He placed a showy kiss on the petals before tossing the flower onto his seat. "By the love of the one who gave me this flower, I swear to abide by the invocation of the right of death."

Jada's brow lifted at the exaggerated meaning of the flower he placed on his council seat. Gabriel began to speak again, but the smile he gave Silvestri was not a nice one. "I will abide by the invocation of death and demand the same. May you die by the sword that you live by."

Jada's hand lifted to her ears at the din of shouts and cheers around them. The streets were filled with fairy pandemonium that had broken out into the streets. Things had escalated and way too fast and had complicated twofold. Forget fighting for them to get home; they were now fighting for their lives. The lives of sixteen pieces rested in her hands, and never had the burden been as heavy as it was now.

Silvestri smiled despite her anger and turned to her side. The Judge who had given her to Gabriel stepped out from behind her throne with a wide smile. He had changed from his Egyptian robes into what looked like a long white tank top and baggy denim jeans. He had a tumbler filled with an amber liquid that barely kept from sloshing over the side of the glass. Jada frowned as she recognized the clothing, but how he wore them was strange to her.

"Thank you for returning from the other side of the briars to do your job. We are ever so grateful for your time and attention." Silvestri's sarcasm was lost on the smiling adjudicator.

"You're welcome, but let's hurry. I was making it rain when I was summoned." He quickly spun, and his formal robes appeared around his form. The book he wrote in at the court and crown floated before him as he took out a quill and tested the tip on his tongue.

"My patience is wearing thin." Silvestri snapped at the Judge as her impatience started to get the better of her.

"Your patience might be thin, but that troll was thick. Get on with it before I make a ruling you won't like." The book's pages glowed and fluttered rapidly, indicating that the Judge was prepared to end everyone on the platform before him.

"Does the Court and Crown accept these terms as a binding promise made between two council members of sound mind and facility?" Silvestri looked at the end of her tether, but like the twins, the Judge did not answer to her.

The quill scratched across the parchment as he wrote the terms of their pact in the book. "The Court and Crown most certainly do. If you will hold out your hands?" The Judge licked the tip of the quill, and the point sharpened, leaving a long line of blood across his tongue.

Gabriel took off his coat as he approached the waiting Judge. He handed it to Valkari, who waited with the platter behind him. He held out his hand, and the Judge sliced a straight line across his palm. As soon as the bloodied point touched the paper, Gabriel's blood scrawled his signature beneath his name. Silvestri stood and held out her hand for the Judge to cut into. The red scrawl of their combined signatures glowed before darkening in their place on the page.

As both Gabriel and Silvestri signed their names, Valkari offered the broken bread to the Judge. He consumed the loaves and sucked his fingers clean.

"The oath has been sealed. Both will abide by its terms or be Judged as apostate of the invocation with a penalty of becoming a piece on the opposing member's board for the duration of their natural life." The Judge closed the book with a decisive snap and turned away from them both. "If you haters will excuse me. I'll be back through the briars just in time to party like it's 1999 with the trolls."

Jada frowned, hoping that was not the year back home. It would mean that she had been in fairy for almost twenty-five years in her world. The Judge pulled a pair of dark shades over his milky white eyes. With another spin, the Judge changed back into his jeans and brown boots. He walked away from the gathered council until he disappeared into thin air upon the third step.

Silvestri watched the Judge disappear, then turned her attention back to Gabriel. "The tournament will begin tomorrow. When the two suns meet in the sky, have your board ready. Mine will be. Now, if it's at all convenient for you, maybe you would like to get some work done for the citizens of Fairy?"

She didn't wait for Gabriel's answer. Silvestri imperiously strode from the platform towards the castle with a toss of the fringe that covered her eye. The other council members rose and followed her to the castle. Without a word said between them. The fairies began to mill around excitedly, talking amongst themselves. Now that the formalities were over, it was time for the capital-wide festivities that accompanied such events.

Gabriel takes his coat from Valkari with a nod of thanks and makes his way back to Jada. Princeton and the rest of the board come up the steps, and once they are all gathered. Gabriel smiles at them, though his smile loses some of its wattages when he sees how close Irshad is standing next to Jada.

"Well, now that the gauntlet has been thrown, you can have the rest of the evening to yourselves. We will leave once the council has finished its business. Enjoy yourselves. You all have earned it, and this is the one night you will have to do as you please. Spare no expense and celebrate every moment you have left before the tournament." Gabriel smiles amidst the cheers of those gathered, and his hands raise to get their attention once more.

"Though you are free to do as you please this evening, remember that running away is punishable by death.

Don't get any ideas. Otherwise, have an amazing day.

Jada, may I speak with you before you leave?" Gabriel steps away from the group as they begin to disperse.

Jada follows as she smooths her dress down in agitation. "I'm not going to run away!"

"I know. You're in love with me. You aren't going anywhere. I just wanted to see what your definition of fun entailed." Jada blinked at how serious Gabriel was.

"Really?" She shook her head in confusion. Her hands rising and falling uselessly at her sides, "I don't know? Dinner and dancing? Maybe find what passes for chocolate in this place?"

Gabriel nods his head with a relieved smile and wags his fingers to punctuate each word. "Excellent good!

Glad to hear it! Well, you have fun doing those things. Stay away from fairy dust!"

He gathers Jada's hands and kisses the back of her fingers before leading her back to Irshad. "Please take care of Jada with your life."

"Don't worry, I will." Irshad's lips quirk up at the end in a half-smile, and he turns to Jada. Taking her arm in his and leading Jada towards the stairs, "Shall we?"

"We shall." She takes a few steps forward and gently releases Irshad's arm before returning to Gabriel. "Take care of yourself in there."

The frown that had etched its way across his lips cleared at her words. He moves to kiss her but pulls himself short as he remembers his promise. He coughs in embarrassment and takes a step back from her. His hand lifted to the back of his head with a wide smile. "Better be careful. It sounds like you're worried about me."

"No, just my investment. You are the only one who can honor the wish I make." Jada turns back to Irshad and places her arm back around his. This time it's her leading him away from Gabriel, as she runs not only from him but her own feelings. She was no longer sure if she was in more danger from the tournament or herself.

Parades continued to fill the streets that that twisted twined through the capital of Rexsarious. Any free space was filled with open-air markets and booths selling spices, meat, and sweet baked goods. Fairy children ran around with thin sticks attached to bubbles with goldfish floating around. Women and men danced around maypoles with flowers in their hair as a kitsune played zithers and shamisens with all nine of its tails. A tall man with eight arms and legs sold golden good luck charms with the words

"Anansi" scrawled on a yellowing sign over his booth. His orange suit and top hat slightly faded in the shimmery light that surrounded him. He lowered his glasses down as Jada rode by and dropped a wink at her as she passed. Jada dipped her head. There was so much for Jada to see.

Every section of the city was a sensory overload of activity.

As they made their way through the city, there was not a door that was closed to them. Each person they passed offered them strong drinks, and each elderly grandma had a son that they wanted Valkari and Jada to meet. Though the atmosphere was jovial, Jada could not help but feel like a fatted calf on its way to slaughter. A sacrifice to their entertainment. Each laugh and every cheer were like a joyous nail laid into their coffins. Just as they were cheering with them today, they were just as likely to be cheering against them tomorrow.

"Valkari!" Princeton held out his hands to his lady love, and Valkari took them gracefully. Jada could only smile at the easy banter between them. They were one team on the same side, and it was beautiful to watch.

"What can I do for you, oh husband mine?

"I have something to show you... you know... over here!" Princeton winked at Jada before gently guiding Valkari away from the group.

Valkari waved at them, leaving Odin, Irshad, and Jada watching them for a moment before continuing their walk through the city.

"Wait until you see this place, Jada! The Rising Phoenix has the strongest drinks and the most beautiful women in the city!" Odin's voice crowd through the streets teeming with fairies that wanted to give them more food and trinkets.

Jada was just in the middle of politely declining one of many offers for a final role in the briars. Her lips twisted ruefully at his words, and she could only shake her head. "Oh well! I guess we must hurry to this paragon of wine, women, and song!"

Odin's arms draped companionably over Jada's shoulder as he continued to lead the way. "Exactly!

That's the spirit! You can be my drinking buddy! Irshad refuses to get a drink with me!"

"I refuse to get drunk with you. There's a difference." Irshad smiled and continued to follow Odin and Jada with an alertness that Odin seemed to lack.

"I refuse to get drunk with you!" Odin's voice rose an octave as he mimicked Irshad's words. "By my beard

and spear, you are so dull before a tournament! Live a little!"

"If I don't get drunk before the tournament, I can live a lot." Irshad shrugged and accepted a cloth bag filled with sweet powdery rolls. He offered one to Jada which she accepted gratefully.

"How many of these tournaments have you both been in?" Jada took a tentative bite of the roll and closed her eyes as the honey-drenched pastry melted on her tongue.

"Too many to count. You're a babe in the woods compared to Irshad and me!" Odin's voice was as loud and boisterous as the street they traveled through.

"Have you ever thought of escaping?" Jada stared at the bag of sweet rolls in Irshad's hand before he passed the bag over to her with a laugh.

"Greedy much?" Irshad dusted off his fingers and shrugged. "When I first got here, I did. However, where would I escape to? There is not a place in a fairy that would not extradite me back to the council, and the trolls are the only fairies that can willfully create fairy rings. They would ask for payment that I couldn't give them."

Jada mulled this over silently as she continued to enjoy her ill-gotten rolls. The trio turned one last corner, and they reached a sign that had a bright fiery orange woman resting in some man's lap. The feathers of her tail are effectively painted as a multi-hued skirt of various reds, yellows, and oranges. It reminded her of Faigen's place, and she suddenly didn't want to go in. However, she loathed ruining what could be that last night for Odin and Irshad due to her squeamishness.

Irshad must have witnessed her discomfort as she leaned in to a whisper. "We don't have to stay, Jada. We can find another more suitable location to drink in."

"What do you mean another place? What's more suitable than a tavern full of bawdy wenches and large cups of ale?" Odin dismissed the idea before Jada could answer and deftly led her through the green swinging doors of the rising Phoenix.

The room that Jada was guided into was filled with drinking, gambling, and more drinking. A spider was just off stage playing several instruments with his long black hairy legs. His free hand tipping his hat to her when their eyes met. On the stage was a tall fairy with translucent pearlescent skin. Her lips were the color of blood, but her voice sounded like that of an angel. Her dark hair twisted and coiled about her form of its own accord as if the strands were beneath water. Everything about the establishment was loud. No matter where Jada looked, something was happening. Odin led her to a table that had been cleared just for them. The moment they sat, large cups of ale materialized in front of them. Jada's eyes almost crossed at the strong sweet scent, and in panic, she looked over at Irshad.

"Eat first, Jada. You don't want to drink anything fairy made on an empty stomach. You won't be fit to lead a prayer, much less your army." Irshad's advice seemed to give her was sound, but it did not stop him from throwing the first cup back as quickly as Odin did.

Odin' finished his drink with a smack of his lips and slamming of the cup on the table. "Don't be shy, Jada; drink up! I'll be on my tenth before you even start on your first!"

"Should you really be drinking that much so quickly? Slow down; we have the whole night." Jada laughed, and her eyes widened at the food that was laid in front of her. She picked up her knife and fork but filled her plate slowly as not to be a hypocrite about the amount of food she was going to inhale.

Buxom servers of all manner of hair colors and sizes started to bring Odin more ale. Each was receiving a lusty kiss for their troubles. "Never lass! I want as much mead as they can bring to this table!

The crowd cheered at his words as Jada looked on nervously. Irshad, however, filled her plate and passed it to her with a laugh. "Don't be too concerned. Odin is famous for being able to drink three times his weight in mead."

"Yes, but will he be able to hold up his weight by the end of the night?" Jada murmured as she watched several cups disappear into his mouth.

Irshad watched Odin sadly for a moment and shook his head. "He'll be fine. He wouldn't want to do anything that would disappoint Yamja after all." "Yamja... the mermaid." Jada blinked and looked at

Odin for a second before turning her attention back to Irshad. "They were close?"

"Were we close? Our love was legendary! For who could love the sea as much as a Viking?" Odin's laugh was boisterous but lacking the joy from earlier. He drank down another cup and wiped away the ale from his lips with the back of his shirt sleeve. His coat having been forgotten long ago. "Now she's gone."

Jada wrestled with telling him the truth, but in the end, decided it was not her secret to keep. He was hurting, and it was her fault. "Well, she's not gone perse. Just not necessarily accessible." Jada coughed and moved the next cup of mead set down before him out of his reach.

"I'm not drunk enough to try to puzzle this out. Irshad makes sense of what she's babbling about." Odin reached for the cup once more, only to have Jada pull it back from him again. Instead, he reached for a giggling barmaid and rained kisses along her shoulder.

Irshad frowned, putting his cup down when he saw how serious Jada looked. His eyes meeting Odin's grief-stricken gaze over her head. "You're saying that Yamja is not dead?"

"She's not dead, but she not mobile." Jada rushed to her explanation at Odin's annoyed scoff, almost wishing she had just said nothing. "There is a grotto on the second floor of the east wing beneath my room. She was turned into a fountain and rests there."

Irshad's mouth opened and closed as he tried to find something to say. He looked back at Odin, who seemed to instantly sober up at her words.

Odin gently set the barmaid down with a quick kiss to the apple of her cheek to remove the sting of his abrupt rejection. His stormy gaze cooling as it rested on Jada."Well, I think I'll turn it in then. That's enough drink to last several lifetimes. Enjoy yourselves this evening."

The giant of a man stood and calmly pushed through the table leaving despite the lament of the crowd around him. His spear at his side as he stiffly disappeared through the swinging doors. Leaving Jada and Irshad to watch him go. They sat in silence for a few moments and quietly finished eating their meal. They thanked the owner of the establishment and made their way out into the night.

"Come on. I'll take you to my favorite place to spend the evening before a tournament. The location is not as loud, but I hope you find it worth it. It reminds me of my home along the Nile, Qustul."

Now that the twin suns had gone down, what had felt like a cool day was now a cold evening. Irshad pulled off his coat and wrapped it loosely around Jada's shoulders as he led her through the city. They made their way into the evening through an area that smelled like fried dough and sugar to a less crowded area that smelled of jasmine and water lilies. As they meandered through the streets, the architecture changed from that of a fishing village to that of sacred temples with Egyptian columns.

There were once rows of wares sold from stalls; there were now lush green hanging gardens.

Firelight lit their way as they moved to a less busy area of the city. The land sloped up at an angle that made Jada feel like she was climbing. Irshad would turn to her and make sure she maintained her balance as they ascended. Once they reached the summit, there was a large ancient tree with two swings that hung from one of its massive branches. Irshad led her to one of the swings. He held out his hand and guided her into the seat before taking the one beside her.

Jada forgot how to breathe as she looked out at the world spread before them. The city was laid out before them like a blanket of stars. Twinkling and glittering in the dark firmament like diamonds cast over black velvet. She could make out some of the buildings, but they were up high enough that she couldn't distinguish one house from another. They sat there in companionable silence for a moment before Jada felt brave enough to ask the question that was weighing on her.

"Do you think that Odin will be okay?" Jada's toe rocked the swing slightly, causing the ropes that held her aloft to twist.

Irshad took a deep breath and shrugged. "I think that he is glad to know that she is still with us, but I don't know how he will react when he sees her."

Jada went silent again for a moment mulling over his words. She pulled his coat about her tighter as a small gust of cold air swept past them. "It's beautiful here. Thank you for showing me this place."

"I am glad to share it with you, but I must admit I have ulterior motives." Irshad pulled his knee up so that his booted foot rested on the swing. He leaned back against the rope so that he could watch Jada's face. "Why are you not using Gabriel's board?" "Irshad, you charmer you." Jada laughed, and this time she lifted her feet to stretch and curl under her to begin swinging.

Irshad quietly laughs and shakes his head. "In another lifetime, I suppose. That doesn't answer my question, though."

"You don't think that we can win?" Jada continued to swing as she tried to find a way to explain the necessity of abandoning Gabriel's merry band of killers.

"That was evasive." Irshad just continued to watch her swing as he patiently waited for an answer. His voice neither lowering in annoyance or lifting in laughter.

"I'm sorry. It wasn't meant to be." Jada slows her swing down with the toe of her shoe and turns in her seat to meet his eyes." If I die I want it to be as myself, and not what Gabriel's board would turn me into."

"You don't want to be a monster then." Irshad's head was canted as if weighing and measuring her words to sift out the truth in them.

Jada's hands wrapped tightly around the ropes of the swing. Her anger of the past three years simmering beneath the surface as it always did. "I know I'm not exactly human any longer, but I want to fight as a human. I don't want to kill anyone else."

"I see." It was Irshad's turn to swing, and it did not escape Jada that he was trying to avoid the rest of the conversation he had started.

"Just say it Irshad." Jada's voice snapped out into the cool air, and when Irshad stopped, his gaze remained out towards the city.

"How do you know you're not already a monster?"

"Gee, thanks!" Jada stood and began to pace indignantly. Her skirt was making the first few steps more of a trial than it should have been.

"You avoid questions beautifully."

"What am I supposed to say to that?" Jada turned towards him, spread her arms helplessly. "I don't think I am? I do know I am nothing like Gabriel's board. Isn't that enough?"

Irshad was quiet as he continued to look out into the city. Jada assumed that he wouldn't answer her, but his low, quiet voice broke the silence once more. "You know, I hadn't expected to live long enough to see this place again. I hadn't expected to live past our first practice session."

"Well, with any luck, we will survive this tournament without becoming monsters." Jada moved back to the swing but didn't sit down, her hands wrapping around the ropes as she laid her cheek on the one to her right.

"Fairies"

"Excuse me?" Jada looked up from her contemplation of the city below in confusion. "Without becoming fairies."

"Well, they are pretty monstrous."

Irshad laughs humorlessly and shakes his head. "No, Jada, to survive the games, you will have to kill. It is the only way you'll become stronger. Each life you take brings you closer to becoming a fairy."

Jada frowns and shakes her head. "So you're saying that we are not humans at all?"

"I am saying that Odin and I are as close as we can get to being a fairy and still retain human sensibilities."

"So, if I want to stay alive, I will have to become a monster."

Irshad pulls his hands distractedly through his long locs. His breath was left his chest in a sharp, frustrated huff of air. " I'm trying to say thank you for being you. Regardless of what you are, or what I will become it is because of you I have this moment."

"You don't think we'll win."

"I don't think it will matter. Winning isn't always winning, Jada. There is a lot we can lose that has nothing to do with our lives." "I will get us home, Irshad."

"Home is very subjective."

"It may be, but it's not negotiable."

Chapter Sixteen

Jada woke up with a deep sense of foreboding. Even Octavius's rhythmic purring wasn't helping her to relax. She wondered if she would miss wardrobe when she had won. If she won. A deliberate shake of her head was made to clear her thoughts. All she could do was focus on today. And it would be a hell of a day. The matches would begin once Silvestri and their board were settled. The council and select members of the nobility would be in attendance. The match for the high council was very secretive. Gabriel as the challenger was responsible for the welfare and general entertainment of everyone who came to the palace. He had spent weeks getting their home ready for the games. Even now she could hear fairies scurrying around outside putting the finishing touches on rooms.

Jada sat up and wrapped her arms around her knees as she pulled them to her chest. There was a good chance that some of them would not be alive by the end of this day. There were so many variables. Her gaze wandered over the room for a moment. She wouldn't see this room for a while. After she helped Gabriel greet the council, she would be staying in the oubliette with Irshad and the rest of the board. The oubliette was a large version of the holding tank that Faigen had. It was filled with the same regenerative crystals that made the healing process faster so that the fighters would be in shape to kill each other some more.

Tossing the covers aside Jada swung her feet from the bed and started getting ready. She took a bath and pinned back her hair. Normally she would be attended by the fairies that she had mentally coined the Bobbsey twins. They were being utilized elsewhere and Jada was not sorry for it. She needed the alone time to get ready for the match. It wasn't going to be like the pits where she only had to worry about getting herself out alive. She had a board full of people to try to save, and the prospect of so much responsibility worried her.

Jada arrived out of the bathroom to see her new armor and Gabriel's sword laying on her bed. She smiled over at Octavius but said nothing. If she did, he would ruin it by spitting something at her. Her eyes wandered over the gold breast and shoulder plates. The grieves were tall enough that they would reach past her knees, but her eyes rolled at the black skirting that would leave her thighs bare.

"It's nice to know that men are men no matter what side of the briars you're on." Jada murmured to herself.

There was a soft knock and one of the Bobbsey twins came in with a smile. "Are you ready to get dressed? I see that my lady has already had her bath."

"Uh sure, let's get this day started!" Jada tried to infuse some enthusiasm into her voice, but the flat look that the fairy gave her said that her effort had been for naught.

The process to get her armor on was quick and unceremonious. Once done the fairy left to attend to other business leaving Jada to wander around the palace until the council got there. She turned to go into her courtyard but stopped short. She hid behind a column and watched as he sat on the edge of the fountain speaking with Yamja.

"There is not a day that goes by that I do not pine for you." The large Viking whispered softly to the stone mermaid. "I will come by each night after the fight. I don't want to miss a chance to say goodbye to you."

Jada's heart twisted at the forlorn tone of his voice. She felt even worse because it was her fault that they were separated. There would never be anything she could do to make amends for it. Silently she edged away from the courtyard to give them back their privacy.

She turned and headed down the next set of stairs that would lead her to the front door. By the level of noise, she knew that it was time to greet the council. Jada stood by the door patiently waiting for Gabriel to show.

"Someone go upstairs and tell Ja..." He saw her by the door and paused in mid-step. His surprise was soon replaced with a smile that was as glorious as the morning they found themselves sharing. Within a few graceful strides he was at her side. Just his very presence eased her nerves and settled her fears. "You're up early, how did you sleep?"

Gabriel placed a sweet if distracted kiss on her temple and looked around with satisfaction. With a nod, the wooden nymphs that were both functional tree and door swung open to a scene that was straight out of a fairytale. Each member of the council was pulled by their own clockwork chariot laden with colorful bags. Every council member wore a blue pants, billowy white shirts, and their customary pins. The soft clop of hooves ended as they reached the door. One by one the council came out along with a personal assistant who was left to see about the luggage. A small fleet of dandelion-looking servants skittered out to bring in various bits of luggage. Jada and Gabriel stepped back to give them a wide berth as they walked into the palace with their leaves full. The occasion had the feel of children being dropped off at an expensive boarding school.

Silvestri's carriage was followed by her board. They looked normal enough right now, but like the other boards, their appearance would change once they got onto the field.

Gabriel turned to Jada and dropped his voice in a conspiratorial whisper. His hands rested lightly on her shoulders as he leaned in. "I'm sorry that I will not get to have breakfast with you. I hope that the feast that I have prepared for you and the others in the oubliette will make up for it."

"Hurry up and get my luggage into this hovel! The sooner I win this tournament the sooner I can get home and wash the stench of failure away." Silvestri's high-pitched voice shouted at her servants.

Gabriel cringed and closed his eyes with a shake of his head. "Truth be told, I'd rather be with you."

Trine and Trinity had ridden with her. They continued their pattern of wearing the same but alternating colors. This time they wore suits of blue and mustard yellow. Trinity laughed and shook his head. "It will be over soon High council Silvestri."

Gabriel's kept his eyes studiously on Jada's until Silvestri finished shouting. Jada chuckled at the quick roll of his pale gold eyes. At the sound of her laugh, the side of his lip quirked, and he shook his head.

"I see that you are not going to be any help this morning."

"Absolutely none." Jada laughed and leaned over to look out the door. "Here she comes."

Gabriel fixed his face and turned around to greet Silvestri with a smile. To look at them you wouldn't know that they loathed each other. Their bright politician-like smiles on full display as they greeted each other with two quick kisses on the cheek.

Silvestri gave a friendly squeeze to his hands. "Gabriel darling, wonderful to see you. I see that you even brought your pet! Does she plan on doing any tricks? There's not a pole, but I'm sure she's used to making do"

"I'd rather do tricks than be one." Jada mumbled under breath, but not too low that the evil fairy couldn't hear her.

"I beg your pardon?" Silvestri's violet eyes widened in shock, and her mouth opened and closed a few times at Jada's audacity. "Gabriel, are you going to just stand there, and let her speak to me that way?"

"Not at all" Gabriel made his face stern despite the struggle he was having to keep his smile down. "Jada as punishment you will not be allowed to have breakfast with us."

Silvestri smiled sweetly at Jada at her small victory with a lift of her brow and followed the large dandelions that waited for her at the door. Nero strode in and bowed to them both. He was wearing a white dress shirt and simple black pants. Jada guessed he only wore his bdsm outfits when Silvestri made social calls.

"Councilman Gabriel, Silvestri's board and myself are honored to be here." He turned to Jada and took her hand placing a polite kiss on the back. "Lady Jada, I look forward to meeting you on the field of battle."

Jada bowed her head in thanks. "Yeah, I wish we could have met under different circumstances. But good luck, I guess."

Nero smiled and turned to follow Silvestri, and Jada gave a sad but deep sigh. Gabriel watched her for a few moments, and before discreetly taking her hand and holding it behind his back. The next councilman was Barron. The attractive man looked just as severe as he did when Jada first saw him. Now that he was standing, he was outright imposing. The beautiful black spirals of his hair had Jada slightly in her feelings about them. She nodded deeply from her place at Gabriel's side. Barron ignored her and focused on Gabriel.

"Gabriel, I see that you have everything ready and well in hand." Barron's thunderous voice seemed to echo around the airy foyer.

"Thank you, Barron, if you follow the flower sprites, they will show you to your quarters.

Barron nodded and walked by without looking back or saying anything to Jada. She looked over at Gabriel out of the corner of her eye, and he just laughed and shrugged.

"As far as he is concerned you are just a servant. Of course, if you were to say yes to marrying me, he would have to acknowledge you as my wife." He smiled and held up his hands at the way Jada's eyes narrowed. "I'm just putting it out there."

Jada rolled her eyes and focused on the next councilman. It was the Grimali the one who had abandoned Devanshi over the briars. She tried to keep the frown from her face, but it was difficult. There wasn't any love on either side between Devanshi and her, but it was horrid to abandon a woman in dangerous situation.

"Council Grimali welcome. I trust your ride was comfortable. " Though Gabriel's voice was polite, it had dropped several degrees as he shook the man's hand.

"It was comfortable enough. It would have been more comfortable had you put Devanshi and me in the same carriage." Grimali pouted but walked in with a faint look of surprise. "I say, it's nicer here than I thought it would be."

Jada turned to say something to the arrogant fairy, but the soft squeeze of Gabriel's hand kept her firmly and quietly by his side. She could deal with them snubbing her, but there was something about them being rude to Gabriel that made Jada see red.

"I don't like your friends." Jada murmured quietly.

"We're not all bad, Grimali is just one of the worst." A soft musical voice had Jada dropping her gaze to the short woman standing by Gabriel's side. She too had a slight look of disgust as she watched Grimali walk away. "I'm Ezuli. It is a pleasure to meet you. I have heard so much about you."

"Was any of it good?" Jada gave the woman a tentative smile. Ezuli was the first of the fairies that came close to what she pictured when she thought of a fairy. She smelled of the sky just before it rained and sugar. Her large delicate moth like wings cheerly fanned out behind her.

"Not at all. None of it. " Ezuli laughed at Jada's crestfallen expression and released Gabriel's hands to take hers. "It's how I knew I would like you. Gabriel, your home is beautiful. Thank you for hosting us."

"As always, it's my pleasure, Ezuli. Please the sprites will take you to your room. Once you are settled in, breakfast will be waiting for you." Gabriel smiled and watched the dandelions take her away.

"She seems nice." Jada said once she was out of earshot.

"Yes, she is, but we are on very different sides of the fairy political spectrum I'm afraid." Gabriel shrugged as if he truly regretted the truth of that statement. "She wants to abolish the games."

Jada watched him for a few minutes and frowned. "Why would that be bad? Who wouldn't want to abolish such a barbaric practice?"

"Really Gabriel, that human is getting far too out of line. You should give her to Trine and Trinity. They would whip her into shape in no time." Jada didn't have to turn around to recognize Devanshi's voice. "We keep the games little human because if not for the games there would be an all-out war in Fairy. The centuries before the games were a time of bloodshed and horror. The game gives us order."

Gabriel placed two quick kisses on Devanshi's cheeks that she returned with a flourish. "Gabriel, everything looks beautiful!"

"Thank you Devanshi, as always you have my devotion and affection for all the work you do on the council." Gabriel bowed and handed her off to the dandelion sprites that waited with her bags.

He looked over at Jada with an amused smile. "Don't be jealous. I love you more than life itself."

"Thanks for that, and I'm not at all jealous. Just send my wedding invite over the briars. I'll work hard not to be there." Jada made a show of smoothing out the nonexistent wrinkles in armor. "What did she mean the centuries before the games?"

"Fairy has always been both beautiful and dangerous. It was once fraught with wars, and fairies died every day. After so much bloodshed the seven kingdoms came up with this method of keeping the peace."

"Are all the kingdoms represented here?" Jada asked curiously as they waited for the next councilman.

"Not any longer. Dims losing his seat to me leaves one out. The kingdom of Kanari." Gabriel frowned and looked out the door to see what was taking the councilman so long.

"How many represent your kingdom?"

"I am the first in four hundred years to represent the Kingdom of Astryd. Without a member on the council, a kingdom suffers greatly." Gabriel's eyes contracted in some memory he did not share. Jada watched him pull his smile back on and settle in a place like a mask.

"It is the way of things. Councilman Kionah. Welcome to my home."

"Thank you. I am sorry I took so long. The wind was telling me that there will be a large storm soon." Kionah looked over at Jada with a smile and wink that had her brushing back an errant curl behind her ear.

"Not a problem at all and thank you for the warning. I will tell everyone to prepare for it." It was Gabriel's turn to side-eye Jada.

"Good luck Jada, I hope you do well in the games." Kionah walked away leaving the scent of burning wood and suede behind him.

"Thank you." Jada watched the man walk away and missed the slight cough that Gabriel made to get her attention.

"So, you have a type." With a long-suffering sigh, Gabriel gently took her arm and guided her towards the oubliette where she would get ready with the rest of the board. Leaving the other fairies to take care of clearing everything away.

"Wait what?" Jada turned around to look at him with her brows raised in indignation. "I don't know what you're implying, but I have absolutely no idea what you're talking about!"

"Yeah okay, "Thank you" Gabriel's voice went up several octaves to mimic her voice. He tucked one of his curls behind his ear and fluttering his thick lashes as he imitated her. Guiding her gently through the doors that would take them to the oubliette. "Spare me the indignation."

"If you mean gentlemanly and polite. Sure okay, That's just my type." Jada defended herself in indignation. It was what had drawn Jada to him once upon a time.

Gabriel's brow lifted as he leaned his head to the side, his snake-like gaze studying her in amusement. "Oh, is that what that mongrel is?"

"His name is Irshad, and what's wrong? Jealous?"

"Immensely." Gabriel nodded and shrugged unapologetically. "I have and do not make any secret about how I want your time all to myself."

Jada dropped her eyes from his silently. He was telling her his truth, and like all the other declarations of love, she had no idea of what to do with them. If she was honest with herself, she begrudged the way he was so sure of his feelings when it came to her. She was always in a state of confusion about what she felt for him. The air was still pleasant, but the temperature dropped considerably as they made their way down to meet the others.

Since she had no answer for his declaration, she opted to ignore it, and changed the subject. "Did you build the oubliette, or did it come with the castle?"

Gabriel allowed her to change the subject as he laced his fingers through hers. "It came with the palace actually. This villa is well over four hundred years old."

"The last time someone from your kingdom held a council seat," Jada said grimly as the corridors took them deeper underground. The walls had started to glow light blue amidst the firelight. Soon the torches disappeared as the crystals got larger. The light blue glow of the walls leading them to the oubliette.

"Jada, I don't take what you and the board are about to do lightly. I know that what I am asking you to do is both dangerous and traumatic. However, know that I am not having you do anything that I did not have to do to get here." Gabriel released her as he brought her into a large open area surrounded by large blue crystals.

The other members of the board were gathered at a large table filled with unimaginable amounts of food. Jada's eyes went wide at the overflowing table. Irshad and Odin laughed at one end of the table, and the other pieces talked amongst themselves. Minus the lone basilisk that came from Gabriel's board. He was off to the side eating quietly. He was one of the few pieces that did not have an army. He was his own army.

"I will see you out there then." Jada dropped his arm and began walking towards the table. Only to be pulled back into Gabriel's arms in a deep hug. His head dropped into the crook of her neck, and the long strands of his hair tickled her skin. "Gabriel! Everyone is watching!"

"Let them. I also don't make any secret about the fact that you belong to me." Gabriel continued to hold her as he spoke into her neck. Jada was about to snap at him but remembered what would come after the feast. He was trying to say goodbye.

"Don't worry. I'm sure everyone knows. You say it repeatedly and loud enough." Jada patted his arm consolingly with a laugh. "I'm sure there is not a fairy, wardrobe, firefly, popsicle, or beta fish for a hundred miles that doesn't know who I "belong" to."

"But do you know?" The soft hiss of his voice was made in frustration as he released her. "Go to your board. Fight well, I will see you after the match.

Jada watched him go with something akin to regret before turning to the board that was silently watching her. She smiled at them nervously and sat down next to the Basilisk. "Did he put out enough food?"

Valkari smiled and shook her head in amazement at

all the food. "As far as boards go, I feel spoiled right now!"

Princeton handed Jada a plate that was as piled high as his. "My love, you shouldn't feel anything. He isn't feeding us. He's feeding hot stuff over here!"

Princeton smiled and winked over at Jada as he began to eat what looked to be his third plate. Jada just marveled at how someone so thin could put away so much.

"Prince! Filter!" Valkari hissed beneath her smile. " Well, at least she's willing to share her spoils with the rest of us!"

Princeton narrowed his eyes at Valkari, before throwing a grape at Jada which she caught and took a bite out of. Valkari laughed and Princeton blinked in surprise. "Man!"

Jada laughed and turned to the basilisk and held out her hand. "I'm Jada, as I'm sure you know. You're from Gabriel's board. What's your name?"

The basilisk had green eyes that watched her for a minute. His hand rubbed across his bald head uncomfortably. He didn't seem like he was used to being addressed like a person. Or at least he hadn't been addressed like one in a long time. "Jonas."

"A pleasure, umm have you had to battle anyone on Silvestri's board before?" Jada asked another question before he could go back into his shell. She didn't want him or anyone else going out there and feeling undervalued.

"Noah, he is the werewolf. His army is very strong." Jonas' voice was low and scratchy. It was as if he didn't remember how to use it.

Princeton nodded picking up the conversation. "Yeah, he's kind of a jerk, but to be fair he was made that way. Word on the street is that Silvestri doesn't treat her pieces very well."

"She doesn't, I was on her board before she became high council. She lost a duel to Dima, so had to give me up. She does horrible things to the pieces that fail her." The knight Tomas shook out his dark brown hair as he spoke. The tip of his ears pointed like Irshad's and Odin's. He was almost a fairy as well.

"Oh, that makes sense you're attrac..." Jada closed her mouth and stuck some cake in it. "You're an awesome Bishop."

Tomas laughed and nodded his head. "Thank you, Silvestri is known for having the most attractive board in seven kingdoms."

"Yeah, it was why she was after Princeton. She was trying to complete her collection." Valkari gave an annoyed roll of her eyes, and Princeton nudged her playfully. Jada could see that Valkari had very strong feelings about the situation.

"Can you be mad at her for having good taste!' Princeton brushed his shoulder off and popped the collar of his shirt. " It's not easy being pretty."

The table laughed as they continued to eat the feast Gabriel had laid out. No one was shy or reticent about trying everything that was on the table. They wanted to leave the room with no regrets.

"What do you plan on wishing for if you win." Odin asked as the feast started to whine down. He watched her intently waiting for something that Jada could only guess at.

"I plan on wishing everyone who wants to go, back home." Jada shrugged, unsure how to proceed. Odin seemed to be searching for something and didn't seem to be finding it.

"How noble." Odin picked up a green apple and a knife from the table. His booted feet lifted to drop onto the table and leaned back. "So, you are going to skip the chance to be with your murdering fairy lover to set all of us free."

"Yes, because it's what I want also. " Jada's eyes met the grey blue of his steadily. She wasn't sure what made him so unsure suddenly, but all she could do was prove it to him. "When we win, I will use the wish to take us back home."

Odin cut into his apple and crunched down into the slice. Chewing slowly then bringing his attention back to Jada with a shrug. "I guess we'll see won't we."

Chapter Seventeen

Trine stood in the center of the board. He had dressed for the occasion in a bright Magenta and yellow suit. The sunny ruffles at his wrist swayed in the cool breeze. It was a beautiful day. One better suited to road trips with friends or days at the beach with your family. It was not a day that she would have chosen to have a battle to the death, but she was not in charge. They were. Jada looked towards the palace where the assembly was gathered. The dais from which Gabriel and the council watched was filled with fairy nobility. There were platforms along the cliffside with tables laden with hors-d'œuvre and alcohol. Some even dipped their spoons into a sparkly white substance that Jada assumed was fairy dust. It was a social gathering that none of the working-class fairies had been invited to. They went about their lives with no knowledge of the horrors that were performed to keep their kingdom peaceful.

Jada took a deep breath and looked out on to the feel. Something flashed into view just outside of her peripheral vision. She turned bringing up Gabriel's sword, and the figure caught her arm before she swung. Her breath caught in her throat until she realized that it was Gabriel standing before with a large smile. "I could have killed you."

"Have I told you how much I love your confidence? It's adorable!" Gabriel laughed and took her hands in his. The evil fairy leaned down to rest his forehead against hers. "I'm just here to wish you luck. Though if you had used my board, you wouldn't need it."

"I'm not about to argue with you Gabriel. Your board is filled with psychopaths." Jada snapped and turned her attention back towards the field. She glanced Irshad who was watching her in concern, and Odin who rolled his eyes before looking out at the other team. His demeanor towards her had done a complete about turn, and she wasn't sure what to do about it."

"Here, those are called winners Jada. Gabriel sighed and looked out at the board across from them. He held up his hand in acquiescence and stepped back. "You're right. I don't want to argue with you. Just..." He pulled her forward and gave Jada a quick peck on her lips before releasing her. "Stay alive. You promised to kill me after all. "

Jada brushed her lips with the tips of her fingers with irritation and brought her attention to her most immediate problem. Once the twin suns met, she would be at war with Nero. Another place she did not want to be. Everyone was as ready as they could be, but it was no longer about practice it would be about who had the better team. She glanced over at Odin's stoic face. He no longer trusted her, and she wasn't sure what had happened between last night, and this morning to cause the rift. He was looking straight across at the mask wearing Nero, the king of Silvestri's board. Her eyes widened slightly as she met the bright blue of Nero's. He was focused on her, and his attention only shifted when Trine appeared on the board. The sky on Jada's side of the board started to darken. It was almost time, and Trine held up his hands.

"Welcome to the high council seat tournament. The winner of this tournament will decide who will hold the high council seat for the next seven years." Trine had to stop speaking amidst the cheers of the gathered nobility. Once the crowd died down, he smiled revealing rows of jagged teeth and continued. "The winner will be determined by the board who wins the best out of seven matches. One for each kingdom."

Both Nero and Jada approached the middle of the board. He played the role of a king on his board but would be leading the match. Jada thought the queen would be leading the match for Gabriel's board. They reached Trine and stopped. They faced each other, and Jada had to arch her neck to look Nero in the eyes.

Jada shrugged helplessly, unsure of what to say. What did condemned souls say to other condemned souls? "Well, I can't wish you luck, but I sincerely hope you survive."

Nero smiled took her hand in his, and Jada assumed they were about to shake on it. However, Nero pulled her forward into a deep kiss. The crowd cheered as his wings wrapped about her. Jada was surprised for the first two seconds but quickly pulled away.

"So, consent has never been a thing here in the world of fairy huh?" Jada angrily sputtered, and nervously looked over her shoulder in Gabriel's direction and back at Nero. "Are you trying to get yourself killed?"

"Yes." Jada's lips parted in surprise at Nero's unexpected affirmative. Seeing that she was bereft of witty comebacks he lifted his clawed fingers to gently tuck an errant coil behind her ear.

Jada turned sharply and pinched the bridge of her nose as she moved back to her square. Stars began to appear overhead, and Jada took a deep breath readying herself for the game. Jada glanced at the dais one last time. She found it hard not to resent how well-rested both Gabriel and Silvestri looked. Them and their sadistic audience had time for frivolity, but Jada did not. They had a match to win and focusing on how unfair the world was would do nothing but get her or her friends killed.

"The loser of this tournament will die along with their board." Trine made the announcement of pending death with relish. The appearance of the pieces changed to match their fighting avatar the closer the suns came to being one. Trine turned to the dais to address the council. High council Silvestri are you ready?"

"Yes, let's get this farce over with." Silvestri turned her attention away from the board to dip her own spoon into the sparkling mound of fairy dust.

Trine moved his attention to Gabriel. "Councilman Gabriel. Are you ready?"

"More than." Gabriel lifted his glass from his place beside Devanshi. A picture of serenity and peace. If he was nervous, he didn't show it.

"Then I Inquisitor Trine proclaim the games open.

When the twin suns come together the match will start. May the best fairy win!" Trine backflipped out of site and there was thunderous applause.

There was palpable excitement amongst all of the players. Even those of Gabriel's board seem to come alive once the match was declared open. Jada frowned and shook her head. Her plan was to get them all back safely over the briars. However, from the look on Nero's face, she might have to settle for most of her board. The suns hit their zenith plunging Jada's side of the board in the artificial night. The game had officially begun. There was a very real chance she could die today. The protections only kept them safe outside of the games. On the field of battle, no life was sacred. She cleared her head to focus on the game. She had bigger problems than Nero's death wish, and it was the welfare of her team.

The sky was set aflame as the suns conjoined and

Nero turned to a pawn on his board. "Pawn to E4."

At the command of his voice, a large gray spider with long black hair and the torso of a man made his way to the designated square. Once all six of his hairy brown legs carried him to a stop he looked up at the sky, and Jada looked over as well. Immediately her skin began to crawl at the army that the spider man called forth spiders the size of Pomeranians parachuted from the sky. There were so many that they blotted out the sun until they all landed around their ruler. The spider man spread his arms out as if presenting his children for show. His smile revealed black teeth and pincers that seemed to clap in anticipation of the fight to come.

"Jonas to E6 please." Jada ignored her misgivings; there was no more time to have any.

Jonas smiled in amusement at politely being asked to move to a square. He began to walk toward his square causing the fields to quake. With each step he took, he became larger, and his body stretched out until he slithered across the ground. The basilisk that Jonas turned into no longer looked like the Jonas that had eaten with them. He took up almost half his field. His emerald skin glinted in the fire of the suns. The serpent that used to be Jonas opened his jaws and released a loud angry hiss.

"Pawn to E5." This time, Nero's command was directed to a large silver and sunny yellow bird that took to the sky. Lightning began to strike the ground as the large bird flew to its square. The flap of his wings caused two of its feathers to fall from its plumage. The wings never landed though. The feathers soon turned into birds that filled the air with the sound of thunder. They landed in a triangular formation on the field. Casting baleful looks at Gabriel's board.

Jada took a deep breath. She knew she could do this. "Irshad to C6, if you please."

Irshad bowed, and his jackal-like features were soon covered by the helmet he pulled on. He lifted and waved his staff forward. An eerie laugh broke the silence followed by another. The hyenas slowly peeled from the darkness around them. They started off in a quick lope that soon turned into an all-out run. Irshad took a step and disappeared only to reappear in the correct square. The hyenas snarled and laughed at the other board, their backs arched and bristled in barely restrained rage.

"Bishop to C4" Nero called forth an army of Goblins. They marched out onto the field in a controlled square column. The green eight-foot-tall monster's faces were streaked with what looked like ash. Their torso was left bare and streaked with the ash that covered their faces. They chanted something in a language that Jada didn't know, but the sound was no less terrible for its secrecy. They were wearing pelts around their loins that didn't look entirely made of animal furs.

Jada recoiled in disgust and turned her attention back to her board to keep from retching. " Princeton, may I ask you to go to F6."

Princeton gave her an amused salute before tugging on the black tailed tuxedo jacket that ended at the back of his thighs. He blew a kiss to Valkari and pulled out his flute. He began to play a short scale, and four ghostly figures rose from the ground. As he walked four figures with white skulls that protruded from their grey skin pulled out various string instruments. The spectral foursome followed him to F6, and Princeton pulled his

313

flute away from his lips; he stretched the instrument until it became a conductor's wand.

He turned to the string quartet with the most serious look Jada had ever seen on his face. "If you would be so kind as to turn to Vivaldi's Juditha Triumphs. We have some people to murder."

Nero's ever-present smile widened as he watched the moves, she was making on the board. He looks over at another piece and waves his hand forward. "Knight to G5."

The small trio of thunderbirds lifted into the sky in a blur of silver and yellow. Lightning arced across the clouds. Jada frowned as their flight took them to the requested square. It put them in direct opposition of red and white armored Arthur.

"Asane to D5 please and thanks! " Jada refused to dehumanize Gabriel's pieces. They had names and they mattered. They would never be broken and forgotten like useless toys.

Red tattooed fingers lifted to part a mass of curly dark hair from large amber eyes. She blinked slowly looking left then right before she smiled with a broken grin. Bare feet the color of cinnamon slowly stepped forward. The white shrouds she wore swayed in the cool wind that wrapped around them. As Asane moved, a large snowy owl settled on her shoulder. Fingertips that looked as if they had been dipped in brick dust brushed along the owl's feathers. She quietly peered at the owl and the wind began to pick up from the gentle breeze from moments earlier. Suddenly white crystalline strings unfurled around her. The breeze picked up as thousands of owls came and lifted Asane from the ground by the strings. They flew her over to her field and landed around her.

Jada watched the cloud of owls take Asane to her square, and not for the first time she wondered how everyone's army got to be so large. she would have to discuss it with Irshad later. For now, she would focus on the business that was keeping her alive.

"Pawn... I'll call you Arachnan. If you would make the owls in D5 feel more welcomed." Nero bows and waves his hand forward.

The spider man laughed and curtsied daintily mocking Jada and her board. Arachnan's pincers spread wide, and a blast of gooey webbing spewed from his lips. Once the webbing landed in the square with Asane the multitude of spiders ran around his form and skitter across the sticky bridge.

"Parlimentos" Asane screams and with a resounding screech, the owls arch into the sky and dive towards the bridge. The moment the arachnids land on the square the owls begin to pick them off. Another set of owls swoop in to sever the sticky bridge.

In turn, the spiders spew their webbing using the strands to parachute to the ground where they are met with another round of snowy owls. The spiders seemed to chatter amongst each other as began to construct a large web made on the backs of spiders that remained in stationary pillars on the ground. Owls who could not maneuver fast enough were caught and devoured. Other owls would catch the spiders and throw them into the webs. The spiders would cannibalize their army thinking it was the owls they had caught.

The field they fought in was a mix of feathers and webbing. Asane was so caught up in the maneuvers of her familiars she barely missed being stabbed by Arachnan's dagger-like legs. Asane rolled and produced an crepe myrtle can that she spun between her hands. Asane began blocking Arachnan's attacks. The owl that had lifted from her shoulder screeched and flew into the spider king's face to gouge out three of his eyes. Arachnan knocked the bird away in a screech of pain.

Asane looked back at her owls and saw that they were losing the fight. Silvester had ages for her pieces to amass their armies. The owls were holding them off, but they were not able to attack. They would get tired soon, and they would lose the fight. Asane lifted her staff, and the wind picked up once more. The owl that had been resting on her shoulder screeched in alarm, and all of the owls begin to fly back to her. Another whisper of wind and she and the owls were gone.

The fairies cheered and boo'ed at the first sign of bloodshed and the subsequent departure of Asane. Jada's teeth ground in anger at the glee the fairies took in their pain. She was glad that Asane left the fight instead of trying to finish it. Jada grimly came to terms with the fact that if she wanted to keep her team safe, she would have to kill Silvestri's. They had shown that they had no problem killing hers. Jada watched the spiders crawl over Arachnan to create an webbed eye patch for the eyes he lost. A night in the oubliette and the spider would be fine, and ready to kill another of her pieces. Jada wasn't going to give him the chance.

"Irshad, D5 please." Jada ignored the smile on Nero's face. She would not get drawn into a tit for tat with him, but she would protect her board.

The hyena's muscles bunch and trigger beneath their brown and black spotted coats. The desire for bloodshed was so at odds with the man who led them. Irshad lifted his staff and with a laughing bark the first wave hyenas take off into a dead run towards Arachnan and his spider army. The hyenas run and leap over both the owl and spider carcasses that littered the ground. Their creepy laughter turned into a yelp by those who ran into the large web that the spiders had erected before.

The hyenas that followed used their fallen comrades to crawl on top of and scale the webbed wall. Jumping from the backs of captured hyenas and the backs of the spiders that were eating them until they were able to land on the other side of the wall. Soon the gossamer wall fell apart amidst the barking laughs of the Hyenas. The legion of blood-thirsty quadrupeds moved forward. The spiders spewed more webbing to try to catch as many of the hyenas as they could, but the sheer number of them kept them on the defensive much like they had done the owls. They began rending the spiders that held to the wall to pieces.

Irshad and the rest of his army surged forward once the webbed wall had come down. The spiders began to retreat in a mass of hairy black legs and terrified squeaks. Arachnan reared back on his hind legs to prepare to engage Irshad in hand-to-hand combat. Arachnan watched in rage as the hyenas began tearing apart and tossing spiders aside to clear a safe path for Irshad to travel through. Once the way had been cleared the overzealous hyenas caught hold of Archnan's legs and began to rip them from his haunches. The bark of shaky laughter from the hyenas as Arachnan tried to use what was left of his opposing legs to get away made Jada frown in concern. Irshad's army was so unlike him.

Irshad watched for a moment and took a running leap into the air. As he came down his staff landed in what was left of Arachnan's eyes to put him out of his misery. The large spider flailed before whatever life he still had dissipated completely. The spiders screamed in anguish and began to fall over in a dramatic ripple of lost life. Irshad stood surveying the toll the battle took on his army, and suddenly dropped to one knee on the ground. A golden glow washed over him, and Jada could only look on in frantic confusion. Irshad's chest heavily rose and fell until the glow faded and he was able to stand once more.

Nero had the first frown on his face that Jada had seen since the first night they met each other. Though the scowl was one of contemplation it seemed to remind him that Gabriel's board was no joke. The majority of Gabriel's team had been on a winning board. He would have to take them seriously. The loss of Arachnan however did not seem to cause him any exceptional grief. The melody of his deep voice was almost bored as he gave the next command. "Pawn to F7."

The thunderous birds lifted from the ground and lightning began to strike the ground around Arthur. She was on the night side of the board, so she was not going to be as powerful as she would have been had she been playing on the day side. Nevertheless, Arthur held up her red and white shield, and the griffin that was etched on the front began to glow. Hundreds of griffins flew out of the shield to stand in front of her. The proud chimera-like beast roaring through their beaks at the massive birds flew towards their leader. The nobility was screaming themselves hoarse with adulation, and Jada assumed Arthur was a crowd favorite.

The cascades of lightning narrowly missed striking Arthur as her army of griffins took flight. They met in the sky in a collision of fur and feathers. The thunderbirds would catch the griffins in their vise-like beaks and break their backs before tossing them aside. The griffins overwhelmed the last bird and the silvery and yellow plumage soon disappeared amidst a pile of angry cryptids. The other birds screeched at the loss of their fallen comrade. The lightning began to come down in earnest around the griffins. The first and presumably the strongest of the thunderbirds took off towards the white knight, while the other began keeping the griffins busy. Sending a rain of lightning on the griffins who were tearing the fallen bird apart.

Arthur had been kneeling on the ground praying. When the lightning struck directly in front of her, she rose and unsheathed her sword. To Arthur's credit, she stood tall and strong against the onslaught of lightning. She neither flinched nor coward at the strikes being made around her. She summoned a horse from her shield and mounted the black stallion before taking off towards the thunderbird. She met the bird head-on and began swinging her sword as if fighting a dragon. Arthur landed a strike over the bird's beak, and the monster pulled back to take flight with an angry squawk. Once in the air it turned and dove towards Arthur. Her horse reared back in an attempt to kick the bird but knocked Arthur off instead. The knight rolled losing her helmet and lifted her shield to prevent being fried by a vengeful bolt of lightning.

The other bird was barely keeping its beak above water. The swarm of griffins were tearing out its feathers. It was keeping itself alive but was unable to aid in the attack against Arthur. However, the griffins found themselves in the same position. They were able to keep the bird from aiding its brother but were not able to help Arthur in her fight. By the end of the match, the griffins that were left stood snarling at the bloodied but alive thunderbird. Arthur stood as her long chestnut hair whipped about her shoulders with the gale of wind produced by the thunderbird's wings. She fought the bird to a standstill, and the thunderbirds took the square with a tired, but victorious call.

The knight had just left the field when Jada began to give the next order when Odin's voice rang out before hers "King to F7" Odin emphasized the word king.

Jada almost gave herself whiplash at the audacity of the storm bringer. The air began to fill with the call of crows as the feathered beast poured from the tattoos on Odin's chest. The crows began to fly around the thunderbirds in a dense circle that made the birds draw closer and lash out with strikes of lightning. He was on the night side of the board, and his power rose twofold. Odin jumped into the air and landed in a graceful crouch in front of the thunderbirds. His tall frame unfolded from the ground, and he moved with the grace of someone who knew they were going to win. His spear appeared in his hands, and he calmly sauntered over to the bird that was still tired from its last match.

The thunderbird must have thought their chances of winning were low as well. They retreated from the field in a flurry of feathers and bolts of lightning.

Nero's frown had been replaced with gales of laughter. Odin had embarrassed her and everyone on the field knew it. Jada shook with fury, but the move had already been made. the brittle calls of the crows grated along with her already ragged nerves. Odin would have won that fight, but at what cost to the bored?

As if Nero read her mind, he turned and bows to the raven-haired queen at his side. "Queen to F3"

The queen curtsied and the woman turned her dark hollow eyes towards her location. The sheer white gown was a sobering reminder that the world of fairy cared very little about what they put their pieces through. Every time she moved the gauzy gown would shift from being see-through to being opaque. She silently moved across the field without calling an army. Her red lips curling into a cruel smile as she faced Odin.

"Check." Nero's voice was smug, but then again, he had a right to be. One of Jada's own pieces made it possible for her to lose this match.

"Odin to G8!" Odin had taken a step towards the queen, but Jada's command had him angrily looking over his shoulder at her. There had been no trace of request in

Jada's voice as she snapped at Odin. Her rage was a living breathing entity beneath her skin.

Odin glared and looked for all the world as a pouty child as he moved as Jada bid. "By my beard, if you didn't have Gabriel's cock wrapped around your fingers..."

"You'd be dead. Do as you're told." Jada pointedly turns her attention from Odin to focus on the board.

She ignored the grim look on Irshad's face as well. They would discuss it after the match was over. Or not, she was not exactly inclined to be conciliatory right at that moment. For now, she would castle Odin for his own good. Nero had sacrificed his knight for a reason, and now she could see that he was just trying to make way for his queen.

Nero looked mildly disappointed that he would be denied the chance to kill her king but went back to the business of playing. "Bishop to D5."

At the sound of a horn, the goblins began running towards Irshad's square. They were met with teeth and claws of thousands of hyenas. His army had grown even larger since the last time Irshad had called them. Irshad took his time meeting the leader of the Goblins that invaded his field. He was almost lazy in his assurance of besting the goblins that came toward him

If only to herself Jada admitted that she preferred the way Gabriel moved. It was graceful and methodical. Every movement was meant to convey or provoke a different reaction. However, there was something to be said about Irshad's fluid savagery. The way his muscles moved like liquid beneath his skin as he swung his staff. It seemed as if he was almost dancing through the goblins that threw themselves at him to keep their leader safe.

The hyenas looked like ants crawling and ripping goblins apart limb from limb. At one-point Irshad was just walking through the carnage as he made his way to the goblin leader. When the bishop and the knight met the fight was brutal and frightening. There was so much blood Jada wasn't sure who belonged to who.

The goblin would slice into Irshad's arm, and in turn, Irshad would swing his staff into the goblin's jaw, dislocating it from its sockets. The goblin was strong, but he was clearly not a trained fighter. Irshad turned around and hit the goblin's arm with so much force the bone broke leaving the arm to hang like uselessly swing at its side.

"Goblins to the oubliette. We call this match and take the square." Nero watched in annoyance as both Irshad, and the goblin left the field. His cold gaze followed the goblin until it disappeared cradling its damaged arm. Jada did not want to be the goblin when Nero got back to the oubliette. A large Manticore traded places with the bishop. "We request the use of an alternative."

"Queen to D5." Jada moved to the field that Irshad had just vacated to meet the snarling manticore. The beast simultaneously snarled and hissed at her presence. Jada lifted Gabriel's sword as the manticore's human-like face stretched into a hateful smile.

"I will savor every bit of the flesh I lick away from your bones." The manticore's gravelly voice purred as his scorpion tail wagged in excitement.

"I'm honored." Jada's flat tone of Jada's voice underscored what the roll of her eyes could not say aloud. She waited for the Manticore to make the first move.

They both began to move in a slow circle waiting to see which would make the first move. The Manticore didn't need an army, he was almost as strong as her entire army by himself. The manticore's tail struck, and Jada barely missed being impaled by the scorpion tail. She swung at the tail in retaliation, and nothing happened. Her sword bounced off the exoskeleton on his tail with a force that made her awkwardly stumble back.

"You should be. Not everyone has the honor of being sustenance for one as glorious as I." The manticore snarled at her and reared back. His tail swinging at her once more as poison oozed from the tip.

The manticore struck out at Jada with a claw that she barely blocked. He swiped again and missed, but the back of his paw caught her and knocked her across the field. Her body skidding and bounced over the ground. Jada shook out her head, trying to clear, and felt her bruised ribs scream in protest as she got her bearings. The manticore leaped, and Jada rolled out just in time to keep from being stabbed with his tail. Jada rolled across the ground in a full dodge, only to bring up Gabriel's sword as the manticore struck out at her with his paw.

Her skeletons would try to make create barriers between her and the angry monster, but to no avail. The manticore continued to strike out at her with his claws and tail. The skeletons ran over to fight the manticore off. Jada pulled herself up and wasn't sure if the sound that she heard was the roar of the crowd or the ringing in her ears. The manticore knocked away the skeleton and ran for her at full speed. Jada caught his mane and pulled herself onto his back. She spun wards and sliced off his tail where luxurious fur met his scales.

"My tail, my beautiful tail. I will kill you!" The manticore's human-like scream made her blood run cold. He jumped, knocking Jada off his back and dislodged the sword from her hands. The skeletons gathered around Jada as the manticore rolled angrily around on the ground. His venomous tail flopping uselessly beside him. The manticore lifted himself onto his haunches, his body seething with rage. "After I have killed you, I will leave your body to the crows!"

The ground beneath them shook with the manticore's furious roar. He began prowling toward her. Jada felt the same level of frustration that the manticore was feeling. Her mind running a thousand miles a minute as she tried to come up with a plan. Cutting off his tail had been a lucky strike. He was still physically stronger than her. Although with her army they were of the same level of strength. She had to hurry and think of something before he wore her out.

The manticore lunged again and struck out with its razor-like claws. Her army surged forward, and he began knocking them away in his effort to get to her. Jada took a sharp inhale of breath and ran at the manticore. The manticore roared and stood on his hind legs thinking she was going to attack from above.

However, she jumped and rolled between his legs. She took off running to where his tail laid uselessly on the ground. Her opponent shouted angrily and began running after her.

She leaped as the manticore swung at her legs and raked his claws down her thigh tearing skin until it exposed her bones. Jada fell a few yards away from his tail with a hiss of pain. She grit her teeth and begins crawling forward. The manticore laughed and lazily moved toward her.

"Such a weak little human. It's hard to see what all the fuss was about." His voice grated on Jada's nerves, but she continued to crawl forward. Her lame leg barely helping her push herself along. "I am going to make this as painful as possible. You're welcome."

"Thanks." Jada could almost reach out and touch it. "I'll remember your generosity when I kill you. "

"That's a lot of bravado for someone who is trying to slither off the field." The manticore paused and sat back on his haunches watching her crawl in amusement. "You are truly pathetic."

Jada dropped tiredly to the ground next to the tail. She had lost a lot of blood, and her breathing was coming in ragged gasps. The manticore was ready to pounce, and she had to come "Yeah? Well, your mom's a snow leopard."

The manticore leaped from the ground with a vengeful growl. Jada pushed herself over and grabbed the scorpion's tail. She rolled over on her back just as the manticore landed with a sharp snap of his teeth. The crowd screamed, and for a time that was the only sound.

Silvestri picked her head up from the table from snorting a line of fairy dust. Wiping off her nose. "Well killing your toy took less time than I thought it would."

Gabriel frowned as he watched Silvestri and shook his head in disapproval. "I think Jada will be fine. You however might want to slow down. It's not even midday."

The crowd watched the field in silence. The skeletons stiffly turned towards the manticore waiting like the rest of the audience. The manticore stood, with a proud smile, and slowly the veins beneath his fur began to bubble and fill with black. His eyes turned grey and roll to the back of his head. The crowd gasps as the brute goes limp and tips over revealing Jada barely breathing on the ground.

Silvestri knocks over the table filled with fairy dust, and Gabriel smiles calmly from his seat. The crowd is cheering, as Gabriel's board takes a deep sigh of relief. Silvestri rounds on Gabriel angrily, her eyes narrowing on him as he smugly watches the field.

"When this is over, I will eat that bitch's heart out with a spoon!" Silvestri wipes her nose once more and looks to the field.

Gabriel didn't respond, he just continued to watch the field with a wide smile. "Then we will see what we will see."

Jada stares up at the sky but tosses the scorpion tail off to the side. She tiredly laid her head back on the ground. She took a deep breath and suddenly her body began to glow. She gasped and squirmed as the light wrapped around her body. The world felt like Christmas, bills paid on time, and happiness all wrapped into one. Her wounds began to close, and her body was lifted from the ground. She laughed and wriggled some as the feeling flowed through her. She never felt anything like this and wasn't sure if she should be enjoying the manticores death this much. Her turn ended, and her attention moved back across the field for their next challenge.

Nero was in good spirits as he politely sent his queen to attack her. "Queen to D5."

The siren turned her hollow eyes towards Jada, and all the warmth that Jada had felt moments before left her. She landed on the ground as the siren floated across the field toward her. A skeleton handed her Gabriel's sword that she tiredly took from his boney hands. As the siren entered the field her blood-red lips moved into a soft smile. The spectral woman continued to move until she was halfway through the field. Jada didn't see an army, which meant that the siren was strong enough to be her own. She watched the ghostly woman warily from her spot behind the skeletons.

The siren stopped and her lips parted. What started as a whisper ended in a high melancholy note. The sound became louder and stronger the longer she held it. Jada heard the note but didn't realize anything was amiss until she tried to take a step towards the other queen. Her feet were stuck to the ground, and she couldn't move at all. Jada looked up at her opponent and the siren only smiled before launching into a song.

"There once was a lass all bonnie and blithe. The dear child knew not a day of strife." The siren lifted her hand beckoning Jada forward. "She waltzed through the meadows with a basket in hand singing, way oh merry ai yi!"

Tears began to well in Jada's eyes at the high pure sound of the siren's song. When the siren sang about waltzing through the meadows Jada's feet began to move in the direction of the siren. She tried to force herself to be still, but the lure of the siren's song was too powerful.

"One day the lass met a man all handsome and tall. He had seen her waltzing and had come to call. He saw her waltzing and had come by to call." To Jada the siren's voice sounded like cool winds and corn cob pipes. The smell of crackling fires and rain falling through the trees filled her senses. Jada continued to move forward as the siren continued her song as if nothing was amiss. "He asked for her hand by the light of the moon singing way oh merry ai yi!"

The siren's mouth closed, but Jada could still hear the song in her head. She was powerless to stop herself from moving. She couldn't even scream for her army. it was as if the same power that controlled her feet froze her vocal cords.

"They married in June with her father's full blessing. He gave her away without too much pressure." The siren's voice danced through Jada's head, but the siren herself had stopped physically speaking. The corners of her mouth split open as her jaw unhinged from its hollows. Tentacles unfurled from her mouth over brittle ragged teeth. "They danced through the mountains in love as can be. He dropped her off a mountain and kept her dowry."

Jada had covered half of the distance that was left between them despite her inner struggling. She could faintly hear fairies screaming at her to move or run away. A few yards more and she would get eaten by Appalachian Barbie.

"The lass is still dancing through meadows and mountains. Singing way oh merry ai yi!" The siren's tongue snapped out to take off Jada's head, but a skeleton pulled her back sharply.

The skeleton of the ogre silently placed his arm to stop Jada from moving any further. Jada screamed aloud and struggled to get around the giant skeleton, but the other skeletons began dragging her back across the field as she struggled against them. He watched her with empty eyes as more and more skeletons pulled themselves out of the ground. Her army becoming twice the size it was at the beginning of the match. Each new row of skeletons drew her further back from the siren, building a blockade between both queens.

The siren screamed in rage and tried to break through the mass army of skeletons. The tentacles in her face swung wildly trying to get to Jada. However, once they had the sobbing Jada secured, they turned towards the siren and unsheathed their swords. Half of the segment breaking off to march towards the siren.

"Well, that's enough of that. We've taken the square, leave her for now." Nero was almost giddy with excitement.

The siren bowed her head in acquiescence and smirked at Jada as her skeletons pulled her from the field to place her behind Nero. Jada glared at his back despite the excellent view of his broad shoulders. "Jada, what would Gabriel say?"

"That he would kill you if you touched me."

Nero turned to her with a bright smile, and a wink before turning his attention back to the board. "Promises. Promises."

With Jada off the field, Odin happily took control of the board. "Bishop to E6."

Tomas walked to the square Odin called out with a shrug of his shoulders. Jada guessed Odin saw how his earlier moment of impulsivity had made him vulnerable.

Nero focuses on the board and Jada watches him get back to the business of winning this match. His bored voice calling out his next move with no enthusiasm. "Queen to E6."

Tomas, like the rest of the board, had watched the sirens bout with Jada, and immediately put a ravine between them. The siren screamed angrily, but with the distance between them, her song wouldn't work. The siren sulkily took the square and Tomas took his place beside Jada with a smile.

"Fancy meeting you here!" Tomas laughed but kept his attention on the board.

"Tomas." Jada greeted him and crossed her arms in frustration as she watched the moves that were being made without them.

Nero sighed and shook his head in disgust at the ease of his win. "Check."

"We accept the check. Our board is done." Odin, seeing that he had no more moves, reluctantly conceded the match. He sharply turned away from the board and faded away.

Trine jumped back onto the board, and his jagged teeth were on full display as he announced the winner. "The first round goes to Silvestri.

The crowd cheered at the end of the match and made their way back to the palace. There was a party that they all had to get ready for. Silvestri blew Nero a kiss and confidently walked away from the table she had flipped over. Pieces from both sides followed suit. Tomas looked at Jada who nodded and he walked away into nothingness back to the oubliette.

Nero turns to Jada with a slow sweep of his that began at her eyes and ended somewhere below her waist. Jada's brow lifts as she waits for him to say something after finishing his appraisal. Instead, he turns away without saying anything. He leaves her alone on the board. Leaving Jada to take a deep steadying breath as she waited for what was to come.

"Just say it, Gabriel."

"Say what my pet? I told you so? I did, but I'm quite gratified at how this match turned out." Gabriel lifted his hands to rub along the tops of her arms and over her shoulders comfortingly. "You managed to suss out several of the other board's abilities and kill off two of

Silvestri's pieces. You also finally made your army bigger!"

Jada didn't relax because she knew what was coming. Gabriel leaned over and placed a kiss on her forehead and leaned back to look at her. His smile was beautiful, but his words were quite serious. " Though I expect a better showing tomorrow. All in all I was very entertained."

Jada sighed and allowed herself to relax fractionally but looked up at Gabriel through her lashes. Her eyes closing as he pulled her further into his embrace, her cheek tiredly resting against his shoulder. "Odin is going to be a problem, isn't he?"

"Yes" The soft hiss at the end of his words meant that he was at least partially angry with her failure. His arms tighten around her for a moment before he releases her to take a step back.

"I will handle it." Jada felt oddly bereft of his touch but was grateful that he stepped back. She didn't want Gabriel handling Odin himself.

"See that you do. I can't kill any of you, now that the tournament has started, but I can make you wish to die during the interim." He kept the distance between them but took her hand. "Come on, since you refuse to satisfy any of my appetites I might as well feed yours."

Jada rolled her eyes but allowed him to lead her away from the field. If the action didn't have the same bite that it normally would, and it scared her. She didn't take his hand and ignored the slight quirk of his lips as she walked past him. If she wasn't careful, she would lose herself here in the world of fairy. She just hoped she could keep her own world together just a little longer.

Chapter Eighteen

After the spaceship settled into place over the field, Jada continued to consider her options. There were so many beings that lived simultaneously over the briars. Monsters that only lived in folklore she had read as a child and failed science experiments lived side by side. In the world of fairy, they were all ready to kill you. After releasing the deep breath, she made her next move. "Jonas to E6, please"

The blindfolded basilisk hissed angrily at being disturbed, but obediently made his way to the designated square. With each step his human body stretched and grew until instead of steps the giant serpent slithered into place. Jonas let a threatening hiss as his eyes closed waited for his next set or instructions.

"Pawn to G4." At Nero's command a tribe of centaurs marched to their field. The crashing sound of their hooves and armor noisily bringing them out onto the board. They settled, and their heavy hooves pawed anxiously at the ground. Their muscles bunched and relaxed as they readied themselves for a fight.

The match up to this point had been quick and brutal. Nero had basically been tossing pawns at her. Jada assumed that Silvestri had given him orders to finish her quickly. Too bad for them both, she planned on winning this round. Jada had been fighting as many of the fights as she personally to keep her board alive. They would make it back over the hedge sound if not whole.

There had been more deaths on the board then Jada had wanted. Irshad and Odin had not been wrong when they said she would have very little choice but to kill the other pieces. None of her opponents had wanted to give up. They were all adamant on fighting to the death. Nero was not leaving her any options that involved keeping his board intact either. She could not figure out Nero's strategy. There was no rhyme or reason to the moves he was making.

"Queen to H4" Jada moved from the empty square with a frown. With a wave of Gabriel's sword, the massive army of skeletons marched forward. With each kill her army got bigger, and more of a threat with each turn. The dancer did not know what law of physics the world of fairy was breaking to fit the evergrowing army into each square, but they never ran out of room. Her hand lifted and was consumed with fire. That was another change. Her control of fire had gotten better. She was faster, stronger, and with each change her enjoyment of the game grew. It had become almost fun to see how far she could push herself. Even her movements had become more confident, almost predatory.

She leaped hovered above the ground before landing neatly into the square. Something else that was new. She could leap high into the air and gracefully slow her descent to the ground. Her eyes met Nero's across the board. Her brow lifted over a gratified smile. "Check"

Nero had no place to go and from the smile on his face he had no place he would rather be. He his lightly bronzed arms languidly stretched above his head. He pulled the domino mask down over his blue eyes.

Throwing it to the side as he calmly walked forward. "King to F2."

Jada's lips parted in surprise. Nero was coming for her, and not the other way around. Nero was still in check, but this move would place him in check mate. His eyes stayed on hers as he moved towards his chosen square. She watched him, and she started walking as well. Something inside of her was goading her into engaging him. Once his turn ended, she would make the call to go to F2 as well. She could end this today or be ended today. She did not think she was strong enough, but the power flowing through her veins said to try her luck. That power was telling her to meet him and have the fight her body was screaming for. Regardless of if her newfound power told her how much stronger then she he was.

"Check mate." Jada smiled as Nero finished his turn. She was already leaving her square to engage. "Let's dance…"

"We abstain." Silvestri's words were tight, but it was Nero who Jada could not take her eyes from. "The match is Gabriel's!"

The vibrant blue of Nero's eyes burned angrily at Silvestri. He had wanted the same fight that Jada had. More than if the way he stiffly dismissed his board with a wave of his hand was any indication. Silvestri stared back at him, and he turned sharply on his heel and followed his board off the field. Silvestri looked over Jada coldly licking the powder away from the corner of her lip. She stormed away from the balcony in flurry of dark blue satin and lace. Gabriel lifted his glass and took a deep satisfied sip of wine as she went by.

Jada released a breath she had not realized she had been holding. The anticipation was still there, but so was the knowledge that she might not make it out alive. She bounced on her toes trying to shake off the adrenaline that ricocheted around her system. Unfortunately, it excited her.

"Jada, you need to be more careful." Irshad's calm voice broke her reverie, and she turned her attention to him. "I know you want to keep us safe from the monsters, but to save us from them you may become one."

So Irshad saw her desire to kill and throw caution away growing as well. Jada pulled on a bright smile to cover the emotions that raged through her and nodded. "Of course, Irshad. I promise not to take too many chances. I have to get us back over the briars."

"Home." Irshad's voice was gentle, but the reprimand was still here. "You have to get all of us home."

"Yes sorry, Irshad. I'm sorry." Jada's words were rushed, but they sounded hollow even to her. Her hands lifted in apologetic surrender. When had she stopped thinking of her world as home? "I meant exactly that. I promise to get us home!"

"If you and Nero could get a room and hash your differences out there it would save us all from dying." Odin's snarky voice snapped Jada's attention away from her mistake. He angrily brushed into her shoulder as he went by without a backwards glance.

Jada watched him go by. That same energy that egged her into battles on the field goaded her to follow him and remind him who was queen of their board. Her body had even turned and had taken a step towards him before she even realized what she was doing. She shook the rage away, and forcibly turned towards Irshad with a frown. "What did I do to offend him this time?"

Irshad was also watching Odin walk off with a disturbed frown. He moved forward smoothly inserting himself between his king and queen with a shake of his head. He had been watching her body's response, and it seemed he felt the need to head off trouble before it started. "I'm honestly not sure. He has never been like this. Although he doesn't have Yamja to keep him levelheaded any longer."

"Irshad you should go to the oubliette. It's going to be a busy day tomorrow." Gabriel's voice pulled their attention away from Odin. Thankfully, he ignored the way Irshad took the same step forward Jada had towards Odin earlier.

This time it was Jada stepping between the two of them. She turned to Irshad with a reassuring smile. "Go ahead. I'll be alright and will follow you soon."

Irshad gave her a look out of the corner of his eyes but turned and disappeared to the oubliette as well. Jada watched him go with a worried heart, but as always Gabriel was there to take her mind away from her team.

"That dog is trying my patience, Jada." Gabriel's voice was flat, and Jada turned to face him in exasperation.

"Stop calling him names." She looked up at him and realized how her body had started to orient itself to his position. It did not matter where he was in the area her senses automatically reached out to locate him. "What do you want Gabriel?"

"We both know you're not mad at me." Gabriel took her hand and gently stroked soothing circles over into her palm. His gaze raking over her as he checked her bruises in concern. "Anyway, I came over to congratulate you on winning the match."

"Your faith in me is humbling." Jada nervously but gently pulled her hand away before she started to enjoy his touch more then she already was. "If you'll excuse me, I should head out and…"

"Get ready for the ball." Gabriel interrupted her with a smile, and gently placed his hand at the small of her back as he led her in the opposite direction of the oubliette.

Jada half turned to look back at him shock. "The what now?"

Gabriel laughed and slowly pulled her into his arms giving her the option to resist if she wanted to. In turn, she carefully eased into his embrace warily." I am throwing a masquerade ball. You and Odin will be my plus ones."

Jada frowned, not wanting to deal with anymore of Odin's attitude. Much more prodding from him and they would have a fight. In honesty, she wasn't sure she wouldn't be the first to take a swing at him. Not with the way she had been feeling lately. "I think Irshad would be the better choice. He is much less volatile."

Gabriel's face suddenly contorted in rage for just a moment before his face smoothed out into something more cordial. Jada would have thought she imagined it if it wasn't for the way his pupils remain contracted. He smiled, but his voice had taken on the soft hiss it did when he was angry. "Go to your room and get dressed. Odin will be there to pick you up soon."

Jada watched his eyes searching them for something and running when she found it. There was that emotion again. "How will I know who you are if we are in costume?"

Gabriel laughed and gently disengaged the embrace trying to be mindful of her recent fight. "Don't

pretend you won't know."

Gabriel walked away leaving her on the balcony, and Jada sighed. Her brow creased, and her hand cupped her lips as she shouted out after him. "If nothing else you have the audacity."

"If you would just admit how you feel, I could show you what else I have going for me." Gabriel's amused voice floated back to her, and Jada shook her head in exasperation. "I will see you tonight. I hope you enjoy your costume."

Jada allowed him to leave before making her own way to her room. She should be resting up in the oubliette, but something about the rules of hospitality required her presence at certain events. She ascended the stairs of the palatial villa that comprised her home. Her thoughts filled with the matches and her board. There was so much crowding her head vying for her attention. But at the center of her thoughts was Gabriel. He was like the sun her world revolved around. She barely noticed the macabre decorations that the fairies were throwing up around her.

Once she made it back to her room, she immediately set about removing her armor. She closed the door, and she heard a soft purring that made her cheeks lift in a fond smile. Octavius was sleeping soundly and tiptoed past the wardrobe as not to disturb him. She had just taken the last step that would have cleared her path to the bathroom, but the wardrobe door opened and slapped her soundly on the rear.

Jada yelped and rounded on the sassy wardrobe indignantly. "Your mom was made of toothpicks!"

Octavius did not bother to respond; he simply spit a towel at her and went back to napping. Jada tossed him a dirty look before heading on to take her bath. She would deal with him later.

The fairies must have been expecting her because the bath was already drawn and steaming pleasantly into the air. She climbed down into the tub and sank as far as she possibly could into the lily of the valley scented water. Jada leaned back against the tub and allowed her muscles to slacken into its liquid warmth. It was the first time she had allowed herself to relax since last night. It was also the first time she had time to think of anything but death since the matches.

"Stupid fairies and their stupid power hunger!" Jada petulantly slapped the water with a vehemence caused the water to ripple around her in agitation. A vase filled with flowers shattered and disintegrated off to her side. It was another manifestation of how powerful she was getting. Energy just seemed to break free from her at any given moment. Like her body was not enough to contain it. She dunked herself underwater in anger to soak her hair through. She would need to learn how to control her powers soon or she could hurt someone.

"Then there was Gabriel." Jada leaned back against the tub once more and allowed her head to rest back on the edge of the tub. That was a whole other set of emotions she had no desire to explore but found no less exciting. Jada had no idea how she could both admire and hate someone at the same time. She didn't want to call it love, but it was a lot warmer and fuzzier than she should feel about the man who kidnapped her.

Jada sighed and shook her head. "What in the

Stockholm syndrome am I going to do?" She murmured to herself as the two fairies that normally attended her room came in. One washed and detangled her hair with a wide tooth comb while the other rubbed and massaged her limbs. Jada was in heaven in the middle of this hell, but for a while she was willing to let go of her anger and live in the moment.

Octavius opened and closed his doors repeatedly to warn them that they were running out of time. Jada was wrapped in a towel and led to the vanity where the first fairy twisted her curls into a chignon, and kohled her eyes. The other fairy laid out her dress. It was a full blood red ball gown that left her shoulders bar but plunge into a sweetheart neckline. The ruby like brocade would wrap around her form like a glove. She stood and allowed them to help her get dressed.

"Is this me?" When she looked in the mirror her red lips parted in surprise. Jada didn't recognize herself. She knew the person in the mirror was her but not her. The person in the mirror was her, but this version of her was strong, self-assured, and powerful. She looked regal. Like she belonged here and nowhere else. The fairy that put on her makeup had dusted her exposed skin in gold. Her mahogany shoulders almost glowed in the light of her room. The heavy diamonds in her ears fell in large crystalline tear drops against her cheeks. The matching necklace was a cascade of fiery rubies and diamonds that dripped down her chest to end in the valley between her breasts.

A high-pitched whistle came from Octavius as she continued to look herself over. She smiled and winked over her shimmering shoulder at the wardrobe. "You're welcome."

The first fairy smiled and took a step back to grab her mask. It was a dark gold domino mask that had dainty horns protruding from the forehead. The mask was pure gold with little ruby tears beneath the eyes and above her brows. She brought the mask down over Jada's dark eyes and tied the blood red ribbons behind her head. The other father attached a set of black bat like wings that flapped and spread of their own accord to her dress. Then a diamond encrusted crown was placed on top of her head. She shone like their midday sun.

There was a sharp nock on the door, and Odin barged in before she could allow him entrance. Jada's eyes narrowed at the disrespect but ignored that and chose the the route that would keep him alive longer. "You look nice."

She wasn't lying. Odin wore a crow mask and a dark grey suit covered by a smokey cloak that seemed to be made of an even darker grey mist. The costume accentuated his broad shoulders, and his height. He looked down at her, with a hatred that almost made her take a step back. He nodded slowly and stepped outside of the door with a wave of his hand. "You ready?"

"As I'll ever be." Jada felt a sense of Deja vu. As they walked through the bright candlelit halls of Gabriel's home. All the preparations had been made and all of the servants were settling into their normal functions. As Jada and Odin made their way to the hall where they first met Silvestri. Odin didn't offer his arm like he did before, but Jada had no desire to touch him. They were no longer comrades, and he was the one who chose this path.

Trinity and Trine stepped out from behind two pillars on either side of the hall, and they circled around them with twin leers.

"Aren't you a sight to behold." Trinity was dressed as a clown. The royal purple of his custom was offset by black polka dots that ran the length of his outfit. His hair pulled into a polished pompadour.

"Yes, you are definitely a feather in Gabriel's cap!" Trine continued his counterclockwise circles in his own clown costume that was black with purple polka dots. The lecherous lilt to his waspish voice made Jada not want to know what either was thinking when they saw her. "But a burr in Silvestri's saddle."

"We have been having the most amazing time since you were dragged over the briars or carried rather." Trinity snickered as he stopped in front of them.

"More fun than we have had in centuries." Trine smiled, baring mottled shark-like teeth. Their aim was to scare her, and for some reason it wasn't working.

"I'm glad to be of service," Jada watched them silently trying not to roast them where they stood. They were looking for an excuse to attack her, and she refused to give them one. She would never allow them to hurt Gabriel through her. She smiled, and their smiles lessened but remained. Their eyes bleeding into a shade of red that matched the rubies at her neck. They weren't finished and would continue to court a fight as long as she stood there. Unfortunately for them she was dying to give them what they asked for.

"What a coincidence, accident, happenstance!" Bane came up behind Jada and Odin. He took Jada's arm and led her away from the evil twins. Their teeth still bared in their evil smiles as they moved by. Even Odin relaxed his grip on his spear and adjusted his mask back over his eyes.

"Bane lovely to see you." Jada grits her teeth but forced herself to be calm. Now Bane was the lesser of three evils. The other two were going to end in bloodshed, and scarily enough she welcomed it.

"Yes, isn't it. But it was not niceties, generosity, altruism that brought this on." Bane was quite dapper in his dark green military coat. His long black hair pulled into a low ponytail that fell down his back like a dark river. He looked like a prince, but according to Gabriel that was probably not too far off. Bane belonged to the same nobility that Gabriel had to claw his way into.

"You expect a favor from Gabriel." Jada said flatly as she continued to walk by Bane 's side.

"From you actually." Bane led her into the ballroom with a bright smile. Jada looked over at him, and he dipped his head. A razor like nail gently traced the side of her mask. He was close enough to kiss her, but he just hovered. "Tell Gabriel what just happened.

Also, tell him an eye for an eye."

Bane took a step back and bowed gallantly before leaving her standing in the doorway of the great hall. She turned and Jada had to shield her eyes against the brightness of the room. The lamps were filled with fireflies that danced along with the music that wafted through the large hall. There were horns and wings everywhere she looked. She looked around and found that Odin had slinked off without saying anything.

She mentally shrugged and made her way into the ball. Jada was actually glad not to be in his presence any longer. He had probably gone to spend time with Yamja, and that she would not begrudge him no matter how irritated she was with him.

She waded through tight clusters of dancing fairies. There were masks and feathers, pearls, and dresses. Jada was amazed at the sight before her. Princeton stood on a platform where the thrones had been and conducted a full orchestra. He was supplied with one, as to not put the fairies at the party in danger. Heaven forbid one of the pieces decided they wanted revenge for how they were treated. Princeton caught her eyes, and he gave her a discreet thumbs up as she passed by. Jada gave him a bright smile, letting him know that she was okay for now. It was like watching a movie. A cinematic masterpiece that she was now a part of. As she made her way through the ball, she wondered how she would ever find a way to leave the world fairy behind.

"If it isn't Gabriel's little pet." Devanshi's sultry voice whispered over her shoulder. She slinked from behind Jada in a large peacock blue dress reminiscent of the dresses that Jada had seen Marie Antoinette wear in her history books. Her inky hair was piled in a gravity defying pouf and ringlets that beautifully framed her face. The large white feathered fan that matched the feathers in her hair was held over her lips, as she looked Jada over with the same level of scrutiny.

"Councilwoman Devanshi, you look lovely this evening." Jada refused to get pulled into a fight with a council member. Especially one that was clearly a noncombatant and was looking for a reason to separate her from Gabriel. "Are you enjoying the ball?"

"Now now Devanshi. Don't be bitter, you made a promise to Gabriel to be good." The stout man Jada recognized as Grimali chided Devanshi with a wide mocking smile. His stubby hands removed the plague doctor mask he wore. The black shrouds he wore shifted and moved like smoke around his body. He didn't bother to look at Jada and made a point of turning his back to her. Though silent the message of Jada not being worth his notice was loud and clear. "Anyway, once the games are over, maybe Silvestri will give Gabriel to you."

Jada's blood began to boil at the insinuation that she would lose the tournament. Silvestri would get her hands on Gabriel over her dead body, and the bodies of both of their boards. She was about to say something scathing when Kionah came up beside her in a grand swish of his black, red lined cape. He held out a rose and bowed his head politely acknowledging her existence in a way that Grimali had not. Jada took the rose and curtsied, momentarily losing her anger.

"So, you think that Silvestri will win?" Councilman Kionah's voice was polite if doubting. He was not one for costumes it seemed. He wore an understated black tuxedo, and white Venetian mask that only covered his eyes. The only item that lent any frivolity to his outfit was the tall top hat that he held in his hands. He was standing beside Jada which forced Grimali to turn and face her. He looked up at Kionah in irritation, but his tone was polite as he addressed him.

"Of course, she will win. Have you seen Gabriel's board? I can't imagine what he was thinking." Grimali laughed, and this time his eyes met Jada's and passed a decisive sweep over her gown. "Or was he thinking at all?"

"His board won today." Ezuli walked over to the group that was now forming and stood on the other side of Jada. She patted Jada's hand comfortingly before continuing. "Not only did they win, Silvestri lost a lot of her board today."

Jada personally thought Ezuli stole the show from the majority of the fairies gathered. She was wearing a black corset that ended in a matching ballerina tutu. The fluffy material fell to her knees leaving her brown legs bare. The black silver lined heels that she wore were impossibly high. They made the diminutive fairy almost as tall as Jada. Ezuli tossed her curled hair over her shoulder, and the movement exposed the straps that held the voluptuous fairy's shoulders. Her eyes twinkled behind her simple black mask. Her head tilted in a way that made the decorative silver feathers that lined her mask and shoulders quiver.

"Gabriel was lucky today. Nero was overconfident. I've been telling Silvestri that she gives her doll too much Freedom." A deep sonorous baritone joined the conversation, and Jada turned to see Councilman Barron standing on the other side of Grimali. He also ignored Jada and continued to talk about her as if she wasn't there which gave her ample time to look him over. He had foregone the mask to paint an ivory skull over his face.

351

The crown of his afro was still perfect. His tall lean form was completely at home in the charcoal grey suit he wore. "After Silvestri is done with him I doubt he'll lose another match."

Jada glared up at him and he smiled with a shrug that said he was not at all sorry. They were toys to him, and the way he spoke reminded her of why she had to get her board back over the briars. Silvestri couldn't physically harm Nero right now, but as Irshad said, there were plenty of way to hurt someone that had nothing to do with the body.

"I'm sure she's punishing him as we speak. It's probably why she's late to the party." Devanshi smiled as she continued to needle Jada about Nero's fate. "I'd hate to be him right now."

They continued to talk about the different ways they punished their pieces for losing. Ezuli and Kionah engaged her in polite conversation as the other three spoke about the board pieces as if she wasn't standing there. Jada's shoulders rolled in an effort to keep from doing something about it. A fact that did not go unnoticed by Barron.

"Look at her getting angry. I don't know why Gabriel refused to discipline his pet." Barron's voice sounded weary. As if he had the world of board punishments well in hand.

"Gabriel's pet queen is hot blooded I see." Grimali leered over at her, watching as Jada's fingers curled into her palms creating fists even as she did her best to ignore them. "I bet Gabriel is enjoying that regularly."

"Gabriel wouldn't lower himself in that way!"

Devanshi's voice was scandalized. Or at least scandalized with the idea that he would do those things with Jada.

Kionah gently pulled Jada further away from the trio, but they continued their hateful conversation amongst themselves. Ezuli shook her head in disgust. "The three of you are absolutely vile!"

"Oh, you don't sleep with your pieces?" Grimali laughed as he picked away nonexistent dust from his clothes. "That would explain why you're always so uptight."

"Of course, I don..." Ezuli angry reply was cut off by the appalled voice Barron.

"I certainly don't sleep with my pieces. Would you make love with the hounds you hunt with? Absolutely obscene." Barron scoffed with a slow shake of his head. "You know that when you lay with dogs you'll likely come up with fleas."

"Apologize to Ezuli at once, both of you. She is a council member, and you will show her the respect that she deserves." Kionah's clear deep voice snatched the attention of the other three. "You can also apologize to Gabriel's queen. You are in his home and will respect everyone and everything in it."

Jada was too busy thinking about how the council members viewed their boards to enjoy their pouty fake apologies. Things, that's all the pieces they captured and brought over were to them. Just toys to be broken and thrown away whenever they were done with them. Jada was keeping a very tenuous grip on her powers, but with the added strength came a loss of control that she wouldn't gain until had a chance to learn what it could do out on the field. Jada couldn't trust herself to speak. Not when she didn't know what would pass through her lips. She was sure she was strong enough to hurt them now, but not strong enough to kill them.

Nero's movements were stiff as he joined their little party. His bare chest was covered with welts, and his eyes were filled with an angry fire that promised retribution. His gaze flickered to Jada's, and his lips curled into momentary sneer. The pale brown his bare torso was lacerated in angry crosshatch patterns. Jada's eyes widened and moved to Silvestri angrily as the fairy approached.

Silvestri laughed and shook her head in a way that made her asymmetrical hair toss dramatically over amazing cheekbones. "You have an entirely too much nerve for a human. Gabriel does not do enough to keep you in your place.

"He gives me the freedom to win, and that's all that counts." The group goes quiet and Jada watches Silvestri's eyes narrow behind her mask. Jada smiled and took a step forward. Jada's eyes narrowed on Silvestri, and as she looked back over the abused Nero. She had to stop herself from taking a step forward to check on him personally. The act would be seen as aggressive, and she was already going to be making enough trouble for Gabriel this evening. "You and your little council friends are cowards. You don't have the nerve to kill each other, so you use us instead of ponying up and doing it yourselves."

"I will skin you alive, you simple strumpet. You should be grateful for this council and tournament. This is probably the longest you ever kept your clothes on. I wouldn't expect a human stripper to understand manners and breeding." The smile that accompanied Silvestri's condescending words was benevolent. As if explaining life lessons to someone extremely slow.

"At least I was paid to be seen. I didn't have to buy a stable that can't stand me." The longer she spoke the more disrespectful her mouth was getting, and she knew that she was probably crossing a line. She glanced over at Nero's torn skin and remembered that she did not care.

Silvestri looked down her nose at Jada, which was impressive considering the fairy's diminutive size. "Grubby bitch."

"Vapid whore." Jada in turn did the same. When in Rome after all.

"When I win this tournament and secure my throne once more. I will let Gabriel watch me skin you alive before I sever his head." Silvestri's words were nasty despite the sweet tone of her voice. It was as if Silvestri was not threatening her or Gabriel's life. Just having polite conversation with a servant.

"When I win this tournament for Gabriel, I will use my wish to free your board and let them do to you what you've done to them" Jada snapped and took that step forward. She was not concerned about how Silvestri threatened her, but something about her threatening Gabriel made her see a shade of red that was darker than the dress she wore. It did not matter if Jada regularly threatened Gabriel's life, Silvestri couldn't. He did not belong to her.

Silvestri's hand snakes out to slap Jada across the face, but a white gloved hand catches her arm. Jada knew who the hand belonged to and allowed her eyes to wander over the bone white covered arm to a gold mask that matched hers. Gabriel was resplendent in a white coat that was edged in gold. It hung open over a golden button up shirt that some sadist left unbuttoned at the top. The mask he wore was coordinated with the mask she wore. However, the face was a bone white that matched his coat, and the golden horns curled out back from his temples instead. The snout of the mask was snake-like giving the mask a dragon-like look. Jada probably would have swooned if she was not keyed up on rage and hate.

"Councilwoman Silvestri, I will thank you not to harm any more pieces this evening. Mine or yours." Gabriel gave Nero a pointed once over before gently dropping her hand. He looked around with a wide smile beneath his mask. "Is everyone enjoying the party?

"The rules clearly state that no one can harm any pieces during the tournament. Though I had a momentary lapse of poor behavior in moving to strike your trollop, I have not touched my dear Nero." Silvestri turned and moved back a step to stand next to Nero. Her fingers lightly danced over one of his bloodier welts. "The rules however say nothing about him hurting himself. Isn't that correct inquisitor Trinity?"

Trinity's grotesque smile made the grease paint on his face crack with its hateful grin. "That is most correct,

High Council Silvestri."

Jada took a step forward ready to commit murder, and Gabriel quickly stepped forward. "So, they don't. Excuse me for assuming High council Silvestri."

Silvestri sneered, and her gaze moved to Jada. "Not at all Gabriel. You have commoner manners, and that is to be expected. However, you are supposed to be offering me hospitatliy, and your strumpet isn't very welcoming."

Gabriel smiled with a nod. "I agree she hasn't. Jada, expect to be punished later."

"No now!" It was Silvestri's turn to take an aggressive step towards Gabriel.

Jada's hand went to Gabriel's sword, and he lifted his hands to stop her from drawing it. "I will decide how to punish my pieces. The rules you are so excellently acquainted with only state that I need to make amends. Not as to how. Is that not correct, Inquisitor Trine?"

"Yes, councilman Gabriel. That is unfortunately correct." Trine pouted disappointedly, and his balloon-like form deflated in on itself. "Quite unfortunately"

"Now if you will excuse me, I will be taking Jada to the dance floor to discuss a suitable punishment." Gabriel took Jada's hand and gently led her to the center dance floor past the small crowd that had gathered to watch the argument. Leaving Silvestri to splutter angrily.

Gabriel pulled Jada gently into his arms and eased her into slowly dancing with him. "My life has certainly not been dull since you came into it."

"What is my punishment going to be?" Jada followed his lead in the dance, but she wanted to get whatever he was going to come up with out of the way.

Gabriel didn't say anything for a moment. A quick quirk of his lips was the only sign that he was even paying attention to her. The moved over the dance floor in a slow waltz that took them through throngs of costumed figures. Beastly faces made of paper, and beasts that wore human faces laughed and frolicked around them.

"Bane saved me from the twins as Odin and I came to the party. He told me to tell you Sùil airson sùil." Jada watched a slow smile spread across Gabriel's beautiful face. "What does it mean?"

"An Eye for an Eye." Gabriel replied with a soft laugh, and continued to move them through the circle of dancers. "You look ravishing in that dress.

"Are you not concerned?" Jada fingers tightened around his shoulders in frustration. It felt like her entire world was spinning out of control. Valkari chose it."

"No." He glanced over at Princeton, who was making kissy faces at Valkari, who was directing Gabriel's fleet of fairies by the dessert table. He pulled Jada closer as they continued to dance. His chin was resting against her temple. You have a good eye for choosing players."

"Can I wish for the games to stop?"

Gabriel slowed their pace, and gently rocked them back and forth. Jada did not think he would answer her question for a minute, but a deep breath of air was taken before being released on a deep frustrated sigh. His words were soft, but the hiss against her ear told her that she had made him angry.

"Do you notice that when you are in my arms all you can think about is other men?" Gabriel's angry whisper danced across her ear. "It's one of your more frustrating qualities."

Jada had to close her eyes against the wave of disappointment that radiated from his voice. The sound of his disapproval made her want to back down, but she could not if she wanted to save her board. Her gaze lifted to his, and Gabriel took a step back, but continued swaying with her, so that they would not cause a scene.

"Gabriel, can you just give me a straight answer?" Jada was tired. She hated walking on this tightrope of love and hatred that he had her walking on. Gabriel drew her back into his embrace and they continued to sway to the music that filled the hall. People surrounded them, and Jada could not feel more alone than she did right that instant. Outwardly and even mentally, she was ready to defy him at every turn. Her heart was singing a completely different song that she could no longer close her ears to.

"How spoiled you've gotten. Is that my fault?" The dangerous hum of Gabriel's voice, brushed across her shoulder as she continued to sway. A line of short perfunctory kisses was laid against her shoulder, as if he could not help himself despite his anger. "I give you the freedom to build your own board, to walk freely within the palace, and train with that mongrel as you wish. I have let the little disrespectful things you do, including the way you allow Nero to touch you slide. Despite, mind you, that here in this world I am well within my rights to physically act as I wish. Now here you are, ordering me to help you dismantle the exact thing that I have been working so hard to achieve. The very process that will allow me to effect change here in the land of Fairy. Have I made a mistake by allowing you so much freedom?"

They continued to dance, but movements were stiff and polite. There was none of the warmth that had filled his movements before. The tip of Jada's tongue lashed over suddenly dry lips. She may have taken things a step too far, but she was not going to withdraw the question. With his reaction, it appeared that she certainly could make that very wish.

"Gabriel, I am very grateful for the..." She paused looking for the right words to describe his attitude toward her. "Grace, that you have shown me."

"Are you?" Gabriel's serpent-like eyes met hers. Every ounce of his anger telegraphed in his eyes, despite the smile that hovered on his lips. "I don't think you are. I think you need a reminder of how lucky you are."

They continued to dance for a few minutes. He held her at arm's length, and Jada felt like she was being chastised for stealing from a meta-physical cookie jar. She knew she had not done anything wrong, but it did not feel that way. The way he held and spoke to her made her feel as disappointed in herself as his tone suggested she should be. They danced for about two songs. His gaze never left hers as they moved together. After a time, his smile grew, and she shook her head as they continued to dance. Whatever was coming was not going to be good.

"It wouldn't matter if you made a wish to end the games, not really." Gabriel did not speak as if he was talking to her. More like he was thinking to himself about how her wish would affect his ambitions. Gabriel pulled her closer, and the low hiss of voice curled around her ear sending another shiver along her spine. "You could wish the games away, but then they would move to one-on-one duels. Can you imagine the number of people that would die then? Fairy and human alike?"

He continued to hold her close, allowing his words to sink in." Jada hated the warm satisfaction in his voice. It was as if he had been waiting to find a way to hurt her and found just the way of doing it. That easy assurance that came from knowing that they would always be one-step ahead. He knew it would be enough to stop her from taking the chance. They continued to swirl and moved through the other guests, as if nothing was wrong.

Seeing that his words had their desired effect his smile widened, and his lips dropped a short kiss just under her ear. "Now as for your punishment." Jada's head snapped up to look into his reptilian gaze. His irises expanded and contracted in dark amusement as he watched her. "I want the heads of three of Silvestri's pieces. This will be in compensation for her insulting me, and your selfish behavior. You have been a very bad girl this evening."

Jada's fingers curled into the fabric of his coat angrily but continued their embrace. Her mood swung back towards murderous, and her voice was stiff despite the strained smile on her face. They were putting on a show, and she would play her part in effort not to

draw any more of his ire then necessary. "And if I refuse?"

Gabriel's viper-like teeth flashed as he smiled down at her. His fingers lifting to trace his thumb along her bottom lip and her jaw. "Then I will kill the mutt you enjoy spending so much time with. He is becoming tiresome."

"You can't harm him during the games." Jada's angry hiss was barely below a whisper as they swayed together.

It felt like the walls of the ball room were closing in on her. He knew she did not want to kill anyone, but he knew she would do it to protect one of her own. "Gabriel be reasonable I…"

"I am being reasonable." The forked tip of his tongue danced across her ear before he gently bit into the lobe. Jada felt her body go weak for a moment before shaking herself out of it. He smiled down at her in amusement, having caught her reaction. "I can't hurt you. I love you too much. It would emotionally hurt me to see you harmed. However, I feel no such compunction about having the pooch kill himself to save you or maybe Valkari. Can you imagine how Princeton would feel?"

Jada jerked back as if he had struck her with his words. Her mouth parted in soundless shock, and she looked over at Princeton. He was leading the orchestra but watching her dance with Gabriel in concern. Her attention shifted back to Gabriel's cruel smile. She dropped her eyes and nodded without another word. She would do what she had to do to keep her board together.

"As you wish, Councilmen Gabriel." Jada took a step back and mockingly curtsied once the song ended. They both stepped away from each other, and he took her hand leading her back to council where a worried Valkari had moved to wait on her. Apparently, she had been watching the exchange along with her husband.

Gabriel's brow lifted, and he nodded at the formalness of her tone. He gallantly brought her to Valkari and bowed to them both with a smile. He turned to Devanshi and held out his hand to her. Devanshi took it with a flourish and winked at Jada on her way by. Jada resisted the urge to do something childish like trip her. She watched them head to the ballroom floor shaking with suppressed rage. Her fingers curled into fists so hard they created small moons where her nails met the flesh of her palm.

They watched them dance for a few minutes before Valkari turned to Jada with a worried expression on her face. "Is everything okay?"

Jada took a deep breath and pulled her attention from Gabriel. She smiled and shook her head. There was no reason to burden the rest of the board with her problems. "Yes, I think I'm going to turn in for the evening. Tell Odin if you see him, please?"

Before Valkari could reply Jada made her way through the throng of dancers. Her thoughts as stormy as the expression on her face. She would have to kill three pieces tomorrow. Though not innocent, they had nothing to do with what was going on between her and Gabriel. She continued to trace her steps back through the halls past bustling servants. She lifted the heavy dress away from her feet as she began to ascend the stairs. Her thoughts running a mile a minute in the solitude she was grateful for. Away from everyone else Jada could admit that she did not exactly hate idea of feeling the euphoria that came with winning. She certainly would rather not kill, but she could not deny the level of excitement that spread though her veins at the prospect of winning.

Was she becoming a monster Irshad warned her about? She hated to think so, but she could not deny the way she felt when she fought. Neither could she ignore the way she started to understand and appreciate Gabriel despite the hate that churned inside of her. How was she going to protect her board, and not become one of the things she hated the most? She continued to move up the stairs, and her thoughts were no clearer as she reached the second floor. On her way to her room, Jada came upon one of the many mirrors in the hall. She peered into it prepared to see smudged make up, and an angry flush to her skin. What she found was her reflection smugly smiling back at her. Jada's lips parted in silent horror as the mirrored image stroked it's forked tongue of over her lips and blew Jada a kiss.

Chapter Nineteen

The weather was as sour as Jada's mood. The sky was filled with large dark gray storm clouds that obscured the twin suns that had joined in the sky. They were halfway through the game, and Jada had not found a way to complete her mission yet. Dark eyes wandered over her team, and her heart twisted as she watched the way Valkari nervously watched Princeton on the field. Odin was of course glowering straight ahead, while Irshad spent his time looking over the players. She had picked this board she knew that they would be compassionate and get the job done. They would kill but they were not killers.

Her gaze traveled over to Nero who was another problem entirely. He didn't so much enjoy killing as he did sacrificing his players. Jada had still not found any rhyme or reason to his game methods. Despite the angry red bruises that crisscrossed along his skin he played like there was nothing wrong. Not even a wince could be seen as he expertly moved his pieces around the board. The clouds had started to sprinkle drops of freezing water across the fields. Jada marveled at how there were no rules for how the weather acted during a match.

The last match had been a brutal one. Irshad had taken down an entire circus with his team of hyenas. If Jada wanted to keep Irshad winning she would need to complete her mission. She suffered no delusions about how serious Gabriel was about killing Irshad in a fit of jealous rage.

"Pawn to G4." Nero called out, and a huge toga wearing minotaur with a ring in his nose marched out onto the field. Once he landed in the square he bleated, and suddenly stone pillars shot from the ground soon to be connected by beige stone walls. The walls twisted and shifted until an entire maze had been constructed around him.

Jada's body almost sagged in relief when she saw a chance to complete Gabriel's mandate. She had three lives to take, and they weren't going to take themselves. "Queen to G4!"

She ignored the sharp way Irshad turned to look at her and the surprise on Princeton's face. The board was too crowded anyway. She was just doing her part to make more room for them to maneuver. The minotaur bleated from the center of the maze, and Jada shook her head. The fool thought that she was going to rush into the maze with her army and allow whatever traps he had to pick them off one by one. Red lips painted lips curled in amusement as her army began to spring up around her. They crawled up from the ground and she waited until they settled. She pointed towards the maze once she made sure that she had every last soldier available to her.

"Please fine me a way through the maze." Jada's voice was smug as she made the request. The skeletons began marching, but each step her army took had them sinking back into the ground.

Jada waited until she started hearing the screams before making her way into the maze. The further she moved through the corridors and walkways the more bodies she saw. If she made a wrong turn a smaller minotaur would jump out only to be taken down by the skeletons that jumped out of the ground and slaughtered them. She came to a dead end and a golden bull materialized from the wall. The bull stamped its hooves and charged straight at her. She calmly watched the bull come toward her unaffected by its charge. As a larger skeleton sliced the bull in half before sinking back into the ground to find other traps throughout the maze.

"Come out, come out, wherever you are!" Jada's singsong voice rang out as she entered the center of the maze.

The minotaur was lazily lounging on a stone chair in the middle of the courtyard. He looked up at her in surprise, and Jada assumed it was because she had arrived with nary a scratch on her person. He rose angrily and picked up a golden ax. He was easily three heads taller than Odin, and twice as wide. His large muscles flexed as he swung the axe over his shoulder as he stepped forward. His heavy horns spreading out over his shoulders.

"What have you done to my army?" The minotaur's gravelly voice asked curiously as he looked behind her.

Jada pulled Gabriel's sword from its scabbard, and slowly began to circle the Minotaur. A slow smile curling her lips, as she shrugged. "Stand up and find out."

The miniature took his axe in his hand and began stamping toward her. "You'll pa…"

She cut the Minotaur off with a wave of her hand. "Yes, yes, pay, regrets, and punishments. Get a move on I have two more heads to collect before the end of this match, and you're wasting my very valuable time."

The Minotaur pulled out his axe and rushed towards Jada with an angry snarl. She almost lost her footing as the ground shook beneath her feet. He leaned in as he swung at her, and she narrowly missed getting her throat sliced open with his axe. He reared back and blinked owlishly at her with wide human eyes.

"This is impossible." He watched her warily, and Jada had to smile. He clearly did not expect her to be so fast.

They trade swings for a while. Each looking for an opening that would give them the upper hand in the fight. The Minotaur was stating to tire, and Jada found it easy to dodge the heavy swings of his axe. It was almost laughable how clumsy of a fighter the mountain of a bull was.

"Her head canted to the side her eyes washing over him in boredom. "You have never actually fought a fair fight before, have you? They have all been too tired after running this gauntlet to give it their all by the time they get to you." Jada quickly reached up to grab the bull by the ring in his nose. Pulling him down so that his eyes were level with hers. "I hate bullies and cowards. You and Silvestri are both."

She jerks the ring out of his nose and the Minotaur rears his head back with a loud bleating scream. Jada gave the bull a satisfied smile before lunging in to carve a new smile into his neck. The bull dropped his axe to try to hold his neck together. His heavy body falling to the ground amidst soundless bleats of rage. Jada watched the monster until it laid still. Her shoulders rolling in agitation. It was not so much as what the Minotaur's death made her feel, but the lack of what she was feeling that concerned her. As the walls of the maze began falling around them. Jada began to glow. With the rush of power flowing through her she felt as if she was floating. Her army left the grounds and returned double the size with the addition of the skeletal remains of the minotaur's that her army had vanquished. The skeleton seemed to be disoriented, and soon lifted their boney muzzles to the sky braying loudly as they mourned their new reality.

She looked directly at Gabriel as she dropped the first head to the ground. Then turned her back on him completely as her attention turned to Silvestri's king. Nero's beautiful smile was a frightening thing to behold. So out of place amid the death and carnage that laid before him. What was even more frightening was that she looked forward to fighting him just as much as he was looking forward to fighting her. Her hand waved toward the field inviting him to make his next move.

Nero's smiled widened as he bowed his head in acquiesced to her challenge. "Pawn to H4."

"Queen to H4." Jada hissed as Nero threw another pawn into her path. That was not at all, what she had wanted, and Nero knew it. She was almost insulted that he did not come himself.

"Jada stop!" Jada ignored Irshad's voice as she made her way to the designated square. She had a head to collect, or he would not be there to reprimand her tomorrow.

Jada watched in curiosity as a forest popped up in front of her. She warily led her army in and suddenly the trees uprooted themselves. Long wooden arms began to flinger her soldiers every which way. They were on the dayside of the board and her army was weaker. They were not as fast as the trees that were now tossing them through the air.

Jada sighed and held out her hand. The fire started as the small blaze that it always did, but this time it developed into a massive column that she was now strong enough to manipulate with both hands. The trees heard the rush of flames and slowly began to back away as she calmly walked forward. Some even started to run in the other direction, but their size made it more of a hurried shamble. She looked into the frightened eyes of the trees that watched her and lifted the flames to her lips with a smile. Taking a deep breath before they puckered and blew the fire out over the startled forest.

She would never forget the wooden screams of the trees as the fire washed over them. The broken nightmarish sound would give her nightmares for the rest of her life.

The trees were running around through the square, which only fanned the flames higher. Jada felt a momentary pang of regret but was soon forgotten as the next rush of power stretched through her limbs and lifted her from the ground. Her childlike laugh was giddy as her fingers curled into her curls feeling the newly pointed tips of her ears. She bit back a moan at the warm sear of pleasure as the power spread beneath her skin. The lives of her opponents forgotten in the ecstasy of almost limitless power.

When she landed her army had grown once more, but this time they had full armor on. She did not bother looking back at Gabriel to show off the head she collected. If he wanted it, he could damn well come pick it up himself. She was busy.

"Knight to H4!" Nero called out his next move with a laugh that was as unhinged as Jada's had been. His excitement at the murder of his comrades should have set off at least some warning bells, but Jada was too far in the throes of chasing that next high of power.

There was a howl, and hundreds of large timber wolves the size of horses descend into her square. Jada calmly looked at her army with a smile. "Show me."

The skeletons began building a wall with their newly gilded shields. Their fleshless jaws gaping and snapping against dry teeth as they called out orders to each other. The skeleton that used to be Blyssed created a phalanx that had each of the shields mounted upon each other like scales. Each point where the shields met was a spear or sword ready to stab the wolves as they attacked. Jada nodded approvingly, but her attention was caught by another howl. She moved towards the wall that waited for the oncoming wolves, and two of the skeletons dropped their shields so she could look out.

There was a man on the other side of the wall. He was unfortunately attractive. Jada was already in mourning of how she was going to have to mess up the man's overly beautiful face. The werewolf in questions had dark waves cut in a low-cut Caesar. The broadshouldered caramel statue of a man's full lips spread in a bright smile that was as beautiful as the dawn. He looked like someone who belonged in the VIP section of Karnach, and not some field ready to maul someone to death with his army. He looked like expensive sex and cognac. Jada instantly regretted the actions she was about to take. He pulled his green military jacket away from his muscular frame, and it left him in a white tank top. His dark jeans hung low on his hips, and Jada shook her head at the waste of it all.

He walked out in front of the line his wolves made, and the wattage of his smile seemed to brighten as he saw her through the wall of shields. His hand lifted, and two of his fingers curled back to beckon her over. "Mira. Come out, and let's talk."

"Nah. I mean I will come out, but there won't be any talking." Jada still had a job to do, and she refused to get taken in by another pretty face.

He gave a surprised laugh and shook his head. The man smiled, and his gold-capped canines glinted in the sun that shone over his side of the board. His hand rubbed over waves of his hair that could make someone seasick. When he looked back up at her, his dark eyes had a bright yellow ring circled his irises, and she knew playtime was ending. Jada resisted the urge to look back at Gabriel; she knew what she had to do. However, they had not lied when they spoke of Silvestri's fondness for beautiful men.

"It's a shame really I was going to kill you gently. A doll like you deserves to die with a smile on her face." Jada's eyes narrowed as she tried to place his accent. The suit and the quick way some of the words cut off placed her in the mind of New York. The endearment he used reminded her of slang from old film noir movies. She assumed he was taken during the Harlem Renaissance.

"It's okay, I like it rough." Jada shrugged, and waited for him to make a move.

"Oh it will be, just know that this could have went an entirely different way." He looked back out over his snarling wolves, and a fond smile tugged at the corner of his mouth. "How about we do this. I am sure you do not want any of your army hurt. I would rather not get any of my friends killed. How about we do this one on one?"

Jada nodded and the shields peeled back to allow her to walk forward. Once she was about a hundred yards away her sword lifted and nodded. "Let's hurry. I have places to be."

The man ran up to her just as she finished preparing herself for the fight. Jada turned, and as she was about to stab him, he disappeared. They continued like that for a while. Jada was taking heavy damage because the man was so fast. With all the winning she had been doing, she had managed to forget that she could bleed. Her cockiness was costing her, and she would have to hurry

374

and figure out another plan of attack before she was as dead. He suddenly appears behind her and pulls her into his arms. His tongue slowly dragging along the pulse in her neck.

"It's a shame really. I could have toyed with you for hours." The soft hum of regret, grated on Jada's nerves, but she was angrier with herself then she was at him. He had not been caught off guard, she had. She could feel the blood trickle down her arm from the multiple hits the werewolf had landed.

Jada quickly took stock of her position and made a quick decision. She returned his sunny smile with an even brighter one of her own. She half turned in his embrace, and her hands slid behind his neck pulling him closer. "There's still time."

Her lips connected with his, and the wolf gave a soft growl of approval at her sudden submission. His hands slowly caress the curves of her waist as he pulls her back against him. The world smiles into the kiss and tries to pull away from her to catch his breath. Only Jada would not let him go. In fact, his body was starting to disintegrate at his feet. Jada held on tighter as he started to scream into the kiss, it was her turn to hum in approval as he tried in vain to pull away from her. Her tongue languidly gliding against his capped fangs as they disappeared along with the rest of him.

Without his arms, holding her Jada fell to the ground with a sharp laugh. The skeletons at once came to stand around her protectively. The light engulfed her once more, and she could not stop laughing at the tickle of power that roiled through her once more. The light teased her senses until she spent upon the ground pulling in deep breaths. She gave a happy sigh and rolled up from the ground with the help of the skeletons that stood at her side. Her army had grown once more, and slowly black snake began to etch their way onto the shields of her army. A sudden memory of the snake that escaped its cage at Herr Drosselmier's took away some of the joy that she had felt moments before.

Despite her curiosity at what the new symbol on their shield meant, her gaze traveled unbidden to Nero. Her smile spread as it was her move, and she had a clear path to him. His mile widened and his arms spread as if welcoming her home. Her smile was a match for his as she spoke her next move.

"Queen to E..."

"We call the match. Gabriel's pet won." Both Nero and Jada turned to glare balefully at Silvestri as she yet again delayed the inevitable. Something in their eyes must have scared her because she sobered all the way up from her fairy dust induced binge. Quickly making her way from the dais where the other council members watched her soberly from their seats.

Nero turned angrily away from the field, and Jada could not say that she was not as upset. The fight would have been a glorious one. She now understood what Odin meant when he said he wanted a worthy battle to die in.

"Jada."

Jada turns sharply holding her sword up to Irshad's neck. She hastily took it down with a guilty cough. "I'm sorry

Irshad. I am still hyped up from the fight. I would never hurt you."

Irshad waved her off with apology impatiently, as he looked her over. "Understandable, are you okay?"

Jada guessed she looked a fright. The last fight had not been easy, and she had barely come out of it alive. She smiled tiredly and tried to gather her adrenaline scattered thoughts. "Irshad, I feel like I could fly!"

Irshad pulled in a deep breath visibly trying to keep his temper down. "Jada you can't keep doing this to yourself."

"If I hadn't kept doing this Gabriel would have had you kill yourself!" Jada snapped as his sensible words rained on her murder-fueled parade.

"And I'm grateful, but I would rather be dead then you become what I am. Even worse what Nero is. I at least care about the loss of life I'm causing." Irshad returned her argument just as heatedly. He was clearly in no mood to back down from this argument.

"And what am I Irshad?" Jada's clipped words were a sharp staccato against the grinding of her teeth. If he wanted to fight, she would give him one. After all of the work and effort she expended to continue his existence!

Irshad's voice dropped to a gentler tone, and he sadly shook his head. "On the verge of becoming a monster.

Do not let Gabriel use us to twist you, Jada.

Remember who you are and where you came from."

Jada lips parted, and no sound came from them for a moment. She took a second to listen to what he was saying, and she was not sure what to believe about herself any longer. "Do I Irshad? Do I want to go back to that cesspool of racism, sexism, war, and bigotry? At least here, I can see them coming at me. At least when I'm used here there is a reward that's twice the amount of pain, I have to suffer for it!"

"But there you are free." Irshad's hand lift to tuck a curl gently behind her ear. His dark yes gazing earnestly into hers. His worried gaze focusing deeply into her eyes. "There you can say no."

Jada abruptly turns from Irshad and takes a deep breath. She was feeling too many emotions in a short span of time. She did not know how to process all the information that was being thrown at her. "I hear you Irshad. Go back to the oubliette. I will be on my way soon."

"Take care." Irshad wraps his arms around her in a hug that her body complexly relaxed into. He nodded curtly to her and disappearing off the field. Leaving her thinking about what he had said.

"I was honestly hopping that you would fail." Jada turns back around sharply to see Gabriel watching her in irritated amusement where Irshad once stood. "I truly hate how much time you spend with that dog. All of them actually."

"They are my family." Jada snapped not in any mood for his jealousy. It was his fault she was in this mess in the first place.

Gabriel's head leaned to the side as his eyes contracted. He studied her for a moment. "Am I not your family?"

Jada gives him a slow shake of her head. "You belong to Devanshi, and the council who sanction these murder games. So, no."

Gabriel pulls her roughly into his embrace and buries his nose into her jasmine scented coils. "Why do you fight what we both know you feel? Do you think that puppy, and your family of broken toys can give you what I can?"

"Gabriel, please let me go." Jada was hard pressed to fight what she was feeling. When he held her, she was forced to confront some uncomfortable truths about the way she felt for him.

His arms wrapped even tighter around her and a placed a frustrated kiss at the top of head. "Never! You're mine, and we both know there is no one else for either of us!"

Jada pulls out roughly out of his arms pulling in deep breaths to staunch the flow of feelings she had for him. Inwardly grimacing at the blood, she left on his white suit. "We are toxic together Gabriel, why can't you see that?"

Gabriel's hand raked back through his hair in agitation. "We are powerful together, Jada. I watched that last transformation and I burned right beside you. You are becoming as powerful as Nero, and I could eat every second of it with a spoon. I could not take my eyes off you. Do not let that "family" of defective dolls make you afraid of who you are!"

"I am not a monster." Jada's words tremored despite the way she pulled his jacket tightly around her shoulders. Her eyes closing as if it could shield herself from the effect his words were having on her.

Gabriel, sighs, and pulls out an expensive looking linen handkerchief to clear away some of the blood on her face and arms. "You are everything I dream about at night. If that makes you a monster, so be it! The only one that makes you feel bad about who you are

becoming is you, and that puppy you refuse to let me kill."

"I am the same person I was when I got here Gabriel!" Jada snapped waving her hands over herself. "What you see is what you have always gotten!"

Gabriel laugh was derisive and humorless. He peeled his jacket away and draped it around her shoulders. Parts of armor had come loose during the fight. His hands lifted gently to trace along her ears and his fingers laced together behind her neck. The warm honey of his gaze was humorless as he looked into her eyes. His lips quirking up at the end at whatever he saw reflected at him. "You are not at all the same person you were when you got here. You used to stumble over yourself trying to tell Theo your nightly playlist. Now you would murder him while Leticia watched because the volume was too high. You have changed, and you will continue to change with each win."

"Stop touching me."

Gabriel immediately dropped his hands from her shoulders and took a step back. "As you wish, but what I said was no less true."

Jada sharply tuned away from him, and she disappeared from the field to the safety of the oubliette. Everyone looked up as she came in, and she gave them a tentative smile. The weight of keeping everyone alive was starting to wear on her. The adrenaline had worn off, and all she wanted to do was to recuperate in silence. She ignored Odin's angry glare, as she moved to her own seat amongst the large glowing crystals. He was a problem for another day, right now she just wanted to get lost in the blue glow of the crystals. She caught her reflection in the crystals as she settled into her seat. Her lips parted on a scream of angry frustration. Her black serpentine eyes reflected the golden irises of the monster she was becoming.

Chapter Twenty

Q ueen to E5! Check!" Nero's voice called out the
command, but his eyes never left Jada's. Jada was
fine with it because her eyes never left his on this
bright sunny afternoon. She had been having trouble with
Odin trying to usurp her board from beneath her, and it
was taking everything in her not to go over to his square
and kill him for the other the team. Playing his way would
get one of them all killed.

"Silvestri takes the match!" Gabriel smiled and stretched
before turning and guiding Devanshi towards the
mansion. The other board members soon disappearing
behind him.

The tip of Jada's tongue brushes along the inside of her
cheek in irritation. She looked up just long enough to see

Nero give her a slow nod towards the center of the field. She returned it and began to walk towards the center of the field. He clearly had something to say.

"You're playing will despite the... distractions."

Nero's amused voice grated on what was left on Jada's nerves, and she returned the smile with one of her own. However, admittedly it was not as friendly.

"You mean Odin trying to undermine me at every turn?" Jada rolled her eyes towards the heavens hoping they would give her the strength she was not finding on the ground. "I do have seem to have a habit of collecting frustrating men. He has a bigger death wish then you do it seems." C

Nero smiled and shrugged his pale brown shoulders." We cannot all belong to a council member that loves them the way Gabriel loves you.

"Silvestri seems quite partial to you." Jada frowned in confusion up at Nero. "I do believe that was her calling that match when I was getting ready to meet you in your square."

"It is the other way around I'm afraid. It is I who am in love with her." This time Nero's smile was quite melancholy, and Jada had to bite back any retorts about the Silvestri's lovability. Her own voice rising

inside of her head to whisper "Pot meet kettle and all."

"Then why the death wish?" Jada sheathed Gabriel's sword; the match was over so there was no reason to have it out any longer. She was in no danger from Nero outside of the match and neither was he from her.

"I want to die before she does. I know her time is ending. The nightmares I have been having about it keep me from enjoying what time I have left with her. I want to get off this ride before its inevitable stop." Nero stopped speaking and for a moment the electric blue of his eyes seemed to focus on something, only he could see. "I'm tired of killing people to keep this machine running for someone who refuses to stray from this path."

Jada shook her head vehemently; he was ruining at least part of her plan to save him. "How can you be so sure? What if you win?"

"We won't win, Jada. I knew the moment Gabriel waltzed you into Drosselmier's shop that it was over. Today's win just prolonging the inescapable conclusion to this act."

"Then why did you save me that day? Why not just throw the matches if you're so sure?" Jada was floundering trying to figure out how to rescue someone that had no desire to be saved. She was so tired of feeling helpless in the lives of the people she cared for.

Nero seemed to focus on something over her shoulder, and a ghost of his normal smile tugged his lips. "Because I will do nothing that harms Silvestri. She is my North star. I envy how you and Gabriel love each

other so openly. Maybe I will have that in the next life."

"Or this one!" She ignored the comment about

Gabriel, but Jada refused to give up on saving him. "I could use my wish to take you home with us! A place where there are women who would be only too glad to love you! They would cook you breakfast, wash your clothes, and give you children! With you doing very little but smiling. Help me help you!"

"You still believe the world beyond the briars is your home?" Nero's head tossed back as a genuine laughed filled his chest. He pulled her into a sad hug and began rocking her back and forth. "I never thought of you as someone who lied to themselves."

Jada leaned forward resting her forehead on his shoulder and shook her head. It was nice to speak to someone who was in the same boat that she was regardless of how fast they were both sinking. "It's where we are from Nero."

He stopped rocking her to lean back, waiting until she lifted her eyes to meet his. "But is it your home Jada?"

Jada just looked into his eyes for a moment and tried to stop another angle trying to convince him not to use her to commit suicide. "Why not just tell Silvestri to give up the throne?"

Nero's brow lifted over his sad smile, and he shook his head again. "Do think Gabriel would give up the throne willingly if he, had it?"

"He said he would." The answer she gave was as pouty as it was ridiculous, she could not hate Nero for the laugh he was having at her expense in that moment. The statement was childish even to her. Her chin dropping in frustration at the spot Nero was putting her in. "I know, don't say it."

"He also knew you wouldn't abandon this board. He played you like a fiddle, and I love you for it." Nero released a sigh and gently shook his head. He lets his fingers fall to hers and twined his fingers through them. His thumb stroking along her palm. "You're too good inside, and it hurts you. It is why he loves you. You're nothing like him."

Jada took a deep breath and shook her head in contradiction to his words. "I don't feel good. I feel like a monster."

"Almost." His other hand brushes beneath her chin, so that her eyes met his once more. "Fairy has physically changed you, but it has not taken your soul."

"Do we still have one?"

Nero smiled, and brought the hand that held hers up to his lips in a chaste kiss. "No, we don't, but you do. Even now, you feel guilty about the lives you have taken. Maybe not on the field, but I know you see them when you close your eyes in the oubliette. Tell me you don't."

Jada felt him slipping further and further away, and she was mentally scrambling to find a way to save him. "Nero there has to be another way. It cannot end like this for you! Not after all this!"

"Even now, you're trying to save me." He leans forward and placed a kiss on her forehead. "I wish I had met you sooner. I would have held onto my soul a little longer." Nero releases her he and leaves her in the field.

Once he was gone a few tears rolled down her cheeks. The release of those tears released the dam of emotions she had been holding back since she had come to fairy. Her hands covered her face, and she just allowed herself to be weak in that moment. She just needed that moment alone. Tomorrow would come and she would be strong then. Right now, she just didn't want to be the one holding everything together. Jada fell to her armor covered knees weeping in rage-filled frustration. Nothing was going to plan; it was so painful to watch everything fall apart around her. "I hate it here."

"Who made you cry Jada? I will kill them."

Jada looked up through her tears to see Gabriel, kneeling in front of her in his navy-blue council suit. Ignoring the grass stains, he was getting on his knees as he watches her in grim concern. She crawls forward and wraps her arms about his shoulders. Her body shuddering against his as she continues to cry into his linen covered shoulder. "Jada precious, what's wrong. Tell me where it hurts. Who did this to you?" His hands tenderly stroke through her coils until her sobs ebb into soft sniffles and hiccups. Just whispering soothing nonsense while his hand rubs her back in soothing circles. At least until she pushed him away and began hitting him in the chest.

"You! This is your fault! I hate you! I wish I had never met you! You made me love you, and then turned me into a monster. I hate you so much I can't see straight!" Each sentence was met with a strike against his chest. Jada was seething, and there was nothing better to take her rage out on then the person who caused it.

"Jada, calm down what happened?" Gabriel catches her fist as she went in for a few more strikes. His gold eyes sweeping over her in concern.

"You! You're what happened!" Jada yanks her hands back and stands up so she could pace back and forth. Her words more for herself then him. "I hate you, and I hate myself because I don't hate you the way I should!"

Gabriel continued to kneel on the ground watching her walk back and forth during her tirade. After a few moments of listening his lips tug at the corners but kept his expression politely attentive. "So, what you're saying is that you love me?"

"No! What I said is that I hated you! Haven't you been listening? I can't stand you, but I can't go a day without wondering about you!" Jada continued her agitated pacing, not really paying that much attention to Gabriel. If she were then she would notice the way he stood and pulled off his jacket before tossing it to the ground. She turned to pace the other way still angrily calling him out on the mess he had made of her life. "I am so tired of everything! Gabriel. I'm tired of fighting in this tournament to go to a place I'm not sure I want to be any more. I'm tired of fighting with Odin and trying to save Nero. I'm tired of fighting whatever nonsense this is that I feel for you!"

Had Jada been paying attention to anything other than the ire that continued to spill past her lips she would have also dodged the arms that grabbed her shoulders and spun her around. She jerked back only to be hauled into the circle of Gabriel's embrace. Jada glared up at him with just as much rage, but it did not seem to affect Gabriel in the slightest or the smile that broke across his face like the sun. "So, does that mean that I can kiss you now?"

"No! You absolutely may not!" Jada took a step back but did not get very far with gentle press of Gabriel's arms around her. Her golden irises flash up at him, and her hands rest on his chest pushing him back. "Let me go!"

Gabriel laughed, but did not release her. He just smiled and continued to watch her face as continued with his questions. His arms tightened around her and he slowly began to rock her back and forth. "Are you staying here with me over the briars?"

"Yes, but I'm sending Irshad and the others back with my wish!" Her defiant glare dared him to disagree, and from the bemused look on Gabriel's face she need not have bothered with the silent threat of her anger.

"Of course, of course, It will save me the trouble of kill them." He smiled at the sharp thump to his chest from a fist that was much smaller than his was. "I'm kidding. Kidding!" His lips tugged even wider at the disbelieving scowl Jada's face. "Okay I'm not, but we don't have to worry about that now if you're staying here!"

Jada parted her lips to say something, and whatever it had been lost with the taste of Gabriel's lips against hers. She allowed herself to get lost in his touch and ignored every consequence she knew would be coming. At that moment, she didn't care. Her fingers greedily pulled him forward, and his arms wrapped about her tighter. Neither wanted to let go, but eventually both needed air.

"What happens next?" Jada laced her fingers behind his neck unsure of what to do, but reluctant to lose contact with him. There were so many variables to consider, and so many things that could go wrong. But she was glad to at least have this decision made.

Gabriel continued to press reassuring kisses over her neck and jaw line. His fingers curling into her dark coils despite the way she gently pulled back. Her chin lifting, so that he could look down into her eyes. He sighed in impatient happiness and shook his head. "What do you mean? We plan our wedding and move you to my… ah actually" Gabriel kept one arm wrapped around her waist, but his other hand sheepishly scratched the back of his head. "I'll stay in your room. There is an orgy happening in mine right now."

Jada pushed back against Gabriel's chest in annoyance. "Gabriel, seriously!"

Gabriel laughed unashamedly with a shrug. "What? I wasn't going to participate …much"

"You know something…" Jada pulled out of his arms and turned to walk away. "Just forget it."

Gabriel sobered, and pulled her back into him arms with a cheery laugh. He leaned in and brushed his nose across hers and pulled in a deep breath as his shoulders relaxed. "What comes next is up to you. I know that I love you. That I have always loved you, and that you feel the same. Come on, let's go make plans before you change your mind. You know how fickle you women folk are."

Jada laughed as she was pulled away from the field, but she looked up in time to see Odin glaring down at them from the courtyard containing Yamja's fountain. The grey blue of his eyes promised a storm that she was no longer afraid of. She watched him for a moment before turning her attention back to Gabriel and her future. She would deal with Odin tomorrow. Jada swore silently swore on Odin's life there would not be.

Chapter Twenty One

Pawn to F4!" Nero makes his move, and Jada could not help but notice how serene he looked. As if, he had made his confession and was ready to die. It was too bad for him that Jada had other plans for him. The spaceship slowly meandered onto the field, and not for the first time Jada wondered what would jump out if anyone ever engaged it.

"Arthur to E5." Jada eagerly moved her pawn forward and Irshad lifted his brow but said nothing. Jada felt guilty, but when they won the tournament, he would understand. They would all understand. Arthur looked puzzled but moved as she was bid. The last fight hadn't her with many griffins, but she moved without complaint.

"Pawn to E5." Nero looked up at her in surprise at how easily she sacrificed the knight. The centaurs confidently rushed onto the field. The fight was brutal, but Arthur would live.

"We are requesting an alternate. Asher if you would take her place, please." A dashing musketeer came onto the board. He swept his hat from his perfectly coifed tight black curls and bowed to Jada. Jada nodded to the musketeer but did not look at the rest of her team. She knew they were giving her the same looks that Irshad was. They would just have to trust the process. She would save all of them; they just had to hold on for a little more. Arthur was roughed up, but she and the rest of her griffins would live

"D7 to D6." Jada smiled, she admittedly was being a little reckless, but she knew she could win this one. Then they could end the whole tournament a lot sooner if they played more aggressively. She took steadying breath that was released in the mantra that she had been saying to herself all morning. "Everything is under control; I just have to keep winning."

"Look at her sacrificing the board to be with her lover." Odin snapped angrily as he watched Hazel rush out onto the field on a carriage pulled by deer. He looked back at Jada with sullen fury as she continued to make questionable moves on the board.

Jada grits her teeth and ignores Odin's commentary. She also watched Hazel move to her square. She had always though the hedge witch with her orange curls and freckles was cute. Like she had stepped right out of a Grimm's fairytale. She was one also one of the weaker players. She wouldn't last very long in a fight, and it was best to move her now. Jada turned her head to glance over at Odin with a lift of her brow but said nothing. Dismissing him from her thoughts completely she focused on Nero, and his board nothing else mattered right now.

Nero frowned at her aggressive moves and turns to a large black tortoise that he had developed earlier in the match. "Pawn to D6."

Another pawn was taken from Jada, as the tortoise pulled his legs and feet in and rolled over the army of rabbits that the hedge which called to the field. There were a few casualties, but it was fine. She needed to remove the weaker ones to alternates for the next fights. This way they would live to see the end of the tournament. Her methods looked horrible, but the results would be worth it. They were not taking any hits that Jada would not take herself. The game was about to get rough, and she would rather them be a little hurt and survive then be on the field and end up dead.

"We require our next alternate Lilly. If you would take the lovely Hazel's place!" Jada's smile was almost blinding in its intensity. One more move, and this match would be hers. "Bishop to D6" Jada called moving Valkari forward and out of her way. She was almost out of her cage. "Come on, just a little more."

"Knight to C3" Nero watched Jada with the first signs of temper that she had ever seen from him. A large man with an axe moved towards the field. His body was covered with blood, and his slightly balding head was red from the sun. As he walked dark red figures bubbled up from the ground behind. He lurched forward watching

Gabriel's board with empty sockets where they should have been eyes.

"Yes!" The Jada hissed as she moved forward. "Queen to H4."

Both Odin and Irshad looked as if they were about to have a stroke on the field as they turned to look at her. She laughed as her skeletal army made their way to the designated square putting herself in the direct line of fire.

Nero's angry confusion was palpable. He was looking for a trick as he scoured the board but could not see anything in her moves. "Pawn to G3." A tall spindly man with the head of a pumpkin strode out onto the field. His dry wooden fingers sprinkled hay all around him as he walked to his designated square. When the hay landed the scattered bits pulled themselves together until they formed an army of scarecrows.

What he found was Jada ready to wage war on behalf of her promises. "Queen to G3."

"Jada stop!" Irshad shouted at her from across the board, but she was busy moving towards her objective of winning this last fight.

The pumpkin head's mouth hinged open and short bursts of fire puffed from its knobby orange teeth as it laughed at her approaching army. The scarecrows shivered sharing in their leader's amusement. Hay falling from their limbs as they shambled forward. Jada assumed that if they had been on the night side of the board more scarecrows would be produced. Not that it left her lot of room to gloat. Her own army was at a disadvantage on the day side of the board. They would not be able to regenerate here.

The pumpkin head covered his fiery mouth and gave a high-pitched snicker. "Are you going to show me a trick? I think I'll give your head to Lady Silvestri as a treat." The pumpkin head stretched before waving his flannel covered army forward with a wave of his pitchfork. They moved in front of him, as their jagged burlap maws laughed in dry imitation of the Silvestri's knight. "I will be gracious and make your death quick. You can thank me by putting your sword down and giving up."

"Thank you, but I think I'll take my chances." Jada laugh was almost giddy as she walked ahead of her army. Her army had gotten so large that the sound of their armor was clinked a dirge that rang out behind her. The skeleton army lifting their shields and weapons as they marched forward. Their bleached bones almost glowing in the sun's bright light.

The pumpkin head laughs, and his head almost unhinged as fire bursts through his carved smile. His army laughs but the sound was just the shuddering of burlap against straw. "I'll make you wish you had!"

His scarecrows moved into a sharp run from their shambles and the first scarecrow fell beneath Jada's sword soon followed by another. Each scarecrow scattered and knit itself back together. Jada frowned and continued to swing. Her army was having the same problem. Their swords and spears would cut through the straw dolls only to have the holes fill back in.

"This shouldn't be happening." She glared across at the smiling pumpkin head, who leered at her from behind his. Her skeletons were starting to take the worst of fight. Even the size of her army was no match for their oddly regenerative power.

"You look confused" The pumpkin head shifted until he became humanoid. The resulting change produced a tall sun-tanned farmer with dark blond hair, and hazel eyes. He was chewing on piece of straw as he walked toward her. Once he reached her, his hand lifted to tip his hat to her. His bright white smile beaming at her. "I am stronger on the night side; however, my army belongs to the day. You ready to give up now? I'd hate to kill such a pretty lady."

Jada allowed her gaze to sweep over the attractive shirtless man but refrained from allowing her eyes to roll. "Silvestri must have raided a male revue for her board."

The former pumpkin head laughed which set off another shiver of silent laughter from his army. "I was working on my homestead in Kansas actually. So how about giving up? I'll put in a good word for you with Silvestri."

Jada could hear her army becoming frustrated. However, the man was being polite and that was something that she hadn't received all day. "No but thank you. I am going to extend the same offer to you as well. Please give up. Id would really rather you live."

The farmer laughed and soon the pitch returned to the high give that belonged to the pumpkin head. His body stretched back into his spindly arms and orange head. The pumpkin head was finding it hard to catch his breath, and his stick fingers had to wipe away a few pumpkin seeds from his eyes. "Your army is falling by the dozen. You will be alone soon. What deal could you possibly offer me on the day side of the board?"

"Then we will create our own darkness. Drag them to hell!" Jada shouts at her army, and the skeletons drop their weapons and grab the scarecrows by their arms and legs. The frantic dry screams rustle through the air as the skeletons pull them beneath the ground.

The pumpkin head's high-pitched giggle soon turns into a full roar. He swings his pitchfork down at her, and she rolls out of the way before she is impaled on the sharp metallic tongs. Lifting her sword in time to block another strike. The muscles in her arms vibrated with the force of his strikes. She wouldn't be able to take too many of those before she lost the use of her arm completely.

'Give. Me. Back. My. Army!" The pumpkin head screamed at her. Each staccato word was punctuated with a strike. It was all Jada could do to keep from being stabbed on the ground. They are mine! Give them back!"

"Silvestri's army is certainly high strung." Jada sweeps the pumpkin heads legs from beneath him. She scrambles up and begins to stomp down into the sticks that held his wrist together. The dry twigs splintered and cracked, but he pulled his arm out, and she rolled out of the way.

"I will…" The pumpkin head mouth opens only to have a spear push through the back of his throat. Soon row after row of spear pushed through his body. The skeletons had come back up, now impaled him waiting for Jada to inflict the final blow.

Jada was tired, so she simply cut off his head.

Watching it roll onto the ground until the fire went out. She looked into the hollow eyes of the ogre skeleton and lifted her brow. "What took you so long?"

Ignoring the mass shrug of her army she sank to the ground waiting for the rush of warmth and rapture that came from killing her opponent. Only there was no warmth and no rapture. Just a searing white-hot pain that spread through her limbs. The pain was so great that she dropped to dropped back onto the ground in agony. She began to scream but the sound was cut off by another moan of pain as the fire began to burn through skin. Her heart hammered against her chest as if trying to burst through her rib cage. Every one of her limbs were on fire. Her clothes no match for the flame that engulfed her.

"Jada!" Irshad's voice sounded so far way in the rushing between Jada's ears.

She writhed on the ground as the same fire that consumed her soon engulfed her skeletons. The army turning to piles of ash all around her. Her arm stretched out as she tried to reach out to them. Her fingers began to blister and the flesh fell away from her bones, soon the pain began to subside as the blaze cauterized the nerve endings they exposed and melted away.

"Nero! Kill her now!" Silvestri's shrill voice galvanized Nero into uncertain action as he reluctantly performed as he was bid. "Pawn to G3!"

A warlock came out onto the field with a swish of his dark red tunic. His eyes were empty black sockets that blindly made his way towards Jada's square with his army of dark paladins. With each step, every blade of grass within three yards withered and died beneath his sandaled feet. Soon a large mass of locust collected in the sky screeching and flying towards Jada.

"Jada get up!" Princeton called out as Jada was still laying on the ground weakly staring up at the sky. Only blinking when the first red droplets fell over her raw skin. She could only watch as the sky became angry with dark clouds that churned and filled the air with a shower of blood. She had thought that she couldn't feel any more pain, but the blood that stung her kin let her know how wrong she was.

The hum of millions of locust wings became louder as the arched up into the sky to gather above her preparing to strike her down. She looked up at them with a tired smile as she watched all her plans dissolving in front of her eyes.

"It's over, I can't." Jada tiredly whispered towards the sky. She could hear the screams for her to get up, but all she could focus on was all the losses. Her heart was slowing down, and she was so tired. Her mind swirled with all the things she could not accomplish.

Her board? Gone. Her freedom? Gone. Her life? Over. Gabriel? Gone.

Her eyes close as the horde of locusts descended. Another drop of blood hit her cheek; she screams as her back arches from the ground. Her skin began to ripple and replace itself with a fine coat of black scales. A deep gasp of air pulls into her lungs, and sharp piercing scream echoes and pulses out around the board. Every locust disintegrates as they rush down into the trajectory of her scream. Her hands rest on the bloody ground, and she slowly pulls herself up into a sitting position. There was no euphoria with this change, only pain, and she intended to share every moment of that pain with her opponent. Jada moves to her knees, lifting the back of her hand to brush away the blood from her chin. Her fingers curl around Gabriel's sword, and she pulls herself up from the ground. The first steps were torture, but it did not matter. She had to keep moving. She had to win.

The tip of Gabriel's sword slowly dragged across the ground as she made her way towards her enemy. As she walks by the piles of ash that used to be her army, hands covered in rotted flesh began to pull themselves up from the ground. The clinking and clanking of polished brass rang out around her as she continued to make her way towards the warlock. Her armor that burned away replaced themselves into a black formfitting halter and pants that looked like leather until one came close and saw the scales. The brass fittings at her elbows and knees matched the plates that covered her shoulders. Her ears shifted into fine points at the top, and her hair reverted to the curly afro that she had when she first came to Fairy.

Skeletons of varying sizes fell in step behind her had gained flesh, but their eyes remained as hollow as those of the warlock before them. Their skin was a dry mottled grey that peeled back away from their teeth exposing the fangs that each of them had grown. Her army had grown so large that it was amazing that the warlock had found room to keep his army there. The flesh forms began to beat their spears and swords against their shields as she walked by. Their focus was drawn to the paladins that stood to oppose them.

Jada stood in front of her army and lifted Gabriel's sword into the sky. The forked tip of her tongue brushed over her lips as she faced the warlock with all the angry power that flowed through her veins. Her dark serpentine gaze moved over the army with an air of boredom, as she knew they were no match for her current incarnation. Her eyes met Nero's wide eyes with the disappointment she felt at the move he made to kill her while she was incapacitated. Nero looked ashamed, but there was another emotion there. For the first time since she had known Nero, he looked afraid. Whether it was of her or for her would remain to be seen. With a swing of the sword, her army surged forward toward the paladin army.

The paladin's must have wanted a quick death with the way they practically threw themselves in front of her army. Even if they had been excellent swordsmen there were overrun by the sheer numbers of the living dead that became a plague onto them. For herself as she walked through the battle the paladins closest to her burst into flame only to crawl from their incinerated remains to fight their brethren.

As she came closer, the warlock pulled out a dagger from the rope that held his tunic together. "I see Gabriel's whore learned a trick that doesn't require a pole."

"I was going to just kill you before, but now I'm going to make it painful." Jada hissed as she walked around him. Waiting for hum to start the dance that would end his life.

"You won't get the chance harlot." The warlock shouts at her before he lunges forward.

Jada deflects his first swing and clicks her cleft tongue repeatedly against the roof of her mouth. "Not very agile, are you? If you were not about to die, I could have taught you some stretches. C'est la vie, and all that."

The warlock swings, again and this time the deflection comes with a kick to the center of his chest that sends him flying to the ground. "Are you even trying?"

The warlock grunts in angry frustration as he picks himself up out of the dirt, and a ball of fire collects in his hands. "Let's see if you're still cocky after I burn you to a crisp."

Jada sighs and shakes her head. "You don't want to do that."

"Oh, believe me I do!" His hands shove the ball of fire towards Jada in a torrential column of flames. The fire was so large, and consuming Jada's form seemed to disappear within the blaze. The warlock soon tired and allowed the flames to dissipate.

Jada stood closer to him then when the fire started and leaned forward with dark smile. The forked tip of her tongue stroking over his ear. "Boo!"

They continued to fight. The warlock nicked her a few times, and each cut swelled with signs of disease that spread from the wounds. He dropped to the ground and rolled away as his dagger grazed her leg. Jada hissed angrily and cut off a few of his fingers in retaliation. The warlock screamed in rage and began fighting in earnest.

Flinging fireballs and thrusting his dagger in clumsy stabs that would leave him off balance. In one such swing, Jada side stepped past a fireball, and used Gabriel's sword to pull the warlock's ankle from under him. He pulled his arm back to aim another fireball at her, only to have his hand lopped off with the sword. He dropped the dagger with a scream and held his arm at the now cauterized stump that used to be his hand.

"You bi..." The warlock's words were cut off as Jada removed his head from his body.

"Check, and the next person that brings up me being a stripper is going to die. How all of you can sit on high to judge me, while you kill people is insane! I will tolerate it no longer!" Jada snapped across the board to Nero then turned to the council that sat watching her soberly from their dais. "From anyone."

Jada dropped to the ground, next to the beheaded warlock in exhaustion. A booted foot petulantly kicking the head away from her. Her army moved to stand around her, waiting for the next command. She sat on the ground, examining the festered cuts that ran along her legs and arms in aggravation. She looked up at her army, and the shiny brass of their shields were once emblazoned with a snake now had cobra in their stead.

"We are calling an alternate." Nero came out to the field, and Jada's army drew close effectively cutting off his access to her. "Jada, please tell your army to let me in. Allow me to tend to your wounds."

"Let him through guys. We won the match, but he took the square. I'm safe for now." Jada's sour voice called out to the living dead, and they unwillingly let Nero through ready to attack if necessary.

"What am I going to do with you?" Nero squatted down to look at her with a shake of his head. He slid his arm beneath her and carried her back towards his side of the board.

"My hero." Jada cooed mockingly as she watched her wounds close up as he carried her over the board. Though the cuts remained as large angry red welts over her skin.

"Jada you don't understand what you did to yourself." Nero's low voice was subdued and reproachful as he carried her towards his square.

"I know exactly what I'm doing. I'm saving all of you." Jada hummed happily in the comfort of Nero's arms. Now that the fight was over she could afford to be gracious. "This isn't the time or place, but did anyone ever tell you that you're kind of cute when you're grumpy?"

"Yes. But that's not the point Jada" Nero sighed with an angry roll of his eyes. He carried her to his square and turned toward Irshad who was now in control of the Gabriel's board. She was captured not killed. So, for the time being she belonged to him. "Who is going to save you?"

"Deyani to G3." Irshad snaps angrily as he continues to play the game in Jada's stead.

The Naga that slithered over the ground with her army and made quick work of the witch hunters that Nero had alternated. His entire board seemed to be shell shocked by the loss of the warlock. As if the prospect of losing had never occurred to them before. The army raised their weapons in a triumphant hiss that grew louder as her army was augmented by the witch hunter's army.

Once the witch hunter was vanquished, Irshad turned his attention back to Jada. He stalked forward across the field intent on retrieving his queen from enemy hands. "Check mate, this match is over!"

Nero's brows raise in amusement at Irshad's declaration of the match being over but bows with Jada in his arms. "We abstain and agree."

Jada's eyes closed and she turned to Nero with a whisper. She could practically feel the wrath Irshad was projecting in her direction. "I can't see Irshad's face does he look upset?"

"Positively incensed, and I don't think it's at me." Nero smiles down at Jada who gingerly looks over her shoulder at a scowling oncoming Irshad.

A deep sigh fills and releases from Jada's lungs as she sends up a quick prayer. "Nope, that's all for me."

"You deserve his ire, you know."

"I think you're wrong." Jada's voice was pouty, as she knew the fire and brimstone that was coming her way. "I think all of you should trust me."

Nero's brow lifted as he calmly watched Irshad storm over. His arms tightened around her as he carries her over to Irshad. "It's not you we don't trust Jada."

Irshad meets them in the middle of the field, and immediately pulls Jada from Nero's arms. "Thank you for seeing to the care of our rather impulsive queen"

"It's my pleasure." Nero bows to them both and walks away disappearing from the field with a smile.

Leaving Jada to the fiery wrath of knight.

"Jada."

Jada held up her hands to forestall the anger that was directed at her. "Okay Irshad, hear me out."

"I'm waiting."

Jada could see the strings that were barely holding his patience together and hurried into her explanation. "I thought that if we could shorten this tournament less of us would die right? So, I did, I had not counted on turning into this. "She waves a hand over her new self. "Have I told you how handsome you are? I feel you should cut me some slack because we won, and I'm injured!"

He did not argue, but Irshad's eyes narrowed as he looked down at her from the circle of his arms. She gave Irshad her most winning smile, and he continued to frown at her. As he turned back towards their side of the field Jada watched as his scowl deepened at something behind her. By the shiver of rage that rippled through Irshad's muscles, she knew it was Gabriel. She twisted to confirm her guess, and she had been right. Gabriel stood at the edge of the board waiting for them to come back with a tight smile. Irshad set her down between them, but his glare never left Gabriel.

"Thank you for seeing to her care."

Irshad scoffs and leans his head over and cracks his neck as if preparing for violence. "Someone needs to. Everyone else just wants to use her."

"You're trying my patience, mongrel. You're lucky

Jada is fond of you."

Irshad gently moved Jada from between them and took a step towards Gabriel. "When I'm free. I will make you pay for everything you have done to my friends and I."

"If you survive, you're welcome to try. Now give me what is mine and go back to the oubliette. We have no more need for you." Gabriel smiles and pulls Jada behind him leaving the space free for Irshad.

"Or I could do it now." Irshad smiles and his staff appears in his hands. He twirls the bow in his hands but draws up short when Jada moves in between them. Jada places her hand on his chest hoping to sooth Irshad's well-deserved anger. Though the soft growl he gave her was a warning to move out of the way.

"Irshad don't worry. I will be okay. Everything is alright and under control. I have a plan. Just trust me for a little while longer. I see you in the oubliette soon!" Jada was practically tripping over her words to staunch the fight she knew was brewing. "Please make sure the others are okay and apologize for me."

Irshad looks down and searches her new eyes for a moment. He grits his teeth, and furiously turns away from her. Disappearing from the field leaving Jada alone with Gabriel. Gabriel gathers her in his arms, and slowly begins gently rocking her in his arms.

"He's going to be a problem, Jada." His gaze never leaves the space where Irshad once stood. He places a kiss on the top of her head and begins smoothing his hands over her angry red skin. Dropping soft kisses over each of the cuts along her arms.

"No, Irshad and the others are going back over the briars soon. He'll forget all about me and this place." Jada whispered sadly as she thought about the day, she would lose her family. Her body relaxes some at the touch of his lips against her skin. Her arms moved to wrap around his shoulders trying to ignore the heady rush of desire that flooded her every time she was in Gabriel's proximity.

"I don't think anyone could forget you, Jada." Gabriel's hands skimmed down her sides to rest at her hips. Gently pulling her back into him, so that her neck was more accessible to the trail of kisses he was trying to make. His fingers gently dipping beneath the band of her new pants.

"Wait, I'm sorry. I'm not ready." Jada stepped away with a shake of her head. Doing her best to calm her accelerating heart. She had to keep her head. The tournament was not over, and she didn't want to be any more distracted by Gabriel's touch then she already was,

Gabriel smiled and pulled her back and up into his arms. "Then I will wait until you are. We have eternity together after all. Come on, I want to see to your wounds myself."

Jada laughed with joy as he carried her up the dais stairs. "Okay, but I can't be with you long. Tomorrow is a big day."

Gabriel's golden eyes narrowed slid over to her before giving her a strained smile. "I'll have you back to your makeshift family soon." His fingers cupped beneath her chin to rest a soft kiss on her forehead. "Promise!"

Chapter Twenty Two

J ada. You don't look very good." Valkari placed a
worried hand over Jada's forehead. "You're burning
up!"

Jada nodded and gave Valkari a weak smile. "Yeah, I
think whatever that warlock poisoned me with hasn't
worked its way out my system. It didn't help that I missed
getting back to the oubliette since Gabriel needed my
presence at the council get together."

Irshad brushed past Jada without saying a word. Valkari
gave her a sympathetic smile and patted her on the back.
Most of the board was ready to mutiny. It looked like
only Princeton and Valkari was willing to give her the
benefit of the doubt concerning her plan. He could have
also just been busy getting ready for the match. Jada was

not sure; the fever was making it hard for her to think. Making her see things that were not there.

She slumped back as she took a step forward. Princeton and Valkari caught her and set her back on her feet. Princeton's thick curls shook in worried agitation. "I don't know Queen bee; you may need an alternate. You can't fight like this."

"Gabriel really should have known better." Valkari's gaze slid up to the dais where Gabriel was watching them without comment or expression at the reproachful look. "You're as hot as an oven!"

Jada smiled and waved them off. "It'll be fine. I will get you out of here. I promise."

"Jada, stop worrying about us, and worry about you." Princeton snapped and pulled a handkerchief out of his pocket to dab over Jada's clammy skin. "You're not alone. Just let us handle the match today."

"Oh, is the harlot sick?" Odin walked past them to the king's position. "Then I'll be taking over today. She can watch how a real match is run."

"Odin…" Both the warning and threat in her voice was real. Jada was over Odin and his cute comments.

"Don't say another word. We cannot trust Gabriel's toy to win this match. Look at how she sacrificed us to go play footsie with Nero. She's insatiable!" Odin stretched fur covered arms and focused his attention over the field where Nero was watching them with great interest. "Just stand there and look pretty... actually with the way you look right now just stand there."

Jada's temper rose to the surface. It was like a living breathing thing that wanted to cut out the Viking's throat. "Odin, your skirts showing. Just say what you have to say and be done with it."

Odin storms over to get directly into her face. "While you've been getting cozy with your slave owner you've forgotten how he's been treating us. Who has died because of him, and how you got here. The things he has taken from us, hell the things you took from me! I pine for Yamja every night while you cuddle with her murderer next to the fire. When he is done with you, I hope he kills you in your sleep. It's kinder than what happened to Yamja"

Jada rubbed her fingers together to keep from turning Odin into ash. She knew he was hurting but she was not going to keep taking his abuse. Not with her half killing herself to get them all back over the briars. "Everything I do is to make penance for the suffering all of you have felt. I don't sleep at night…"

Odin scoffs. "You don't sleep because you're riding Gabriel every night. Do not act as if this is all for us. Just stand back and I will take care of us."

Jada laughed in his face but waved him forward. "Then by all means. I hope you do a better job of leading them then you did at the last tournament. That is how you and the people you love got here right? Because you failed?"

Odin stiffened, and he looked like he wanted to hit her. If Jada was honest, she wanted him to, she wanted the excuse to incinerate him where he stood. However, Irshad's calm voice pulled them both out of the fight that was about to take place between them. "The suns are almost in place."

Everyone took their places and prepared for the match. Jada had nothing to do, but to wait and pray that Odin knew what he was doing. Her gaze moved over to Irshad, and his lips were set in a grim line as he looked out over the other board. Odin's crows lifted from his shoulders and began to circle the board. The caw of Odin's crows gave her a chill and suddenly Jada had a bad feeling about this game.

Nero dispassionately looked over his board as if the argument on her side of the board had not happened.

He turned amidst the cries of Odin's crows. "Pawn to E4."

"Pawn to E5." The relish in Odin's voice was hard to miss. A strike of lightning arced across the sky as the wind began to pick up. The sky was beginning to fill with foreboding clouds that blotted out the twin suns.

"Knight to F3." Nero frowned disapprovingly as he saw Odin calling the board's moves today. Jada frowned at the aggressive moves both kings were making.

"Knight to F6." Odin's laugh filled the board as the wind began to toss around his beard and cloak.

Princeton moved out to the board with a look in Valkari's direction. He pressed his lips to the tips of his fingers and blew her a kiss. Jada grits her teeth as she watched helplessly from her square. This was not going to go well, and the ripple of ferocity that scattered across the board told her so.

"Knight to E5." Nero's cyclops completely decimates Odin's pawn as it moves into their square. Jada cries out as the cyclops makes quick work of the Asher and his musketeers leaving only one alive. Only because he ran back to remove Asher from the field to get her to safety.

"Odin stop this!" Jada called out as best as she could above the rising winds. "You're going to get someone killed!"

"What wrong Jada? Afraid I'm going to hurt your little Nero?" Odin laughed. "Good I intend to! Pawn to D6!"

"Odin what are you doing?" Irshad shouts to Odin as loud as he can despite the rush of wind that carries his voice away. Frantically trying to reign in his blood brother in. However his hands are tied by the rules of the game.

Nero makes eye contact with Jada, as he calls out his next play as if punishing her for not being his opponent. "Knight to F7."

"King to F7." Odin had moved Princeton out of the way to open the space for himself to come onto the board. His tattoos glowed and even more crows began to peel from his body. The rush of crows preceded Odin as they continued to pull from the tattoos on his chest. The black column of screams and feathers circled around the cyclops pecking and tearing at his flesh. The Cyclops angrily swatted them away but continued to move forward towards Odin.

The mass of birds made the square almost invisible. Were it not for the cyclops swinging his axe none would be able to see what was happening at all. Odin picked up his spear and ran into a leap that had him landing point down into the cyclops's eye. The beast tried to toss Odin away, but the spear was lodged too far in. Odin stood on the Cyclops brow and jerked the spear back in a way that made the Cyclops head bump back along his shoulders. The crows flew by, and as a column tore at its neck until the skin tore apart. Leaving the cyclops throat exposed to the open air.

Jada took a deep relieved sigh as Odin made it through his match. She watched Odin glow, and now that the cyclops was dead. The lightning began to strike in streams around Odin as he stood on what was left of his opponent. The wind rushed around to lift him in the air as the rush of power that followed death flowed through him. His crows circled around him before splitting into two creating a larger force for him to take into battle.

"Bishop to C4. Check." Nero's bored voice reminded everyone that they were still in a match. Taking the chance to exploit Odin's exuberance.

"Pawn to D5." Odin finally realizes the mistake of leaving himself open and moves a pawn to cover himself.

"Pawn to D5." Nero emotionlessly takes the square like the match had become too easy for him.

"Knight to D5." Odin calls out trying to put more distance between himself and the approaching enemy's board.

"Prince!" Valkari's worried voice followed her husband into battle.

Princeton's string Quartet began to play as the match started. Princeton didn't even turn around. The music that filled the air had the army of goblins dancing until dropped and died from exhaustion. Those that still moved began fighting their teammates once the song moved into the next movement. Jada felt as if she couldn't breathe as she watched Princeton's match. When it was finally over, Jada felt as if she had aged ten years. There was a rush of power, and the quartet turned into a full orchestra. Princeton popped his new tuxedo collar and winked over at tearfully relieved but smiling Valkari.

Nero's eyes remain steady on Jada's as he calls his next move. Something draws Jada's attention to the queen at Nero's side, and the way that she smiled, made something in Jada's stomach turn. It felt twisted, like the queen would destroy anything she touched. The siren smiled and focused on Odin playing checkers instead of playing chess. Not to check, but to kill. "Queen to F7."

Jada tore her gaze from the Queen to scream out across the board. "Odin cover your ears!"

The Siren steps out onto the board and begins to sing. The crows fly out in a rush towards her, and though they are cutting her arms, and legs they cannot stop her song. Odin's tattoos glow once more, and his wolves leap out to circle their dazed king.

"Yamja..." Odin drops his spear and comes forward. The wolves are caught between trying to hold Odin back and attacking the siren. As soon as one has him subdued, he knocks them away, and the other tries to catch him. They are so preoccupied with him, that they cannot effectively attack the siren.

"Odin, wake up! That's not Yamja!" Snap out of it!" Irshad yells at him trying in vain to wake Odin out of his desperate fugue. Desperately trying to get him to listen to his wolves.

The wolves finally wrestle Odin to the ground, whining and snapping at the siren as she comes closer. One runs at her, and she catches the canine by the neck and snaps it to the side. Dropping the wolf on the ground. The wolf holding Odin releasing a long pitiful wail at the site of his brother.

"Odin! Yamja is in the courtyard. That's not her!" Jada screams out, and Odin seems to blink his eyes trying to clear his head.

"The courtyard." Odin seems to swim in and out of consciousness as he tries to pull himself together. "That's not Yamja… My Yamja…" Odin's eyes cloud over again as the siren reaches him and strokes her pale hand along his cheek. He turns his lips into her hand and kisses it reverently. Yamja, I miss you so much it hurts."

The siren continues singing until her lip's rests on Odin's. His body begins to glow and goes translucent as she begins to suck his soul away. Jada watches as Odin's skull becomes visible through his skin, and shakes her head violently.

"Fenrir break them apart hurry!" Jada calls out to the wolf who lunges at the siren biting into her arms and thighs wrestling them apart. Unfortunately, the damage had been done leaving no question of who the victor of that match was.

Gabriel rises from the table with a languid stretch. "The match I believe belongs to Silvestri."

"That was mature of you Gabriel, are you well?" Silvestri smiles trying not to gloat about Nero's win.

Gabriel smiles with a shrug as he watches his board break and run to Odin's square. "Quite well. I can be benevolent about this match. You're already won the tournament for me."

Gabriel's board rushes out to Odin as his wolf whimpers over his dying brother and leader. Jada slides to her knees next to him trying to keep him there. "Odin... Odin! Wake up do not die on us! Hurry, we have to get him to the oubliette!" Jada was trying to keep hold in her tears, but her voice began breaking.

Odin placed his hands on her and shook his head. "Don't. take me to the courtyard Jada. I want to be with her."

Irshad and Princeton hoisted the large Viking from the ground and rushed him off the field, as the rest of the team gathered his wolf friend. Jada led them through the palace and to the courtyard as quickly as she could. The statue stared off into the distance towards the boards. The storm must have alerted her that something was wrong. They pulled Odin through the fountain's water to rest at Yamja's feet. Odin's arms moved to her knees to wrap about them with a relieved smile.

Odin's breath was becoming labored, His coughs containing specks of blood. "Irshad. Kill me."

"Don't, spend your last moment with Yamja." Irshad snapped when he tried to see to Geri's brother.

"I will be with Yamja forever now, but my wolves and crows will be dead." Odin laughs, but the action causes him to cough violently. "Take them brother. I know that they will protect you as well as they have protected me."

Irshad looked to Yamja uneasily, but he found no answers in her still gaze. Odin coughed again, but his voice was angry. "Hurry before that wench gets my army. They will use it against you tomorrow in the last fight. I don't want my wolves fighting against their loved ones."

Odin's crows rest on Irshad's shoulders and Fenrir nudges his leg, as he worriedly looks back at his brother. Irshad reluctantly walks over to Odin and pulls out his staff. He leans over and places a kiss on Odin's head and wraps his arms around Odin' shoulder in a hug. Odin's eyes met Jada's and he smiled before Irshad quickly shoved the spear through his heart. Odin smiles and slumps back against Yamja's legs. His wolf howled in mourning amidst the wrecked screech of his crows. His tattoos glowed before appearing on Irshad in a rush of energy. The two crows that rested on Irshad's shoulder and the wolves disappeared leaving Gabriel's board crying in the courtyard. Jada walked over to Irshad and wrapped her arms around him as he sobbed at the loss of his brother. Though the embrace did not last long, because Irshad threw her off as he suddenly screamed in pain.

Jada grabbed his flailing arms and pulled him from the fountain. The group tried to hold his arms down as he writhed on the ground much the same way Jada had done. His beautiful dark skin became sleek black fur. Gold cuffs encircled his wrist and ankles. His face became elongated into razor sharp canines. They held him until he laid painfully panting on the ground.

Jada looked back at Odin and saw that Yamja had moved so that her arms wrapped around Odin. Her lips were placed against his in a loving kiss. The basilisk walked over to the fountain, and turned Odin to stone, and Jada looked up at him gratefully with a watery smile. "That was kind. Thank you."

The Jonah looked uncomfortable with the praise and shrugged. "I was human once." He walked away, only to be replaced by Valkari and Princeton.

She wiped her eyes from the circle of Princeton's arms, but Jada could see that Valkari was as ready to fight as she was. "What's the plan now?"

Jada looked back at Irshad who was still on the ground through his change, and Jada fists balled angrily. "Tonight? We go back to the oubliette. Tomorrow? We finish this.

Chapter Twenty Three

In it would be the last match of the tournament. Both Trinity and Trine were there to wave the match their alternating blue and white suits. Fairies from all over the seven kingdoms were in attendance, as the last tournament was open to the entire public. It was almost time for the suns to conjoin. The deluge of rain from yesterday's match left the grass sparkling in the sun's light. Despite the rain this day was bright and cheerful. And the audience was full, every fairy that could pile into the area, but stay off the fields was there. They had every right to be excited. This day would determine who would be the one in charge for the next seven years.

"It's such a beautiful day." Valkari's voice was grim as she took the Knight's position left by Irshad. She took a deep breath and pulled a needle from her hair preparing for the fight before them.

"Misleading, isn't it?" Jada gave a ghost of a smile as she looked over her board. They knew what was at stake, and everyone was as determined to go home as Jada was to get them there.

Jada glanced to her side where Irshad now stood in Odin's square. The board had unanimously named him king, and Jada knew they had made the right choice. She watched him run his fingers against the new tattoos along the side of his face. They all needed time to mourn Odin, but with the ways of this world there was none. They had to wake up to some fresh new hell every morning. Jada planned on making that stop today.

Her eyes met Nero's, and his smug gaze had glanced over at Irshad's new position on the board. He lifted his broad shoulders in a shrug and turned his attention to Trinity and Trine as they made their speech for the last match of the tournament.

"We announce this last game of the tournament open."

"Winner will take all."

Nero gave her a mocking bow which Jada only returned with a nod of her head. Her attention focused on the siren at his side whose red lips curved in a hateful smile. She would not be able to bring Odin back, but she would make sure that he was avenged. Jada looked up at the sky, and as the twin suns conjoined. The match would officially begin, and she was ready to get it over with.

"Pawn to E4 " Nero called out his first move beginning the match with one of his more aggressive moves. The band of elves moved silently towards the square.

"Lilly to E7." Jada called Lilly and her army of golems to the square.

Nero's brow rose, and he looked out across his board trying to decide which was the best route to kill her with. "Yetis to D4."

"Valkari to D5." Jada moved Valkari who gave her husband a serene smile before calmy moving to the board.

"Knight to C3." Nero watched as the square filled with water and the tentacles of a kraken emerged. Angrily waving its limbs in the salty water that filled the square.

"Ezra to E4 if you would." Jada smiled at the surprise on Nero's beautiful face. If he wanted to be aggressive, she would show him aggressive. She was going to pull him kicking and screaming out of Silvestri's clutches. Ezra adjusted his top hat and cane and moved to the square. The elves ran forward only to be sucked into the void of Ezra's hat. Taking the square and removing the player from the board with a smile.

The crowds cheering grated on Jada's nerves, but she didn't have time to focus on them. They were nothing and would be a distant memory for her board soon. Every hateful inch of them could walk into Gabriel's Ocean for all she cared. Nero didn't seem to be enjoying their loud prattling either. Their eyes met in shared irritation before the next move was called. The cheers were for the deaths of their friends, and there was nothing glorious about fighting for them.

"Knight to E4." Nero repaid in kind, but the frown on his face said he thought he would be the first to attack. The Kraken came, and Ezra pulled himself into his hat and disappeared from the square.

"Valkari to F6 one more time please" Jada moved Valkari moved to the open square that would allow her out onto the board.

"Knight to F7" Nero removed the Pegasus army that stood protecting Irshad.

Jada smiled at Nero with a shrug. "Irshad to F7."

Irshad's body rippled into his new incarnation as an Anubis. His short sleek black fur shone in the sunlight. Cropped ears flicked forward as impressive shoulders rolled beneath his gold breast plate. His onyx helmet fanned out like the rays of a black sun rimmed in gold. The tattoos on his face glowed, and he was soon flanked by four grey figures. Two humanoid hawks and two larger humanlike wolves at his side. There was a collective gasp from the gathered fairies as he moved to his new square, and the kraken that filled it with his army of jackal men.

Irshad watched the kraken create a whirlpool, and one by one his new generals jumped into the water spears first. They came up and used the metal plates that now covered their feet to ride the waves that swirled down into the water depths. Irshad soon followed, and for a moment no one could see anything. The crowd had drawn silent, and Jada watched the swirl water for her king and his generals. There was a loud tortured sound like the blare of thousands of trumpets sounding off in agony. The water churned and turned red before going still. The crows murmured worriedly until the water dissipated. Leaving Irshad and his generals to walk out of the water scraped up but alive. The crowd cheered and Jada tried not to be too smug about the win.

Nero looked over at Jada with a surprised but condescending smile. "You had him kill your king just so my queen couldn't collect the spoils of her battle? That was exceptionally cold blooded of you. I am impressed. Is this why Gabriel chose you?"

"You'll see why he chose me when I win." Jada shrugged. "Stop stalling. It's your move.

"If you win." Nero turned his attention back to the board. "Knight to G5." Nero puts his demon knight in play to taunt her.

Jada rolls her eyes. Irshad could easily take the next night, but she was saving him for much bigger fish. It would not do to wear him down with smaller fights. "King castles to G8"

Irshad did not look exceptionally happy about the move but moved behind a mere slip of a robot in a black and red polka dot dress and red head wrap. Her name was Tedra. She had short cropped brown hair and looked to be about twenty. Her smile was slightly creepy, but she had been very nice every time Jada spoke to her. Her power had something to do with the electronic ladybugs that intermittently crawled over her arms. Jada was not sure how she got to be on their board, but she was the alternate that the others had chosen. Jada decided to trust them but kept an eye on her. Tedra gave an out of place giggle as Irshad moved behind her for protection. Her small hands move to cover her wide smile.

Even Nero looked mildly uncomfortable as he looked at the young lady. He looked over at Jada, who could only shrug. He shook his head as he called out his next move. "Knight to E6 then."

Jada's teeth ground as he killed one of the alternates that took the field to replace Asher. Nero would pay for that, and she would do it personally.

"Queen to E8." Jada called out her next move and took to the field. Now that Irshad was protected Jada could move about the board freely.

"Knight to C7." Nero took Vashi's square, but luckily he and his genie survived. He was trying to goad her into making a mistake, but Jada only smiled.

"Jonah to B4!" Jada calls the basilisk away from his square to clear her path to Nero. She was going to end this.

"Coming for me directly, are we? You are full of surprises today. Alright then, Pawn to C3. Let us end this." Nero smiles and clears the pawn that stood in her way. His hand lifted, and his finger curled back inviting her forward.

"Let's. Queen to E1." Jada's army begins to pull themselves out of the ground. The air was filled with the clanging of swords against shields and the shouts of the dead. The troll zombie stepped out and growled something that sent the massive army moving forward behind Jada.

Nero waited patiently for her to reach his square before taking out a small wooden music box. His fingers wound a golden key and laid it on the ground. The latch opened, and the hinge of the lid lifted to reveal a small clockwork ballerina that suspiciously look like Silvestri. A small drawer slides forward, and five miniature brown tin soldiers hopped out. Their little bayonet resting at their side as they helped their red and white uniformed companions out of the box.

A drummer and a standard bearer that held Silvestri's flag hopped out and adjusted their uniforms. The drummer began to tap out a sharp beat that pulled the tin soldiers together. They began to march forward, and soon more figures began to march out the box. With each step the soldiers grew until they were as tall as Irshad and Princeton. The field was soon filled with beautiful dark soldiers with bright pink spots painted on their cheeks. Their black boots fell in line with the beat of the quad drums that marched beside them.

Jada watched as the next wave of Nero's army left the box. It was the same soldiers, but they flew out of the box on the back of black swans. Jada did not want to be impressed, but she had known that this fight would not be an easy one. The swans took flight and hovered over his army waiting for the word to charge. Nero waited until his army was completely on the field, before materializing his scythe in his hands. He stepped forward with a smile and waited for Jada to be ready.

Jada sighed, shook her head, her dark serpentine eyes pleading with him. "Nero, cede the match. Let me help you! I don't want to kill you."

"Oh, but I want you to." Nero laughed and spun his scythe between his fingers. "Let's see what you, and your new army is made of."

"Nero! I can help you. Let me use my wish to send you and your board home with the others!" Jada was desperate to reach him. His army appeared stronger, but she knew her army would overwhelm his by sheer numbers. His only hope to win and save Silvestri was to kill her.

"You think we would be able to integrate back into the world we left? Don't make me laugh." Nero smiled and waved his army forward. "Silvestri is my home. Just as Gabriel is yours. Now let the best piece win!"

Nero's soldiers ran out to meet Jada's army, and they clashed in the middle of the field. There were so many people on the field that Jada had the lost track of Nero. She looked up to see his scythe swinging and made a beeline towards where she assumed he was. Jada dodge through soldiers blasting them away with fire and stepping over the slain members of her army. Nero's army had the home field advantage, as they were on the day side of the board. Once her soldiers died, they were lost to her as they could not regenerate. It mitigated some of advantage she had of numbers.

Bodies burned and screamed around her. For every step she took there was a soldier trying to be a hero. She dodged bayonets and swords. The smoke from the field began to fill the air until they were fighting through a layer of black clouds and heat. Jada wiped the sweat from her brow doing her best not to inhale too much of the smoke. She felt something come up behind her and turned just in time to block Nero's scythe with Gabriel's sword. His large black wings flapped around them. His feverish blue eyes stared down into hers, and she knew that she would not be able to save him. He had no desire to be saved.

Her foot lifted and kicked him back a few steps. Nero caught himself with his wings before he fell, but not before Jada lunged up to swing at him. The tip of the sword grazing his stomach. Nero's hand rests along the line of blood that welled across his abdomen. He lifts his hand to look at the blood now coating his fingers. Jada watched the tangle of emotions that danced across his beautiful face. The fact that he could die seemed to become real for him.

His gaze moved from his hand to her eyes and smiled. Jada watched his sanity abandon him as his powerful wings lifted him towards the sky. Jada took a deep breath, and jumped up to meet him, her body to his surprise hovering just in front of him. His eyes widened as he saw her flying, and something seemed to shake loose inside of him. He shot forward, with a swing of his scythe, and Jada had just enough time to block him. They bounced through the air, and over the ground. Jada landed on the grass just to have to jump back from the arc of Gabriel's scythe. Nero would dodge backwards as Jada swung barely missed severing his perfect nose from his face. She rolled back and landed in a crouch.

Nero rolled away into a wave of smoke, and Jada pulled in as much air into her lungs as she could. The smoke was starting to make it hard to breathe. If she were not careful, she would pass out long before Nero had the chance to kill her. The air around her swirled, and Nero lunged out of the smoke to tackle her to the ground. They tumbled over and bounced over the ground with the force of Nero's trajectory.

Jada's head swam as she tried to get her bearings beneath the weight of Nero's body. Nero sat up, and Jada's eyes widened as she focused on him. Nero frowned at her expression and followed her eyes down to his chest where Gabriel's sword protruded from his rib cage. Nero sat back in surprise, and he looked back at Jada in wonder.

"Nero, Nero stay with me. Let me get you to the oubliette!" She scrambled up to catch him by his shoulders before he fell back injuring himself further. Jada frantically looked around for someone to help her. A task made difficult by the tears that kept filling her eyes. "We can fix this. We can still get you back over the briars!"

Nero watched her face, and his pale brown fingers lifted to brush away the tears that fell down her sootstreaked cheeks. He shook his head and smiled at her. The battle continued to rage on around them, but they were lost in each other. "You won."

Jada shook her head desperately. Her hand lifted to wrap around the hilt of the sword, but she jerked her hand back. Pulling it out would cause more damage, and she already felt helpless. "No, I mean yes. I mean do not worry about that right now! We have to get you…"

"Jada, Jada…shhh. It is okay, beloved. I am ready to go. I'm so tired." Nero wrapped his hands around the hilt of the sword, and grimaced as he pulled the sword out. Blood began to rush through the wound with the fresh damage done to his internal organs. He laid back into Jada's arms and smiled up at her. "Thank you."

Nero's breathing became labored, and his eyes drifted close. Jada held him as his life shuddered away. When he went still in her arms Jada gently laid him on the ground. She watched as his arm flared and burned into ash through the thinning smoke. Swans fell from the sky along with their riders. Disintegrating into grey mounds that their carcasses pulled themselves out of. There was that normal rush of power that followed as another player died, but Jada could not take any pleasure in this win.

The smoke began to clear, and the crowd began to lose itself in cheers. The smokey air filled with confetti and brightly colored streamers. Gabriel was now high councilman, and the world of fairy rejoiced. Jada watched the celebration in disgust at how little they cared for the lives lost on the field or the man who just dies in her arms.

Jada found Irshad who had been searching for her through the smoke. He looked at Nero and shook his head. His arms immediately went around Jada's shoulders comfortingly as she began to cry in his arms.

"It's okay Jada. It's over now. It's all over. We're free." Irshad's hand softly rubbed her arms as she tried to console his crying queen.

"Irshad I…" Jada's apology was interrupted by the sound of a high pitched inhuman scream from the dais where the council sat. The sound was so heartbreaking that Jada's eyes began to fill with more tears. She knew who the scream belonged to, and she knew it was coming for her.

"No. it's not over. Not all."

Chapter Twenty Four

Silvestri appeared on the field in a beautiful black gown. She looked like a vengeful goddess as the material flowed around her feet. She dropped to her knees next to Nero and roughly pulled him away from Jada and into her lap. Her arms cradling his head in distress. The distraught fairy wailed in agony over the death of Nero as black tears fell from her eyes. Her board watched on in shock as Silvestri lost herself to grief over her king's prone body. The air was as clear as the billows of smoke allowed, giving the entire world of fairy a view of the carnage that was wrought on the field of battle.

Jada watched Silvestri in anger for a moment before she wearily turned away with Irshad deciding to leave the displaced councilwoman to her grief. "Irshad, go back to the others and tell them it's over."

Irshad bowed and ran back to the night side of the board. The fairies that watched from their seats along the cliff continued their celebration. Plates of fairy dust were passed around, and the sounds of corks popping from bottles could be heard despite Silvestri's loud sobs. Jada watched for a few moments and turned away. However, she only took about two steps before something hot slammed into the middle of her back.

"Where... do you think... you're going?" Silvestri's deathly calm voice queried Jada's charred form.

Jada rolled over on the ravages of her back and watched Silvestri stand from her place beside Nero. Her clawed hand tore away the council pin that laid at her breast. Silvestri threw the silver piece at Jada's face. The edge of the pin creating a deep cut beneath Jada's eye.

"You know." Silvestri's ragged laugh made Jada's blood run cold. She walked towards Jada with an angry smile on her lips and shrugged her shoulders. "I don't really mind losing. I was honestly getting bored of running this world of junkies and gold grubbing narcissists. Gabriel can have the throne. He won't have it for long."

Jada rolled to grab Gabriel's sword only to be kicked in the chest back into her prone position on the ground. Silvestri kicked the wind out Jada's chest, and she fought to pull air back into her lungs. She was still

tired from the fight with Nero, and Jada was finding it hard to get her bearings through the pain she was in.

Silvestri stood a few yards away from Jada, and her hand began to fill with a bright light the color of stars. "What he won't have is you. I will not condone his happiness when you deprived me of mine!"

Jada was floating in and out of consciousness. She tried to make her ravaged body move, but she did not have the strength. The glow from Silvestri's hand became so bright that it forced Jada to squint her eyes against the sharp light.

"You'll give Nero my love when you see him won't you?" Silvestri giggled and pulled back her hand to strike Jada down.

The light became so bright that Jada tiredly lifted her arms to shield them from the light. When the energy was released, she felt the force of the blast, but received none of the pain that Jada knew would come with it. Just as Jada began to accept the inevitability of her death two things happened. Jada felt a warm energy envelope her body that made her feel safe. Then the soft familiar brush of material against her legs. Jada tiredly blinked up to see Gabriel standing in front of her. He leaned down to pick up his sword. Wiping away Neo's blood from the blade before facing Silvestri.

"That's enough Silvestri. You lost. Clear your dead from the field and accept your fate." Gabriel's voice was soft, but stern as the rest of the board appeared onto the field. There were mixed reactions about the world that they had stepped into, but none of them contradicted Gabriel's claim.

"But Gabriel, how can you be the head of a council that doesn't exist?" Silvestri's deranged smile widens as she looks over the board and the revelers beyond its borders.

"In fact. How do you expect to rule over any of these people when they are all dead?"

As Silvestri spoke, her eyes darkened and hollowed out. Her skin dissolved from its beautiful dark brown to an abyssal black that was covered in star light. It was as if the galaxy had found a new home in her flesh. She was a being of pure darkness that radiated hatred. Her body lifted from the field and the afternoon sky was blotted out as night spread over the board. Stars that normally danced and twinkled in the sky suddenly came whistling down from the heavens hitting the board and members of the audience.

Silvestri turned to her army as she floated above them "Your lives are forfeit with the end of this match. If you have any chance of survival, I suggest you kill everyone on the board. I no longer can or even want to save you."

Her board looked around at each other, and suddenly armies of all sizes began to rise and appear on the day side of the board. The council and the twins huddled on the field. They had not brought their armies, as they had not expected their lives to be in any danger. It would also be a chance to get revenge on the very beings that brought them here. Jada gave a dry painful laugh at the irony of them dying on the very grounds that gave them power. It would be a fitting end to all of them.

Gabriel looked down at Jada in amusement. "Petty." The fairies began to scream as comets began to crash into their tables, and there was a mad exodus from the places they had been sitting at. The stars began tearing up the board around them. At this rate there would not be a palace to shelter in after Silvestri got through.

"Valkari now!" Princeton's voice bellowed out distantly. Jada wanted to tell them to save themselves, but she did not even have the strength to try. She could hear the song of the siren moving towards them.

Valkari appeared pulled up into a chariot next to Jada. Jada watched in confusion as Valkari and moved to stand in front of Jada and Gabriel. She lifted a royal purple gris-gris bag that hung from at her side. Nimble fingers pulled a deck of cards from the pouch and began to shuffle quickly.

Jada could hear the distant sounds of Silvestri's queen coming towards them. Her voice was faint against the stars that were tearing up the ground around them in bright fissures of rock and light. The ground shook as Silvestri rained death down around everyone gathered there.

"Valkari take the others and run!" Jada's parched throat ached as she tried to get Valkari to safety. Her voice came out in a soft croaking whisper.

"No mam, we are all leaving here together!" She glanced back at Jada with a wink. "Anyway, I think our luck is about to change!"

Valkari shuffled once more and pulled out the

Hierophant in reverse. "Well at least hers will."

Valkari lifted the card out towards the siren that was singing her way across the board. The card began to glow in her hand, lifting from her fingers until the square stretched into a doorway next to them. Irshad walked out and moved towards the siren that was making her way towards them.

The siren's song faltered for a minute, but soon came back loud and strong. Irshad's army of human jackals rushed through the door behind him. Dodging stars and making a beeline towards the siren. The siren's song changed, and her appearance began to shift from the body of a lithe beautiful woman to a large bird with the siren's beautiful face. The siren screeched and used her tongue to lash out at Irshad's army. Knocking them away as she made her way towards the council.

The tattoo on Irshad faces glows as he runs towards the siren. The two hawks and the wolves holding down the sirens tentacles as the rest of Irshad's army covered her like ants. Irshad ran into a jump that brought him down on top of the siren. The tip of his staff slicing the monster in two as he came down. His army howled in victory, but they had little time to rejoice there was a legion of mummies coming their way. Jonah slithered by, and Irshad rushed onto his back as they dived deeper into the fight of for their life.

Jada squinted at Valkari in confusion trying to fight off the effects of pain and blood loss she was feeling. "Remind me what your army does?"

"I'm a fortune teller. I can channel other armies based on who is on the board. For instance…" Valkari shuffled her cards again, and this time she pulled the star card. Princeton walked out with a wide smile as he moved to take care of another oncoming army. "The power is unpredictable though."

Jada's brows lifted as she was suitably impressed. "Can you channel Silvestri's power?"

Valkari looked up to the sky with a frown. Silvestri was tearing into the palace and countryside with abandon. Comets whizzed past them as she made Gabriel watch the destruction of everything he built. The fairies that had been spectating were either escaping or unable to escape. "She unfortunately is not on the board."

"Of course, that would be too easy" Jada was fading, and she was not sure how much longer she was going to stay conscious under the conditions. "What are we going to do? There is going to be only so much of the palace she is going to destroy before she gets tired and comes this way."

Fairies from a corner of the seven kingdoms were screaming as they tried to get away from Silvestri's retribution. The stars continued to whistle through the stands and tables scattering fairies and rocks everywhere. Valkari continued to shuffle until one card jumped out of her hands. She kneeled to pick up the card, and her gaze lifted to Gabriel who smiled, with a shrug. He took off his cloak and kneeled to wrap the material around Jada.

"You don't have to do anything else. We will take care of it. Rest." Gabriel dropped a kiss on Jada's head and took off his coat. He handed it to Valkari with a bow and started walking away. "If the council will begin evacuating people and seeing to the wounded, I'll take care of Silvestri."

Gabriel's words seem to remind them that they too also had powers. They galvanized into action and disappeared from the field to do as they were told. He began to walk towards Silvestri with a roll of his sleeves. Grabbing his sword before stepping into the sky as if climbing up a set of invisible stairs. "Valkari, if you would be so kind as to keep an eye on Jada, please?"

"Valkari, what card did you pull?" Jada asked as Valkari kneeled to tuck Gabriel's coat tighter around her.

"Death."

Gabriel calmly walked into the sky where Silvestri was still slinging stars at the spectators and now at the council that was trying to save them. She was laughing, and murdering people recklessly. He sighed impatiently as he stood before her. A soft warning hiss was made to get her attention, and Silvestri focused on Gabriel with another laugh.

"Gabriel how nice of you to finally join me. I had planned on killing your little pet before I killed you, but the other way around is just as good." She flung a star at him that he side stepped impatiently.

"It's over Silvestri" Gabriel continued to walk towards her. Using his sword to block and parry the worst of the starburst she threw at him. One whizzed by so close that it buzzed his ear tossing his dark curls about around his head. The tip of his tongue brushed along the inside of his cheek followed by annoyed hiss. "That was rude."

"Do not think your paltry powers will work on me

Gabriel. You are not powerful enough to stop me by yourself. In fact, why don't we all go. I'll take everyone with me." Silvestri stopped throwing stars and went still.

Her body began to swirl with celestial lightning and seemed to collapse in on itself. Instead of stars being thrown out, her body started to bring everything in as if a dark hole had been opened in the middle of her chest.

Instead of fighting the force that threatened to suck him into Silvestri's abyss. Jada watched as Gabriel purposefully moved towards her. He started to glow, and soon the halo around him was as bright as the stars that Silvestri had thrown. Gabriel dodged the rocks, and chairs that Silvestri was pulling into herself as she self-destructed and took the world with her. The light that radiated around him illuminated Silvestri's form, and he grabbed onto her wrist. He stepped behind her and pulled her back against his chest. Jada could not tell what he whispered into her ear, but she could see the broken sob that wracked Silvestri's body. His lips parted, and his teeth sank into the pulse point in her neck injecting his venom into her body. The force that had started to pull all of them towards her slowed down, until it stopped completely.

Silvestri slumped down, and Gabriel scooped up her legs bridal style. He walked back down out of the sky to where Jada and Valkari waited for him. Valkari watched him uneasily as he stepped down out of the air and glanced at Jada worriedly. Gabriel gave them both a heart stopping smile and turned to see what the council was up to.

They had followed Gabriel's directions and saved what they could of the populace. When they saw Silvestri in his arms. The fairies gave a loud cheer as their savior made it safely to the ground. The council reappeared on the board, and Trinity rushed over to take Silvestri out of his arms.

"Burry Silvestri next to Nero. She was a member of this council and should be honored as such." He paused to listen to the distant sound of the last of Silvestri's army being defeated by his board as Trine collected Nero from the ground. They both bowed to Gabriel and disappeared from the board leaving the rest of the formalities to the council.

The judge stepped onto the field and lifted his drink that he managed to keep from spilling up to Gabriel. The other council members bowed their heads, and some looked less than happy to do so. "Well done and well played. High councilman Gabriel. You have won the tournament and observed the right of hospitality."

"Thank you, I'm honored." I only hope to lead with dignity and fairness." Gabriel walked past the council to scoop Jada up from the ground. "If you all will excuse me, I have to see to the care of my board. In three days, we will hold the coronation and wish ceremony."

Ezuli walked up to Jada and handed her Nero's scythe with a slight smile. "You have saved us all. If you have a need for me, invoke my name. I will answer."

Jada bowed her head in thanks, and tiredly relaxed in Gabriel's arms. The rest of the board were waiting for them at the edge of the field. All of them in various stages of pain, but relieved for the tournament to be over and alive at the end of it. Minus the tiny ladybug holing robot who giggled and waved at Jada as she arrived in Gabriel's arms.

Gabriel stood before them and bowed with a bright smile. "Well done all of you. Rest well. We will all soon receive that which we deserve."

Chapter Twenty Five

Octavius was busy spitting out items of clothing at Jada as she tried to get ready in the makeshift tent that had served as her room. She was not sure how the bucket of firewood managed to survive the onslaught of stars, but here he was frantically tossing creamy white shoes at her.

"Slow down you pile of planks!" Jada snapped in irritation as she glared at the dresser.

Octavius purred sadly and opened its doors allowing her to pull out a shawl that matched her shoes. Jada frowned in confusion, and gently took the item from the caverns of Octavius shelves

"Oh, Octavius, did I hurt your feelings? what's wrong?" Jada gently closed the door and rubbed her hands along his wooden sides. Octavius huffed and opened and closed its doors as if crossing his metaphorical arms. "Do you think I'm leaving? No, I'm staying here with you and Gabriel."

Octavius seemed to perk up, and his drawers opened. A thin shelf slides out revealing gems and necklaces that he began spitting out at her in earnest. Jada tried to catch all of them, but he was throwing so much at her it was hard to keep up. She put on what she could and slid the rest into her pocket to store later she was running out of time.

"So, you had all of this inside there, and let me go out sans finery? You old toy box!" Jada watched Octavius purr happily out of the side of her eye as she made her way to the door with a grumble. The grumble soon turned into a sigh, as she mentally berated herself for stopping at the door. Odin was not coming. She would have to make her way to the makeshift stage by herself. Another causality of an unnecessary war wrought by fairy kind.

Jada wrapped the shawl about her shoulders tightly and resented the cheerful buzz of the fairy court that waited for the granting of the wish. They had their security but at the cost of the lives that they had enslaved. It was on such dark thoughts that she became aware of a new set of steps that moved beside her.

"What can I do for you Bane?" Jada's voice was as stiff and as unwelcoming as she felt.

Bane's red lips curled back revealing the rows of jagged teeth in a semblance of a smile. "So, my liege, my sovereign, my queen. Off to close this chapter and into a new fever dream, hallucination, nightmare?

"Actually, I'm staying. So, like it or not we will be seeing more of each other. But that is an unfortunate fact, not an invitation." Jada continued walking assuming he would understand the brush off and fade back into the shadows.

"My how quickly we forget where we come from." Bane's high-pitched giggle ended on a soft amused growl. "What of the girl you were so blindly devoted to? What was her name?"

Jada stopped and glared at him. The familiar anger raises her blood pressure. "You know very well what Kedra's name was. You killed her after all."

"No, not me, not at all." Bane's smile grew wider as he stopped to face her. His hands moved behind his back as he waited patiently for her to ask the necessary questions.

"Are you accusing the trolls of killing her? Does that make it any different or absolve you of everything that happened that night?" Jada snipped and Bane 's smile was a full-on grin as he watched her work out what he was not saying aloud. Waiting on her to come to the conclusion he knew she would eventually get to. The bottom of her stomach dropped as she realized what he was leaving unsaid. "Gabriel. You're saying that Gabriel killed her."

"How well, do you think you know him? Did you think you were invincible, unaffected, impervious to his ambitions? How conceited!" Bane laughed and took his arm to hers gently ushering her forward towards the makeshift stage.

"You're lying." Jada said the words aloud more for herself then for him. Following his forced lead to the stage. "You're just saying that to cast doubt on Gabriel, so that you can drive a wedge between us."

"Am I?" Bane led her between the tents, until they reached a break that would lead her out into the center of those gathered. "Then by all means. Ask him yourself."

Bane bowed and after doing the damage he aimed to do joined the general audience. She stiffly walked out to where her board waited with wide smiles. They were ready to leave fairy, and it would be her wish that set them free. The coronation had already concluded giving Gabriel the right of granting the wish. The judge had already given them clothes that would allow them to blend into whatever era they would be walking into. They would start brand new lives, and Jada could not help but smile at them. Her gaze moved over to Gabriel and her heart hurt with how fast it was beating at the sight of him.

She would love him forever, and she hated herself at that moment. There would never be anyone else for her but him. He stepped over and took her hands placing quick kisses at the tips of her fingers. It never ceased to amaze her how he could make her feel like a queen. Jada stood before him waiting for him to begin the ceremony.

"Jada, my queen. You have won the tournament and slayed your dragon. You have led my board to victory. You are allowed one wish that will be granted without question. What do you ask of the council?" Jada' eyes misted over at Gabriel's words. She looked back at her expectant board.

"May I ask a question before I make my wish?" Everything inside of Jada screamed at her to not ask. To let everything go, but in the end, she knew she could not. To accept the dream that Gabriel had spun for her during the nights of cuddling in his arms would be to ignore everything that made her who she was.

Ever the consummate actor Gabriel smiled hastily concealing his confusion with a nod. "Of course, my queen. I can deny you nothing."

"Did you kill Kedra?"

The way Gabriel's smile froze, and his golden gaze contracted told Jada everything she needed to know. He did not even have to say it out loud. He had never lied to her; it had been her lying to herself. Her fingers laced within his as she took a step towards him. She gave him a watery smile and took a deep shaky breath.

"My wish is that Octavius, this board, and I shall return over the briars to live in peace." At Jada's words the gathered fairies began to murmur.

"Jada. I love you."

"With this last kiss I wish you joy and bid you goodbye." The words were halting but said with a finality that her heart rebelled against.

"Jada do not do this."

"Please abide by your pact in good faith and grant my wish." Jada spoke the last words of the right of wishes, her gaze meeting the fury of his as she lifted on her toes to seal the bargain with a kiss.

He accepted the kiss but pulled her forward in an angry hug. This furious hiss of his voice brushing along her ear.

"I'll allow you to play human for now. You will see that the world over the briars is no longer your home. Go playhouse with your puppy. You'll return to me soon."

The Judge's fangs were exposed in a wide smile as he stepped between them. Jada ignored the look of angry betrayal on Gabriel's face and turned to the judge as he made his ruling. "By the power invested in me I acquiesce to your wish. Goodbye Queen Jada. You have been most entertaining.

Chapter Twenty Six

A reluctant Theo used a fairy ring to bring them back across the briars. The judge dropped them back off in Dallas at the very spot that Jada had been taken from. The world looked so different than the one she had left. The buildings were so tall and filled with glass. There were so many lights, and there was music floating through the night air. The new surroundings were a balm against the memory of Bane's smug smile and the quiet rage on Gabriel's face. She and the rest of the board peered around trying to get their bearings. They looked like they belonged, but she looked out of place with her cream-colored gown and shawl.

"So... we're back?" Valkari looked around with wide eyes at the city before her. Her expression matched the look on the rest of their faces. The world looked nothing like this when any of them had left it.

"But what are we back to?" Princeton took Valkari's hand, and pulled her closer in anxiety, as if shielding her from the world they found themselves in.

"How long have you been away, Jada?" Irshad turned to Jada and asked as he too looked around wide eyed at what the new world was showing him.

Jada looked around to see a new stand. It was almost pitiful how grateful she was to recognize something. "Ummm lets see... The date in this newspaper says that I've been gone... forty years."

"So now we have a when and where, but not what we are going to do." Irshad spoke as he helped Jada over a puddle of water. They had begun walking as their large group was starting to draw too much attention just standing there.

"That's a question as we don't have Id's or money." The bracelet on Jada's hand glinted in the neon light that lined the streets, and she took a deep breath in relief. "Okay we need to find a pawn shop. Hopefully we can hawk this and find a place to stay for a few days to make plans. Then find a more reputable place tomorrow."

"But then what?" Princeton asked, staying very close to Valkari as he searched for the instrument less music that filled the air. "You want to make plans, but for what? We are warriors in a land with no battles. What are we collectively planning to do in a few days? Will we be going our separate ways?"

"This is true. What is our next move?" Irshad asked her curiously as he watched a group of men in suits chatter on their phone as they walked by.

Jada frowned at Princeton's words. Never in her wildest dreams did she think she would have to let them go. That she would not see them again. Some selfish part of her had thought she could keep her new family. She floundered for a few minutes trying to figure out something to say.

"I'm staying with Jada. She would be lost without me anyway." A soft masculine voice piped up behind them. Jada turned to see a tall young man smiling down at her. His bright brown eyes twinkled down at her as he seemed to be taking everything in stride. His outfit had so many pockets that jingled and clinked as he moved.

Jada took in the cornrows and tried to figure out how she would be lost without a twenty something sleeping on the new couch she was going to buy. "I'm sorry, were you one of the alternates?"

The young man rolled his eyes towards the sky. "See what I mean? Lost! I am Octavius. It'll be nice to have you call me something other than some colorful euphemism for wood."

Jada laughed and launched herself into his arms for a hug. The fairies had made good on their promise to release them all. Her heavy heart lightened some at the first sound of good news they had since they arrived.

"Don't get sappy. The canine asked a question. Octavius grinned as Irshad shot him a look, and he turned to Jada. "You saved us. Now what?"

Jada looked at the smiling faces around and felt humbled by the trust they put in her. She looked around and saw the sign for a strip club not too far away. "They will need to place someone in the position left open by Gabriel. They will start stealing people again."

"So, you want to stop them." Jonas asked with a surprise smile.

"No Jonas." She turned to Irshad with a smile. "I want to build our own board."

The End?

About the Author

There is beauty in everything no matter how stark the world is, and Lorraine strives to find a way to make that world come to life. Lorraine Williams is first and foremost someone who loves to write. She is a novelist who has a special place in her heart for all things fantasy and horror. She is based in Texas, and her stories take place within the gentle rolling hills of the South and Southwest. She is a travel addict who enjoy incorporating the worlds that she visits and their many wonders into her writing. She has always wanted to see more African American presence in fantasy, and decided to be the change she wanted to see.

Her debut novel Fairy Dust and Stripper Heels combines two things that she adores fairies and urban fantasy. She loves weaving the fantastical into the mundane and finding magic in the everyday. It is the first in a novel in her Through the Briar's Series.

You can find Lorraine on her Instagram @WritersCrush. Stop by for writing advice and other useful writing tips. You can also watch her create a novel real time her website www.WritersCrush.com, and read along and ask questions!

www.ingramcontent.com/pod-product-compliance
Lightning Source LLC
Chambersburg PA
CBHW030849030726
47495CB00005B/1444